KNIGHT ERRANT

*A Knight Errant of
Medieval Chivalric Ideals*

BY MICHAEL SLOAN

Published in the USA by:
BearManor Media
1317 Edgewater Dr #110
Orlando, FL 32804
www.bearmanormedia.com

Perfect ISBN 979-8-88771-157-7
Case ISBN 979-8-88771-158-4
BearManor Media, Orlando, Florida
Printed in the United States of America
Book design by Robbie Adkins, www.adkinsconsult.com

TABLE OF CONTENTS

PURSUIT 1

FOOZ 11

VALLANCE 20

FAIRGROUND 30

SPECTRE 39

ASSASSIN 47

CONSEQUENCES 55

SHERIFF CONWAY 64

ABIGAIL 74

LEDGE 83

TEA BUT NO SYMPATHY 92

CANDY ANNIE 102

DIXIE 111

PRISONER 121

SISTERS 130

GATHERING THE TROOPS 139

PAYBACK 148

DAMSEL'S-IN-DISTRESS 158

KACEY ROSE 168

THE EQUALIZER 177

EVANGELINE 187

GRAVEYARD 199

RESCUE WORKERS 207

LOST 219

ALLISON 229

LABYRINTH 238

AFTERMATH 248

DEATH MATCH 259

NEMESIS 268

RESOLUTION 278

I

PURSUIT

CANDY ANNIE WAS RUNNING for her life. She had eluded her pursuers and had plunged deep into the woods. Tangled branches grasped at her face and her bare arms. She had to fight her way through sharp thorns and flowering shrubs until at last she had broken free. She could hear no sounds of pursuit, but she knew that they were not far behind her. The kidnappers' car was a Volvo 60 Cross Country station wagon that had seen better days. The men who had been stalking her were Jeremiah Reynolds and Jeff Fletcher. Jeremiah was a fat tub of lard who sweated profusely. His body odor alone had been enough to make Candy Annie gag. Fletcher was a powerfully built sadist who was six-foot-four inches tall with a pockmarked face and lackluster eyes.

The Volvo had come to a stop on the deserted country road with Candy Annie still a prisoner. Jeremiah was not concerned about her. He needed to concentrate on his driving. He had to deliver the girl on time and on schedule. Candy Annie had asked Jeff Fletcher if she could take out a small mirror from her purse. Fletcher did not notice the small perfume bottle that was lying beside it. That had been a gift from Mickey Kostmayer. Fletcher had waved a dismissive hand at Candy Annie.

"Go ahead," he said.

Candy Annie turned and sprayed the perfume in Fletcher's face. He howled as the cologne stung his eyes. Jeremiah had screeched to a halt on the country road. That was when Candy Annie had jumped out of the Volvo and ran into the woods. The branches clawed at her face. She had to scramble over them. The foliage was almost impassable. She didn't know which way to turn. There were no signposts. In the end she opted out to continue on down the path which twisted and turned and then was cut off by more prickly brambles and tangled foliage. She kept listening to the silence in the woods. There were no sounds of pursuit now, although she knew that the men from the Volvo must have followed her. She changed direction twice, but that didn't show her where she was headed.

Candy Annie thought back about her panicked flight through the forest and didn't even know how it had all happened. She knew no one in New York City except an older, compassionate black man named Jackson T. Foozelman. Candy Annie loved him fiercely, but she had not seen him in a very long time. She had been friendly with Jeremiah Reynolds who she had seen around the neighborhood. He had a pleasant face with laughter lines around his eyes which were gray and deep-set. He and Candy Annie liked the same café in Manhattan. Jeremiah was a salesman who always carried samples with him. He had run into Candy Annie outside her apartment building and had asked her to accompany him to his car. He needed to pick up some folders he had left behind. Then they could go to the café they liked for a snack.

Candy Annie was a trusting soul and followed Jeremiah to his parked car. The man leaned into the car and grabbed some folders. At that particular moment the street was deserted. Candy Annie had been suddenly grabbed by Fletcher, Jeremiah's partner. She had struggled, but in the end she had been subdued by her captors. She had been thrown into the back of the Volvo. A black hood had been placed over her head. She clawed at it, but Fletcher tightened the noose around her head. He threatened to strangle her if she made a sound. Candy Annie kept her cool, biding her time. Finally the car had come to a stop. Candy Annie had pleaded to have some air. She was choking under the black hood. Fletcher had pulled the hood off her head if she promised to behave. Or the hood would go back on.

That was when her abductors had come to a fork in the road and Candy Annie had thrown the perfume into Fletcher's face. Jeremiah had screeched to a halt. She had managed to escape, but she knew her kidnappers were out searching for her.

Once again Candy Annie listened to the silence in the forest. It was oppressive and relentless. She plunged blindly through the trees and emerged finally at a small lake. A signpost said: *Lake Calm.* Candy Annie noted several cottages that were located around it. She ran down to the water's edge and looked out at the serene lake. That told her nothing. Panic had started to take hold of her. There was a level of hysteria that she had to keep out of her voice. She tried to call for help, then she decided that was a very bad idea.

She thought about Robert McCall. He had been Candy Annie's mentor. He had encouraged her to move into Mickey Kostmayer's apartment at Fifty-Fourth and Second Avenue. He had introduced her to Kostmayer who turned out to be the love of her life. At least, that was what she told herself. Mickey could be irritable and mercurial, but Candy Annie loved that aspect of his nature. She had felt safe with him. Now she was running for her life and the mentors who had nurtured her were all gone.

Candy Annie plunged back into the trees. The thickets closed around her making her progress that much more difficult. The trees in the forest also seemed to close in around her. She turned and twisted and finally came out onto another road. She could see more of the rental homes around her. They were all boarded up. Obviously the secluded lake was a desired spot.

Candy Annie came out to a picturesque house. She made her way to the front door. Thankfully it was unlocked. She opened it and stepped inside. A cozy living room greeted her with book-cases along one wall with a staircase going up to the second floor. There was a 2-piece sofa and loveseat, a Sicily Wood Coffee Table, a Toshiba Stereo System with a CD player. Bluetooth Speakers were in evidence along with a Remote Control. Three steamer chests stood in the house, a dining table and an Everest Floral fabric chair. There was a coffee percolator and a microwave oven in an alcove. A Grandfather Clock was prominently displayed on one wall.

Candy Annie ran through to the modern kitchen and went through the drawers there. She found a 10-inch chef's German Stainless-steel knife with a serrated handle. It had a wicked looking blade. She slipped the knife into the sleeve of her coat. She rummaged through four more drawers in the kitchen, but there was nothing in them. She ransacked the drawers of the bedroom. They were empty. The cabinets were also empty. She did not know what she was looking for. The house was up for sale or lease. The realtor could show up anytime, Candy Annie realized, but with no phone hooked up she would have to wait until she could talk to someone. Which was out of the question.

Her options were severely limited.

Candy Annie didn't know anyone in New York City except Mr. McCall and Mickey Kostmayer. And of course her friend Jackson T. Foozelman. She knew she could not stay in this sanctuary for long. She searched further. A mini-Storage chest held nothing of interest. There was a Rattan Basket that was also empty. She didn't search the upstairs rooms because she knew it was futile.

Candy Annie closed the door to the house and ran down the flagstone path which was adorned with hydrangeas bushes. She had noted a single garage door to one side of the house. She had nothing to lose. She turned the handle and found it was unlocked.

Candy Annie entered a darkened garage. Shelves were lined up along one wall. There was a *Disney Frozen II Toy & Book Organizer*, a *Bear Pillow*, a *Minnie Mouse Play Set*, a *Castle with Turrets with a moat* and a *Unicorn* wrapped up in a blanket. She didn't dig further into the playroom because it was buried beneath an avalanche of discarded dolls.

A 1950 Riley 2.5 convertible roadster took most of the room in the garage. She knew something about old vintage cars. This one was a beauty. It had been lovingly restored. The smell of the upholstery was somehow intoxicating to her. She wondered if the motorcar was drivable. She slid into the plush seats of the Riley and gripped the steering wheel. It had a nice feel to it. She remembered a time when Jackson T. Foozelman, her companion in the sewer tunnels, had arrived in her subway space dressed up to the nines. He had been wearing a cravat and a fancy waistcoat. His shoes were polished to a high gloss. He had splashed some cologne on his face. He had told an amazed Candy Annie that a friend of his, also from the subway tunnels, had loaned him his sports car for twenty-four hours. He was going to take it out for a spin to see how it handled. He wanted Candy Annie to accompany him. At first Candy Annie had demurred, saying she could not possibly emerge from her cocoon to go out in the *Outside World*. But the old man had insisted. It would do both of them a world of good. Candy Annie had relented. She changed her clothes, which meant she was wearing a new pair of stone-washed jeans and sandals on her feet. Fooz had led her through the labyrinth of subway passageways until they had emerged near Forty-Second Street and Times Square. There was the restored, vintage 1950 Riley 2.5 convertible roadster waiting for them. Candy Annie had been enchanted. She did not know if Jackson T. Foozelman could even drive! But she climbed into the roadster and off they went. It was one of the best experiences that Candy Annie had ever had. Fooz had driven to the Bowery, then up to Brooklyn, with a pit stop at the *Metropolitan Museum of Art*. Then he had carried on to Chelsea and Fifth Avenue and on through Central Park. Fooz had returned the car back to where he had left it. Candy Annie had been elated. She had told Fooz it was the best day she ever spent in her life. The old man had been very pleased. After that reality had set in for both of them. They had returned to their sewer tunnels beneath the Manhattan streets. But it had been a great treat for Candy Annie that she'd never forgotten.

She closed the door into the garage and was immediately attacked by Jeremiah and Fletcher. She had not been paying attention to where her pursuers had emerged from the forest. She took the kitchen knife she had concealed in her sleeve and tried to stab Jeremiah with it. He wrenched the wicked looking blade contemptuously out of her hands. Fletcher picked it up and slapped Candy Annie's face, bringing tears to her eyes. Jeremiah and Fletcher manhandled her back to their Volvo. Fletcher threw her into the back seat and climbed in after her. He dragged the black hood back over her head and punched her in the stomach. She doubled over in agony, gasping for breath. Jeremiah climbed back into the driver's seat and burned rubber getting out of there.

Candy was left in a world of pain and grief.

There was no one going to save her this time.

*   *   *   *

Robert McCall ran to the Montreal train that was standing in the station. He had booked a seat in the First-Class section where he had left Rebecca Sinclair. Roger Forrester, Rebecca's ex-husband, had just climbed onto the train carriage. McCall caught up with him while he was still on the platform between the two railway cars. He grabbed Forrester from behind. He used a back fist to the man's forehead to stun the pineal gland and paralyze his arm through the median nerve. A sword-hand to his throat finished him off. Forrester slumped down into McCall's arms. He carried him down the short metal stairs off the train and heaved him onto his shoulder in a fireman's lift. There was a waiting room opposite the train which was deserted at this time. McCall dumped Forrester into the restroom, sitting him up and locking the restroom door. It would be some time before any of the other passengers were even aware of his presence. McCall moved back through the deserted waiting room and back onto the train platform. More passengers were still boarding. McCall climbed the metal stairs and entered the coach compartment where he found Rebecca Sinclair sitting with her laptop at a table. She smiled at him.

"I thought you weren't going to make it to the train on time!" Then she looked at his face with some concern. "Is everything all right?"

"Everything is just fine," McCall assured her.

The train pulled out of Montreal Station, gaining momentum. McCall sat back down beside Rebecca Sinclair who was reading an article about Steve Jobs. McCall told her he was going to walk down the various carriages again as the view of the city unfolded. Rebecca just nodded, engrossed in her reading about the bonuses the senior R&D executives had received which were based on the company's performance numbers rather the costs from a particular product. McCall got back to his feet and proceeded to make another sweep of the train.

It took him another half-an-hour to find the explosive device.

Which told McCall that Samantha Gregson must have planted the device somewhere on board the train before it had left the station.

A cigar box had been placed under one of seats which was deserted at this moment. McCall opened it. It was filled with explosives contained in small glass jars held tightly together. He closed the cigar box. He dialed a phone number on his cell phone as he made his way down the train coaches and out on the moving platform between two of the train carriages. It only took Michael Ralton, known to his friends and enemies as "Gunner", one ring to answer.

"Gunner," he said, which was the way he had answered all his calls.

"Gunner, it's Robert McCall. I am travelling on a train between Montreal and New York City. Samantha Gregson has placed a cigar box of explosives under one of the seats. It is filled with a murky substance contained in four glass mason jars fitted with safety levers. There is a timer with multi-colored wires protruding from it, all of them connected."

"How much time do we have?" Gunner asked him.

"The timer on the device is counting down from one minute and twelve seconds."

"Don't touch that one!" Gunner said, quickly. "The liquid is probably held tight in the jars with some kind of TNT mixture. How many wires are affixed to the kill switch?"

"Ten," McCall said, tersely.

"Is there a red button on the timer?"

"There is."

"The wires will have been wired in a random order."

"That doesn't help me, Gunner. Less than a minute."

"Is there a safety lever on the glass jars?"

McCall assessed his cell phone. "Yes, there is."

"Take a photograph of it."

McCall took a photograph of the device and sent it to Gunner's phone. "Got it," he said. "Forty seconds," McCall said, "and counting."

"Pull the fluorescent wire out," Gunner said.

"You're sure?"

"Just do it!"

McCall pulled the wire out. He only realized in that moment that his face was awash with perspiration. "Six seconds left on the timer," he murmured. "I'd say that was a good call, Gunner."

"You still need to deal with the four bottles filled with some kind of liquid," Gunner said. "Probably nitroglycerin or a nitric oxide mixture. Who is trying to kill you?"

"I can't be sure," McCall said. "Maybe Samantha Gregson."

"That's a name I'm not familiar with."

"She tried to kill me when I rescued Deva Montgomery and tried to rescue Daniel Blake at the Chateau Krarzinsky in Russia. She has been gunning for me ever since."

"Let me know if there's anything I can do with that situation," Gunner said.

"I just have to watch my back," McCall said.

"I know the feeling," Gunner said. "Stay safe."

He hung up.

The train was racing through some trees. McCall noted there was an open stretch of wasteland coming up. He waited three seconds and then hurled the cigar box as far as he could throw it. The explosive charge detonated in a fiery explosion. A huge elm and some cottonwood trees had ignited with it. McCall thought the local the fire department could handle the aftermath. He put an emergency call to them. Then he moved back down the carriage. He searched the train again while the passengers took a five-minute break. He was looking for a second explosive device that Samantha Gregson could have concealed on the train, but he found no sign of it. He returned to where Rebecca Sinclair was sitting as the train pulled out of Westport Station. She looked suddenly frightened.

"What was that explosion?"

"Nothing for you to concern yourself about," McCall said.

"What caused it?"

"A faulty circuit that I was dealing with on the train. I disarmed it. No harm done."

"I was looking for my husband when the train pulled out," Rebecca said. "But I didn't see him anywhere."

"You won't. Consider him missing in action," McCall said.

Rebecca relaxed, but she knew she was not getting the whole story. She took his hand.

"Thank God for you," she murmured, softly.

And she kissed him. When they broke, Rebecca still had hold of McCall's hand. "I feel safe as long as I am with you."

"Keep that thought," McCall said, but he knew it was a promise he couldn't keep.

The train made another stop in Albany and then it had reached its destination in New York City. McCall and Rebecca emerged into the chaos of the Penn Station.

"This is where I need to leave you," McCall said.

She stopped in the crush of people and her anxiety level was heightened.

"Why would you do that?"

"I don't have a choice," McCall said. "I have some business to take care of in the city. I'm going to put you on the train for Washington D.C. You'll be fine. I will be handing you over to a very good friend of mine. Her name is Emma Marshall. She works for my old boss in D.C. You will be in good hands with her. You'll like her. She is sassy and feisty and basically a hoodlum, but she will make sure you are taken care of. You can trust her with your life."

"So this is an 'Equalizer' kind of a thing?" Rebecca asked him.

"Something like that. Wait for me right here."

McCall left her in the crush of people while he bought her a ticket for the D.C. train. He had checked out the passengers, but he did not see anyone threatening. When he returned to Rebecca she seemed composed. He handed her the ticket. She moved into his arms and kissed him again. When they parted she had a strange expression on her face. "Why don't I think I will ever see you again?"

"You will," McCall promised her. "This is a temporary parting."

Rebecca kissed him once more, then she abruptly left him as if she had been overwhelmed with emotion. He watched her until she was safely on board the D.C. train. She did not look back. McCall waited until the train had pulled out of the station on its way to Washington D.C., then he disappeared into the crowd of people jamming the concourse.

*   *   *   *

When McCall exited Penn Station, Samantha Gregson was waiting for him. She had realized that her grand scheme to kill him on the train from Montreal to New York City had failed. He must have found the explosive device and disarmed it. She was parked in a side street with Khalid Rehman Mohammed doing the driving. He was a soulless urban guerilla although he thought of himself as a freedom fighter. He had succeeded *Abu Bakr Al-Baghdadi* as one of the leaders of ISIS. Beside him, Samantha was seething. McCall picked up a cab at Grand Central Station and it turned onto 34th Street. Beside her, Khalid Rehman Mohammed pulled out into the traffic. He had a tracking device he had fitted in the car so he could monitor McCall's movements.

"At least we have found out that he is in New York City." The terrorist chose his next words carefully. "You are going to a lot of trouble to kill one man. He is a retired spy. He is of no use to anyone. Why do you care so much about him?"

"He threw out a gauntlet in my face," Samantha said, spitting out the words. "I want him killed."

"I will take care of it," he promised her.

"Keep behind McCall," Samantha hissed. "See where he goes. He is not expecting any trouble."

"So this is a matter of honor for you," Khalid Rehman Moham-mad said.

"Yes, it is," Samantha said. "I have at least two more of my *Memento Mori* operatives that I can call upon. You know both of them. I want Robert McCall followed. If he goes to ground somewhere in the city, I want him found."

"Then what are you going to do?"

"Keep tracking him. At a certain point he will make a mistake."

"That could take time," the terrorist said.

"It won't be tomorrow. Or the next day. As long as we are track-ing him, he is vulnerable. I will know when the time is right." She turned to face him. "Do you have a problem with that?"

Khalid Rehan Mohammed smiled and it chilled Samantha's blood. "Not in the least," he said, softly.

‖

TWO

MᴄCᴀʟʟ ᴛᴏᴏᴋ ᴀ ᴄᴀʙ from Grand Central Station to the Liberty Belle Hotel which was situated on 66ᵗʰ Street. He walked through the lobby doors and felt like he was home. Chloe was behind the desk dressed her in usual outfit of grey slacks with a pale blue shirt and an emblem of the hotel stitched on it. She wore a silver name badge on her lapel. Her colleague, Lisa, also wore a silver name badge. They had been with the hotel for as long as McCall could remember. Right now they were dealing with an unruly mob of guests, all of them clamoring for attention. McCall acknowledged Chloe and moved to the entrance to the ornate bar off the lobby. Bookshelves lined the walls with classic editions in leather-bound volumes. McCall noted that in addition to *Charles Dickens, War and Peace, Don Quixote, The Three Musketeers* and *Moby Dick*, a few more volumes had been added: *Homer: The Iliad & The Odyssey,* an *Edgar Allan Poe Collection* and a *Jules Verne Collection* that included *Twenty Thousand Leagues Under The Sea, A Journey to the Center of the Earth, Mysterious Island* and *Around the World in Eighty Days.* The bar was jam-packed with guests. McCall looked around, but he did not see Sam Kinney. Usually by this time the old Spymaster was holding court with his friends and acquaintances, his "cronies" as he called them, but not tonight.

Chloe entered the bar and moved directly to McCall. He noted there was an urgency about her which resonated with him immediately. "Mr. McCall, I am so glad you see you! I was told you had checked out of the hotel."

"I did," McCall said, "but Sam Kinney has managed to keep my suite booked for a least a year in case I returned. I expected to see him here in the Library Bar or behind the reception desk."

Chloe reached into her pocket and handed McCall his room key. "I had just been waiting for your return. I haven't seen Sam in three days, which for Sam is a lifetime. He rarely leaves the hotel."

"Maybe he is just taking some time off."

"No, he would have called."

"I have been away for a few days," McCall said. "Let me check my hotel suite. Maybe he left a note for me. Is my suite still located on the 17th floor?"

"It is," Chloe said. "But I can't shake the feeling that something terrible has happened to Sam."

"Hope for the best,' McCall said, "plan for the worst."

"He has simply disappeared. I am sick with worry about him. Please find him, Mr. McCall. He is someone very precious to all of us at the hotel. Oh, you have a friend waiting for you in the lobby."

Chloe gave McCall an impromptu kiss on the check and then moved to an entrance that opened up back into the Library Bar. When McCall reentered the lobby she was dealing with more of the guest's outrageous demands.

Mickey Kostmayer was waiting on one of the sofas in the reception area. He immediately got to his feet and gave McCall a hug. When they broke McCall noted there were dark circles under his eyes. Obviously he hadn't gotten any sleep in the past forty-eight hours. He was an insomniac at the best of times.

"No word on Candy Annie?" McCall asked him.

"Nothing. It's as if she had vanished into thin air," Kostmayer said. "She hasn't been home for three days." He looked over at the busy reception area where Chloe and Lisa were dealing with more customers, as if he was trying to find a clue he had overlooked. "I didn't even know where to look for her. She rarely left her apartment. It was a safe haven for her."

"She might have returned to her home for whatever reason," McCall said.

Kostmayer looked at him. "You think she was living back in the sewers below Manhattan?"

"It's a possibility."

"That's a life she left behind her."

"Maybe she went back to her roots because the walls were closing in on her," McCall said. "She needed to find a comfort zone. That is where she would logically go."

"Would she have gone to see Jackson T. Foozelman?" Kostmayer asked. "I can't believe she would return to the subway tunnels."

"It's worth a shot," McCall said.

"You know how to get below the streets where Candy Annie once lived?"

"There is an entrance at Times Square."

Kostmayer smiled. "You're full of surprises, McCall."

McCall left his luggage with Chloe behind the reception desk and he and Kostmayer moved out of the hotel. McCall found the manhole cover on Lexington Avenue and Forty-Second Street. It took him and Kostmayer a few minutes to slide it into position. They climbed down the rusting red pipes and Kostmayer slid the manhole cover back into place. They reached the bottom of the iron ladder. Work lights illuminated the sewer tunnel. Claustrophobia immediately assailed them. The sewer tunnels stretched on both sides of the passageway.

"I've never been here before," Kostmayer said. "Where did you find the entrance?"

"Candy Annie lived beneath these subway tunnels for years," McCall said.

"Until you rescued her and brought her into the real world," Kostmayer said. "How did ever you manage to do that?"

"Need to know." McCall said.

"Sure, you've got your secrets," Kostmayer said. "I've got mine. So tell me what is in your mind."

McCall nodded. "Fair enough. I'm looking for answers that may lead us to Candy Annie. The only person I can think of is Jackson T. Foozelman."

Kostmayer nodded. "I'm way ahead of you. Let's do this."

McCall led the way through the subway tunnels which were lit by halogen lights. The ambiance was fetid and heavy. Overall a phosphorescent radiance permeated the dank passageways. McCall remembered his way through the maze and came to an iron door that had a mural of the *Williamsburg Bridge* emblazon on

13

it. A young girl and her mother were surrounded by fields of daisies. A golden retriever had been painted on the wall at the little girl's feet. Since the last time McCall had visited the vaulted space a new mural had been drawn of a *New York City skyscraper* with the *Met Life* building prominently displayed.

The sewer corridors led to a maze that twisted and turned in the underground passages. Finally McCall and Kostmayer came to the vaulted room with the metal steps connecting them. That emptied onto a park-like setting where artificial grass lawns, a badminton court and several deck chairs had been spaced at intervals. People were scattered throughout the space, some of them sitting in the deckchairs or relaxing on blankets. Halogen Night Security Flood Lights illuminated the tunnels that were suspended from the high-vaulted ceiling. Some of the residents were reading books and magazines as if they did not have a care in the world. Maybe this was the real world, McCall thought to himself. Maybe the pretend world was the one that had been manufactured. A few of the homeless citizens glanced up at them as he and Kostmayer made their way across the "lawn", but they were wary. They clearly wondered what the interlopers were doing here in their space.

There was a beautiful, older women sitting in a deckchair reading a paperback copy of a *Harry Potter* book called: *Prisoner of Azkaban*. Kostmayer thought she was probably in her sixties but held herself with grace and style. She looked like she had worked on a farm all her life. Her skin was tanned and leathery and her cornflower blue eyes blazed with life. Her back was ramrod straight. She was wearing faded blue jeans and a cowboy shirt with horseshoes embroidered on the front and back of it. She wore Nike blue running shoes with a white swoosh on them. She also had a Walther PPK 9 mm pistol tucked into her belt. When she looked up at McCall her voice had the husky whisky timber of a chain-smoker. She looked surprised at seeing him, but McCall knew that she had been following him from the time he had reached the badminton court and the artificial grass lawns. He remembered her name was Alicia.

"Nice to see you again, Mr. McCall," she said.

"And you too, Alicia." McCall nodded at Kostmayer. "This is Mickey Kostmayer, a colleague of mine."

Alicia glanced at Kostmayer, somewhat disdainfully, then turned her attention back to McCall. "What brings you back into Braker's territory?"

"I am searching for a friend of mine who used to have a niche down here in the subway tunnels," he said. "You will remember her. Candy Annie?"

"I remember her very well," she said. "A gracious and gentle soul. But it's my information that she is no longer with us in the subway system."

"I brought her up into what I call the *real* world," McCall said.

"How did it work out for her?"

"It worked out very well for a time. Then Candy Annie disappeared. She has been missing for three days."

Alicia got to her feet. She took the Walther PPK 9 mm pistol out of her belt so that it was pointing down at the ground. "Missing how?" she demanded.

"She had been living in the *real* world for some time now," McCall said.

"And you believe she has returned here to the sewer tunnels?"

"It's a possibility. We are on our way to see Jackson T. Foozleman who might have some intel on Candy Annie's whereabouts."

"Mr. Foozleman will not be a help to you in your quest," Alicia said, somewhat enigmatically. "But you're welcome to try to find him. I will put the word out, but it is a closed society down here in the sewer tunnels. Candy Annie did not return to the subway tunnels once she had been liberated. I would have known if that had happened."

"You keep track of all of the people here below ground?" Kostmayer asked her mildly.

Alicia glanced at him. "I make it my business to know where all of my flock are at any given time." She returned her gaze back to McCall. "You will find Candy Annie, Mr. McCall. In my heart I know that."

"Keep that thought," he said.

"God bless you and keep you safe. Do you know the way out of this rabbit warren?"

"I do."

Alicia sat down again in her deckchair and picked up her *Prisoner of Azkaban* book. Her Walther PPK 9 mm pistol was back in her lap. McCall and Kostmayer moved over to where a set of steel stairs descended into the darkness.

"That gal is a real ball breaker," Kostmayer muttered.

"She's got a big heart," McCall said. "That's all I care about."

"Where do we find Jackson T. Foozelman?"

"At the end of this next passageway, if I remember correctly," McCall said.

Kostmayer said: "Would Candy Annie really have returned to the subway tunnels down here?"

"She would if she was visiting Fooz," he said. "They got very close."

Ten minutes later McCall found Jackson T. Foozelman in his study beneath the Manhattan streets. He remembered that it had been decorated like a Victorian parlor from the pages of the *Strand Magazine*. A Victorian curio cabinet stood in one corner filled with porcelain bells of all kinds. Fooz had been collecting them since he came out of the army. There was a *Hammond Access Chair*, a *Victorian chaise longue*, a *Victorian seven-drawer armoire in antique white*, all the drawers open, filled with knickknacks which the old man had collected from junk stores. There was a *Queen Anne Cheval six-foot mirror* and a *Pulaski Victorian Cherry Cabinet*. McCall noted an *Old Streamer Trunk* which hadn't been opened since the recent Boer War. Fooz kept a *Lucinda Sleigh Bed* along one wall with, incongruously, a full-size oversized Comforter with a Flamingos sheet set and a patterned quilt on it from Pennsylvania. There were various editions of *The New York Times Crossword* discarded on end tables.

Leather-bound editions were in evidence of the Classics including *Ancient Greek Philosophers, Grimm's Complete Fairy Tales*, a *Jules Verne collection*, an *Edgar Allan Poe collection* and Classic Westerns like *"Hondo", "Gunfight at the OK Corral"* and *"The Magnificent Seven"*. Fooz had added more furniture to the already cluttered space including a cedar gazebo with a steel hardtop in black which was in pieces. An ornate coffee table in charcoal was beside it and a collection of ornate walking canes including a *Bat Masterson Han-*

dle in black beech wood. There was a bed with a colorful quilt on it, two leather chairs and a rocking horse. A bookshelf and a TV screen, circa 1990s, was in a corner. A mural had been added to the wall. *Palm Trees Silhouetted At Sunset.* A sink had been hooked up to a large tank and a shower stall had been erected. Ceiling pipes carried hot water and there was a small toilet also hooked up.

Jackson T. Foozelman was lying in his signature black jeans, black NYU torn T-shirt and his heavy brown workman's boots. His skeletal face was even more emaciated than McCall had remembered. A *Jim Beam Devil's Cut* bourbon bottle beside him was almost empty. The old man had virtually passed out on his couch. His hair was sticking up like it had been scrambled by an eggbeater. His eyes were bleary and unfocused. He had been shooting up heroin. That much was clear to McCall.

"I have only seen Fooz like this once," McCall said, angrily. "He promised me he would get his act together." He took hold of the old man and shook him. "I need you to focus, Fooz. Candy Annie is missing. When was the last time you saw her?"

Fooz looked up at McCall through a haze of alcohol. He shook the old man again in frustration like he was shaking a rag doll. "I need you to understand what I am saying! I need you to sober up. When was the last time you saw her?"

"Take it easy, McCall," Kostmayer warned him. "You won't get anything out of him like that."

McCall hauled the old man upright. He was awake now, although not functioning very well. He glanced at McCall and then at Kostmayer, trying to get them into focus in his mind. He didn't recognize Mickey Kostmayer at first, but he was focused on McCall's face and that shock of recognition seemed to be sobering him fast.

"Mr. McCall," he murmured. "Always good to see you. I must have been dozing. I forget your colleague's name?"

"Mickey Kostmayer."

"Nice to meet you, sir. I've been a little under the weather. Be right as rain once I get my sea legs back under me."

McCall was amazed how quickly Fooz had sobered up. He motioned for Kostmayer to bring him a mug of coffee which Fooz percolated constantly. The old man reached for it with trembling hands, practically gulping it down.

"Take it slow," McCall advised him.

"I will surely do that," Fooz said. He looked around him as if he were seeing the sewer tunnels for the first time. "This is the most beautiful subway station in all of Manhattan. Like it was a metro in Paris or on the Riviera someplace."

"Focus, Fooz," McCall said. "Drink your coffee."

Fooz held the mug in his shaking hands like it was a lifesaver. "I saw a movie one time," he murmured. "The hero poured heaps of salt into his coffee. I think it was Bing Crosby and he needed to sober up real fast."

"When was the last time you saw Canny Annie?" Kostmayer asked, brusquely.

Mickey Kostmayer was not much on small talk, McCall realized.

"Musta been a few weeks ago," Jackson T. Foozelman said. "I miss her terribly. But I'm heartened to know that she is living up in the real world now."

"We don't know where she is," McCall said. "She's been missing for several days."

All of the color seemed to have drained out of Fooz's face. He looked at Robert McCall as if his world has just come apart. Which it had. "She is missing?" the old man asked. The revelation had obviously rocked him to the core. "But that isn't possible. I just saw her. Well, maybe that was a few weeks ago. I tend to lose time down here in the sewer tunnels. The days and weeks merge together. Candy Annie is truly missing?"

"She is," McCall said. "Do you have any idea where she could have gone?"

"No, sir, I surely don't."

He motioned at the coffee mug and Kostmayer filled it up for him. Fooz drank the scalding coffee right down in more huge gulps. He had finally sobered up to the point where he could function. He glanced around the niche as if it were a suite at the Venetian Resort in Las Vegas.

"I won't let anyone to enter this space," old man said. "I had some folks who wanted to move in, a family of four, nice people, but for some reason I knew I just could not give it up. Too many memories of Candy Annie. I left the place just the way it was."

Whatever had sobered Fooz up it was still working. He was a little unsteady on his feet, but McCall gave him a chance to get his bearings. "Candy Annie had been coming to see me," the old black man said. "Just for old time's sake. But that was weeks ago." The effects of the narcotic were slowly wearing off. "She was coming to say goodbye to me."

"Why should she do that?" McCall said.

"It was in her nature to come and see me from time to time," Fooz said. "Kind of look in on me. She is a caring person. You know that." Now Fooz got shakily to his feet. "You can trust me, Mr. McCall. What happened this afternoon was an error in judgment on my part which I sincerely regret. It will not happen again. That much I can promise you."

"Did Candy Annie have a special place here in the subway tunnels?" McCall asked.

"Yes, sir, she did, although she had not been back there for a long time."

"Can you take us there?" Kostmayer asked him.

"Yes, sir. I certainly can." Fooz nodded, as if he was making a promise to himself. "I will not let you down again, Mr. McCall. Follow me."

Whatever had sobered Fooz up it was still working. McCall gave him a chance to get his bearings. Then the old man moved out of the *Strand Magazine*-style rooms and into the beginning of the sewer tunnels.

McCall and Kostmayer followed him.

III

VALLANCE

Fooz led the way to another series of tunnels laid out in a haphazardly fashion until at last he came to the passageway he wanted. Then he paused, listening intently. The tracks had started to vibrate like it was a living entity.

"Subway train!" Fooz warned. "We can beat it if you crank it but watch your steps or you'll be in its path!"

McCall and Kostmayer jumped down onto the subway tracks. Water trickled obscenely down the clammy walls. The air was thick with the debilitating moisture. A phosphorescent radiance danced across the tracks. The moaning sound that had begun as a crescendo was vibrating wildly. Fooz grabbed McCall's and Kostmayer's arms and literally propelled them to the other side into one of the niches cut into the subway wall. The subway train thundered past the niche and then just as quickly it was gone, echoing through the tunnels like an afterthought.

McCall and Kostmayer scrambled over the tracks and plunged into another subway passage. "Keep with me," Fooz said. "Other side of this is a storm tunnel. We'll cross the viaduct there, then we'll traverse these passageways and go down several stairs here. Hopefully they won't be flooded."

A keening wind greeted them. It was bitterly cold. Finally the three of them emerged into a brick tunnel. Halogen lights were spaced at regular intervals, most of them dark, but an occasional light burned in the recesses. McCall had his bearings back. He led the way to a niche that went back seventeen feet into the tunnels. Once upon a time this cellar space had belonged to Candy Annie. The room had been furnished just as McCall had remembered it. There was a bed with a colorful quilt on it, two leather chairs and an antique rocking horse. There was a bookshelf and a TV screen, circa 1990s. A sink had been hooked up to a large tank and a shower stall had been installed. Ceiling pipes carried hot water and there was a small toilet also hooked up.

"I haven't ventured into this space since Candy Annie moved out," Fooz said. "Too many memories are crowding into me. She lived here in these sewer tunnels for a long time. When it was time for her to leave, with your help, Mr. McCall, I felt a joy in her spirits I cannot describe. She had come to terms with her destiny."

Kostmayer looked around the space. "Why would Candy Annie move out? She doesn't live here anymore below the streets. She was staying in an apartment on Fifty-Fourth Avenue on 2nd Avenue until three days ago. What would have induced her to leave?"

"That is what we have to find out," McCall said.

He and Kostmayer searched the space, not that there was much of it. Then McCall noted that a coffee table was lower that it should have been by about one foot. McCall knelt beside it, feeling for a catch that would release it. He found a hidden compartment which dropped down from the table. Kostmayer joined him. McCall reached inside and brought out a small, leather-bound notebook. He flipped through the pages of the diary while Kostmayer looked over his shoulder. Fooz held back, as if these pages were a sacred text that he was not permitted to read. McCall turned the notebook pages. There were notations in a kind of chicken scrawl that he could barely decipher. It did not even look like Candy Annie's writing with words crossed out and arrows going in different directions. It did not make sense to McCall except in a few places where the notes were written in the margins. McCall came upon a late entry right at the back of the notebook. He made out the words: *General Store* and *Banning* with various maps with directions that seemed to lead nowhere. In another margin the words *General Store* were listed once again and the words *Feed Bin* were highlighted in red with names like: *Banner Elk, Deep End* and *Seven Devils*. It looked to McCall as if the roads were all grouped in a rural area. The notations in McCall's hands were just the idle thoughts of a vulnerable young girl, but toward the end Candy Annie's narrative became more heartfelt and meaningful.

"It *is* in Candy Annie's handwriting," McCall said.

"But can you make out any of this text?" Kostmayer asked him. "It doesn't make sense to me."

"Nor to me," McCall said. "But at least we have found a few clues."

"Candy Annie used to devour candy," Kostmayer remarked. "Gummy Bears, Jelly Babies, Nougat Swirls, Chocolate Frogs, Lollipops and Tootsie Rolls'. So there is no question that this diary *did* belong to her."

"But she may have ditched it," McCall said. "Just because the diary belonged to Candy Annie it doesn't mean the entries were still meaningful to her." McCall turned to Jackson T. Foozelman. "Can I trust you to let me know if you hear from our damsel-in-distress?"

"I will surely do that," Fooz promised him. "Just bring Candy Annie back home. That is all I ask of you."

McCall put a hand on Fooz's bony arm. The old man's eyes were burning into McCall's with a burning passion. "We'll find her."

Fooz nodded. "I know you will."

"I wish I had your conviction," Kostmayer said. "But so far Fooz hasn't done anything to get us closer to Candy Annie. I think this is a dead end."

"That thinking won't get us anywhere," McCall said, shortly. "You have to have faith that we will find her."

McCall and Kostmayer moved out of the *Strand Magazine*-style rooms with Fooz into the beginning of the sewer tunnels. Once again the spectacular arches, skylights and chandeliers led to a maze that twisted and turned. If Fooz had not been leading the way they would have been hopefully lost. Finally they came to a vaulted room with more metal steps connecting them. That emptied onto a park-like setting with its artificial grass lawns, a badminton court and several deck chairs spaced at intervals. McCall noted that he and Kostmayer had accessed a different part of the tunnels. Fooz went ahead. People were still scattered throughout the space in deckchairs. Halogen Night Security Flood Lights illuminated the rabbit-warren that was suspended from the high-vaulted ceiling. There were different residents here who were reading books and magazines as if they had given up hope that their lives could be altered in any way. Maybe this was the real world, McCall thought to himself. Maybe the pretend world was the one that had been manufactured for them. A few of the homeless citizens glanced up at them as they made their way across the "lawn", but they were wary. They clearly wondered what the interlopers were doing here in their space.

"These folks give me the creeps," Kostmayer murmured in a low voice.

"They have nowhere else to go," McCall said. "Cut them some slack. One of these days we might find ourselves hanging out at picnic tables like this one because we have nowhere else to go."

"A charming thought," Kostmayer said, darkly. "It doesn't get us any closer to finding Candy Annie."

"I guess patience isn't your strong suit," McCall murmured.

"You just figured that out?"

"Try focusing on where Candy Anne could be."

"I'm working on it," Kostmayer muttered. "But she could be anywhere."

"We've ruled out the underground tunnels," McCall said. "That has given us a starting point. And we have Candy Annie's diary. We have to work with the information we've got."

"I know you're right," Kostmayer sighed. "But that doesn't help my anxiety level from going through the roof."

"We'll find her," McCall said. "This is just the first skirmish."

McCall and Kostmayer finally came out in one of the larger tunnels. Fooz led them to the iron rungs that led up to the manhole cover. Having delivered them to their destination, Fooz eased back a little. He felt ashamed of his behavior. He made a promise to himself that it would never happen again. He needed to return to his own space which was decorated like a Victorian parlor with a mural of *Sherlock Holmes* on one of the walls to keep him company.

McCall and Mickey Kostmayer climbed up the iron ladder. Between them they manhandled the manhole to one side. They climbed up into Times Square and wrestled the manhole back in place. The people in Times Square did not pay the slightest bit of attention to them.

These were New Yorkers.

"Now what?" Kostmayer said. "Candy Annie doesn't live below the streets anymore. She was staying in my appartment on Fifty-Fourth Avenue and 2nd Avenue until three days ago. What would have induced her to leave?"

"Think of her like she was the Marshal of Tombstone," McCall said. "She knows the town and where all the bodies are buried. Candy Annie did not return to the tunnels. I am certain of that now. I am going to search all the usual places for her. There used to be an old-fashioned Soda Fountain in Queens she loved to go to."

Kostmayer nodded. "Eddie's Sweet Shop in Forest Hills."

"That's the one. Check it out."

"What else was on your list?"

"She liked to go to the chess tables in Central Park," McCall said. "She liked to visit the bronze sculpture of the *Mad Hatter and the White Rabbit* where Alice was sitting on a giant mushroom looking at a pocket watch with the *Cheshire Cat and the Door Mouse* looking on."

"She also spent a lot of time at the American Museum & Natural History," Kostmayer said. "They have a new exhibit of the perpetually dark ocean and sea creatures that never see the sunlight. Her favorites were the sea squid and the angelfish."

"She would also go to see matinees of Broadway shows," McCall said. "*The Lion King* was a favorite of hers. *Wicked* and *Harry Potter and the Cursed Child* was another. The staff at the theater let her sneak into a matinee of *Phantom of the Opera* once in a while. She had seen that show maybe ten or twelve times."

"That gives me a direction to go in," Kostmayer said. "Where are you going to be?"

"I need to find us an ally who would be sympathetic to our cause," McCall said.

"Who would that be?"

"It's a long shot," McCall admitted.

"You're not going to tell me the identity of this ally?"

"Not until I am sure he is on board. I'll meet you back in your apartment in two hours."

"Good enough."

Mickey Kostmayer disappeared into the crowd around Times Square.

McCall walked over to Broadway and 50th Street. A four-story brick building faced the street. There was one entrance to a foyer which was drab and looked like it had been there since the Pilgrims landed. McCall found a set of stairs that led down to a basement. He tried one of the doorways and pushed inside. The basement had four fire-escapes hugging the brick walls around him. Two more of the skeletal steel ladders had snaked down from the far side of the room. Lighted windows flared in them. A figure was climbing up from the fire escape. He was merely a silhouette in the shrouded gloom. Then the figure suddenly fired a burst from a sub-machinegun and strafed the open window. His victim staggered and fell onto the fire escape. Above him a gangster appeared. He was dressed in black wearing white suspenders and a wide tie with spats and a fedora. He held a Chicago-style sub-machinegun and opened up on the figure clinging on the skeletal ladder. The G-Man, who looked like Kevin Costner to McCall, fired back, sending the gangster crashing down into the dented trash cans below. Then the lights blacked out on the fire escape, leaving the antagonists once again in darkness. When the lights brightened again the scene had reset itself. The two figures had miraculously recovered. They flew up to the two top windows. Both of them were poised to repeat the exercise over and over again.

McCall moved through the doorway of the basement room and found himself in a shooting gallery. A room had been furnished like a scene from the Old West with an old-fashioned General Store, a jail set, a barber's pole where 5 cent-and-ten-cent groceries were labeled. More life-size figures with *Interactive animation and Laser Targets* had been placed in the Old West setting. Motorized steel target systems were mounted on the counters. 22. rifles had been placed with them with rimfire targets. Mechanized ducks travelled across the massive shooting gallery. More targets were lined up on the counters: *Coyotes Howling at the Moon*, a *Cast-Iron Buffalo* and more *Gunfighters from the Old West*. There was also a *Grizzly Bear*, a *Snoopy Target*, the *Red Baron* and a *Flying Goose*

Gallery Target. Shooters were all lined up at the tables to take their turns at scoring a bullseye.

McCall found Hayden Vallance at one of the targets that displayed scenes from *Gunfight at the OK Corral* where the bullseyes were staggered over an old-fashioned style poker hand. The sharpshooters had to shoot out the *Ace of Spades* from each target. Vallance turned to McCall, surprised to find him on a shooting range.

"What kind of a rifle were you using in that simulation?" McCall asked.

"A Riger MKIII Rimfire pistol," Hayden said. "It can be handled with one hand. All of the shots with a spatter impact can hit the targets."

"What's your best score?"

"Seventy-five percent gets you into the high stakes game with a marksman classification," he said. "With a 95 percent rating you are off the charts. Eighty-two percent is considered high, but I am working on a perfect score. But you did not come here to discuss percent points with me. You must have a good reason for seeking me out."

"A circumstance that I did not allow for brought me back to New York City," McCall said.

"I am listening."

"I need a favor."

Vallance shook his head. "I don't do favors," he said, shortly.

"That's the mercenary talking. I wouldn't ask if it wasn't important."

"Why do I have the feeling I am going to regret this?" Vallance murmured. He set the rifle on the counter. "Come with me."

McCall and Hayden Vallance moved through the echoing shooting gallery and exited the building. There was a pub on the corner of Broadway and W 55th Street called the *Robin Hood* that Vallance frequented. He and McCall entered and sat down at a table in the raucous ambiance. McCall thought about Hayden Vallance. He had rescued McCall, his friend Granny and Deva Montgomery from the Chateau Krazinski in Plyon Privolzhsia on the Volva River in Russia. A journalist named Daniel Blake had been killed by a sniper's bullet in the melee that had followed. Both

McCall and Vallance had been affected by it. Vallance had brought McCall, Granny and Deva Montgomery home. He knew McCall well enough to know that at some point he would seek redemption from this assassin whose name was Samantha Gregson. But that was not Vallance's problem. As far as he knew, Samantha Gregson was alive and well and was probably still stalking McCall. But that was not his problem, either. Hayden Vallance had other priorities that needed his attention. He respected and admired Robert McCall, but Vallance was a mercenary who fought other people's wars. He was, as McCall once described him, a loner who didn't allow his feelings to interfere with his lifestyle. He was ruthless and expedient, but there was a small part of his lethal expertise that McCall admired. He had a big heart, even though he would always deny it.

Their waitress, a pert, elfin honey named Colleen who Vallance admitted he had spent some quality time with, moved over to their table.

"Nice to see you again," she said to Vallance. "You haven't been around lately."

"People to see, bad guys to deal with."

Colleen was used to Vallance's quirky sense of humor. "What can I get you guys?"

Vallance ordered the Shepherd's Pie. McCall ordered some popcorn shrimp.

"Good choices," Colleen said and moved away.

Vallance's cell phone rang. He answered it, listened, said: "All right" and hung up.

"Bad news?" McCall asked.

"Nothing I can't handle."

Hayden Vallance lapsed into silence, glancing at the raucous ambiance around them. McCall let him have his space. The mercenary was mercurial and temperamental. Vallance had once picked up McCall from Syria where he had been trying to rescue a wounded US marine named Captain Josh Coleman. Vallance had been traveling in a M1-24 helicopter, firing at the insurgents while McCall had climbed aboard the chopper. They had made it out of that hellhole, but Captain Josh Coleman had been killed in the firefight. Vallance had flown to South Korea to pick McCall and Granny up when they had been incarcerated in a prison camp in North Korea. Liz Montgomery, a photojournalist, had managed to escape from the camp. Her sister Deva had also escaped with them. Vallance had brought them all home. So McCall had a lot of time for Hayden Vallance. But he knew there were dark places that Vallance frequented in his mind where no one else could venture. Not even McCall. He was a dangerous friend and an even more dangerous enemy.

The waitress arrived at the same time with Vallance's Shepherd's Pie and McCall's Popcorn Shrimp. She smiled at McCall. "I know Hayden's order before the chef does. Enjoy," she said and wandered to where more customers were seated in the pub.

Vallance followed her with his eyes. "A dynamite ass," he remarked. "And those legs are spectacular."

He started wolfing down his Shepherd's Pie which he ate with relish. McCall took some bites of his Popcorn Shrimp.

He waited.

"I heard that you had pulled stakes and disappeared into the wilds of Alaska," Vallance said. "You took a trip to Vancouver where you were last seen crossing the Caplano Suspension Bridge. But that was where my intel ends. I lost track of you in the Boreal Forests on your way to Montreal. But you came back for a reason. I am not sure I want to hear it."

"You do or you wouldn't be sitting here with me."

"I am going to lead a peace-keeping mission," Vallance said. "I am trying to find some missionaries in the Republic of Amenia which became independent in 1991 during the dissolution of the Soviet Union. I have a few clues, but nothing I can take to the bank."

"But you could postpone that trip if you needed to," McCall said.

"Get to the point," Vallance said.

"You remember my friend Candy Annie?"

"I remember her name. I heard you rescued her from the sewer system where she had been living beneath the streets of New York City and introduced her to a bright new future," Vallance said. "I got that from Mickey Kostmayer, but it was all heresy. I have never met Candy Annie, although her name appealed to me."

"She has been missing for the last three days," McCall said. "Maybe longer. Her friends are concerned about her."

Vallance glanced up from his Shepherd's Pie. "You don't have friends, McCall," he said, tersely. "You have acquaintances and enemies."

"That's true," McCall agreed. "But I am calling in the favor."

"I don't do favors. I collect markers that I cash in."

McCall let that go. He knew that wasn't true. The mercenary went back to his Shepherd's Pie, but McCall knew he had touched a nerve.

Once again he waited for Hayden Vallance to respond.

IV

FAIRGROUND

Finally Vallance succumbed to the silence. "You have no idea where Candy Annie is?" he asked.

"A couple of clues," McCall said, "nothing more."

"But you are going to find her and rescue her."

"That's the general idea."

"You have a way with words, McCall," Vallance said. "Only you could appeal to my conscience."

"I was under the impression you didn't have one."

"Smoke and mirrors," Vallance said, ironically.

McCall smiled. "I understand. Do you still have your Global 6000 Vista Jet?"

"I do."

McCall got to his feet. "I'll be in touch," he said and left Hayden Vallance to finish his breakfast.

Back at the Liberty Belle Hotel the lobby was jammed with guests who were all clamoring for attention. Chloe and Lisa were dealing with the unruly mob with their usual style and finesse. McCall took the elevator up to the 17th Floor. He entered his hotel suite. It was in darkness. He did not make a sound as he listened to the stillness around him. He turned on some lights. Everything was exactly the same as when he had left it. McCall opened the refrigerator. A bottle of champagne was chilling, a Yellow Label Brit 91 Champagne which Sam Kinney had been saving for McCall's return. Everything seemed to be in order, then McCall noticed a note that had been left for him under the suite door. He picked it up and unfolded it. It was written in Sam Kinney's distinctive chicken scrawl. It had an address on it of a fairground located somewhere in the city. The note had been written in haste. It gave no clue as to where Sam Kinney could be located. Which meant that the old spymaster was also missing. McCall took out his cell phone and accessed a number.

Then once again he waited.

* * * *

Mickey Kostmayer entered his apartment on Fifty-Second Avenue and Lexington and turned on all of the lights. He had found nothing in his search for Candy Annie. It was his intention to pack a small suitcase and wait for McCall's phone call. He had just started on it when there was a knock at his front door. Kostmayer lifted his Walther PPK 9mm pistol from his bag and moved to the front door. When he opened it he found Jackson T. Foozelman standing on the threshold. The old man looked haggard and drained of all emotion. Kostmayer sighed, ushering him inside. He put the Walther PPK pistol behind him in his belt.

"Sorry, Fooz, I wasn't expecting you. This is not a good time for you to come visiting."

Kostmayer returned to the bedroom and continued his packing. Fooz came to the threshold of the room. He appeared ill-at-ease and hesitant. His face had a haunted look to it.

Kostmayer could relate. He had been incarcerated in a prison camp just over the North Korean border from which he had escaped. The sense-memory of that trauma had stayed with him for a long time. He never wanted his freedom compromised again. Alcohol had been his choice for most of his clandestine career in the spy business. He had resolved to cut back on the martinis and the Bloody Mary's. To see Jackson T. Foozelman in this sorry state affected Kostmayer in the worse way. His attitude softened to the old man. "I know you are worried about Candy Annie."

"I got her a little present," Fooz said, as if distracted. "A charm bracelet. I have been saving it for just the right moment to give it to her. Now I don't know what to do with it."

"I am sure Candy Annie will love it," Kostmayer said, patiently. "Wait until you can slip it on her wrist."

"I will surely do that." The old man was struggling with his words. And his tears. "I need to get something off my chest."

Kostmayer sighed and continued with his packing. "What's that, Fooz?"

"It's a decision I have been wrestling with for a long time. Candy Annie lived with me ever since she was persuaded by Mr. McCall to venture out into the streets for good. But it was not just that."

"Then what is it?" Kostmayer was getting impatient again. "You're talking in riddles."

"I am going to just come out with it," Fooz said." He paused, as if for shock value, then he said: "Candy Annie is my daughter."

Kostmayer turned his full attention back to Fooz. "You can't be serious."

"Yes, sir. Candy Annie is my real daughter."

It took Kostmayer a couple of minutes for the shock to sink in. "Does McCall know about this?"

"No, sir. No one does," Fooz said. "I know it is hard to believe. I can see exactly what you are thinking. I am an old black man a little touched in the head who imagines that a child as beautiful as Candy Annie could be his. I was in the hospital when she was born. A nurse brought her to me. She was three days old. Her birth mother was a white girl who had been hooked on smack. The infant was so small and helpless and had been bawling her head off. I knew the mother was in a bad way. She was not going to make it through the night. The nurse let me hold my daughter and I fell in love with her right there and then. I had been visiting the doctor who used to live under the streets of Manhattan, so we were kindred spirits. He said he would facilitate the paperwork. Otherwise the child was going to be taken to a clinic somewhere in New York City and I would never see her again."

Fooz paused, as if trying to get his breath back. Kostmayer was still reeling from the import of the old man's words.

"Go on."

"The deal was done," Fooz said. "I assured my doctor friend that I would take good care of this special person. He asked me if I realized what kind of a responsibility I was committing to. I told him I knew the risks. Two days after that Annie---that was her name---was home with me."

"But you could not have looked out for her when you were living under the streets of Manhattan," Kostmayer objected.

"I left her in the care of a nurse who had nursed me back to health some time back," Fooz said. "Her name was Colleen Desmond. Annie spent the first few years of her young life in this gal's care. She worked at a nearby clinic catering to the needy. My friend who had helped me got sick and, sad to say, passed away. By that time Annie was five years old and feisty, but very withdrawn into herself. Finally I brought her home to live with me below the New York City streets. After that Candy Annie---she had been calling herself *Candy Annie* by that time---and I had bonded. I never told her who she really was. That ship had already sailed. You know the rest."

In light of Fooz's stunning revelation, which Kostmayer did not really believe, he was even more determined to find out what happened to Candy Annie. She had once told him that she was in love with him. Kostmayer had dismissed that sentiment as cavalier and just something Candy Annie said in the heat of the moment when they were making love. Finally he just shook his head. "I am sure you thought that was the right thing to do for her, Fooz."

"It was the only thing I could do for my daughter," Fooz admitted. "She had lived with me ever since that time. Then she was persuaded by Mr. McCall to venture out into the streets of New York City for good. I miss her something terrible.

"Who else knows about this?" Kostmayer asked.

"Only you. Not even McCall knows about it." Fooz took Kostmayer's arm and tightened it until Kostmayer thought the circulation had been cut off. "Bring her home to me. That's all I ask."

"I'll do my best," Kostmayer promised him.

Before Kostmayer could move, Fooz had exited the bedroom. By the time Kostmayer got to the front door it was closing. He opened it and heard Jackson T. Foozerman's clattering down the stairs and out the front door of the apartment building. Kostmayer slowly closed the door. He tried to reach Robert McCall, but the phone went right to voicemail.

He went back to his packing.

If Fooz's words were true it weighed heavily on him.

*   *   *   *

Ten minutes later Jimmy Murphy pulled up to the Liberty Belle Hotel. He was driving a late model Lexus. Jimmy was a retired spy that McCall had said reminded him of a ferret with watery eyes and a cunning face. He was five-ten, a hundred and sixty pounds with high cheekbones and luminous green eyes. He was no longer in what he called the 'spook' business, leaving that to other stalwart souls to carry on the tradition for him. He wore a green track suit and orange Nikes. Jimmy had given up trying to placate his wife Sarah when it came to the subject of Robert McCall. She was convinced that Jimmy put his life in jeopardy every time he went out of his way to deal with him. It was a good way for him to get killed. But her husband had stopped listening to her warnings. There was a bond between Robert McCall and Jimmy Murphy that Sarah could not explain. Whatever it was, it took her husband out of the security business and left him seriously vulnerable. That, in her eyes, was a dangerous course for him to navigate.

"Where to?" Jimmy asked.

"We're going out of the city," McCall said. "The route takes us past Westchester to Middletown on the Hudson River in Tarrytown. It's about half a mile south of the Tappan Zee Bridge before you get to Lyndhurst Manson."

"What is out there?"

"I'll know more when we get there," McCall said.

"I live to serve," the retried spy said.

He fired up the Lexus and headed out of Manhattan.

McCall had lapsed into silence. Jimmy knew his passenger well enough to know that he could be introspective and withdrawn. The countryside got wilder the further Jimmy drove out of New York City. Crape Myrtie trees, American Red Maple and Poplars stretched out in front of them. Soon thick hedges and overgrown shrubbery had petered out. In another hour a skeletal *Amusement Park* emerged like a mirage out of a grey mist that had descended on them. It was fenced off with barbed wire, but in many places that had been trampled to the ground.

"The fair is right here ahead of us," McCall said.

Jimmy leaned forward, fascinated with what he was seeing. "I didn't know a fairground even *existed* in this place."

"It was abandoned in the winter of 2014," McCall said. "I only came upon it when I was searching for Control after he had been abducted. Since then the fairground has deteriorated ever further."

"Would now be a good time for me to ask who we're looking for?"

"Sam Kinney," McCall said. "He works at the reception desk at the Liberty Belle Hotel. He has also been missing for the last three days."

"You think he'll turn up at some abandoned fairground?"

"It's the only clue I have for finding him."

"Works for me," Jimmy said

He parked and he and McCall got out. Barbed wire enclosed the facility, rising to a height of eight feet. McCall found a break where the fencing had been trampled almost to the ground. They climbed over it and found themselves in another world. Around them the ghostly reminders of the fairground had been left to rot. A huge wooden rollercoaster towered above the vendor's stalls. There were significant gaps in the coaster where parts of it had collapsed. Several wooden buildings were grouped around the attractions with names like *The Shredder*, *The Hellraiser* and the *Nightmare Scream*. Dodgem cars with gaping mouths painted on them swung haphazardly in the brisk wind. Witches on flying broomsticks swooped down on wires in front of the sepulchral *Haunted House*. A gigantic *Ferris Wheel* dominated the scene, but most of the rides around it had crumbled or disintegrated.

"I wouldn't want to here in the middle of the night," Jimmy murmured.

"Too late for that," McCall said, softly. "We're being watched."

"By zombies or living folk?"

"Hard to say. They're just shapes in the darkness. They're not threatening yet, but they could be."

"It's always an experience working with you McCall," Jimmy said. "Abandoned fairgrounds and murderous night creatures are always high on my 'to do' list."

"Just keep focused," McCall said.

"Too bad I'm not packing a gun," Jimmy said. "But Sarah tends to frown if I leave the house carrying a loaded weapon. She thinks I am going to shoot someone unless I have a good reason to curtail my natural instincts."

"Keep your distance from the fairground folks if we encounter any of them," McCall said. "I don't know if Sam Kinney is here or not. Just keep your eyes peeled."

"Any idea why he should be here at this fairground?"

"No."

"Was the note written by Sam?" Jimmy asked.

"Hard to say," McCall said. "His notes have all been left for me over the years in Sam's chicken-scratch scrawl. This one may not have been legitimate, but I need to check it out."

McCall came to a *Fortune Teller's Booth* where a wizened crone cackled over a loudspeaker system. He noted that the *Hall of Mirrors* had been shattered. Daggers of glass had been carelessly strewn around the ride. Jimmy noted an aquarium that no longer held any fish. A corkscrew ride that had once sent its passengers on a wild ride through a *Dinosaur-Themed Land* lay ahead. A *Tyrannosaurus Rex*, an *Allosaurus* and a *Velociraptor* towered above a lagoon. For the most part the creatures in the park were in pieces. They had all been dismantled or destroyed. There was a fake graveyard with crosses from *Boot Hill* in the *Old West*. Wooden windmills turned lazily at intervals. A Paddle Steamer had run aground in a lagoon where more ferocious beasts were hidden in the huge trees. The steamboat listed precariously on its side. The only ride that seemed to be intact was a *Pirate Ship* with full sails billowing against a manufactured wind. It was anchored to a concrete platform that gave it the illusion of being fixed in one place. The entire fairground had a desolate air of palpable destruction.

McCall and Jimmy moved to where the *Ghost Train* glistened in the fractured moonlight. Large oil drums were spaced at intervals. In their ghostly glow people moved in and out of the shadows. Their shapes were ill-defined in the darkness. McCall reckoned there have might be ten or twelve homeless denizens cloaked by the fires which burned lower as the iron drums were being slowly consumed. He put out a hand and gripped Jimmy's arm.

"I want you to wait for me here," McCall said, tersely.

"You might need some backup."

"Nothing I can't handle," he said. "Keep your distance from the itinerant souls that are surrounding you. If they suddenly come at you in a rush, retreat further back into the fairground."

"Sounds like good advice," Jimmy said. "What happens if they are murderous and life-threatening?"

"Improvise," McCall said.

He slipped away from Jimmy and climbed up onto the *Ghost Train* platform. There was a set of double doors that led him into pitch blackness. He allowed his eyes to adjust to the gloom before he proceeded further. Skeletons leaped out at him triggered by unseen rising platforms. Ghouls and demons swirled around the walls which were projections with no substance. A huge *Black Widow Spider* hung from the ceiling in a glowing translucent web. Shrieks and maniacal laughter echoed from speakers hidden in the walls. McCall stepped over the overturned *Ghost Train*. The tracks had long since been removed from the ride. He came to the *Sky Wheel Ride* which was at an angle on its side. He clambered over the *Teacups Ride* which no longer spun its passengers around until they were dizzy. He turned a corner and came to set of double doors that opened out into a study straight out of *Sherlock Holmes' "A Study in Scarlet"*. The great detective sat in an ornate armchair puffing on a pipe while he brought a magnified glass out to examine some clues. *Dr. Watson* sat opposite him in a wing-backed chair wearing a trimmed grey moustache and a Homburg hat. The animation on the ride was minimal, but the figures of *Sherlock Holmes* and *Dr. Watson* were skillfully brought to life. McCall pushed open a mauve door and stepped out into an eerie graveyard with crypts and headstones that was filled with an undulating fog.

Some figures emerged on the edge of the graveyard as if they had been summoned from the *Gates of Hell*. They circled McCall in a tight group. They were wielding tire irons, lengths of chain, switchblades and one of them was carrying an M48 Cobra crossbow with steel-tipped aluminum arrows and self-cocking bolts. They were all young, not more than twenty-five, with the unnerving look of predators.

They attacked suddenly and without warning. McCall disarmed one of them who had been carrying a tire iron. The youth collapsed to the ground. The second assailant swung a metal chain at McCall's head. He sidestepped the vicious blow and sent the assailant to his knees. He grabbed a switchblade knife from the third assailant's hand. Using a butterfly kick McCall threw him against a brick wall. The blade shattered. The youth staggered away. The remaining hoodlum was carrying the ornate crossbow. McCall disarmed him, sending him down to his knees.

The crossbow clattered to the ground.

McCall turned in a circle to face more of the savage attackers.

V

SPECTRE

A YOUNG WOMAN IN HER mid-twenties emerged from the shadows and picked up the crossbow. McCall thought her sunken cheeks looked as if they had been ravaged with drugs. Her hair was jet black and cut short in bangs on her head. She wore stonewashed jeans, a denim shirt and a pair of classic Croc Tie-Dye sandals. Several bracelets caught the pale light as she turned them around on her wrists. She wore a *Lord's Prayer Bracelet* and a *Leather Stainless-Steel Necklace*. Several nose-rings protruded from her face. Tattoos glistened on her neck and across the upper part of her breasts. McCall noted a prowling *Black Panther* and a verse from the *Bible*: *They Will Soar on Wings like Eagles – Isaiah 40:31*. More tattoos adorned the girl's arms including myriad black butterflies and a beautiful naked girl with folded wings wearing fishnet stockings. A menacing serpent was crawling out of a skull on her chest. The girl's shirt was unbuttoned all the way down to her navel. Her pubic hair was on display and curled visibly beneath her lace panties. On her breasts was another tattoo: "*Winged Skulls*" along with a *Skeleton* and *Four Guttering Candles*. Beneath them was yet another tattoo with the name: *Kacey Rose* in letters of blood. Kacey, if that was really her name, had a husky quality to her voice of honey and cigarettes.

The youth got to his feet but backed away when the teenage girl turned the crossbow onto him. "Back off," she said, "or I'll put this crossbow so deep in your heart they'll have to remove it with a spoon."

"That crossbow belongs to me," the youth protested.

"You gave your privileges away when you turned into an ass-licking creep. We have rules, Xander, and one of them is to keep away from the fairground guests. You got a problem with that then you can find me with the junkyard dogs and the weasels who prowl the darkness."

The youth just stared at Kacey, then at McCall. Then he faded back into the overlapping shadows in the fairground.

"Xander and his playmates are going to be so pissed with you for doing that," Kacey said.

"I'll get over it," McCall said.

She turned the crossbow over in her hands and offered it to him. "This will be safer with you than with me."

McCall's took the crossbow from her. "Would you have actually fired that crossbow at him?"

"I guess we'll never know. Xander is a scum-sucking predator, but he has connections in the fairground."

"So your life may be threatened?"

Kacey shrugged. "It may be. I'll deal with it."

McCall released the trigger mechanism on the crossbow. He removed the quarrels and disassembled the stock until it was in three pieces. Then he broke the pieces in his hands. He removed the deadly bolt and set the pieces and the trigger down on the ground.

"You took a chance with Xander," McCall said.

"The weasel has been undressing me with his eyes ever since I came to the fairground," she said. "I let him look and once in a while I let him fondle me because that gives me a rush. No big deal. Does that shock you?"

"Are you trying to shock me?" McCall asked.

"I don't really care what you do. In this fairground the jackals and the scavengers tear at each other. I just have to stay out of their way."

McCall shook his head. "That's a pretty cynical attitude."

"It's called survival," Kacey said. "Do you have a problem with that?"

"Not unless it gets you killed," McCall said.

Kacey gave McCall an appraising look. "You're pretty foxy for an old dude. I have the feeling you could have jammed that crossbow bolt right up Xander's ass. He has been intimidating the fairground folks for a long time."

"Are you going to be all right?" McCall asked her.

"Why shouldn't I be?"

"These predators will be back," he said. "They didn't like you interfering in their lives. I won't always be around."

"So you have rescued me?"

"I think it's a question of you rescuing me," McCall said, dryly. "How many of these hoodlums are there roving throughout the fairground?"

"I don't keep count," Kacey said. "For the most part they leave me alone and I leave them alone."

"But they'll be back when you're not expecting an attack."

"I will deal with it when they do. Why are you concerned for my well-being?" she asked. "I can take care of myself. I don't need a father-figure to find me in the shadows."

"Do you know the parable of the two wolves?" McCall asked her. "One was evil: Anger, envy, guilt, disappointment and a false ego. The other was benevolent: Joy, peace, hope and a sense of serenity that lifted the spirits. They snarled and tore into one another. Which of them would eventually triumph?"

"The evil wolf," Kacey said, immediately.

"They *both* did," McCall said. "Because they were the *same wolf*."

Kacey thought about that. "That's kind of beautiful in a twisted way."

"It is scary because the real world can be a scary place," he said.

"I'll take my chances," she said. "*Life is short and soon it will end. Death comes quickly and respects no one.*"

"Where did you hear that?"

"It's a poem. Or a nursery rhyme. I can't remember which. It stayed with me."

"Do you have a home to go to?" he asked her. She shrugged. "Only the one I have here in the fairground."

"What's your name?" McCall asked.

"It's Kacey Rose. Take a closer look at my breasts if you need to. Get it out of your system." She opened her shirt and pulled it away from her chest, revealing her large breasts. "Xander, that's the dude with the attitude problem, couldn't take his eyes away from them. Kind of gross, but the vermin in the fairground are like that."

"I'm guessing that Kacey Rose is not your real name," McCall said.

"How do you know what my real name is?" she challenged. "I prowl the streets with the reptiles and the madmen. The only alliance I have is to keep away from strangers."

"That can be a lonely place to find yourself."

"I manage okay," Kacey said. "Tell me your name."

"It's Robert McCall."

She held out her hand and McCall took it. Her handshake was pliant and warm. "Nice to meet you, Mr. McCall."

"How long have you been homeless?"

She released her hand as if it had been burned. "I have a home," she said as if suddenly defensive. "I choose not to go there. I make my own rules."

"I didn't mean to offend you," McCall said.

"I was all right before you did your dog-and-pony act," Kacey said. "You were just trying to do your good deed for the night. I get it. I should have let you take your chances in the dark. Take a good look at my breasts or my tattoos or anything else that takes your fancy, then leave me alone."

"I'd say your anger is directed at yourself," he said.

"So you're going to psychoanalyze me now? Wow, that's so cool!" Then she was in his face. "I have been on my own a long time and I like it that way."

"That won't last forever," McCall said. "You need to rethink your priorities. Find out what will give you a purpose in your life."

"Are you my guardian angel now?"

"Just a little friendly advice."

"What do you want from me?"

McCall shrugged. "Just for you to be safe."

"You are not responsible for my dark moods," Kacey said, but the words had a hollow ring to them. "Now get out of my face."

She turned away. She reminded McCall of "*Andel*" who once had taken care of him when he had recovered from the epic fight with an assassin named Jovan Durkovic above the Chateau Krarzinski in Prague. "Maybe I'll sleep better at night," he said. "Knowing that you're safe."

"You are not anyone special to me," she said and spit the words at him.

She slid the Lord's Prayer leather bracelet higher on her wrist.

McCall let that go. As she rightly said, she was not his concern. "A friend of mine has been hurt," he told her. "I believe he is somewhere in the fairground."

Kacey turned back to him. "What's his name?"

"Sam Kinney."

"Have you got a picture of your friend?"

McCall took out his cell phone and scrolled down to a picture of Sam. He turned it around to show Kacey. She nodded immediately. "Sure, I know this old dude! He was here in the fairground. I came across him last night. He must have been trying to escape from someone."

"That could very well be."

"What was he doing in an old disused fairground in the first place?" Kacey demanded. "He is lucky that the degenerates who inhabit this place didn't steal his shoes."

"He may be held against his will," McCall said.

"Is that right?" she asked, her tone mocking.

"Sam is a trusting soul," he said, evenly. "He wouldn't have been looking for trouble."

"I can relate to that," Kacey said. "Sorry, I was being a brat. I can take you to your friend. The maze can be deceiving. You'd had better follow me."

She turned and was immediately swallowed up in the shadows that threatened to consume her. McCall followed her through the maze of burning oil drums. The abandoned vendors' stalls were all gone now. Kacey stopped at the wooden façade belonging to the *Hall of Mirrors*. Miraculously the structure was still standing. There were three entrances to the maze. Mirrors were set at regular intervals. The myriad reflections elongated or flattened or stretched them, often with hilarious effects. Kacey plunged into the maze. McCall followed her, ignoring the mirror reflections that assailed him on all sides.

She came to a dark corner of the surrealistic setting.

McCall saw Sam Kinny was lying on the polished floor.

"This is how I found him," Kacey said. "I didn't know if he was dead or just passed out."

McCall knelt beside the old spymaster, feeling for a pulse in his neck. It was there, but very faint. "How long has he been here in the *Hall of Mirrors*?"

"Maybe a day or more," Kacey said. "Not any longer than that. I check out the fairground at least one time a day. To make sure that Xander and his pals have not been in here starting trouble."

McCall picked Sam and heaved him over his shoulder. He moved through the *Hall of Mirrors* with Kacey until he was outside in the fairground. He set Sam gently down on the ground.

"Will your friend be all right?" Kacey asked with genuine concern.

"He will be if I can get him into an ER," McCall said.

"What was he doing here in the first place?" she demanded.

"I don't know the answer to that."

"Your friend is lucky to be alive."

"He may have been looking for me," McCall said.

"Why would he have been doing that?" Kacey asked.

"I have enemies. We'll just leave it at that."

McCall looked up to see Jimmy pulling the Lexis to one side of the fairground gates. He straightened. Kacey followed his gaze.

"Who's this dude?"

"The cavalry," he said.

He took a card from his pocket and handed it to Kacey.

"What's this for?" she asked, as if she had been insulted.

"You can reach me anytime, day or night," McCall said. "If you need to."

"Why should I have to do that? I have to live on my wits and my nerves in this place. I have learned to control my own destiny."

"I gathered that," McCall said, ironically.

"What else do you want from me?"

"Not a thing," he said. "Toss the card or keep it."

Kacey suddenly nodded. "I get it now. You're a cop."

McCall shook his head. "Not a cop."

"You act like one. I know all the signs. You're a private eye like *Sam Spade* or *Spencer* looking for salvation. Too bad you won't find any with me."

"This tough guy act only goes so far," McCall said. "I see a frightened young woman trying to find her way through the shadows. If you don't need a lifeline, that's fine. But sooner or later you're going to need a friend. And I don't mean the lowlifes and vermin you are running away from."

"Will you be my salvation?" she asked, caustically.

"I will try to help you," he said. "That is all I am offering."

"It's too late for that." Kacey's voice was ragged with emotion. "Take your compassion somewhere else."

Jimmie jogged over to them. "I took a shortcut through the grounds. Just turn right at the *Ferris Wheel* until you come to the *Ghost Town Ride*." He looked over at Kacey Rose. "Where did you pick up the babe?"

"The 'babe' has a name," Kacey said, acidly.

McCall sensed a frightened edge to her voice that had not been there before. "This is Jimmy Murphy," he said. "He has been helping me locate a missing girl."

"What's her name?"

"It won't mean anything to you."

"Try me."

"It's Candy Annie."

Kacey shook her heard. "I don't know her," she said. "Sorry I can't help you."

She turned away, humming a strange, haunting tune as if she was not aware of it. "Nice to meet you. Mr. McCall." She looked down at Sam Kinney's prone figure. "Sorry about your friend. Let me know if he lives or dies."

"Don't let those snakes and madmen get to you," McCall said. "You have my card. Get in touch with me sometime."

Kacey took the card and looked at it. "*The Equalizer*. That's kind of a cool name. There are more of the walking dead prowling the fairground. They'll be watching you. You had better get your friend to the ER before he dies," she added, softly.

Then she disappeared into the darkness.

Jimmy said: "That's a Hellion waiting to happen."

"She's just scared," McCall said. "The fairground can be very intimidating."

"Does this gal have a hold on you?"

"Not yet," McCall said. "I never saw her until tonight."

Jimmy knelt down beside Sam. "By the way, I got a call on my cell phone. Mickey Kostmayer has been looking for you. He wants you to take a cab to Saint-Luke's Lutheran church on 8th Avenue in Hell's Kitchen. It sounded pretty urgent, but that is Mickey Kostmayer's MO. He is waiting for you."

"Okay," McCall said.

Jimmy felt for a pulse. "I'd say Sam is in a bad way."

"Let's get him into the car."

Jimmy hefted old Spymaster up in his arms. He was little more than a husk. "Sarah has probably got tracker dogs and search teams out searching for me," he said. "Unless you are going to be named in the divorce proceedings, I had better head for the nearest hospital."

McCall and Jimmy headed to where the Lexus was parked. They loaded Sam Kinney onto the back seat and McCall slid in beside him. Jimmy climbed into the driver's side.

"I found a way out of this fairground," he said. "I drove right past the *Sherlock Holmes* exhibition and the *Eerie Graveyard* and that was when I saw you standing in the shadows with that babe with the tattoos. What's her name?"

"Kacey Rose."

"Her real name or is that a handle?"

McCall shrugged. "Could have been both."

"She looks kind of fragile," Jimmy said.

"She is," McCall said.

"When are you going to stop caring for people you don't even know?" Jimmy demanded. Then he nodded. "I guess that's an "Equalizer" problem. You will have to deal with it yourself."

"Let's get out of this place," McCall said.

"Suits me. Deserted fairgrounds are not my idea of a fun place to be." Jimmy fired up the Lexus and they drove away from the fairground.

VI

ASSASSIN

JIMMY DROVE THROUGH THE countryside until he was back in the city and pulled up outside the Lenox Hill Hospital. McCall jumped out and lifted Sam Kinney back into his arms. Jimmy parked the Lexus beside the curb.

"Wait for me here," McCall said.

He carried Sam into the ER where two interns and a doctor were on call. The triage nurse immediately hooked Sam up to an intravenous catheter. One of the other doctors took McCall to one side as Sam was wheeled into an examination room. He explained that Sam was suffering from dehydration and was running a high fever. McCall knew he was prone to respiratory infections. The doctor, whose name badge said Dr. Martin Bernstein, told McCall he might have a subarachnoid embolism and a subarachnoid hemorrhage. The old man's blood pressure had dropped from Hy 110 systolic to 90 Hy systolic which could mean that he was having a heart attack. Dr. Bernstein moved though the double doors advising McCall to take a seat. He would update him on Sam Kinney's diagnosis and condition.

McCall waited for three hours in the ER until Dr. Bernstein returned. Sam was out of danger and resting in one of the hospital rooms on the sixth floor.

"Your friend had pneumonia caused by acute respiratory distress in both lungs," Dr. Bernstein said. "I performed a spectrum culture test to identity the cause of the infection. I also performed a bronchoscopy and inserted a camera into the airwaves to help in diagnosing the causative agent. I drained the fluid out of his lungs. I performed a CT scan and an x-ray to make sure there was no damage to the lungs. Sam is sleeping now. I don't want him to be disturbed until morning. Then he can have visitors."

"Thank you, doctor," McCall said. "I'm very grateful to you."

"It was touch-and-go there for a while," Dr. Bernstein admitted. "But Sam is a fighter and that helped him in his recovery."

McCall shook the doctor's hand. "I'll come back tomorrow."

He walked out of the hospital and climbed back into the Lexus where Jimmy had parked. He looked at McCall.

"What's the verdict?"

"He's going to pull through," McCall said.

Jimmy started the car. "Where to, or shouldn't I ask?"

"I need to get over to Kostmayer's apartment on Fifty-Fourth and Second Avenue," McCall said. He had a fleeting memory there that he had check out. "Mickey may still be there. I have a key that he gave me for emergencies."

Jimmy nodded and started the car. Twenty minutes he was outside the apartment. "Do you need any back-up?"

"Not this time," McCall said.

He did not know how prophetic those words would be.

"Let me know what has happened to Candy Annie," Jimmy said. "She sounds like a special lady."

"She is," McCall said.

McCall got out of the car and Jimmy drove away. McCall entered the apartment at Fifty-Fourth and Lexington and climbed the stairs to Kostmayer's apartment. He let himself in and found the apartment in shadows. He didn't know if Mickey had been back there or not. He might have been chasing out some leads for their quest. The shades at the windows effectively shut out the sunlight. McCall looked around the familiar room that Candy Annie now called home. He knew exactly what he was looking for.

He remembered how Candy Annie had expressed her gratitude for him early in their relationship by unbuttoning her shirt and exposing her breasts. McCall had appreciated the gesture, but he had gently re-buttoned her shirt, telling her that friends did not take advantage of each other. At the time she had been at a loss for words. She wanted to thank her mentor for literally saving her life and rescuing her from beneath the Manhattan streets. He had told her that no thanks were necessary. She was now part of his extended family. McCall would always be there to help her. That was before Candy Annie and Mickey Kostmayer had become friends and, ultimately, lovers. McCall had nurtured that relationship. He thought they made a great couple. He knew Candy Annie was blissfully happy with Kostmayer, but McCall did not believe their relationship was going to last. He did not believe that Mickey Kostmayer did, either. The Company agent was headstrong and mercurial. That impassioned and reckless behavior had got him into trouble more times than McCall could count. Mickey had escaped from a North Korean prison camp where he had been incarcerated before McCall and his friend Granny had destroyed the camp in a blazing inferno. But that emotional trauma had stayed with Kostmayer and it was not going away anytime soon. It was an anguish that Mickey tried to bury deep in his psyche, but McCall thought it was a losing battle. Sooner or later Kostmayer would turn on the people who meant the most to him. That had not happened yet, and McCall hoped it would not happen anytime soon. But Kostmayer was vulnerable. His trauma was on a razor's edge. McCall knew he needed his help if he was going to locate Candy Annie and bring her home.

McCall did not turn on the lights in the apartment. He glanced down at the small desk in a corner of the bedroom. Candy Annie had various display lipsticks on it and an enamel nail polish-remover bottle. There was liquid lipstick coffee mascara, a fast-drying nail lacquer, banana powder and pomade eyebrow make-up. A hairbrush and a letter-opener were neatly placed beside some diamond earrings. There was a vintage dressing table holding a mirrored tray. McCall noted several scented candles and a glass perfume bottle. The drawers in the dressing table were curiously empty. Candy Annie had not collected much in the way of trinkets or keepsakes. The bathroom door was ajar, but the lights were turned out.

Candy Annie had a four-poster canopy with a chestnut rocking chair in front of it. A wooden ladder like the kind the Mexican soldiers had scaled the Alamo with was placed in front of it. McCall moved the ladder to one side and moved the bed six inches until it was resting at the wall. He just had to find a particular spot on the polished floor of the bedroom. The item was concealed in a loose floorboard which could be lifted up if you knew where to look. It was her special place to hide her treasures, such as they were, which she had collected over the years of living under the Manhattan streets. McCall had never questioned her about it, nor had Mickey Kostmayer. Candy Annie had her own secrets.

McCall found a slightly raised floorboard in the bedroom. He pried it open and lifted it up. He felt beneath it and extracted a small six-by-twelve package that fitted snugly under the floorboard. It was covered in brown wrapping paper. McCall got to his feet and unwrapped it. Inside was an antique *Coral Cameo Pearl and Diamond Brooch in 14K Gold* in the likeness of a young woman. She had flowers in her hair and was set in the sloping surface with of a bezel. It was augmented with old European cut diamonds and elaborate detailing. McCall was engrossed with examining the cameo brooch.

He never heard the intruder.

For once in his life Robert McCall had no awareness of impeding danger.

The assassin moved out of the darkened bathroom. He was wearing soft leather moccasins that did not make a sound. McCall turned the cameo over. A small piece of paper drifted down onto the bed. McCall unfolded it. It was a photograph of Candy Annie when she was a teenager, the colors so faded that they were almost non-existent. A name was written on the back of the photograph that said: *Meadow Springs. Minnesota*, but nothing else.

That was when the attacker looped the strangling garrote around McCall's throat and tightened it.

The would-be assassin possessed tremendous strength. McCall was not prepared for it. He writhed under the punishing pressure that was being exerted. He felt consciousness quickly rushing away from him. He would black out within seconds unless he broke the man's hold. He had one tactical advantage. The moccasins the man was wearing were soft and pliable. McCall stomped down at the assassin's exposed right ankle. That broke the hold on McCall's throat. He used a rising right backhand which took the attacker completely by surprise. At the same time he fell into a crouch, using the assassin's weight like a weapon, found purchase on the silk shirt he was wearing and threw him over his shoulder. He staggered, but the attacker was quickly on his feet. McCall grabbed his assailant's throat in a reverse choke, known as *The Sleeper*, but the would-be assassin broke free and rushed at him. He was a compact, powerful man with grey deep-set eyes and high cheekbones that gave him an almost Oriental look. He was dressed in black. His hands were his most telling feature, almost delicate in the way he moved them.

The assassin's rigid right hand grabbed McCall's throat again in an upward right palm strike. A reverse neck kick threatened to smash McCall's cheekbone.

The bigger man grabbed hold of McCall's throat once again and squeezed.

McCall was ready for that. He countered with some hook kicks and a crescent-style kick. Then he smashed a roundhouse elbow into the assassin's face. The attacker swung back unexpectedly with an axe-kick that almost took the top of McCall's head off. The *Hadaka Eagle Claw* maneuvers came at McCall fast and in frighteningly close quarters. It caused compressive asphyxia that McCall had to fight off if he was going to survive.

Once again he broke free from the assassin's grip on his throat. The assassin punched him in the heart which could easily have cracked several of his ribs. McCall narrowly missed a *Muay Thai flying Elbow* that the attacker threw at him. It left him dazed and disoriented.

McCall was fighting losing consciousness fast.

Suddenly he reared back, taking the assassin with him, crashing into the small dressing table in the bedroom. The assassin had not prepared for the sudden move. McCall scattered the various lipsticks and perfume bottles on the dressing table. He unscrewed the top of the nail polish-remover and threw it into the man's eyes. He howled with rage, involuntarily squeezing his eyes shut. McCall turned around with the small perfume bottle in his hands and emptied it into the man's face. The assassin sank to his knees, momentary blinded. McCall wrapped his arms around the assassin's throat and squeezed hard, wrenching the man's head to one side. The color drained out of his face. His lips turned blue, his eyes bulging as he tried to get enough air to breathe.

McCall broke the man's neck.

He slumped down to the floor.

McCall looked down at him and realized that he had never seen him before in his life.

His pulse rate was high and he tried to bring it down a little. He took several gasping deep breaths, trying to clear his head. He stumbled to his feet. He was breathing hard. The unexpected savage fight had taken its toll on him. He allowed his traumatic throat muscles to calm down. Then he knelt down beside the sprawled assassin. He found no ID on him. Samantha Gregson had tried to kill McCall on the train bound for New York City. The attempt had failed, but that did not mean Samantha Gregson would not try again. He just had not expected the next attack to come so quickly.

McCall lifted the prone assassin onto his feet, dragged him into the bathroom and dumped him in the bathtub. He reached down for the assassin's wrist and pulled it back. A tattoo was prominent there that said: *Memento Mori*. McCall had expected to find it, but even so it was a shock to his system. He did not think there would be any further attempts on his life, but these hired killers were relentless.

McCall considered how ephemeral all mortal things were. He had escaped death twice dealing with these *Memento Mori* killers. He did not think he could tempt fate again. The close call with the assassin had rattled him. He thought about Kacey Rose and the haunting tune that she had murmured to him in the fairground: "*Life is short and soon it will end. Death comes quickly and respects no one.*" If a hired killer had come for McCall in the fairground, Kacey Rose would be dead. So would Jimmy Murphy, Sam Kinney and probably Mickey Kostmayer as well. It gave McCall a reflective pause as he dragged more air into his lungs. He would have to monitor his enemies more closely. Kasey Rose had been an innocent acquaintance in his life. Now her life could be in danger.

McCall emerged into the bedroom. He picked up the cameo piece of jewelry that had dropped onto the floor. Carefully, he rewrapped it and put it into his jacket pocket. He moved out of the darkened apartment. He called Jimmy Murphy on his cell phone. He answered it on the second ring.

"This can't be good," Jimmy said. "I only left you half-an-hour ago, McCall. How can you get in trouble in that short space of time?"

McCall told him what happened. Jimmy's wry humor left him immediately. "I can be at your apartment in fifteen minutes. I have a key. Do you know who this assassin was?"

"No idea," McCall said. "I believe the killer was sent by Samantha Gregson. If he was, this is the second time she has tried to kill me within twenty-four hours."

"What are you going to do about it?"

"She won't try again. She'll bide her time. Wait for the right moment."

"And what happens then?" Jimmy demanded.

"I'll deal with it."

"As long as you're safe. By the way, I got a text message from Mickey Kostmayer. He was on his way to Saint-Luke's Lutheran Church on West Forty-Six Street in Hell's Kitchen."

"What is he doing there?" McCall asked, alarmed.

"He just said to get down to Saint-Luke's as quickly as you can."

"I'm on my way. You'll take care of things at the apartment?"

"I live to serve," Jimmy said.

McCall severed the connection and took a cab to Hell's Kitchen. When he stepped out of the cab paramedics were working on Father David Kostmayer. Mickey Kostmayer moved from the ambulance and jogged over to McCall. The pastor had been severely beaten. There were bruises on his face and both of his arms. His right eye had almost closed up. He was obviously in a lot of pain.

"This is how I found him," Kostmayer said. "He had been the victim of a vicious attack. He was crawling on the floor and trying to get onto his feet when I entered the church. He was dazed and in a bad way, but he was coherent. At first he did not know who I was, but then he focused on me. I've only seen him a few times at his church when I introduced him to Candy Annie."

McCall nodded and moved over to where the paramedics were about to transfer David Kostmayer into the back of the ambulance. "Give us a minute," McCall asked them. He clutched David Kostmayer's hand. "You don't know me, pastor, but my name is Robert McCall."

"I know exactly who you are," the pastor said, his voice faint but getting stronger. "Mickey Kostmayer is one of my practitioners. He has been very active in the church. Two men came into the church as I was preparing for a Sunday service. They said they were friends of Candy Annie, but I knew immediately they were lying through their teeth. I had never seen them before. I doubted they had ever set foot in a church unless it was to rob it. I have learned a few tricks being around Mickey Kostmayer and the spy business and I could sense their tension as soon as they entered."

"What happened?" McCall asked.

"Candy Annie was going to wrap gifts for the children's hospitals," David Kostmayer said. "We get regular donations from all around the world shipped here to my little corner of Heaven on 8th Avenue. But Candy Annie had not shown up either at the church or at my basement facility on 46th Street. I had not seen her for over a week and that was not like her. She was happiest when she was wrapping the gifts for the less fortunate souls."

One of the paramedics, whose name was Colleen Torres, finished strapping Father David Kostmayer on the gurney. She moved over to McCall and Kostmayer. "We need to get our patient into the ambulance. You can follow us."

VII

CONSEQUENCES

McCALL TOOK A STEP BACK as the ambulance was loaded up. The paramedics closed the back doors, one of them moving inside, the other one running to the front. They took off with the sirens blaring and the lights flashing.

"That makes two attacks in a few hours," McCall said.

"Where was the first one?" Kostmayer asked.

"At your apartment on Fifty-Fourth and Second Avenue. An assassin tried to kill me."

"What happened?"

"Obviously he didn't succeed, but it was a near thing," McCall said.

"There is something else you are not telling me?"

Sometimes McCall was amazed at how intuitive Kostmayer was. He told him what had happened in the fairground and where he had found Sam Kinney. He also described Kacey Rose.

"Did you recognize this angel of mercy?"

"I had never seen her before," McCall said. "She led me to where Sam Kinney was sprawled in the *Hall of Mirrors*. It wasn't a set-up."

"Then what was it?"

McCall just shook his head. "Something else. A sixth sense that brought her to me."

"But you did meet her at the fairground?"

"I did. But there was a reason why Kacey Rose found me," McCall said. "It was as if she had been waiting for me."

"Was she stalking you?"

"I wouldn't put it that way."

"But for some reason you need to find her again?"

"She'll find me," McCall said, enigmatically.

"I love it when you talk in riddles," Kostmayer said. "Is Sam going to make it?"

"The ER doctor thought he was going to pull through."

"Where does that leave it between you and Samantha Gregson?"

"She'll take another shot at getting me killed," McCall said. "You leave that to me. Right now Candy Annie is still missing. We have to find her."

"So we're back to square one," Kostmayer said.

"We have one clue," McCall said. "It's an address in Meadow Springs in Minnesota. It may come to nothing, but we haven't got a lot of options right now. Hayden Vallance is going to take us there."

"I don't trust him," Kostmayer said. "He'll sell us out to the highest bidder."

"Cut him some slack," McCall said. "Granny trusted him to find Deva Montgomery and Daniel Blake when he and I were coming under fire at the Chateau Krarzinski in Russia. Vallance got us out there in a hurry. He has no loyalties to anyone except perhaps to me. I have called in the favor. He is going to pick us up tomorrow and fly us to Chicago. We'll proceed there to Meadow Springs."

"A pretty long shot," Kostmayer said.

"It's the only one we've got right now."

"You're the boss."

"There is one last thing."

"What's that?"

"Vallance said he found a chapter of the Church of Jesus Christ of Latter Saints who have a parish in Meadow Springs," McCall said. "They emigrated from Utah and have a policy that strictly forbids tobacco, alcohol, coffee and tea."

Kostmayer stared at him. "*Mormons?* You can't be serious."

"Deadly serious. Candy Annie is very religious," McCall reminded him. "Vallance believes that was what started Candy Annie on her current path to salvation. It's a way of life the Mennonite Church has chosen. But was it the life that Candy Annie would have chosen?"

"It can't be," Kostmayer said.

"Are you sure of that? We don't really know anything about her. Maybe that pushed her over the edge. We won't know unless we can find her."

"Fair enough," Kostmayer said. "What happens now?"

"We rendezvous with Hayden Vallance in the morning."

"He has his own agenda," Kostmayer said. "He'd sell us out the first chance he had."

"You may be selling him short," McCall said. "He's mellowed over the years. See you in the morning."

McCall left the Company Agent there. Mickey Kostmayer returned to his apartment on Fifty-Fourth Street and Second Avenue and turned on all the lights. There was no sign of the fight that happened between the *Memento Mori* assassin and Robert McCall. Kostmayer thought that Jimmy Murphy, a friend of McCall's, had probably come in and removed all signs of the skirmish. Kostmayer dragged an overnight bag from the closet in the bedroom, dropped it onto the bed and started to pack it. He was not going to bring much with him. This was a rescue mission and he wanted to travel light.

For some reason the idea of a sect like the *Mormons* being involved with Candy Annie filled him with a sense of dread.

That morning Hayden Vallance picked up McCall and Kostmayer at the West 30th Street Heliport. The Global 6000 Vista Jet took off and soared over the New York City skyline heading for the Midwest. In the conference suite in the Lear Jet Kostmayer related to McCall his conversation with Jackson T. Foozelman about Candy Annie.

"She never once broached the subject when we were together," Kostmayer insisted. "Candy Annie had been living under the streets of Manhattan for years. When she emerged into the real world she was not sophisticated or street savvy, but she relied on her common sense and her inherent grace and style."

"What else did she say?" McCall asked.

"She said she was going home," Kostmayer said, simply. "But she never got that far."

McCall nodded. He did not believe for a minute that Jackson T. Foozelman was really Candy Annie's father. Fooz was prone to exaggeration at the best of times and could weave extraordinary stories when he was on a roll. But McCall was not so sure. Kostmayer's story had a ring of truth to it. Or perhaps that was what McCall wanted to believe. He would reserve judgment until he found out the truth.

Hayden Vallance landed the Global 6000 Visa Jet at the Crystal Airport in Minnesota. He parked the helicopter in a hanger which he had secured in advance. McCall found Kostmayer and himself two rental cars. The first one was a 2021 Ford Explorer Timberline with 18" wheels embossed with a laser-etched logo. The second rental car was McCall's favorite model, a Jaguar F-Type Convertible coupe in Salsa Red. Vallance would drive the Ford Explorer and McCall and Kostmayer would drive the Jaguar. Crystal Airport in Minnesota was about 30 miles from Meadow Springs. They drove in two cars. When they reached their destination they stopped at a diner, the Appolla Grill on Main Street in Clear Lake, Iowa.

The waitress who served them looked like she had worked in the restaurant for sixty years. But McCall put her age somewhere in the mid-forties. She wore a name badge that said *Dixie*. She was paper-thin with tattoos up and down her arms including the words *Cowgirl Up* with entwined silver horseshoes, a motif of Doc Holliday that said: *I am Your Huckleberry* and the words *Marlboro Man* with what looked like James Dean lighting up. She spoke with a western drawl and wore jeans, a western plaid shirt and cowboy boots. McCall thought she looked like Alicia, the elegant matriarch from beneath the New York City streets. They could have been sisters.

"You folks here for the rodeo?" Dixie asked them.

"We're strangers here," McCall said. "Are you familiar with a town called Meadow Springs?"

"Sure. It's a Mormon town about ten miles from here."

"You're sure it's a Mormon hangout?" Kostmayer asked.

"Of course I'm sure," Dixie said. "They got chapters throughout this area. They mostly keep to themselves. They got a pretty good Grocery Store on Shills Mills Road in the Blue Ridge Mountains in Boone. You could travel to the Appalachian State University for the annul Arts Festival or take in the Rosen Concert Hall if you have a mind to hear some good classical music. That is all I can tell you about my recollections on Meadow Springs. I've worked here for twenty years at the Appolla Grill. Ain't worth spit." She sized up Hayden Vallance and grinned. "If you are aiming to stay for a while, I am not doing anything between now and death."

"I'll keep that in mind," Vallance said, wryly.

"What's your poison?" she asked them.

Hayden Vallance ordered corned beef hash, potatoes, bell peppers and scrambled eggs. Kostmayer had a classic Reuben corned beef and fried eggs. He added biscuits and gravy to his order. McCall ordered poached eggs, avocado, turkey burgers and bell peppers. He opened a folded map of Meadows Springs and spread it across the table while they waited for their food to arrive. He glanced at Kostmayer.

"When we get to our destination, find a bed-and-breakfast place on Main Street and check in. The Sheriff's Office is right there." McCall looked at Vallance. "Do you have intel on him?"

"I have," he said. "None of it good. I accessed some of my mercenary sources. The Sheriff in Meadow Springs is a good-ol' boy named Jethro Conrad. He runs the town with an iron fist. My contact said he was also into drug trafficking, but he couldn't prove that. The FBI and I have a love/hate relationship," Vallance added. "Mercenaries are not high on their list of priorities. I did know a Federal Officer who worked out of the Kluczynski Federal Building here in Chicago named Dutch Ryan. He was transferred to Boone, Iowa, where he has been working out of the Government building there and the Des Moines Community College campus. I will reach out to him."

McCall looked over at Mickey Kostmayer. "Pay the local Sheriff a visit. Find out if he has any intel on Candy Annie, but do it discreetly."

"This is not my first rodeo," Kostmayer said. "I know what to do."

At that moment Dixie arrived with their food order. She set the plates out for them. "Enjoy." Then she moved back to where other costumers were waiting. McCall was all business. "Candy Annie trusted people. She was looking for some meaning in her life. Mormons are a closed society where she could have found a home and acceptance. Maybe it was just what she needed to find to give her a sense of purpose. She may have been wrestling with this decision for a long time."

"I don't believe that happened," Kostmayer said.

"We don't know what may have happened to her," McCall reminded him. "None of us really knew Candy Annie that well. She was a free spirit. If she did become enamored with the Mormon way of life, then it is up to us to say God Bless and her let go."

Sometime after that they exited the restaurant. Vallance drove the Ford Explorer and McCall drove the Jaguar F-Type coupe with Kostmayer. In twelve miles they entered Meadows Springs. It was an idyllic, charming little town with a gorgeous downtown street and old, brick houses. The town had its own winery, the *Black Oak Valley*. McCall noted several galleries with picturesque facades, small parks and even a functional lighthouse. Vallance needed to do some exploring in the town.

McCall pulled into the Hyatt Regency bed-and-breakfast suites and parked. He and Kostmayer entered the hotel. It was decorated with rustic flourishes with leather couches, hardbacked chairs and a gleaming hardwood floor. A sweeping staircase climbed to the second floor. The reception desk was oak where the staff wore chic gray slacks and colorful western shirts like John Wayne wore in *The Searchers*. McCall and Kostmayer registered. McCall picked up two antique-style brass keys that looked as if they unlocked pirate chests.

"I've sent the luggage to two of the rooms," McCall said. "We'll pick them up later. Play it easy and charming with the Sheriff."

"You don't have to coach me," Kostmayer said. "Where will you be?"

"Taking a good look at the town," McCall said.

"Seeing if you can run into Candy Annie on the street?"

McCall shrugged. "Hope for the best," he said. "Prepare for the worst."

McCall left Kostmayer on the street. Hayden Vallance drove to the Des Moines Community College Campus. He found his old friend Dutch Ryan at the Kluczynski Federal Building in Chicago at the Loop Station Post Office. Dutch Ryan had a kind of bombastic personality that took no prisoners. He was a bear of a man with a crew cut. He had grey eyes, a rugged countenance and stood five-six feet tall. He was on his way out to attend a meeting on campus when Hayden Vallance had caught up with him. He crushed Vallance's hand in an iron grip.

"Nice to see you again, Vallance. Are you still in the mercenary business?"

"When it suits me."

"That is not a world I would feel very comfortable living in."

"Most folks don't until it affects them personally," Vallance said.

"Walk with me across the campus," Dutch Ryan offered. "I've got a counseling meeting in ten minutes."

Hayden Vallance had to keep pace with the counselor as he strode through the trees as if he was on his way to a fire drill. "Compared to your lifestyle, the pace in this college town is pretty mundane," Ryan said. "We do have an outstanding drama department and the best tennis tournaments in the Midwest with the Oracle Challenger series. We've got the top respiratory therapy program outside of Chicago. For all of us here that is a big deal. I have to be on the baseball field at lunchtime. Everything stops for the DMACC Bears Athletic games. We have a player who just got drafted to the Detroit Tigers."

Hayden took out a picture that Mickey Kostmayer had given him of Candy Annie sitting at the chess tables in Central Park enjoying a picnic. He showed it to Dutch Ryan.

"I am looking for this girl."

Dutch gave the photograph a quick once-over. "Pretty girl. Was she ever enrolled here at the DMACC?"

"Not to my knowledge," Vallance said.

"Then I can't help you. There are over 23,000 students enrolled here. Thirteen hundred of them are female. Who are you looking for?"

"A pattern," Vallance said. "The victim may have been kidnapped. The jury's is still out on that."

"What's her name?"

"She answers to the name of Candy Annie."

Dutch took the photograph and looked at it critically. "I'm sorry, that doesn't ring any bells for me. I don't know her."

He handed the photograph back to Vallance.

"But you do know Sheriff Jethro Conrad?" Vallance asked him.

"Of course I know the Sheriff," Dutch said. "He's a fixture here in Meadow Springs. He throws his weight around a little too much for my taste, but he gets the job done. He's been here for years. What is your interest in him?"

"Just wanted to know what guy he is."

"Look, the Sheriff runs the county," Dutch said. "I am not saying more than that."

"But there is more you could say?"

The counselor paused in his stride, as if sizing Vallance up. "This a small town. We've got the College Campus and a Wal-Mart Neighborhood Market. There's a Safeway Food Market on one corner and an Albertson's on the other. That's all she wrote. Everybody knows everyone else. It's a tight community. The police force here is minimal."

"But the Sheriff is a law unto himself?"

Dutch Ryan looked away. "Sheriff Collins is a piece of work I grant you that. Been rumors about the way he conducts himself that are open to interpretation. Do yourself a favor and stay away from him."

"Your honesty is much appreciated," Vallance told him.

"Don't cross Sheriff Collins," Dutch advised him. "He can be a powerful enemy."

"I'll keep that in mind."

"This is a college town," he said. "The most excitement here is out on the baseball diamond when the Bears are losing, which doesn't happen often, but it does happen. The Bears have a record of sixteen wins and just four losses and I am hoping to improve on that record."

"That's outstanding," Vallance said with no irony in his voice.

"I have another match to judicate," Dutch Ryan said. "That means I have to go back to work. I may have said too much already."

"Not if you're telling the truth."

"I'm telling you to back off," he said. "You never were good at that, Hayden."

Dutch Ryan crossed the rest of the campus toward the Liberal Arts building and was lost in the trees.

"But you've given me a lot to think about," Vallance murmured. "Where do think the Sheriff parks his police cruiser?"

It didn't take Vallance long to find it. It was parked in a lot two doors away from the police station one flight up on the first floor. It was a Ford Crown Victoria 3 5-liter V6 with front wheel drive. It had the lights bar and the words *Police* and *Emergency 9-1-1* on the front of the grille. On the hood the words *Meadow Springs* had been stenciled in blue script. It was adorned with two blue stripes. The police car was unlocked. In a sleepy little town like this, Vallance didn't see the necessity to lock car doors. He slid a backpack from his shoulders and took out some sophisticated radio link equipment. Then he slid into the parked police car.

It had a digital analog two-way XTR350 UHF radio mounted with two speakers. He took the radio link equipment and adapted it with an 8 channels 2KM Android Mobile Phone unit upgrade. He dismantled the FHSS 67 Channels Pseudo Ransom Frequency Hopping feature. He rewired them into the digital analog two-way XTR350 UHF radio speakers. He wired that up with the 8 channels Android Signal Support system. Then he rewired the radio unit back into the two speakers. He placed the radio back on the front seat, slid back out of the car and switched the radio unit on. He got a signal immediately.

Vallance packed back the duffel bag and slipped it across his shoulders. He walked down the ramp to the ground floor and out of the building. He moved over to where the Ford Explorer was parked. He unlocked it and slid inside. He made sure the signal was still strong. He looked over at the Sheriff's Office. Mickey Kostmayer might be already inside.

Valance settled down to wait.

VIII

SHERIFF

WHEN MICKEY KOSTMAYER WAS SHOWN into Sheriff Jethro Conrad's office he was not expecting the reception he received. Jethro Conrad was a throwback to another era. He was a cordial, gregarious, larger-than-life good-old boy whom Kostmayer described as a fugitive from *Smokey and the Bandit*. He was a big man with wavy grey hair and sideburns. His face was craggy and heavy-lined. When he came around his desk there wasn't an ounce of fat on his body. He was lithe and tanned as if he spent a lot of his time outdoors. But Kostmayer detected a subtle shift in the emphasis in his manner. He was sizing his adversary up and his deep-set eyes took in every detail. He reminded Kostmayer of a coiled Black Mamba snake he once had to fight off in the Sahara Desert who could kill with just two drops of venom.

The Sheriff pumped Kostmayer's hand like they were old friends. "I'm Sheriff Jethro Conrad. Good to meet you. What did you say your name was again?"

"Mickey Kostmayer."

"I can't say I've had the pleasure. Please, take a seat."

Kostmayer sat down on a Madison Tufted Wing Back chair as the Sheriff sat back down at his desk. He leaned back and appraised the one-time Company Agent with his easy-going manner.

"What can I do for you, son?"

Kostmayer thought that dropping the good-old-boy routine would be a step in the right direction, but he didn't say so. McCall would have played it differently. But Kostmayer had to play the hand the way it was dealt to him.

"I am looking into the disappearance of a young woman," he said. "She vanished from her apartment in New York City several days ago. I think she may have taken a trip here to Meadows Springs."

"Hate to say it, but young girls don't travel here to our town," Sheriff Conrad said. "Too close to Chicago and too far to have traveled here from the Big Apple. This isn't a destination on anyone's map. It's a nice little town if you are traveling through with time on your hands to visit our local winery or the Community College. You'd be through Meadow Springs in two shakes of a lamb's tail and on your way to somewhere else."

"You have a Mormon presence here, don't you?" Kostmayer asked, casually.

The degree of Sheriff Conrad's affability cooled significantly. "Yes, we have. They're good people leading their lives in the spirit of God. They are very family oriented with strong connections across several generations. I don't judge folks. They leave us alone and we respect their beliefs and family values. Now slow down for me just a tad, son. You wouldn't be asking about the Church of Jesus Christ of Latter-Day Saints unless you had a good reason."

"They might be the key as to why my friend left New York," Kostmayer said.

"Can't say that I am tracking with you," the Sheriff said. "You're going have to spell that out for this country boy."

Kostmayer took the 8x10 photograph out of his jacket pocket and handed it to the Sheriff. There was a flicker of recognition in Conrad's eyes, but then he was working hard on his good-old-boy façade. "I don't know her. Does this filly of yours have a name?"

"To tell you the truth, I don't really know what her name is," Kostmayer confessed. "I have always called her Candy Annie."

Sheriff Conrad laid the photograph on his desk. His demeanor had changed again. "Her name is Anne," he said. "*Not* Candy Annie. Don't rightly know where the 'Candy' got attached. Some kind of nickname, I reckon. Her name is Anne Conrad."

That got Kostmayer's attention. "Anne Conrad?"

"That's right," the Sheriff said. "She is my niece."

Kostmayer took a moment to register the shock of what he had just heard. Finally he said: "I have ever only heard the name Candy Annie when I was talking about her."

Sheriff Conrad sat back in his chair, coolly appraising Kostmayer. "I don't know what handle you gave her, son, but her full name is Anne Grace Conrad."

"When was the last time you saw her?"

"I haven't seen Anne in over twenty years."

"But you're certain this is your niece?"

"That's a pretty old, faded picture you showed me. I guess I could be mistaken, but this old hound dog doesn't have to scratch too deep to know where the bodies are buried. She was a child when I was first laid my eyes on her."

"Where was that?" Kostmayer asked.

"Anne Conrad was living with her mother in Boulder City in Nevada at the time," the Sheriff said. "I lost track of them soon after that. I didn't even receive a postcard from them. They were just acquaintances I got to know over the years. We occasionally get young women who have broken away from the Amish Community here in Meadow Springs when they get to be twenty-one."

"But you're not a member of the Church of Jesus Christ of Latter-day Saints?" Kostmayer asked.

"No, sir. I figure Candy Annie… is that what you call her?"

"That's right."

"I figure Candy Annie broke away from the Amish society a long time ago when she was a child. We may not be even thinking of the same person. She ain't around Meadow Springs any longer. That's for sure." The Sheriff handed back the faded and cracked picture to Kostmayer. "Sorry to have to stomped on your parade, but I have a feeling she is gone forever. Kind of a shame."

"Why is that?"

"I would have liked the opportunity to get to know my niece again."

"If she just walked back into your office would you know who she was?"

"That's the sad part of this," the Sheriff said. "I wouldn't know my niece if I tripped on her in the street. She is just a memory in my mind and a fleeting one at that."

Kostmayer nodded. "I understand."

He put the photograph back into his pocket and got to his feet. The mere fact that Sheriff Collins had even *heard* of Candy Annie filled Kostmayer with hope. But that was something he wasn't going to share with the Sheriff.

"Thanks for taking the time to talk to me," Kostmayer said. Conrad got to his feet and came around the desk. Kostmayer waved him off. "No need to show me out."

"Been real nice talkin' to y'all," the Sheriff said. "Be sure to visit our winery. It's called Valentino's Vineyards. It's about a couple of miles out of town. There is a tasting room that some nice folks run that is not to be missed."

"I'll check it out," Kostmayer said. "Thanks again for your time."

"You're most welcome," Sheriff Collins said. "Sorry if I dredged up some painful memories for you. But you don't get lard unless you boil the hog."

Kostmayer laughed. "I'll remember that."

"Those memories are the ones that bite us in the ass," the Sheriff said. He shook Kostmayer's hand. "You have yourself a fine day."

"I'll do that," Kostmayer assured him.

With that parting shot he exited the office. Sheriff Conrad's entire demeanor changed drastically. He was cold and somewhat ironic. He pressed a button on his desk. One of his deputies entered the office. He was a lean and dour man with close-cropped blonde hair and heavy-lidded eyes. His badge said: *Deputy Jack Foster*.

"The fellah who was in here just now," the Sheriff said. "I want to know where he goes. If he is staying at the hotel in Meadow Springs or if he was just passing through."

"Who is he?"

"Did I not make myself clear?" Collins asked him, a little caustically. "This is a situation I want taken care of."

"I'll see to it, Sheriff," Deputy Foster said.

"The sooner the better."

"Yes, sir."

The Deputy left the office in a hurry.

Sheriff Conrad looked at the place where Mickey Kostmayer had disappeared.

All sorts of alarm bells had gone off in his head.

*   *   *   *

In Meadow Springs McCall had been directed to the Betsy Ross General Store about four miles out of town. When he pulled in a horse was tied at a wooden hitching post. He got out of the Jaguar and made a mental note of his surroundings. A covered wagon was parked beside the Ford Explorer with a horse grazing near it. There was a *1970 Oldsmobile Cutlass Cruiser Station Wagon*, a *Ford Gran Torino Station Wagon* and a *1980 Ford Thunderbird* parked outside the General Store. Wicker baskets stood beside an old-fashioned Coca-Cola cooler. Large barrels of apples, pears, onions, figs, blood oranges and all kinds of fruits were displayed in the baskets. Wagon Wheels had been hung from the porch. A rocking chair stood beside a vintage 1930's *Hawthorne restored bicycle*. A pair of Indian Moccasins were displayed along with several bags of rice and fertilizer.

A few of the Mormon families were moving into the General Store. McCall approached a teenage girl who was feeding her horse sugar beside the covered wagon. She wore jeans and a man's chamois plaid shirt. Gladiator Sandals were on her bare feet. She smiled at McCall and held out more sugar lumps.

"My horse's name is Whiskey. Is that a dreadful name to give to a horse?"

McCall took the proffered sugar and fed it to the horse. "I don't think so. She seems to be enjoying it. What's your name?"

"It's Sariah, spelled with an 'h'. It means 'Princess of the Lord.'"

"That's a very pretty name," he said. He looked around at the other families entering the General Store. "Do most of the Mormons shop here?"

"We prefer to be called the Church of Jesus Christ of Latter-day Saints," she said. "The name 'Mormon' means those of us who have benefited from the teachings of God." She looked over at the entrance to the General Store. "It's not usually crowded like this except at Easter time where His glorious resurrection from the dead is celebrated." She looked back at McCall. "But you're not a true believer."

"I believe in the inherent good in people," McCall said. "Does that count for anything?"

"Sure it does." She smiled at him. "The Lord works in mysterious ways."

"I'm sure that is true." He handed the small 8x10 picture to the teenager. "I am looking for a friend of mine. Her name is Candy Annie. She's about twenty-five. I'm trying to find her." Sariah looked at the photograph and shook her head. "Sorry. I don't know her. Is she a member of our church?"

"Not as far as I know," McCall said.

Sariah studied the photograph more closely. "I see a great sadness in her eyes. She is a troubled soul."

"You can feel that just by looking at her picture?" McCall asked her.

"It's her eyes that give her away," Sariah said.

"You're a remarkable young woman," he said.

Sariah smiled and handed the photograph back to McCall. "Thanks. I hope you find your friend soon."

"I will. Take care of yourself, Sariah."

"I am a child of God," she said simply. "He nurtures us and gives us the strength to endure all of life's calamities." She had finished giving her horse the sugar. "Good boy, Whiskey."

"It was nice to talking to you," McCall said.

"Be at peace," she said.

McCall wondered if he would ever find that peace in his life.

He moved from the girl and pushed the door into the General Store.

He felt he had entered another world.

Several shelves were lined up around a center counter. They had items that McCall had never heard of. Boxes of detergent called *Gold Dusk, Doz* and *Persil* lined the various shelves. There was pure maple sugar, Swan matches, self-raisin-flour, *Old Hickey Overalls* and *Sunbeam Bread for Energy*. There were fishing lures, beef jerky, motor oil, blocks of ice, milk urns and a plethora of American flags. An old typewriter had a shelf of its own beside an old-fashioned antique *National Cash Register*. There were free-standing red gas pumps with the letters ESSO stamped on them.

Rain barrels, old-fashioned brooms and Hoover vacuum cleaners were positioned along one counter. There were vats of onions, herbs and spices, vinegar, red kidney beans and more crates of apples, pears, bananas, plums, cranberries, grapes, mango oranges and kiwi fruits. Grapefruits, passion fruit and bags of refined sugar were also stacked up. Crates were laid out for corn and rice. Also barley and avocados. Some spices were housed in tall glass jars that McCall didn't recognize. There was an assortment of cheese in colorful gift boxes. The grocery had a section for DVDs, but they were all *8-tracks*. There were several cereal boxes. *Quaker Oats* seemed to be the favorite. There was a full-scale *Doll's House* on a stand which pivoted so that the rooms were visible. Sawdust was sprinkled over the floor.

The atmosphere in the General Store was subdued. The Mormons kept to themselves as they shopped. The majority of them were young people. The men wore denim with white shirts with no ties and jeans. McCall noted that all of the men had short hair. The women wore simple blouses or jeans, nothing overt in color or style. He moved over to a central counter where one of the Mormon workers, dressed in muted colors, was wrapping up a package for a young girl. She was laughing at something he had said. She moved with her friends to another part of the store. McCall took a good look at him.

The man was a giant.

He must've weighed in excess of 400 lbs. He was dressed in jeans and a cotton shirt, but on him the shirt looked like a tent. He was barefoot. All of the helpers in the store wore name badges. His name was *Aaron*. He wore several *Indian Bracelets* on both wrists. His eyes were dark brown and sunken deep in the folds of his face. He had a ready smile, but his eyes were wary and guarded. He had sized McCall up from the moment he had walked into the General Store.

"We don't often see strangers here," Aaron said. "What can I do for you?"

"I am looking for this young woman," McCall said.

McCall had Candy Annie's photograph in his hand. He turned it around on the countertop. The Mormon barely glanced at it.

"Don't know her," Aaron said.

"Take a closer look," McCall said, an edge coming into his voice. "You couldn't have made a determination in that space of time."

Aaron picked up the photograph and it made a pretense of examining it. Then he motioned to one of the shoppers in the store. "Take a look at this, Jeremiah."

One of the men moved over to the counter. He was dressed the same as the other men in the General Store in denims and cotton shirts. He was also one of the two men who had kidnapped Candy Annie on the road, although there was no way McCall could have known that.

"Can't say I recognize her," Jeremiah said. "Who is she?"

"A runaway," Aaron said. "I can recognize them a mile away."

Jeremiah nodded and he turned to McCall. "We get a lot of young women who have strayed from their righteous path. Most of them return home where they belong. Wish I could help you, friend, but this is not a member of our church."

"You know them all by sight?" McCall asked.

"The Church of Jesus Christ of Latter-day Saints is a strict and austere society," Aaron said. "We know who our brethren are. They are true believers."

"Are you sure of that?" he asked.

"Absolutely. We are all spirit children of our Heavenly Father," Aaron said, tolerantly.

"That is a noble sentiment," McCall said. "You would know if one of your children of God was missing?"

Aaron handed Candy Annie's picture back to McCall. "We know them all by sight. Your friend is not one of them."

"Good to know," McCall said.

He knew both of the men were lying to his face.

"Anything else we can help you with?" Aaron asked. "I got other customers to serve."

"Not a thing" McCall said. He put Candy Annie's photograph back into his pocket and glanced at Jeremiah. "This is the main road out of Boone, isn't that right?"

"You are way off track," Jeremiah said. "The highway turns back onto itself right after you leave here. You can get lost in these byroads. Folks come here all over the State because it's a way station for the Mormon Society. You need to get back to the main drag and turn around at North Interstate Drive. That will put you back onto Route US-30. If you come to the abandoned Stone Arch Bridge over Honey Creek you've gone too far."

"You're welcome to come back," Aaron said. "I got some aged Hibachi Steaks and Black Trumpet mushrooms on sale and the Halibut Lemon Sauce is a specialty of ours."

"I'll keep that in mind," McCall said.

He moved away from the counter. Jeremiah made sure that McCall had left the store, then he turned around to Aaron. "Put a call in to Sheriff Conrad."

"This guy won't give us any trouble," Aaron said. "He just wandered in from the main road and got lost."

"Call the Sheriff," Jeremiah said again. "I don't like the look of him."

Aaron shrugged, picked up a phone and dialed.

The phone of Sheriff Conway's rang. He picked it up at the second ring. "Sheriff Conway."

Aaron leaned against the counter in the General Store. Jeremiah had departed which, as far as the Sheriff was concerned, was a good thing. He didn't like Jeremiah and he liked his cohort, Jeff Fletcher, even less. But they provided him with invaluable intel from time to time so the Sheriff could not argue with that. It was just something about them that made his skin crawl. He listened to Aaron's disdainful voice while he checked on some paperwork on his desk.

"You say you've never seen this fellah McCall before?"

"That's right, Sheriff. Something about him that doesn't sit right with me."

"And what are you basing this intuition on?" the Sheriff said, somewhat disdainfully. "Just a feeling, is that right?"

Aaron bristled. "I thought you might like to know there has been a stranger in town."

"Duly noted," Sheriff Conway said. "But if you can't run with the big dogs, stay on the porch. I am not going to worry about some fellah who is more than likely visiting Meadow Springs for the first time. If he proves to be a problem, I will deal with it. Thanks you for your concern, son."

The Sheriff hung up and rolled his eyes for Deputy Foster, but something had flashed warning signs for him.

He wondered who exactly McCall was?

IX

ABIGAIL

MICKEY KOSTMAYER MOVED into the lobby of the Hyatt Regency. He picked up his room key from the attractive brunette at the desk and climbed the stairs to the second floor. A Navajo red woven multi-area rug adorned the floors. A couple of end tables and an ornate couch were placed in the corridor. Kostmayer moved over to Room 12, put his key into the lock and pushed inside. The room was in darkness. Heavy drapes hung at the windows. There was a bed in the room with a Southwestern bedspread in Navajo Tribal turquoise with brown and rust colors. Two armchairs in the same motif stood beside a leather couch. Sliding doors led to the oak-paneled closets. A bathroom door stood ajar revealing a sink and a shower with Gold Marble Baroque Mosaic Tiles. A slim balcony hugged the wall outside the window.

Someone was searching Kostmayer's room.

The shadowy figure turned at once. He grabbed Kostmayer and pushed him to the floor. He tried to get away, but Kostmayer caught his foot before he could escape. The intruder fell heavily onto one of the leather couches. Kostmayer scrambled to his feet, but the man was much too fast for him. He came at Kostmayer with a 9" Italian folding stiletto knife. Kostmayer swung away from the assault and grabbed the attacker's arm, locking it. He wrenched the intruder's arm behind his back as if he was going to break it. He disarmed the intruder and the stiletto knife skittered to the floor. The attacker was immensely strong. He wrapped his hands around Kostmayer's throat who writhed under the pressure that was being applied. McCall had once taught him a *Muay Thai* technique that was used on the sharper points of the body. Kostmayer used three methods to break the man's hold: a *Kradot Nueng* Jab, a *Sok Wiang Klap* which was a reverse horizontal elbow strike and the *Mai Soi Dio* which was a forceful uppercut strike. The undercut strike turned the tables. Kostmayer staggered to his feet. The intruder threw open the door to the hotel room. Kostmayer ran out into the corridor, but the man had run down the sweeping staircase to the lobby. Kostmayer followed him, but the attacker had completely vanished. Kostmayer moved toward the back of the hotel where there was a side door. He opened it and stepped out into an alleyway. A heavy wind stirred the debris strewn around the narrow passage between the buildings.

It was deserted.

Kostmayer made his way back through the lobby. The girl at the front desk was a very attractive brunette whose nameplate said *Elizabeth*. She smiled at him. "What can I help you with, Mr. Kostmayer?"

"I was expecting a guest to arrive here at the hotel asking for me."

"The lobby has been quiet just now," she said. "Who were you expecting?"

"Just a friend. Have there been any messages for me?"

"I'll check." She briefly went through her list. "A Robert McCall left a message for you, but he said he was just checking in. Mr. Vallance had been wanting to reach you, but he said he would call back again."

"Thanks, Liz."

Kostmayer ran back to the staircase and mounted the stairs two at a time until he reached his room. He unlocked the door and pulled it closed. He ran to the ornate drapes and opened them. He moved out onto the balcony. It was deserted. Traffic flowed through boulevards. The intruder must have exited the hotel via the back door entrance.

Kostmayer closed the balcony door and locked it. He took some deep breaths, his heart jack hammering in his chest. He did have one quick look at his attacker. He was about six feet tall with laughter lines on his face and brown eyes that were alert and expressive.

Apart from that, Kostmayer had never met him before in his life.

He didn't realize, of course, that it was the *same man* who had terrorized Candy Annie and had thrown her into the back of his Volvo Station Wagon.

But Kostmayer thought he'd recognize the attacker if he saw him again.

Hayden Vallance didn't have long to wait in his Ford Explorer. The Sheriff's Ford Crown Victoria emerged out of the parking structure and made a right turn onto the street. Vallance turned on his radio unit. He adjusted the signal he got from the analog two-way UHF radio speakers and settled down to follow the Sheriff at a discreet distance. It appeared the Sheriff was heading out of town. This could be a wild goose chase, Hayden reminded himself, with the Sheriff just returning to his office. Kostmayer had informed him that the Sheriff was a good-ol'-boy with a lot of charm and a disarming manner. Vallance knew that the Sheriff had been hiding the truth about Candy Annie's disappearance. He was going to see if he could rattle the Sheriff's cage.

McCall found his way back from the Mormon Community Grocery Store to Route US-30. He came upon the Stone Arch Bridge over Honey Creek in Wisconsin north of US-18. He drove over the bridge and came to the Linwood Cemetery behind it. The grounds had a peaceful serenity to them that McCall appreciated. He drove on until he came to the town of Madison and stopped to access a map he bought at the gas station. He had a pretty good idea of where he was headed, but there were switchbacks and signposts along the route. He had to traverse the hills into Perkinsville and skirted around the *Watauga Medical Center*. McCall turned at Goshen Hill and then onto Deerfield Road, but he only had a vague idea of where he was heading.

In four miles McCall came to another halt. He thought he could make out a figure obscured in the oak trees ahead of him. He hesitated, wanting to get back to the main road, but a nagging voice told him to turn around. He fired up the F-Type Jaguar Convertible and took a detour off the main road. In five hundred yards he came to a clearing and halted again. He was surrounded by Red

Oak and Dogwood trees. He saw a young girl moving through the trees leading a Sorrel Quarter horse. The horse was reddish brown in color. There was no saddle on him, but a polypropylene rope with a bowline knot had been tied loosely around the horse's neck. The girl was about twenty-five years old with dark chestnut hair augmented with blonde highlights. She was dressed in high-waist flared jeans, a man's Scotch plaid shirt and no shoes. She was limping a little as if she had been thrown off her horse.

McCall pulled to the side of the road under the trees, got out of the Jaguar and jogged over to the girl. She turned at his approach. She was immediately on her guard, although McCall's manner was not in the least bit threatening.

"You look as if you're lost," he said.

"My horse came up lame," the girl said. "I tried to clean up the hoof with a soft fiber brush, but the nail was embedded in pretty far. I think there might have been a crack in the hoof. I won't know until I can ride it back to the ranch for a closer look. You can give him some sugar if you want."

She had some sugar cubes in her hand. McCall took them, feeding them to the horse.

"What's your horse's name?" McCall asked.

"Powder."

"Good boy, Powder."

The horse gobbled up the rest of the sugar cubes. "Now don't get greedy," the girl chided. "This is your sugar ration for the day."

"How far away do you live from here?" McCall asked her.

"Only three miles. Where did you come from?"

McCall took a shot in the dark. "I was on my way to your ranch."

She straightened up to look at McCall, her eyes filled with suspicion. "No, you weren't. The roads are not signposted. You would have to know your way to the ranch."

"I got directions at the General Store in Meadow Springs on the way here."

"Why would they serve you? You are an outsider."

"I try to blend in," he said, wryly.

"Who are you going to see?"

McCall had no idea, but he was on a roll. "I have a contact here in Meadow Springs that I need to look up."

"You're not a member of our church," the girl said, but her qualms appeared to have subsided somewhat. "It's the Church of Jesus Christ of Latter-day Saints."

"I am familiar with it," McCall said. "But you accept strangers and outcasts who have found salvation, isn't that right?"

"Yes, we do. The light of the Lord shines in all of us," she said. "The Lord is the father of our spirits."

And she bestowed a smile on McCall that somehow seemed to radiate through his whole body.

"That is a beautiful sentiment," he said.

"If we can find atonement, our bodies will be reunited during the time of the Resurrection. But only true believers need apply," she added and suddenly laughed. "Somehow I don't think that includes you, but I am willing to give you the benefit of the doubt."

"My soul has a long way to go to find salvation," McCall said, somewhat ruefully.

"But you're working on it?"

"On and off. I don't want to encourage you to pick up strangers on the road."

"I feel safe with you."

"Why is that?"

She shrugged. "Just a gut instinct. If I am wrong, and you turn out to be an axe-murderer, I will be just mortified."

McCall laughed. "You're on pretty safe ground with me. What is your name?"

"It's Abigail. Abigail Connor. You can find it in the ancient Biblical Hebrew texts. She was the third wife of King David."

"It is a lovely name. Since your horse has come up lame, Abigail, may I escort you home?"

"You certainly may. It's only three miles up the road."

She spent a little more time examining her horse's front leg where she applied a topical analgesic horse liniment to soothe the damaged tendon. She murmured some soothing words to the horse, then she walked over to McCall's Jaguar F-Type Convertible under the elm trees.

"Wow! Cool car!"

"Your mode of transport did leave something to be desired," McCall agreed. "What will you do about your horse?"

"I'll ask the manager of the compound to come back for Powder," Abigail said. "I tied him to that red maple tree. He'll be happy there as long as I don't take too long to come back for him."

McCall opened the Jaguar door for the girl and jogged around to the passenger door. He slid inside and started the engine. Abigail was like a kid in a candy store. She was examining the R52663 5-Disc CD Changer and Audio System. It came with a cassette and an AM/FM Tuner. McCall turned it on for her. The sound was overpowering.

"This is awesome," she said.

McCall fired up the Jaguar Convertible and pulled it back onto the strip of road toward the highway. The radio was currently playing *Simon and Garfunkel's "Bridge Over Troubled Water"*. Abigail's face lit up.

"This is one of my favorite tracks," she enthused. "Garfunkel's voice can touch your soul."

"I think so too," McCall said. "How long have you lived here in Meadow Springs?"

"All my life."

"No vacations, no trips into Chicago or to Wrigley Field to see the White Sox?"

"Nope. I have got everything I need right here."

"How long have you lived in this compound?"

"I moved here when I was two years old," Abigail told him. "I don't really remember anything before then. My mother had lived in the Mormon community all her life. She passed away when the Lord and his angels came for her."

"When was that?" McCall asked.

"Four years ago. We only use pure olive oil to anoint the sick after it has been consecrated and declared sacred. I prayed for my Mom day and night, but in the end she slipped away from me on the fourth night. It was peaceful."

"I'm sorry."

"Don't be," Abigail said. "It is the separation of the soul from the body. Our spirits will continine to exist for all eternity when our spirits return to the soul. Only those left behind feel the crushing sorrow of grief."

"What about your father?"

"He left the church when I was six years old," Abigail said. "I never heard from him again. I blessed him and let him go."

"Those are tough breaks to deal with," McCall said.

Abigail shrugged. "All stepping-stones on our path."

"You are a very resilient young lady."

"I try to be." The next song Abigail pounced on. "Oh, I love this one! '*Bohemian Rhapsody*'! Freddie Mercury! It gives me chills every time I hear it!"

"It's considered classic rock now," McCall said. He turned the sound up a notch. "How's that volume?"

"Groovy."

McCall smiled to himself. There was an endearing quality to this girl that appealed to him. He flashed back to Kacey Rose and found there were similar qualities in both of them. Kacey Rose's demons were darker. He thought Abigail's personality was full of hope and self-esteem.

"Tell me about living in an Amish Community," McCall asked.

"It's cool. I have my religious studies and my chores to do every day at the ranch," Abigail said. "It keeps me very busy."

"No friends at the compound?"

"Sure, lots of them, we all hang out together. That's the wonderful thing about living in the compound. We're all blessed with real friends. There's Ashtyn and Eden and Hannah and Kaidence. My friend Naomi means 'gentle and beautiful'. And my best friend is named Oakley, which means '*Meadows of the Oak Tree*.'"

"Have you ever rebelled at your strict upbringing?" McCall asked.

Abigail hesitated for a moment, looking out the window at the countryside flashing past. "I did run away once when I was seventeen. It was when my Mom passed away. I know she was no longer here, that death is the gateway to immortality and eternal life, but I just couldn't get past the feeling of absolute loneliness. After the funeral I packed my bag and started to hitchhike across the State.

I was scared and lonely, but I was determined to find my path to salvation." She looked back at McCall. "That didn't last very long. I was miserable and feeling super-guilty. Thankfully Sheriff Conrad picked me up on the road."

"So the Sheriff is a good guy?" McCall said.

Abigail looked back at him and shrugged. "He came to my rescue. He has a personality that can grate on you sometimes, but he brought me home and I'll always be grateful to him for that."

"I presume that the Sheriff is based here in Meadow Springs?"

"I don't really know," she said. "I guess so. Oh, I love this song! *'You Light Up My life'!* Kind of corny, I guess, but Debbie Boone's voice kind of soars."

"Go for it," McCall said.

Abigail turned up the radio a little more. He took a photograph out of his jacket pocket. "I want you to look at this photograph."

He handed it to Abigail. He watched her reflection in the rearview mirror. For a moment her eyes had clouded.

"Who is she?"

"A friend of mine," McCall said. "I don't know her real name, but she likes to be called Candy Annie."

"What has happened to her?"

"She disappeared from her apartment in New York City three days ago. I believe she traveled to Meadow Springs, but I don't know for sure."

Abigail's eyes had betrayed her. But she shook her head and handed the photograph back to McCall. "I don't know her."

"Take another look."

"I don't have to do that. I have never seen her before."

McCall put the photograph on the seats between them and turned the radio down a little. "You're lying and I don't believe you do that often," he said, quietly. "If at all. You are a person who values truthfulness."

Abigail looked away to the country road in a gesture of defiance, but she was clearly rattled by McCall's words. "I don't know what you're talking about."

"Yes, you do," McCall said. "You're frightened by something or someone. Tell me who it is and maybe I can help."

She looked back at him. "I don't need anyone's help. My life is just fine as is. I'm sorry about your friend Candy Annie and I hope you find her real soon, but you're just passing through Meadow Springs. I live here."

Abruptly, Abigail turned off the radio. She slid down the seat and turned her attention to the countryside sliding by. In that moment McCall realized he had lost communication with her.

The rest of the journey was conducted in a stony silence.

X

LEDGE

HAYDEN VALANCE HAD REACHED the twelfth stair when he heard voices raised on the stairwell. There were fifteen stairs he had to traverse to reach the top of the staircase. The stairs curved around the Tuscan balustrade that led to the first floor. He stopped immediately. The wooden staircase creaked and groaned under anyone's weight. He had managed to climb up very carefully, one stair at a time, listening for telltale signs of activity. He had carried a small Phillips pocket mini-cassette *Dictation Recorder*. It measured 5" with a built-in microphone. He was taking a chance that the men would not hear him at this distance. Their murmured voices had become indistinct.

It had taken him a good fifteen minutes to reach the curve in the balustrade. The voices were coming from a room on the first floor. At first they had been very faint, but then they had registered more strongly. The building was off Main Street on a side street that Vallance identified as Stratton Street. He realized that the men were right outside the room door. There were three of them as far as Vallance could make out. One of them would be Sheriff Conrad. His distinctive Southern drawl echoed, although his words were indistinct. Vallance had to get closer to the top of the staircase to understand him. The room was a study, not a bedroom. It had solid mahogany-mission style doors. The Sheriff's voice faded which told Vallance it was a large room, perhaps going back the length of the house.

Vallance was not carrying a weapon.

He didn't like using a gun because, in his estimation, they were more trouble than they were worth. Guns jammed on you. They misfired at the wrong moments. Vallance carried a .41 Magnum Smith & Wesson Blackhawk single-action Revolver in his hand luggage, but he used it sparingly. He liked to defy the odds and branding a handgun took all the expertise out of it. Vallance had carried the .41 Magnum Smith & Wesson when he had piloted an M1-24 helicopter to rescue McCall in Syria. He did the same thing when he had flown to Pylos in the Privolzhsky District of Russia and rescued McCall and Daniel Blake. They had been trapped at the Chateau Krarzinski along with Deva Montgomery, Liz Montgomery's sister.

Vallance took another step on the staircase ahead of him.

He waited.

The murmur of voices receded. Vallance took another step onto the staircase. His footfall creaked like a gunshot. He froze and remained perfectly still. The small sounds from the next room receded even further. He took another step at the top of the staircase and waited again. Now there was no sound coming from the room. Vallance moved forward. It was an old staircase and the floorboards creaked under his weight. He reached the door to the office suite. Now there were no sounds coming from inside at all. He listened at the door. Nothing. He pushed on the door handle to no avail. The room was not exactly soundproof, but the recesses went far back. The indistinct words were muted. There was no point in Vallance turning on his mini-cassette Dictation Recorder because the murmurs were too faint to register. He put the mini-cassette recorder into the pocket of his jacket.

Vallance turned to the window at the far end of the corridor. If it was locked he would be out of luck. He moved stealthily toward it, trying not to make any more telltale sounds, but the floorboards still continued to creak. When he reached the window he lifted it.

It was locked.

Vallance shook a small set of keys out of a leather pouch and opened it. It took five minutes for him to spring the lock. He raised the window and stepped out.

Outside there was a narrow window ledge measuring four inches, barely enough to take his weight. It hugged the window casing but there were gaps in it where the window ledge ended and started again six inches farther along. It turned the corner of the window.

Vallance pulled himself up onto the ledge, bracing himself against the window glass. He inched along it, not looking down but keeping his eyes focused in front of him. His feet came to the edge of the building. A brisk wind had come up and threatened to send him tumbling off the ledge. He pressed himself back and finally looked down. There was a six-inch gap between the window ledge and where the next piece of the roof began. It continued right to the end of the building. Vallance had no idea how the windows on the other side were matched up.

He moved very slowly. An inch at a time. He was now at the gap in the window. He pressed himself against the glass. The room beyond was in total darkness. Vallance stepped off the precipice and moved to the next part of the ledge. It was only a few inches to his left. The wind howled in gusts, threatening to send him over the edge. He once again pressed himself flat against the balcony. He worked on his stress levels until they were back under control. He edged slowly until he was at the end of the building. There were two windows there.

The second window was the one he was interested in.

Vallance continued his crab-like walk along the side of the building, looking at the dark window where the lights had been turned out. Finally he came to the edge of the ledge and carefully looked in the last window. Sheriff Conrad was pacing restlessly, talking quietly to two more men in the room. One of them was a heavyset blonde man who was stabbing a finger at the Sheriff. He wore a three-piece suit with a fancy waistcoat and *Laredo Snake Cowboy Boots*. He had unruly black hair that hung down onto his shoulders and little piggy eyes that were encased in flesh. He appeared to be in a towering rage. Sheriff Conrad was doing his best to placate him. Vallance couldn't hear what *Laredo Snake Man* was saying, but he caught the words *"increased heart rate"* and *"respiratory dyspnea"*, which translated to difficulty in breathing. Obviously the patient was in distress and *Laredo Snake Man* was his doctor. The window glass had triple-pane tempered glass to reduce the sound levels. With the wind factor gusting around the building it was difficult for Vallance to hear anything at all. Isolated words were all he could hope for, but that might be all he would need.

Carefully Vallance took the mini-cassette recorder from his jacket pocket. He leaned down and turned it on. The C46 cassette would run 23 minutes. Vallance didn't want to move it once it was in place. Too risky. He just had to be patient. He was spread-eagled in the window trying not to look down. The feeling was somewhat overpowering. But he kept his eyes focused on the actual window ledge.

It was his lifeline.

Vallance had no idea if the mini-cassette recorder was picking anything up or not. Even a few isolated words were worth the risk he was taking. He looked out across the street. At the ground level was a *Subway* restaurant advertising *Buffalo Chicken, Katz's Delicatessen, Hallmark Cards, Meadow Springs Dry Cleaners, Loaves* of *Bread* and the *Cooperstown Bakery*.

A flash of light caught Vallance's attention. He turned back to the narrow edge and realized that the sun was glinting off it. There was movement at the window in the office room. Vallance quickly reached down and picked up the mini-cassette recorder. That would be all he could get with eavesdropping. With the mini-cassette recorder in his hand he sidled past the bright window and moved farther down the narrow ledge until he came to a dark window. The room beyond it was in shadow. Vallance took a chance and leaned down to the window. He raised the window a little which meant the window was not locked. He pulled on the bottom of the sill. There was just room for him. He gripped the top of the window and pulled himself through the opening. Quickly, he shut the window again and listened for signs that the Sheriff has been alerted. It didn't appear he had heard anything. Valance moved through the darkened office and opened the door to the corridor outside.

It was as silent as a tomb.

Vallance wasn't going to push his luck.

He dropped the mini-cassette recorder into his pocket and reached the top of the winding staircase. He went down the stairs quickly. He exited the building and slid into his Ford Explorer. He drove away before anyone could emerge from the suite of offices.

*   *   *   *

For the next two miles McCall stayed on the road as it wound through magnificent oak trees. He emerged from it onto a secondary trail which was not signposted. He followed that for another mile and noted groups of workers in the fields. Their outfits belonged to the Mormon Community. McCall there noted horse-drawn wagons and buggies with metal wheels in several places. There were no cars at all. The workers were tilling the fields. They picked oranges and strawberries. Apples and tomatoes were also being gathered along with potatoes and beans. A few of the workers looked up from their labors to note the red F-Type Jaguar moving some distance from them. If it gave them any concern they didn't show it. Then the car was swallowed up in the forest.

McCall emerged onto another road that wound its way to a cluster of old farm buildings. A ramshackle house had been constructed in white wood that stood five stories high. Around it were two towering grain silos. There were an additional five houses built on the property, most of them in dire need of repair. They all had white walls and some of them had stained-glass windows like in a church. The grounds around the building were unkempt and overgrown. There was an orchard of apple trees that almost blotted out the sky. There were two horse-drawn wagons pulled up with their horses grazing. Old tires were piled up in front of one of the barns. A plow had been abandoned at one of the houses. Grassy paths connected the five houses to one another. A shed had been erected that was jammed with broken furniture. Two volleyball courts had been set up by the Mormons along with a bronze horseshoe set. A croquet set including mallets, hoops and stakes and been laid out on the grass.

Abigail scooted over to McCall and took his arm. "Sorry I have been a super-brat. You were just looking out for my well-being. I understand that. What do you think of our compound? Pretty nifty, isn't it?"

"It is," McCall said. "How many people live here?"

"I've never counted them," she said. "Maybe a hundred or more?"

McCall noted the Amish families on the grounds. The women wore all the same clothing which consisted of solid and colored fabrics with long sleeves. They all had full skirts and aprons and, in some cases, capes that fit snugly around them. The women wore no jewelry of any kind. White prayer bonnets covered their heads.

"What is the significance of the prayer bonnets?" McCall asked.

"It signifies if the women are married or not," Abigail said.

"But you are dressed in jeans and a plaid shirt."

She laughed. "I am a rebel. Don't tell the other women my secret! I would be skinned alive! I will change back to my dress with the long sleeves as soon as I get out of the car."

McCall turned his attention to the men who were mainly in groups. They were all dressed in dark-colored suits and straight-cut coats without lapels. They wore fall trousers, suspenders to keep them up and solid-colored shirts. They wore black socks and laced-up shoes. Everywhere broad-brimmed straw hats were in evidence. McCall noted that none of the men had moustaches.

"What do think of us?" Abigail asked him.

"There is a community spirit that binds these people together," he said. "I like it."

"This is my stop!" Abigail suddenly announced.

McCall brought the Jaguar to a halt. She opened the car door and then, as if on an impulse, she kissed McCall on the cheek and climbed out. McCall climbed out also. A door opened at the main farmhouse and an elegant older woman stepped out onto the raised porch. She had iron-gray hair that was piled high on her head. She was dressed the same way as the other women in a flared skirt with a Victorian 18th Century long-sleeve dress. She wore the starched white apron and a cap on her head. Abigail ran to the front porch and practically dragged the old woman to where McCall was standing.

"Mr. McCall, this is my Aunt Esther," she told him. "She has raised me since I was a child." She indicated McCall. "He came to my rescue when my horse pulled up lame. He drove me here. I have been sharing my Mormon beliefs with him."

"And what are those, pray tell?" Esther said, as if she was intrigued.

"Omniscience, mercy, the path to eternal life," she said earnestly. "And all that good stuff. I had better change back to my Victorian dress and grab my bonnet before Samuel, that's one of the Elders, drags me back here. Aunt Esther will entertain you."

Abigail ran to the main house in the complex and disappeared inside. Her Aunt Esther just shook her head. "That child is like a whirlwind being unleashed by the forces of nature. I declare sometimes I despair of her wanton behavior."

"She seems to be coping well with her new-found freedom," McCall observed.

"One of these days her implacable pig-headedness will be the death of me." She turned back to McCall. "It was kind of you to return our heroine back to the flock. May I offer you some herbal tea, Mr. McCall?"

"That would be very nice of you."

'It is the least I can do since you have been so generous with your time," Esther said. "You can leave your car right there in the driveway. I can promise you that some of the younger boys will be swooning over it," she added with a twinkle in her eyes. "It's a Jaguar F-Type convertible, isn't it?"

McCall smiled as he accompanied the older woman onto the porch. "Yes, it is. But I wouldn't have thought would mean much to you."

"We all have our dreams," Ether said wistfully.

He followed her into the house. Esther disappeared into a kitchen. McCall found himself in an old-fashioned parlor. It was furnished simply with a couch, two armchairs and a dresser above which hung dinner plates with a rose Chintz pink design, four blue Italian 8" Bone China Dessert plates and elk 8" Bone China Salad Plates. In a glass cabinet was more fine China Plates with Sunflower Fields and a large China Plate saying: "*The Joy of the Lord is my strength*". There was a collection of Cherry Blossoms Plates, a set of Southwest 10.5 Dinner Plates with an inscription from Isaiah 4:10 saying: "*For We Walk By Faith Fear Not For I am with you*". A rocking horse stood beside a Vintage-era Steinway piano. The inscription on the piano read: *1893*. There were several quilts laid on low tables that McCall was not familiar with.

A framed photograph caught McCall's eye. He picked it up from the beautiful Steinway piano. It was engraved in the year *1892*, lovingly restored. The photograph was of a much younger Esther when she had been Candy Annie's age. McCall noted a caption at the back of the photograph and the date: *1968*. Beside it was another framed picture of an older girl, perhaps in her forties, dressed a black Victorian 18th Century long-sleeved dress. She wore a single gold cross around her throat. McCall noted there was a striking resemblance between Esther and what must be her younger sister. McCall turned the photograph over and found a date on it, *August 19th, 1988*. He put it back on the Steinway piano with the photograph of Esther when she had been a young girl.

At that moment Esther exited the kitchen carrying a tray of assorted Italian rolled sandwiches, egg salad sandwiches, scones, slices of lemon cake, butter shortbread cookies and Cornish pastries. She put the tray on a table. It had a porcelain Rose-motif tea set with silver sugar tongs and a creamer. McCall moved over to her as she poured the tea.

"You are going to a lot of trouble for a stranger," McCall said.

"It's no trouble at all," Esther scoffed. "Besides, when you enter a Mormon's home you will find his Glory all around you."

McCall sat down at the table and accepted the cup of tea she proffered. She poured herself a cup and handed him a platter of the finger sandwiches and shortbread cookies. "Please help yourself."

McCall accepted one of the Cornish pastries and a slice of the lemon cake. "You set out a wonderful table. Your hospitality is very much appreciated."

"Just Christian charity and the scones are to die for!"

"How long have lived in this compound?" he asked her.

"It feels as if it has been all my life," Esther admitted. "But if truth were told I moved here in the summer of 1950 with my husband Jacob. He's out in the fields right now, but he should be returning home soon."

McCall's attention was drawn to a handmade *Prairie Pioneer Ragdoll* sitting on a rocking chair. It was dressed severely in black wearing a cameo broach and a bonnet. It had black boots and lace trimmings and ribbons in its hair. A string of pearls adorned her throat.

For a moment McCall was taken aback.

The doll did *not have a face*.

XI

TEA BUT NO SYMPATHY

Esther noted the moment and smiled. "That doll is kind of creepy, isn't it? I had one of these dolls when I was a young child. There is a history to it dating back to the 1870's. Mormon children did not believe they needed a face to look at. They just used their imaginations. I have had that doll for a very long time."

"I also noticed the framed photographs on your piano," McCall said.

She followed his gaze and nodded somewhat nostalgically. "Yes, that's me when I was a young girl. I had guys swooning over me. Well, not swooning exactly, I wouldn't want to mislead you, but the Amish suitors made a fuss over me back in the day." She looked back at McCall and smiled. "But don't tell my niece Abigail about that. She just thinks of me as her Auntie Esther, prim and proper, eating delicious scones and trying not to get the strawberry jam on my fingers."

"There are two photographs side by side on your piano," McCall said. "The first one is you as a teenager. The second photograph is of a beautiful woman in her forties. She is also dressed in an 18th Century dress in black with long sleeves. The only augmentation is a gold locket at her throat."

Esther followed his gaze and sighed as if she were overcome with a great sadness. "That photograph is of my sister Ruth. She was truly a free spirit, fiery and boisterous. She wasn't a child of the Mormon faith. I tried to convert her to Christianity, but it was a losing battle. She could not be tamed by anyone. She was thirty years younger than I was. I always looked up to her. She was my big sister and she guided me through the perils of life. I can't really believe she is gone."

"When did she pass away?" McCall asked.

"Sadly, many years ago."

"But you still have the memories of her."

"Of course," she said. "Those memories will always a part of me forever."

"I sense a great sadness in you," McCall said.

Esther turned away as if she was ashamed of her reaction. "There is sadness in all of us, Mr. McCall, isn't there?"

"I guess that is very true," McCall said. "But there's something else bothering you. I can feel it."

"Don't presume to know my every mood and whim," Esther said, reproachfully.

"I wouldn't do that," McCall said, gently.

Esther didn't answer him right away. The door to the porch flew open and Abigail entered. She was dressed in her Mormon attire with a severe long-sleeved 18th Century black dress, an apron and black closed-toe heel shoes. She wore no jewelry. Esther motioned to her.

"Come and join us," Esther said. "I was telling Mr. McCall about our trials and tribulation living here. Not that that would interest anyone in the slightest. I brewed some Ceylon Orange tea. Will you have a cup?"

"You were talking about my Aunt Ruth," Abigail said, as if it were an accusation. "Does Mr. McCall know the whole story?"

"I don't think Mr. McCall needs to hear our whole history," Esther said, somewhat embarrassed. "He is a guest."

"I'd like to hear it," McCall said, quietly.

"My Aunt Ruth was thrown from her horse when she was out riding in the fields," Abigail said. "She hit her head on a rock. At least, that was the story the Elders told us."

"That's enough!" Esther said, as if mortified.

"When did this happen?" McCall asked.

"Four years ago." Abigail moved closer to the table. "I had just come from Bible class when I heard the dreadful news. It was heartbreaking. I couldn't believe that my wonderful Aunt Ruth was really gone. The Elders hushed it all up."

Esther jumped to her feet, appalled at the narrative she was listening to. "You have chores you need to be doing."

But McCall's attention was fixed upon Abigail. "Why would the Elders do that?"

"My Aunt Ruth was a championship rider. She rode in the steeplechase races. There was no way she could have fallen off her horse."

"Accidents do happen, even to the best horsemen," McCall said, gently.

"This was no accident," Abigail said, forcefully. "Sheriff Conrad knows what really happened."

"How does he know that?" McCall asked.

"Because he's my uncle," she said.

McCall looked at Abigail as the weight of her words sank in. He glanced at Esther who still looked mortified. "I will not allow that talk in this house, Abigail," she said. "You know that! This is a family matter."

A voice interrupted from the doorway. "I don't want to interrupt this here hoedown, but what in the world is going on?"

Esther and Abigail turned with McCall to see Sheriff Conrad standing in the doorway He took off his Stetson cowboy hat and gave them the same wolfish smile that he had greeted Mickey Kostmayer with earlier.

*   *   *   *

Mickey Kostmayer met Hayden Vallance in the tavern down the street from the Meadow Springs Hotel. It was lively and raucous. The bar area was packed with people. Vallance noted the waitress who served them was Dixie, the same gal who had served them at the Appolla Grill outside Meadow Springs. He realized she was off-duty and must live somewhere in the town. Kostmayer found Vallance waiting for him at a back table. Vallance acknowledged Dixie, who waved at him, then she went back to animatedly chatting with her friends. He had the mini-cassette tape recorder sitting on the table. Kostmayer sat down beside him. Vallance noted his gaze and nodded at Dixie.

"Who is she again?"

"Our friendly waitress who had liked the look of you in the Appolla Grill," Kostmayer said. "This could be your lucky night."

"I doubt it," Vallance said, wryly. "What did you find out?"

"Nothing," Kostmayer said. "Which left me at point zero. No one in this town wants to talk to me. I rousted the two girls at the reception desk, but they did know anything. I got the same story at the General Store on Main Street and in the deli across the street. No one has ever heard the name 'Candy Annie'. I feel like the hero in 'High Noon' who was trying to find someone in town when all the townspeople had turned against him. Did you have any luck with your enquiries?"

"I figured I would get the same answers you did," Vallance said. "So I didn't wait for that to happen. I followed Sheriff Conrad to an office building off the High Street. I was perched on a ledge on the fourth floor where the Sheriff was meeting with some good old boys. One of them had a severe personality problem who did a lot of shouting, but his voice didn't carry very far. He was immaculately dressed in a fancy waistcoat and *Laredo Snakeskin Cowboy Boots.*"

"Did you get his name?" Kostmayer asked him.

"No, I didn't. Maybe we'll get the answer on the tape. I had a mini-cassette recorder with me so I could try to listen to their conversation."

"You accomplished more than I did," Kostmayer said, ruefully. "All I got were closed doors and a wall of silence. Just as a matter of record, how narrow was the ledge you were on?"

"I tried not to look down," Vallance said, wryly. "The view from four stories down gave me a headache, not to mention vertigo."

Kostmayer tapped the mini-cassette recorder on the table. "What answers did you get?"

"I'm not sure what I got, to tell you the truth," Vallance said. "I've played the tape back twice and it doesn't tell me anything. Put these earpieces on." He handed Kostmayer a headset that could be connected to a USB headphone. "I was not expecting much, but see what you make of it."

Vallance handed Kostmayer a set of the skeletal headphones, took a pair for himself and connected it to the mini-cassette recorder.

The boisterous ambiance immediately receded. They listened hard to what was on the tape, but it was a losing battle. Only snatches of conversation came through clearly enough for them to hear.

Sheriff Conrad's voice was distinctive, but his drawl was muted so very few of the words registered. He appeared to be placating *Laredo Snake Man* who was shouting at him. But that decibel level receded quickly because the two men moved to a room and turned away from the microphone. Kostmayer and Vallance picked up a few more words: *Rendezvous – Mercy County Hospital* (the next word was lost) -- *Meadow Springs Mercantile Bank – Spalding Community Park -- Blackhawk Mission Road.*

Vallance switched off the mini-cassette recorder. He took the earpieces out of his ears and Kostmayer did the same.

"That's it for the recording?" Kostmayer asked.

"That's it," Vallance said. "The rest of the words were all too faint to register."

"Does any of it make sense to you?"

"I did some research while I was waiting for you," Vallance said. "The Spalding Community Park is three miles from here. Picnic tables, a gazebo, a lake, landscaped trees. Nothing for us there. The Meadow Springs Mercantile Bank might be worth a visit. Blackhawk Mission Road is basically a slum area just outside Chicago. All we'll find there are winos, crack dealers and lowlife criminals. On the other hand, the Mercy County Hospital is two miles from here with an outstanding outpatient care including the treatment of Parkinson's Disease, Amyotrophic Lateral Sclerosis (ALS) and other neuromuscular diseases. The only phrases I understood on the tape recorder were '*Increased Heart rate*' and '*Respiratory Dyspnea*' which had to do with elevated breathing."

"Which means what?"

"A patient in that hospital might have had some kind of a seizure or a heart attack in the last twenty-four hours," Vallance said.

"So what?" Kostmayer said. "What does that have to do with us?"

"We have to find a jumping off point," he reminded him. "Or we're not going to get anywhere."

"The tape recording told us nothing," Kostmayer insisted. "We're just back to ground zero."

"It's all we've got," Vallance said, reasonably. "Let's see where this thread takes us."

"Maybe McCall had better luck following up in the town."

Vallance's patience with Kostmayer was getting thin. "I am up for suggestions."

But Kostmayer was no longer listening. In the crush of people around him he had noted that two of the good-old boys had entered the bar area. One of them was stocky with an insolent air. The other was built like a fighter who looked as if he could break the neck of anyone he didn't like as if he were snapping a twig. The two men didn't look in Kostmayer's direction, but their body language was unmistakable. Vallance nodded at them.

"Who are the two Bobby twins?"

"One of them rousted me in my hotel room," Kostmayer said. "Call him *Mad Max*. I don't know who the other one is. Let's call him *Matinee Man*. I figure they are a matched set."

The men stood up from the table and made their way toward the door of the bar. Kostmayer got quickly to his feet, but Vallance put a restraining hand on his arm. "Take it easy, big fellah. They look mean and you've already had a run-in with one of them at your hotel."

"You were the one saying we need to get our act together," Kostmayer said. "I need to follow them and see where that takes me. I'll call you on your cell if I have to. If not, we'll meet back at the Hyatt Regency Suites."

Vallance let him go. Kostmayer hustled out of the bar area. Vallance gave Dixie a fleeting glance as she passed by, then she went back to talking to her friends. Vallance shook his head. "Where is Robert McCall when you need him?" he murmured.

*　　*　　*　　*

McCall walked through the grounds with Sheriff Conrad away from the main ranch houses. More Amish workers had finished their day's work in the fields and were heading for the various locations around the compound. McCall noted that the Members of the Church of Jesus Christ of Latter-day Saints had congregated around two of the volley courts. Basketball courts were also crowded. Further along the grassy expanses a choir practice had begun in earnest. A sense of well-being permeated the activities.

"Nice to see families enjoying themselves," Sheriff Conrad said. "It's backbreaking work out in the fields but once they come home they put their energies into being neighborly and good friends. On the other hand, some folks could steal the nickels off a dead man's eyes. I had a run-in with a young fellah in my office before I headed out here. Name was Kostmayer. He was pumping me for information about some girl he was sweet on. *Candy Annie* I think her name was. That ring a bell with you?"

"As a matter of fact, it does," McCall said. "But I reckon you knew that. She is a good friend. She has been missing for several days and I am trying to locate her."

"You won't find her here in Meadow Springs," the Sheriff said with finality. "I know everyone in this compound. Some of them on a first-name basis. You're wasting your time. Your friend is a runaway. Pure and simple. I know these folks and some of them are friendly and some of them are dumber than church mice. Porch light is on but no one is at home."

"But you know where the bodies are buried," McCall said. "I don't think anything happens here in Meadow Springs that you don't know about. Like the fact that Abigail's sister Ruth took a fall from her horse in the fields here one afternoon and it killed her."

Sheriff Conrad nodded, but there was no sorrow in it. "That happened a long time ago."

"But you don't deny it happened." McCall said. "You would know all of the details, or as much of it as you want to share."

"You're the one who has the floor, son."

"Abigail is your niece," McCall said. "That's right, isn't it?"

"And a sweeter soul never drew a breath in anger."

"Maybe her sister Ruth took a secret to her grave."

"You have a real vivid imagination, son," the Sheriff said, and his tone was no longer folksy. "But all of that is ancient history. Your friend was a runaway. Your time for reminiscences is about up. Best for you to cut your losses and leave Meadow Springs."

McCall wondered when the gloves were going to come off. "I didn't say she was a runaway," he said, evenly. "Just that my friend was missing."

"Are you and I going to do some fancy footwork with each other?" Sheriff Conrad asked him. "Because that will not end well. I can promise you that."

McCall let that go. "So you don't have any idea what has happened to Candy Annie?"

An edge had hardened in the Sheriff's tone. McCall realized that now he was looking at a dangerous predator who ran the county with an iron hand. "No, I don't have any idea what happened to Candy Annie. That was that the filly's name?"

"That's right," McCall said.

Sheriff Conrad got into McCall's face. "We got a saying here in Meadow Springs. *Cowards die daily, the brave just once.* Now I can jump around like grease on a hot skillet all day with you. Or I can arrest you for questioning and we'll do our talking at the Sheriff's office. Your call."

McCall appeared to have backed up a little. "I am not trying to cause you trouble," he said. "I'll take a look around the compound and talk to some of the Elders. If none of them has seen Candy Annie, I will be on my way."

The Sheriff took a step back from McCall. Suddenly he was a good-old-boy again dispensing homespun wisdom and cracker barrel philosophy. "You won't find her at this compound, son, but I'll give you half-an-hour to look for her. There are some of the folks over yonder I need to talk to on Mormon business. When that is done, if I still seeing you lurking around here I'll snap the cuffs on you. I can't say fairer than that. You have yourself a good day now."

The Sheriff strode to where more Amish men were arriving from the fields. He shook hands with several of them. He glanced back at the place where McCall had been standing, but he was no longer there.

*　　*　　*　　*

Kostmayer had to hustle to keep up with the men from the tavern. They had emerged from the bar onto Stratton Street which was located just off the downtown area. One of them was the one Kostmayer had tangled with in the Hyatt Regency suites. He appeared to be in a hurry and strode off down the street. His partner, the one Kostmayer thought as *Mad Max*, and who was built like a Sherman tank, followed him. They turned down an alleyway and were immediately swallowed in shadows. Kostmayer turned the corner right after them. The two men were nowhere to be seen. The alleyway connected to Market Street farther down.

Kostmayer didn't get that far.

One of the men responsible for kidnapping Candy Annie stepped out from a doorway. The other man had been waiting in the entrance to a club called the "*Silver Slipper*". Music echoed from it that spilled out into the street. Kostmayer was trapped between the two men. He might have made a run for it, but that wasn't his style. He held his ground as the two men approached him. He wasn't going to try and talk his way out of the situation. No witty repartee came to his mind anyway. These men were there to hurt him.

Kostmayer wasn't carrying a firearm. That was back in his luggage at the hotel. McCall had taught him that, when in doubt, improvise. He grabbed one of the dented trash cans and swung at his first attacker. He went down onto his knees. Kostmayer finished off the move by smashing the trash can against the man's head. *Matinee Man*, as Kostmayer liked to call him, collapsed to the ground. Kostmayer turned toward the bigger man, whom he thought of as *Mad Max*, who was prepared to do some serious damage to him. He grabbed the trash can out of Kostmayer's grip and tossed it contemptuously away. He lifted Kostmayer right off his feet and smashed him back into a brick wall. Kostmayer felt as if every bone in his body had been broken. He lashed out at the bruiser, but the man avoided the blow with ease. He lifted Kostmayer over his head like a broken doll and hurled him to the ground.

By that time the first man was back on his feet.

Kostmayer stumbled up as *Matinee Man* rained blows against his face and torso.

Mad Max turned him around and wrapped his hands around Kostmayer's throat. He tried to pry the big man's hands from strangling him, but his hold just tightened. Kostmayer felt the world receding away from him. *Mad Max* hit Kostmayer in the kidneys which took the rest of the air out of his lungs.

On a signal from the bigger man, *Matinee Man* let Kostmayer go. *Mad Max* released his hold on him. Kostmayer collapsed to the ground, gasping for breath. *Matinee Man* kicked him several times, breaking several of his ribs. He was going to finish him off, but Kostmayer had passed out. *Mad Max* put a restraining hand on his colleague's arm.

"That's enough. We don't want him bleating like a wounded sheep," Fletcher said.

"Does he scare you?" Jeremiah sneered, his chest heaving with the effort of fighting Kostmayer off.

"It is Robert McCall that scares me," Fletcher said. "He is in Meadow Springs. Which means he followed Candy Annie all the way here. He was at the bar up the street."

"So what?" Jeremiah said.

"So he is a dangerous adversary," Fletcher said. "That's a hassle I don't want to deal with. He's a loose cannon who should be dealt with. We'll deal with him if we have to. We don't want to kill him. Just discourage him from ever coming back."

"He would be better off if I killed him," Jeremiah said.

Fletcher looked down at Kostmayer whose body was not moving. "When he comes to, he'll turn tail and run for the hills," Fletcher said, unconcerned. "If he comes back for another beating, then we'll finish him off."

"He was asking Sheriff Conrad a lot of questions," Jeremiah said. "About our wayward girl."

"Let him ask them," Fletcher said. "McCall and his partners will long be gone from Meadow Springs by that time. Don't sweat it. It's been taken care of."

Jeremiah and Fletcher moved off leaving Kostmayer face down on the ground, unmoving.

XII

CANDY ANNIE

HAYDEN VALLANCE ARRIVED at the Mercy Hospital at 5:50 P.M. He took an elevator to the fourth floor. The muted ambience had resonated with him since he had been a child. The small murmurs of disease worked their way into his very soul. He had been this way as long as he could remember. The specter of death haunted him. He could not attribute it to any specific circumstance that had happened in his life. Just walking into a hospital ward brought with it a sense memory that flooded through him. His father had died at the age of fifty-two and Vallance's brother, whom he been very close to, had passed away a year later. For someone like Hayden Vallance who lived on the edge, he was not prepared to find compassion and sympathy in a hospital. Those emotions were reserved for the living.

But sometimes he was surprised.

The patient Vallance was interested in had been transferred to a room on the fourth floor from ICU. The nurse and doctors on the floor were busy. They didn't even glance up as Vallance made his way to a room at the far end of the ward. He closed the door behind him.

The young man in the room was hooked up to various machines registering his heartbeat, vital signs, myocardial infarctions, signs of asthma, chronic obstructive pulmonary disease, thrombolysis, which was a clot-busting procedure, and short of breath. His pallor was deathly white which suggested anemia. He was probably in his late twenties, Vallance thought, with high cheekbones and ice-blue eyes which were ravaged with illness. Vallance checked his chart and noted that his name was Clifford Morgan.

Vallance sat on the edge of the bed. The patient suddenly opened his eyes. He had a little trouble focusing on Vallance. He seemed confused and disoriented at first, but then his eyes seemed to clear somewhat.

"What are you doing here?" he had asked in a voice that was paper-thin.

Vallance thought it was a strange thing for him to say in the circumstances. It was as if the young man had been expecting him.

"I came to see you, Cliff," Vallance said. "We don't know each other, but I need some vital information. You're the only one who could supply me with it."

"What information is that?"

The youth had trouble forming the sentences. Vallance was aware that the door to the room could open at any moment. "You know a man who could help me," he said. "I have been calling him *Laredo Snake Man* in my mind. He's well-dressed in a suit and tie, long black hair that needs combing, little piggy eyes with a serious attitude problem dealing with authority."

"I know him," the young man said. He had barely been able to get the sentence to form in his throat. "His name is Luther Oppenheimer."

"He came to see you in the hospital in this very room," Vallance said. "He said you were suffering from an increased heart rate and your breathing was labored."

"It is called respiratory dyspnea," the youth said.

It was another sentence he had to spit out between breaths.

"Who is the man who came to see you?" Vallance asked, with some urgency.

"*Laredo Snake Man,*" the young man said, and he actually laughed. "I like that."

That lapsed to a coughing fit. Vallance poured water in a glass and raised it to the young man's lips. He took a sip of it and nodded that he was okay. Vallance set the glass down. He tried again to focus his attention. "*Laredo Snake Man* was very agitated with you. Was he a relative, perhaps?"

"My father," the youth said and that produced another coughing fit. Vallance waited until it had subsided. "What is his name?"

"His name is not important," he said, hoarsely. "He won't even come to visit me here."

"There will be other people who care about you," Vallance said. "Your mother, perhaps? Or a sweetheart who loves you? I could urge her to come here to see you."

"They're gone," he murmured. It sounded like a death rattle. "All of the people who had cared about me are long gone."

"You have been taking a lot of drugs," Vallance said. "I'm not here to judge you. Your father can do that. But now is the time to turn your back on that life. Before it can destroy you."

The young man's voice had gained some strength. "Why should you care? I don't even know you."

"You're right, we don't know each other," Vallance agreed. "But sometimes strangers can offer solace when no one else can. I had a son who passed away when he was a teenager. He fought like hell, but then the life just seeped out of him. That could have destroyed my life if I let it."

"I don't have long to survive," the young man said.

There was no regret in his voice.

"But the drug dealers will survive," Vallance said. "They are responsible for you being in this condition." Vallance didn't know if he had struck a chord, but the young man rose a little more on his pillows. "Maybe there is a way for you to do something that will save another's life."

There was a silence as his words registered. Then the young man reached out for a pad of paper sitting on the end table, and a pen. Vallance picked it up and passed it to him. With a shaking hand the youth wrote seven words on the page and tore it out. He passed it to Vallance before he slumped back against the pillows. Vallance got to his feet. The youth was spent. He had no more energy to give.

"I'm sorry you are so sick," Vallance said, quietly. "I'll come back to see you when my business is finished and see how you are doing."

"Don't be concerned for me," the youth said. "I'm not."

Vallance gave his shoulder a squeeze, but the teenager had no reaction. He had closed his eyes. Vallance moved through the shadows and exited the room.

He waited until he got outside in the street before he unfolded the note and read it.

It said: *BLACKHAWK MISSION ROAD. WAREHOUSE ENTRANCE. COMPASS GROUP DRUG DEAL.*

Vallance consulted his map and found Blackhawk Mission Road. Then he climbed into his Ford Explorer convertible. He fired it up and drove out of the little town on the back roads. The maze of the streets deteriorated quickly into what was in essence a slum area. A warehouse area was flanked by metal bridges with hydraulic devices and forklifts trucks. A rusted sign said: "*Blackhawk Mission Road.* Vallance parked on a side street where pallet trucks were lifting goods in crates to be loaded into the warehouse. There was a fire escape that hugged the building. Vallance climbed the metal stairs until he came to a third level. He tried a metal door which was not locked. He moved inside. It was a vast space with iron catwalks. Metal stairs descended into the interior. Vallance crouched down on one of the staircases to observe the activity below. Workmen were hauling cardboard boxes onto Chevrolet Silverado trucks. The metal frames for the trucks stood eight feet tall. The workforce was supervised by two foremen. One of them was *Laredo Snake Man* wearing his three-piece suit and fancy waistcoat. There was no mistaking him in his hand-tooled cowboy boots.

Vallance didn't know what the cardboard boxes contained, but it was his best guess that they were drugs. Probably cocaine and heroin. His surmise proved to be correct when one of the two men, Jeff Fletcher, joined *Laredo Snake Man* in the warehouse. Vallance would recognize his sneering face even in the low light.

Vallance moved back into shadows of the catwalk before exiting the building.

He was not exactly sure what to do with this new intel.

*   *   *   *

McCall wandered over to the grounds of the compound to where the orchard was situated. Huge apple trees towered up into the sky. Some of the Mormon brethren were sitting on the lawn weaving intricate baskets. A few of them were playing Gemeinhardt flutes and still more were engaged in creating handcrafted quilts. Once again McCall was struck by the simplicity of their work and the sheer joy it brought to the gathered congregation.

Abigail moved through the trees and found him. She took his hand. "I didn't get a chance to say goodbye to you," she said. "How did you make out with Gary Cooper?"

"I can't believe you even know who Gary Cooper *is*," McCall said, smiling.

"Sure I do. I snuck into B movies at a little cinema in Meadow Springs which only catered to diehard western fans," Abigail said. "Gary Cooper was my idol. I also liked Randolph Scott. Do you remember him? He had a steely glint in his eyes and treated the womenfolk with kindness. I saw '*Ride the High Country*' ten times."

"One of the classic movies," McCall agreed. "And Sheriff Conrad is really your uncle?"

"Yeah. He makes my skin crawl," Abigail confessed. "Now that he has been introduced to you, don't turn your back on him. He's a weasel."

"There is a photograph of your Aunt Ruth on your piano," McCall said. "Did you ever get to know her?"

Abigail shook her head. "No, I didn't. But she was feisty as all get out from what I can gather. It was a long time ago that she had been welcomed into the Lord's arms."

"My friend Candy Annie," McCall said, choosing his words carefully, "bears a remarkable resemblance to your late sister Ruth. They could almost have been twins."

"I never thought of her in that way," Abigail confessed.

"Have you given any thought that Ruth could be your *sister*?"

That brought Abigail to a halt. She stared at McCall as the truth of that statement sank in. But she shook her head. "My Aunt Esther would have told me."

"She might have taken that truth and kept in hidden," McCall said. "Your uncle, Sheriff Conrad, has a powerful personality that might overwhelm your Aunt. Look at the two photographs on your mantelpiece in the parlor the next time you visit your Aunt Esther. The resemblance is startling."

"My Aunt Ruth has been with the angels for a long time," Abigail said.

"Not in your heart," McCall said, gently. "Wouldn't you like to know you had a big sister you could turn to?"

"That could never happen," Abigail said, but suddenly the words sounded hollow to her.

"Give it some thought," McCall said. "When I find my friend Candy Annie I will ask her if she has a sister she didn't know about. The answer might surprise you."

"It would terrify me," Abigail said, her voice suddenly shaking with suppressed emotion.

"On the other hand," McCall said, still gentle. "it might be a wonderful blessing."

"My Aunt Ruth was a wonderful person," she said. "She hit her head on a rock in a field one afternoon and it killed her. What was the sense in that?"

"Sometimes there are no easy answers," McCall said. "You have your faith and your belief in God and that will sustain you."

"What if that is not enough?"

"It will be," McCall said.

"How can you be sure?"

McCall shrugged. "I just am."

McCall and Abigail emerged out of the apple orchard and strolled toward the white-walled buildings which surrounded them. The workers from the fields had arrived and were greetings friends. Abigail's attitude had taken on a more somber tone.

"I just realized that this is goodbye," she said. "There is no reason for you to stay in Meadow Springs any longer. I've got prayer study tonight, the *Pearl of Great Price*, which I must learn from cover to cover as it was written to Moses, and after that you will be gone. I hope you find this friend of yours. What was her name again?"

"Candy Annie."

"Cool name. Where will you look for her?"

"At this point I have no idea," McCall confessed.

"But you will search for her until you find her, right?"

"That's right."

"You won't abandon her?

"No."

"I figured that was the case," Abigail said. "She is lucky to have you for a friend. I believe that every person's spirit will be reunited with the body and will no longer be subject to death," she added. "But sometimes my faith abandons me."

She turned suddenly into McCall's arms and hugged him. When they broke, McCall wiped her tears from her face. "You will see your friend Candy Annie again," Abigail said. "I know it."

"From your lips to God's ears," he said and smiled fondly at her.

"I guess there is nothing more to say to each other. Goodbye, Mr. McCall. It has been a blessing to have known you."

Abigail ran from his side until she was swallowed up in the trees.

McCall felt a melancholy sadness at her departure. It was nothing he could put into words. He had felt the same when he had bid farewell to Kacey Rose in the abandoned fairground in New York City. These waifs had touched his heart.

And perhaps Abigail would come to realize that she *did* have a big sister.

McCall looked around at the grounds where more Mormon workers and their families were gathering. There was nothing more he could do there. He walked across to one of the grassy lawns to where his Jaguar F-Type Convertible was waiting. He reached for the door and opened it, but something stopped him. He turned around and looked at the oak trees and the apple orchard and the lawns.

Candy Annie had just stepped out from one of the white-washed buildings.

McCall recognized her elfin figure immediately. She was dressed like the other women in the compound in a full-length long-sleeved 18th Century dress. The only variation that was the dress she wore had a deep burgundy color. She wore a starched white apron and black closed-toe shoes. She wore no jewelry. She appeared isolated to McCall, standing alone as if she had no business to be there, which McCall thought might have been true. He moved away from the Jaguar and jogged through the trees and the apple orchard. He kept Candy Annie in sight, fearing she would suddenly turn around and re-enter the house. But she remained where she was. The other Mormon women kept their distance from her, which McCall thought was calculated. Candy Annie was not a member of their enclosed society. She was an interloper who did not belong in their world.

She had not seen him emerge from the apple orchard because she was looking off to her left where some Mormon women were playing volleyball. McCall jogged across the open field, past three of the white-washed buildings and climbed up onto the big porch. For some reason he did not call out her name "*Candy Annie.*" It did not feel appropriate to him. Instead he said quietly: "Anne".

She turned around and gave a little cry, which could have been elation or despair, McCall was not sure which. His instinct was to go to Candy Annie and embrace her, but that same instinct held him back. Candy Annie was clearly flustered at seeing him, her face going scarlet. Her manner was immediately accusatory.

"What are you doing here?"

"I came to find you," McCall said simply. "I knew you were in some kind of trouble."

"How did you know that?"

"Because you're a good persona and would not have run away without a good reason."

Candy Annie took a deep breath, centering herself, then shook her head. "You don't know me at all. I had good reasons for leaving, but those are personal to me. I am not prepared to share them. You should not have followed me, Mr. McCall. You are here on a mercy mission to rescue me, but the truth is I don't need rescuing."

"I think you do," McCall said.

Candy Annie moved a step closer to him. "I am in the place I need to be. You may not understand it, but I am content within myself. New York City was a scary place for me. I had no friends there. Mickey Kostmayer was a friend, but he had his own personal demons he had to fight. In the end I did not think I could cope with them. I didn't know which way to turn. I returned to my roots."

"So you found solace in the Church of Jesus Christ of Latter-day Saints?" McCall asked her.

"Is that so hard for you to believe?" she asked. "I was lost and alone in the world. The Mormons came to my rescue. They took me in and cared for me. I had never trusted anyone so completely. They are my salvation." She took his arm in hers. "Walk with me?"

McCall walked with her off the porch, heading for the apple orchard. Several more of the Mormons had gathered on the grassy lawns. A game of badminton had started up and croquet hoops were being set up with mallets with colored balls.

"There is an energy here," Candy Annie said. "A vitality that is mirrored in the faces of the brethren."

"How long have you felt this way?" McCall asked. "I never heard you once mention the name 'Mormons' to me."

"I have been following the teaching of the Church of Jesus Christ of Latter-day Saints ever since I was in the subway tunnels," she said. "It sustained me when my spirits were low. I put the doctrine away when I emerged out into the light and found there was a thrilling and challenging world out there. But I always found my way back to the Scriptures."

"What made you pack up your belongings and come to Chicago?" McCall asked.

"I didn't really know where my wanderings would take me," Candy Annie said. "I got off the train in Chicago and hired a rental car. You didn't know I could drive, did you? Fooz taught me when I was living under the New York streets. I never thought I would ever need a car, but it was fun knowing I could drive it. I stopped in a little town called Meadow Springs and fell in love with it. I got to know the people here and their commitment to the Lord. It has been my salvation."

McCall wasn't buying what she was saying. His instinct told him this was all an act on Candy Annie's part. But he was prepared to listen to it until he heard the truth.

XIII

DIXIE

McCALL TOOK CANDY ANNIE'S ARM. "I am happy to hear that you have found some inner peace."

"For the longest time I was content living down in the sewer system," Candy Annie said, her voice vibrant with emotion. "I had my DVDs and my television and my thriller books. I liked *Lee Child* the best. He has a great style of writing. What was the name of his fictional hero? *Reacher*, that was it. I visited with Fooz and I had some good friends in the tunnels. I didn't think life could get better than that. But then I met you, Mr. McCall. You persuaded me to take a chance on life. It was the best decision I have ever made."

Candy Annie paused because one of the Mormon women at the volleyball court allowed the ball to get away from her. She ran after it. Candy Annie picked it up and threw it to her. She acknowledged her with a wave and dashed back to the volleyball game.

"Her name is Hannah," Candy Annie said." It means 'Grace'. I haven't made a lot of friends yet, but I am working on it. It takes time to break the ice."

"You seem to have adjusted to your new life very well," McCall said.

"Living under the streets of New York City takes some getting used to," Candy Annie said. "Just to get out and kick a volleyball around seems like such an accomplishment."

"What will you do now?" McCall asked her.

"The nice thing for me is that I don't have to do anything," Candy Annie said. "I have made some friends here in Meadow Springs. Not many of them I will grant you. I haven't been here for very long. But the Church of Jesus Christ of Latter-day Saints has made me feel welcome. Sheriff Conrad has taken a special interest in me. He has been very supportive and helpful."

McCall glanced over at the wide porch. Sheriff Conway was standing there. His attitude was glacial. He stared at Candy Annie like she was a bug he wanted to squash beneath his cowboy boot. McCall was careful not to make a comment that would get Candy Annie into trouble.

"Small towns like this tend to be wary of strangers," he said.

"I am not a stranger," Candy Annie said. She smiled at him. "I have been accepted into the community for who I am.'

"You are a very special person," McCall said.

"I am not special," Candy Annie said, and she actually blushed. "Only to the people who are special to me. You are at the top of the list, Mr. McCall."

"That's good to hear," McCall said. "I didn't come here alone. I travelled with Hayden Vallance. Do you remember him?"

"I don't think I have ever met him," she said. "I remember you said he was a mercenary who fought other people's battles."

"That's right."

"Why is he here?"

"I needed a travelling companion," McCall said, wryly. "Mickey Kostmayer came with us. He was very anxious to see you again. He didn't say it in so many words, but I believe he is in love with you."

"He is a good person," Candy Annie acknowledged. "Mickey and I bonded some time ago. As for the idea that he is love with me, that is just a fanciful notion. There is nothing there. I have my life now and it fills me with happiness."

They had circled back around to the apple orchard and were on their way back to the white-washed house. McCall noted that Sheriff Conway had not moved from the wide porch where he was obviously waiting for Candy Annie. McCall took Candy Annie's hand.

"This is where I will take my leave of you," McCall said. "I am leaving you in good hands. Sheriff Conrad will take care of you."

Candy Annie looked at the porch and McCall detected a note of panic in her voice.

"I feel as if I have found you and lost you again," Candy Annie said. "You mean more to me than you will ever know."

"Keep that thought," McCall said.

"I feel I should kiss you."

McCall shrugged. "Bring it on."

Candy Annie kissed him. It was not a peck on the cheek, but a lingering goodbye. When they parted McCall smiled. "Just take care of yourself," he said. "You are precious to me. Be safe and be well."

McCall turned to leave. "Be sure to say hi to Jackson T. Foozelman for me," Candy Annie said.

"I will do that."

"And Daniel Blake, too."

McCall nodded. "I will."

He moved toward his Jaguar. Candy Annie climbed up onto the big porch. Her Aunt Esther moved out of the house and gave McCall a wave of farewell. McCall fired up the Jag, turned around and headed back toward town. He caught a fleeting glimpse of Candy Annie on the porch. Sheriff Conrad had put an arm protectively around her shoulders. Candy Annie watched McCall until he was back on the road and out of sight.

McCall turned around when he came to the main road. He took stock of what he knew so far. Daniel Blake and been shot by a sniper's bullet at the Chateau Kharzinski in Russia. Candy Annie knew that. She had deliberately lied to McCall. Still, he had found Candy Annie alive and unharmed. There was nothing more for him to do in Meadow Springs.

Except...

McCall had no doubt in his mind that Sheriff Conrad was holding Candy Annie against her will.

He had agreed to meet Hayden Vallance at the Meadow Springs Tavern where he said he was following up some leads. McCall parked the Jaguar and moved inside. He was greeted by the usual clamor of raised voices. Virtually all the tables were taken and there was a crowd around the bar. McCall looked for Hayden Vallance or Mickey Kostmayer, but he didn't see them. He did recognize Dixie, their ubiquitous server who was clearly off-duty. She was wearing jeans and a western shirt. She had on specular *Cowtown Snakeskin Cowboy Boots*. She grabbed McCall's arm as he moved past her and held him in a vice-like grip.

"Hey there!" Dixie said, grinning. "I thought I recognized a friendly face! I served you at the Apollo Grill over on Main Street. You were with that long cool of water who looked like he ate nails for breakfast!"

McCall smiled at that. "There may be something in that."

"What's his name?"

"Hayden Vallance."

"Well, he got my juices flowing, let me tell you! After work I always stop in at the tavern here for a beer. I am celebrating because I just went out and got myself a new tat."

In addition to her tattooed arms which had inked on them *Cowgirl Up, I am your Huckleberry* and the motif of the *Marlboro Man*, Dixie had added another tattoo of a *Frog Playing a Banjo* against a red setting sun. She grinned at McCall.

"Pretty nifty, don't you think?"

"It defies description," McCall said, wryly.

"Join me for a spell," she said. "I'll catch the eye of the server. She knows my poison. Whiskey straight up with a bourbon chaser."

"I'll take a rain check on that," McCall said. "I am looking for a friend of mine. He said he would meet here."

"What was his name again?"

"Hayden Vallance."

"That's right. Well, good luck finding him in this madhouse. The decibel level in here would deafen a hog-calling contest." At that moment the door to the tavern opened and a new influx of customers arrived. Among them was Vallance. "He just came in," Dixie said. "Can't you wrangle me an invitation with him? I would like to go a few rounds with that hunk."

"His people skills leave something to be desired," McCall said.

"Too bad. It sounds as if it would be a challenge."

"I'll pass the word along," he said. He pushed his way to where Vallance was waiting for him. Dixie downed half of her beer and motioned for some friends to join her at her table. McCall reached Vallance and looked around.

"Where's Mickey?"

"That's a good question," Vallance said. "I left him following a couple of rednecks he had already tangled with here in the tavern. One of them had been searching his hotel room."

"What were they looking for?"

"I'd say evidence of our involvement with Mickey, but that's just a guess."

"What did you find out?"

"Plenty, but it can wait," Vallance said. "I am concerned about Mickey. He went charging out of here following those good-old boys. I would have thought he'd be back here by now."

"Unless they were waiting for him outside on the street," McCall said.

"Why would they do that?" he said. "Mickey Kostmayer is no threat to them."

"We don't know that for sure," McCall said. "We'll split up. You take one side of the street and I'll take the other."

McCall was already moving to the door of the tavern. Vallance kept pace with him. Outside on Stratton Street they split up. McCall headed down the street toward *Katz's Delicatessen* and the *Meadow Springs Cleaners*. Vallance checked out the *Hallmark Cards Store* and the *Cooperstown Bakery*.

It was McCall who saw Kostmayer first. He had stumbled out of a narrow alleyway beneath the façade for the *Silver Slipper Nightclub*. He was swaying on his feet, holding the edge of the alleyway for support. McCall ran across the street and grabbed his arm to stop him from falling. Vallance also grabbed Kostmayer to steady him. The beating he had taken from Jeremiah and Fletcher had taken its toll on him. He was a mess. His face was puffy with contusions. One of his eyes was swollen shut and the other eye was merely a slit. His cheekbones had been severely damaged in the beating and were sunken onto his face. There were myriad bruises and lacerations under both of his eyes where Jeremiah's and Fletcher's fists had pounded on him. Kostmayer looked up blearily. He was having trouble getting McCall and Vallance into focus.

"Do you know where you are?" McCall asked him.

"Yeah," he said, his voice barely registering. "Get me out of the street. Back to the tavern."

McCall supported him on one side and Vallance on the other side. They gently guided Kostmayer across the street. They entered the tavern and were greeted with the usual rowdy ambiance. McCall found a table at the back which had just been vacated by a young couple. Vallance gently helped Kostmayer into a chair. McCall sat down opposite him. Vallance turned a chair around. He reacted with no expression in his eyes, but McCall knew he was seething inside at the severity of the beating Kostmayer had endured. McCall had to practically shake the Company agent to get him to refocus his attention.

"Who did this to you?" McCall asked.

Kostmayer had trouble forming coherent words, but he nodded. "The guy who tossed my hotel room earlier. He had a pal with him. I don't know their names. They were waiting for me in that alleyway in front of the *Silver Slipper Strip Club*."

"They did quite a number on you," Vallance said. "You're lucky to be alive."

"Do you know their names?" McCall asked.

"Yeah. I heard them while I was lying face down in the gutter," Kostmayer said. "One was Jeremiah Reynolds and the other one was Jeff Fletcher. Two thugs just out to have some serious fun at my expense. One of them had searched my hotel room at the Regency Hotel Suites."

"So this wasn't a fight that got out of hand," Vallance said.

Kostmayer shook his head. "They knew who I was," he said. "They were waiting for me."

At that moment Dixie fought her way to the table in the corner. She was clearly appalled at the state that Kostmayer was in. She turned automatically to McCall. "What has happened to your friend? Looks like he's been ridden hard and put away." She put a hand on Kostmayer's shoulder, not quite knocking him to the floor. "You need to get those lacerations seen to."

"I'll be fine," Kostmayer protested.

"Lands sake, look at the state of you! I'll get the first aid kit. There's one behind the bar."

Dixie quickly moved away. Kostmayer shook his head. "I feel like the guy who chases the dolphins and then plays with sharks."

"I'm just glad to see you're all right," McCall said.

Vallance looked at him. "I have some intel for you, if you can leave our wounded soldier for a few minutes."

"Stop mothering me," Kostmayer muttered. "I told you I am going to be fine."

"That isn't the way it looks to me," McCall said.

Dixie was back having grabbed the first aid kid from behind the bar. Vallance got to his feet. "Do your jawing someplace else," Dixie said, taking some bandages out of the first aid kit. "I need to do some serious work on this man's face."

"I'm okay," Kostmayer insisted again, but he looked as if he was going to lose consciousness at any moment.

"Just keep still," Dixie advised him in a hoarse voice. "Give me a chance to work my magic."

McCall stood up and he and Vallance moved away to another table. "I went out to a meeting out of town where members of the Church of Jesus Christ of Latter-day Saints were congregated," McCall said. "More Mormons were playing badminton and creating handcrafted quilts. Some of them were engrossed in weaving baskets. I didn't feel any hostility coming from them. Just the opposite. They struck me as peaceful and benign, but Sheriff Conrad has been agitating them. They are hiding a secret and I would lay odds that it has to do with Candy Annie."

"But you didn't find her," Vallance said.

"I did," McCall said.

"When were you going to tell me this startling news?" he asked, mildly irritated.

"I didn't have time before we found Kostmayer," he said. "She was standing on the big porch at one of the stucco buildings. She hadn't seen me at first."

"Did you talk to her?" Vallance asked.

"I did. She was uptight, not the carefree girl that we know and adore," McCall said. "What did you find out?"

"There is some serious drug traffic going on in this little town," Vallance said. "The supplier is a man named Luther Oppenheimer. It took some time for me to get a handle on him. He was visiting his son at a hospital in Meadow Springs. There was no love lost between father and son. I'd say *Laredo Snake Man*, as I like to call him, was visiting his son because it was a duty call. It was clear to me that it didn't matter whether his son lived or died. Luther was just going through the motions because he thought he had no choice. He is a nasty piece of work."

"What are you going to do about him?" McCall asked.

"I am a mercenary," Vallance reminded him. "Being seen in my company would send some shock waves through the Justice Department. But I do have a relationship with a Federal Marshal named Andy Esterhaus. He is based in Chicago, but I can probably do a little wheeling and dealing to get him to fly out to Meadow Springs."

"A drug bust is a good incentive to bring him here," McCall said. "If he'll look the other way when he is making the raid."

"Leave that to me," Vallance said. "I know how to press some buttons when it comes to the Feds. What will you do now?"

"Go back to the Mormon compound out of town," he said.

"And what are you going to do there? From your description, Sheriff Conrad isn't going to welcome you back with open arms."

"Candy Annie is being held at that compound against her will," McCall said, quietly.

That gave Vallance pause. "Are you sure of that?"

"There's one way for me to find out," McCall said. "You stay close to your Federal contact. Let me know when you sweet talk him into accepting you as one of the good guys."

"Easier said than done," Vallance said, dryly. "Where will you be?"

"I found Candy Annie," McCall said. "I am not going to lose her again."

"Does she mean that much to you?"

"She does."

"You won't have me to watch your back," Vallance warned him.

McCall looked over at Mickey Kostmayer. Dixie had finished tending to his cuts and bruises. His left eye was still virtually closed, and his right eye was no better. Vallance followed his gaze. "In his present condition I would say Mickey would just be a liability to you. But you're the boss. I'll make my phone call to the Justice Department. If you go back to that compound, let me know."

"I'll do that," McCall promised.

Vallance moved away from McCall. Kostmayer stood up. McCall noted he was unsteady on his feet as he moved away from Dixie. "You're done being my nursemaid," he said, brusquely. "But I appreciate it."

"You should have a couple of stitches on that left eye," Dixie said, anxiously.

"I'll be fine."

"Do you know the names of the two men who beat up on you?"

"I never saw either of them before," Kostmayer said.

"I didn't just fall off the cabbage patch, darlin'," Dixie said, tartly. "Those saddle bums were stalking you out in the alleyway. I went out there for a smoke and I caught a glimpse of them."

"A couple of lowlifes," Kostmayer said. "Just leave it at that."

"Just remember, I got your back," she said. "If they come back I'll give you a holler."

"They won't be back," Kostmayer said.

But he took two steps from her and staggered. McCall reached him and held him upright. Dixie grabbed his other arm.

"I'm just a little woozy," Kostmayer protested, but his voice was faint. "Just give me a couple of minutes."

But that didn't happen. He had passed out. McCall and Dixie held him rigidly in their arms. "I just live around the corner from here," Dixie said. "I got an apartment on Stratton Street. It ain't worth spit but I reckon I can lie your friend on the couch in there."

"Let's do it," McCall urged.

They supported Kostmayer between them through the boisterous ambience of the tavern and outside into the street. Dixie led the way around the corner to Stratton Street. She unlocked the front door and proceeded to climb the stairs to a third-floor apartment overlooking the High Street. She led McCall inside. The interior was nicely furnished with cream walls, a couch and two easy leather chairs, walnut shelves and a huge 50" television. The wood floor was mahogany. A bookshelf had dozens of paperback thriller books and a coffee table was strewn with magazines. Stereo speakers were placed one on top of the other and the walls were decorated with various western paintings including a rustic wooden wall plaque of *The Duke* in *"The Searchers"* holding his rifle. A small bedroom could be seen through the ajar door. The place had a rough charm that matched Dixie's personality. McCall carefully laid Mickey Kostmayer down on the couch.

"He's out for the count," Dixie said. McCall looked around. Dixie suddenly looked embarrassed. "It ain't much, but I only moved in a month ago. I'll rustle up some Campbell's chicken soup and some saltine crackers. When he comes to I might even find a steak I can grill with some potatoes and green peppers and a homemade gravy to die for. Your friend needs to get his strength back."

McCall took Dixie's shoulders. "I can see I am leaving Mickey in good hands. If you need to take him to a hospital…"

"We got a clinic over on Mesa Vista Street," Dixie said, "but I reckon we can do without that for now. Your friend is as weak as a kitten. He needs to sleep. Leave him with me."

"Much obliged."

"You can't just be a concerned citizen," Dixie said. "What's your story?"

"I'm here because a friend of mine called Candy Annie is in trouble," McCall said.

"What kind of trouble?"

"The kind that gets you killed."

Dixie nodded. "I figured it was something like that. There's a saying I've always liked. *Don't be afraid to stand up for what you believe in, even if that means you're standing alone.*"

"There is a lot of truth to that," McCall said.

"Hell, honey, I just call the cards the way they have been dealt to me," she said. "I don't know what kind of trouble you and your friends have got yourself in, but I would say it's a humdinger, so you need to get a handle on it."

"I am attempting to do that," McCall said. He looked down at Mickey Kostmayer's unconscious figure on the couch. He leaned down to him. "I'll be back with Candy Annie," he whispered to him. "Just hang tight."

Then he straightened and left Kostmayer with Dixie. He climbed down the steep stairs and let himself out of the apartment building.

XIX

PRISONER

Hayden Vallance knew a Sheriff's car had followed his Ford Explorer for several miles. He was on his way to Chicago where he had arranged a meeting with Andy Esterhaus and several other Federal Officers in the John C. Kluczynski Building on Clark Street in the downtown area. But he never got that far. Vallance had stopped on a country road outside of Cedar Falls where several windmills were placed along a riverbank. A Sheriff's white Ford Explorer had pulled over to the side of the road. Vallance noted it had all the proper decals on it. Two uniformed Officers climbed out of the vehicle. They were carrying the usual utility belts with handcuffs, name badges, radio, flashlights, tasers and, just for fun, pepper spray. One of them approached Vallance's vehicle while his partner waited to use the radio to call in. Vallance lowered his windshield halfway down, automatically reaching into the glove compartment for his license. The first Officer's badge had a gold shield on it with the nameplate: *D. SHAPIRO.* The other Officer's nameplate was lettered: *P. CARUSO.* The first Officer leaned down at the open window. His manner was not friendly, but cordial.

"License and ID," he said. "Please take them out of the wallet."

Vallance knew at once they weren't real cops.

The Officer's nameplate should have had a name on it, not just his initials. The Lightbar on top of the police vehicle should have been red or blue. It had six colors in it. But that wasn't what convinced Vallance that he was dealing with two dangerous criminals. He had seen them for just a fleeting moment in the Meadow Springs Tavern.

He realized they were there to kill him

Vallance handed his driver's license through the open window over to the bogus cop.

"Why have I been pulled over?"

The first Officer looked at Vallance's driver's license perfunctorily, then pocketed it. "Step out of your vehicle, sir."

Vallance climbed out of his Ford Explorer. In his peripheral vision he noted that the other Police Officer had stepped forward. His right hand was resting on the butt of his gun.

"I admit I was going over the speed limit," Vallance said, a little contritely. "But I am in a big hurry."

The first Officer pushed Vallance against the hood of the Explorer. "Lean against the hood of the car, please."

Vallance knew what was coming next and he was prepared for it. Officer Shapiro shook out the handcuffs from his belt. "You have the right to remain silent," he said. "Anything you say can be held against you in a court of law."

Vallance swung around before the bogus first Police Officer had a chance to cuff him. He punched the man in the gut which doubled him over. His handcuffs dropped onto the ground. The second Officer reached to his holster which Vallance noted in passing was a Smith & Wesson Revolver. Vallance disarmed him and kicked him to the ground. His partner had drawn his own gun, a .357 Magnum Revolver. Vallance hadn't expected a move like that. He drew his own Smith & Wesson Revolver from a concealed holster and fired it, blowing the first bogus Police Officer away. The second Police Officer picked up his gun from the road. He aimed it up at Vallance. The mercenary whirled and fired a second shot, shooting the first bogus Officer in the heart. He collapsed into the dirt. Vallance knew both of them were dead. He looked around the stretch of highway which was deserted at this moment.

Vallance dragged the body of the first bogus Police Officer, *D. Shapiro*, to his Ford Explorer and dumped him onto the passenger seat. He picked up the other fallen Police Officer, *P. Caruso*, and dragged him to the Explorer. He opened the rear door and dumped him inside. Vallance slid back into the driver's seat with the two dead men sprawled beside him. He drove the Ford Explorer into some dense shrubbery at the side of the road where their bodies would be hidden. He got out and reached down into their pockets for their ID's, but that told him nothing. He wondered if these

Officers had been responsible for kidnapping Candy Annie, which he thought was a reasonable scenario.

Vallance dragged their bodies out of the Explorer and dumped them in some shrubbery. He ran to where he had parked his Ford Explorer and slid inside. He drove away and put an anonymous call to the local Sheriff's Office and left word where Law Enforcers would find the bodies. Then he drove toward Chicago where he had scheduled his meeting with Andy Easterhaus and several other Federal Officers.

Vallance wasn't going to shed any tears for these brutal kidnappers.

*   *   *   *

McCall parked his Jaguar in the trees to one side of the collection of white-washed buildings in the compound. Six softball games were being played on the grassy slopes around the building. The Mormons were all in high spirits with much laughter and joy emanating from their exuberance. McCall climbed up onto the porch and entered the first building. The furniture inside had a dated and forlorn feeling about it. There were no pictures on the walls. No knickknacks or keepsakes had been saved. The bedrooms, the kitchen and the front parlor all had the same solitary ambiance. The house was virtually deserted. Everyone was out at the softball games that were being played as the sun descended into twilight.

McCall searched the other houses on the estate and found the same lonely isolation. He did come across some of the men and women in the homes who were friendly, but they were guarded in their greetings. McCall told them he was a friend of Esther's and that he was visiting her. That seemed to placate any anxiety on the part of the Mormons he had encountered.

McCall eventually searched all five of the buildings and found nothing that gave him pause. It was like he had entered some 18th Century houses where all the habitants had fled a pandemic leaving just ghosts in their wake. It gave him an eerie, isolated feeling.

McCall had noted three steel grain storage silos that were nestled in the trees. They had flat bottoms with bucket elevators and conveyor belts. He moved over to first one of them which was secured by a brass padlock. McCall glanced around him. The softball games were being played some distance away with a lot of laughter and high spirits. No one was looking at the storage sheds. McCall took a small screwdriver out of his leather jacket. The padlock had a tumbler lock on it. He inserted the blade of the screwdriver and worked it back and forth at different angles. Finally, with some added pressure, the stubborn lock broke open.

McCall hung the lock on the handle of the door and entered the silo. It was in darkness. McCall noted the shape of a figure shrouded in the shadows. He found a light switch and flipped it on, but nothing happened. The lights were controlled by a separate switch. A skylight provided what radiance there was. McCall moved through the ghostly twilight until the figure became more pronounced. Then his stomach turned over.

Candy Annie was hanging up by her wrists.

Her feet were raised off the ground.

The strain on her arms had to be enormous. She twisted slightly one way or the other, her face contorted in agony. McCall quickly reached her and grabbed hold of her legs. Candy Annie looked down at McCall's figure that was obscured in the shadows.

"I'll release you," he said. "Try not to swing any more than you have to."

Candy Annie nodded, but even that brought a grimace to her face. He took out a penknife from his leather coat pocket and opened it. He put his arms around Candy Annie's legs, reached up and severed her restraints. Gently he set her down. He noted her clothes were torn and disheveled. A bruise had darkened on her cheek. There were myriad small contusions around her eyes. A kind of rage coursed through McCall's veins as he held onto her. That someone could torture Candy Annie in this way was so aberrant to him that for a moment he could not even function. As if she had read his mind, Candy Annie raised her hand to gently caress his face.

"I'm all right," she said, but her voice was faint.

"No, you're not!" McCall said, savagely. "Who did this to you?"

"It doesn't matter," she said, softly. "You're here with me now. That is all I care about."

"I need a name," McCall said. He was pretty sure he knew the identity of her kidnapper, but he needed to know for sure.

"It was Sheriff Conrad," Candy Annie said. Tears had suddenly glittered in her eyes. She shook them angrily away. "He hung me up like I was a dumb steer he had roped in a rodeo. He left me dangling here in the dark while he went about his day. He said he would be back to finish the job he had started. There was no rush. I pleaded with him to let me go, but I never heard another word from him."

"I'll make him pay for that," McCall promised her.

"I wanted to tell you all about it, but I was frightened," Candy Annie said. "I gave you one clue that I was sure no one else knew. About Daniel Blake."

"That was a stroke of genius," McCall said. "You did great. I'm proud of you."

"I knew you would find me," she said, softly. "I never gave up hope."

McCall still held her in his arms. "We need to talk."

She nodded. "Okay."

"Can you walk?"

"I'm a little wobbly," Candy Annie said, "but I can walk."

McCall put his around her in the shadows. "Is there another way out of here?"

"I don't know," she said. "You drove away from this place in a totally rad sports car. What was the name of it again?"

McCall thought it was an odd thing for her to say, but she was still disoriented from her ordeal. "It's a Jaguar F-Type convertible."

"Cool wheels," Candy Annie said. "As soon you had left, Sheriff Conway came to find me. He dragged me to this grain silo and locked me in here. I was in the dark forever! But I knew you would figure out where I was."

"Are you sure you can walk?" McCall asked her again.

"I am."

"Fair enough."

They moved through the overlapping shadows to where there was another entrance on the other side of the silo. A weathered door was padlocked. McCall let go of Candy Annie who was still a little unstable.

"I can make it," she said. "But the door is padlocked."

"Not to me," he said.

McCall took out his small screwdriver and worked it back and forth in the padlock. It took him fifteen minutes because the lock was rusty. Finally it split open. McCall opened the heavy door and guided Candy Annie through it, closing it behind them.

"I am frightened I am going to run right into the Sheriff," Candy Annie said.

"That isn't going to happen," McCall said. "There is a back entrance to the main house. I accessed it when I searched the grounds. Stay close to me."

They crossed out of the Poplar trees where the orchard was situated. The Mormon softball games were still going strong. McCall and Candy skirted around the orchard and ran to where the first white-washed house was situated. They were at the back of it. Candy Annie paused, catching her breath.

"My Aunt doesn't go out," Candy Annie told McCall. "She stays close to the big house. In that way she is as much of a prisoner as I am."

"We'll make a dash for the back of the porch," McCall said. "You up for that?"

"I'm up for it."

McCall and Candy Annie sprinted to the back of the first house. None of the Mormons there even looked up at them. They were all too engrossed in their softball games, croquet matches and basket weaving. McCall accessed a back door which opened at his touch. He guided Candy Annie through the door and closed it behind them. They came to a passageway that led into the kitchen. Abigail's Aunt Esther had just finished baking some bread. She whirled around, startled, and then she froze like had seen a ghost. Candy Annie moved tentatively forward.

"Hi, Aunt Esther."

Esther stared at her, nonplussed. Then she threw her arms around her and hugged her. McCall gave them their moment. Esther broke away from her and held her at arm's length.

"Look at you!" Esther said, fighting back tears. "I can't get over the way you have grown! I remember you as a child, very serious and withdrawn. But there was a vitality to you. A mischievous sense of humor." She looked over at McCall. "My other brother Calvin took Anne away with him years ago. I despaired of ever seeing her again."

"My Uncle Calvin dumped me in Brooklyn with some relatives I had never heard of," Candy Annie said. "Calvin didn't stay with me long. Maybe a week and then he was off on his 'travels' as he liked to call them. He never came back. I was homeless for a time, but then I found a life for myself beneath the New York City streets."

"You were living on the streets?" Esther exclaimed, appalled.

"Not a big deal," Candy Annie said. "Mr. McCall knows my history. I adjusted to my new life pretty well. I was very happy there. But in the end the loneliness and the isolation began to eat away at me. I resolved to return back into the real world, but I was frightened." Candy Annie looked over at McCall. "That was when Mr. McCall came into my life. He rescued me from the streets. He found me an apartment in New York City where a friend of his, Mickey Kostmayer, lived. I got to know him. He became a very special friend. I guess could say were a couple. Mr. McCall had left me in good hands."

"But what happened to you after that?" Esther demanded. "What made you return here to Meadow Springs?"

Candy Annie stole a look at McCall who nodded encouragingly. She turned back to her Aunt Esther and suddenly her eyes brimmed with tears. "I was kidnapped from my apartment in New York and brought here to Meadows Springs by some very bad men. They dressed me as an Amish girl so I would be accepted. They kept me a prisoner."

Candy Annie could not go on. Her Aunt Esther put her arms around her niece. Her own eyes had filled with tears. She looked over at McCall as if her heart was breaking.

"What bad men is Anne talking about?"

"None of your Mormon friends," he assured her. "They seem to be fine people. But Sheriff Conrad is a real piece of work. I'm certain the good-old-boy act of his doesn't fool you. He's a dangerous predator."

Esther held Candy Annie close to her. "The Sheriff is a law into himself. But I can't believe he would hold Anne here against her will. Land's sake I didn't know Anne was even *here*. How could she be a prisoner?"

"Anne was putting on an act for Sheriff Conway's benefit," McCall said. "The Mormons who have gathered here would not have known anything about it. Candy Annie would have appeared to them to be a devout disciple."

"Is what you call her?" Esther said. "*Candy Annie?*"

"I guess it is a kind of nickname," she said. "I used to eat a lot of candy when I was living below the streets of New York City. Gummy bears, nougat, Lollypops, M&M's, Mars bars and Werther's candies. But I gave it up before I died of sugar poisoning."

"What kind of a diet is that?" Esther exclaimed.

"Not a good one," she admitted. "That was about the time I started following the teachings of the Church of Jesus Christ of Latter-day Saints. When I got here some of the brethren dressed me in Amish clothes. They assumed I was a member of the church. I had liked it. But that was not who I was."

Finally Esther broke away from Candy Annie and turned to McCall. "What can I do for Anne?"

"Keep her hidden away in this house for as long as possible," McCall said. "It will give us a chance to talk."

"I'll be in the kitchen baking more bread," Esther said. "I won't disturb you unless someone comes calling. But that could happen at any time."

"I'll deal it when that time comes," McCall said.

Candy Annie smiled at her Aunt Esther. "It's so good to see you again," she said and kissed her Aunt.

McCall ushered her out the kitchen into the front parlor. He sat Candy Annie in a big armchair, pulled over a low stool and sat beside her. "You can stay here," he said. "Your Aunt Esther will take care of you. It will take time for the adjustment to sink in, but maybe it would be the best thing for you. You will get to know these Amish people."

"For the longest time I thought that would be the best thing for me," Candy Annie said. "I wanted a family who would accept me for the person I am. But that was a daydream I had when I was depressed or morose. I loved my life in Manhattan. I had found a soul mate in Mickey Kostmayer, even though I knew in my heart that the relationship would not last. He must have been frantic with worry about me. Is he okay?"

McCall didn't want to tell her that he had to leave Mickey Kostmayer in the care of a stranger in Meadow Springs because of a beating he had received from two lowlife hoodlums.

"Mickey ran into some trouble trying to find you," he said. "But he is going to be fine. It is your wellbeing that concerns me the most."

XX

SISTERS

"I just want to go home," Candy Annie said.

"That was what I wanted to hear," McCall told her. "I am going to back to New York City. But I have to take care of business first."

"What business is that?"

"Dealing with Sheriff Conway."

"He'll try to kill you!" Candy Annie said, fearfully.

"I won't give him the chance."

At that moment Abigail came flying into the house. She scooped up some books that she had left on a couch. "I had Bible Study tonight and I had misplaced some of my books. I'm going to be in such trouble."

She stopped short when she saw Candy Annie sitting in the big easy chair. McCall had hoped to drive her away from the compound right after they had their little talk, but that wasn't going to happen now. Candy Annie stood up as Abigail moved deeper into the room.

"Sorry, I didn't see you sitting there," she said. "I'm Abigail."

For some reason Candy Annie felt embarrassed to use the name "*Candy Annie*". She had long ago felt compelled to use her real name. "I'm Anne," she said, somewhat demurely.

"Are you here to see my Aunt Esther?" Abigail asked her.

"No, we just met."

"Anne had been visiting me," McCall said, which was close to the truth.

Abigail came over and shook Candy Annie's hand. "Please to meet you."

"You, too," she said.

"I didn't know we had visitors," Abigail said. "I don't want to be rude, but I really have to dash. I am late for Bible Study as it is."

"What I have to say will not take long," McCall said. Candy Annie looked for help from McCall, not knowing else what to say. McCall thought the time had come to put his cards on the table.

He said: "*Anne is your sister, Abigail.*"

Both of the girls were nonplussed by the revelation. Abigail shook her head, but the words had sunk in. "I don't have a sister," she insisted. "I had a cousin who was thrown off her horse many years ago when she was riding. Maybe you're mistaking her for someone else."

Candy Annie was similarly distressed. "I have no brothers or sisters," she said.

McCall took Abigail's and Candy Annie's arms and gently moved them to the mirror which hung above the dining table. "Take a good look at yourselves," he said. "The similarities are remarkable. If you're not sisters I would be very surprised."

McCall let go of their arms. In the mirror they looked at their reflections with growing realization. Abigail kept staring at Candy Annie's face until she turned beet red. Abigail took hold of Candy Annie's hand and squeezed it tight.

"We do look somewhat alike," she said. She turned around to where McCall was standing. "But *sisters?* You can't be serious."

"I am deadly serious," McCall said. "You have not seen each other until now. It is a secret that your Aunt Esther has lived with for many years. It was time for it to be spoken aloud. You never have to see each other again, but it's my hope that you will find a way to bridge the years and embrace them. After all," he said, "family comes before everything else."

"You could be wrong about this," Abigail said, but in her heart she knew it was the truth.

"I could be," McCall said. "But I'm not."

There was another moment of silence, then Abigail simply embraced her sister. Candy Annie burst to tears and buried her head in Abigail's arms.

"Don't sob!" Abigail said. "I'm having a lot of trouble keeping myself together as it is."

Candy Annie nodded, but she kept her arms wrapped around her sister.

McCall smiled and nodded.

He felt like he had accomplished a rare triumph.

* * * *

The boardroom was crowded with Federal Officers all talking over each other. Tempers flared and egos were stroked. Hayden Vallance stood apart from the melee while the arguments were made for caution and clear thinking. Andy Esterhaus was the mediator, a normally soft-spoken, introspective man in his fifties, but his voice was drowned out by the various egos on display. Matthew Cohen was a brash, firebrand kind of an attorney who liked being argumentative. Ben Reynolds, in his three-piece suit perfectly tailored with an outrageous Paisley Italian-crafted silk tie, waited patiently to put his point across. Gregory Fuller was a good-old boy from Georgia with a pallid personality that made Vallance think of him as a walking corpse. Morgan Lynch was a larger-than-life orator who loved to hear the sound of his own voice. These Justice Officers sat around a large round table drinking coffee and taking potshots at each until Vallance could not stand it any longer. He put his fingers into his mouth and whistled loudly. The Federal Officers reacted as if a siren had suddenly sounded.

"That's enough!" Vallance said. "It's about time for you to get your act together."

All heads turned toward him as if he had not even been in the room.

"How do you propose for us to do that?" Andy Esterhaus asked in his quiet, folksy voice. "We're sitting here debating the pros and cons of a major drug haul and its ramifications like we were a bunch of amateur sleuths unravelling a mystery. As our President once described it, this is a really big deal. Innocent lives are at stake. Let's not lose sight of that."

"I am going to have to consider the source of this intelligence," Matthew Cohen said. "It comes with the word of a mercenary."

"The definition of a mercenary is someone who makes money at the expense of ethics," Vallance said. "I have not done that. If my behavior appears rapacious to you, so be it. I fight for causes that I believe in."

"The ones that include terrorism and coercion," Morgan Lynch said, caustically.

Gregory Fuller had the kind of sonorous voice which made Vallance again think of him as one of the undead. "What reassurances do we have that you are going to lead us to this warehouse?"

"I don't have any to give you," Vallance said.

"What other motive would Mr. Vallance have?" Andy Esterhaus asked, reasonably. "He could easily have walked away from all of us, got in his car and found another conflict to fight and none is us would have been the wiser."

"You bring up a valid point," Morgan Lynch said, his voice cutting through like a scythe. "Mr. Vallance has more than any of us to lose here. I think we should put our petty jealousies aside and come up with a plan to implement a course of action."

"I take it that you have been inside this warehouse and actually seen the drugs?" Ben Reynolds asked.

"I have," Vallance said.

"He can't be certain that this was a drug shipment," Matthew Cohen said. "Not without opening the merchandise and personally examining it. To do that this task force needs to be assured we're not chasing our tails around in circles."

"I say we are the ones who have nothing to lose here," Gregory Fuller said, quietly. "We have to take Mr. Vallance at his word. What other option do we have?"

"None," Andy Esterhaus said, flatly. "Assuming that Mr. Vallance is inclined to move forward with this course of action."

"I wouldn't be here unless I wanted to be," Vallance said. He moved over to the head of the table and spread a map across it. "There is going to be another drug shipment. That's the intel I overheard in that warehouse. We'll have to be in place no later than 10:00 P.M. tonight."

"Which doesn't give us much time to organize a raid," Matthew Cohen said.

That notion was greeted with silence. Finally Ben Reynolds said: "We'll be there when you need us."

"Can you organize that, Andy?" Gregory Fuller asked.

"I have Federal Officers waiting for my call," Andy Esterhaus said. "They can be deployed within a half-an-hour if we can get our act together."

"We're going to have one shot at this," Vallance said. "Let's do it right."

The high-level meeting broke up with various Federal Officers on their cell phones. Ben Reynolds took Hayden Vallance to one side. His manner was flamboyant. "You hogtied those Feds until they didn't know which way was up. Or maybe it was this Paisley floral silk tie that dazzled them. I got about forty more of them at home that are equally outrageous."

"Hard to believe," Vallance said, deadpan.

"We're putting a lot of faith in you, son. I just hope you're not getting my hopes up with a lot of horse putty. The man who has been dealing the drugs is named Luther Oppenheimer. You ever had occasion to run into him?"

"Never had the pleasure," Vallance said.

"He has a son who is lying in a bed at the Saint Anthony's Hospital," Ben Reynolds said. "I was visiting a friend of mine at the time who was in the same Chicago Hospital. Luther Oppenheimer was there to see his son. I don't believe it was a friendly meeting. The man doesn't give a rat's ass about his son being at death's door. I don't believe the young man is going to make it, but that is beside the point. Luther Oppenheimer has a vicious streak in him the size of a Kansas twister."

"I visited with Luther's son," Vallance said, quietly.

That took Ben Reynolds aback. "At the Mercy Hospital?" he asked.

"That's right."

"What were you doing there?"

"A number of reasons," Vallance said. "He is a pretty sick young man."

"At death's door I'd say," Ben said. "But that won't matter to Luther Oppenheimer. He is a rattler who could spit venom and not choke on it."

"So Luther has been dealing drugs as well?"

"In the worst way," Ben said. "We have been trying to nail his hide to the wall for years, but he keeps out of reach. He lives on an island off the coast of Maine and has his own private army."

"Where is this location in Maine?" Vallance asked.

"On Hope Island. A very exclusive address where visitors are not welcome. It is rumored that he keeps several young women at the island as sex slaves who are there to cater to his every whim. But that is only a rumor. I have no proof of that. On the other hand, it wouldn't surprise me none. Luther Oppenheimer deals in human misery."

"Have you ever been to this island?" Vallance asked.

"No, sir. But the island has a mysterious ambiance about it. Luther is a hermit who has shunned the outside world. He does make trips from his island to take care of business."

"Which is the sale of heroin and cocaine," Valance said. "And white slavery."

"There is not a shred of proof to substantiate that claim," Ben said. "He is also in the business of selling arms and Sarin, a nerve pain medication, to the highest bidders. Like you say, a nasty piece of work."

"Someone needs to rattle his cage," Vallance said.

"You aim to take him out?" Ben asked and laughed. "Forget it. You can't touch Luther Oppenheimer. He's got highly paid lawyers and an army of mercenaries guarding him at all times on that island. But the right set of circumstances will nail his ass to the wall. I am counting on that happening."

"Where is this island?" Vallance asked.

"Look son, going after Luther Oppenheimer would be suicide," Ben said. "But if we can take him down in this raid, I am betting the farm that we're going to finally nail his ass to the wall."

"Unless he slips your net," Vallance said. "He might not even be at the warehouse when you close in."

"He'll be there," Ben Reynolds said with conviction. "He's a slippery rascal but tonight we're going to outfox him. With your help," he added.

"I am making no promises," Vallance said, shortly. "All of the circumstances need to come together."

"How long have you been in the mercenary business?" Ben asked him. "If you don't mind my asking?"

"Long enough to see the misery and heartbreak in most people," Vallance said. "It's why I became a mercenary if you want to know the truth."

"So you can be a hero?"

"There is nothing heroic about what I do," Vallance said, shortly. "How many Federal Officers are going to be with you when you spring this trap?"

"About half-a-dozen, the way I figure it," Ben said. "That suit you?"

"Sounds good to me," Vallance said.

Ben Reynolds held out his hand. "Good to be working with you, son."

Vallance shook his hand. "Just be in that warehouse at the appropriate time. You got one shot at getting this right. Don't screw it up."

"I am aware of my responsibilities, sir," Ben Reynolds said, a little chagrined. "I don't need you to teach me how to suck eggs."

That got a laugh from Vallance. "I'll keep that in mind."

Ben Reynolds moved to where one of the Feds, Gregory Fuller, was motioning to him to join him. Hayden Vallance moved out of the boardroom and outside where explosions of neon assailed him.

He had had enough of these Feds to last him a lifetime.

*   *   *   *

McCall went outside on the big porch at the house to check that everything was status quo. The Mormons were playing volleyball and badminton on the grassy lawns. The sounds of their laughter and high spirits were infectious. McCall decided that these were very special people. Their religious views and doctrines were no concern of his. Sheriff Conway was nowhere to be seen. McCall didn't know if he had returned to Meadow Springs or whether he was parked somewhere in the trees or in one of the five buildings that made up the quadrant. He needed to get back on the road as quickly as possible with Candy Annie before Sheriff Conway returned.

He retraced his steps back into the big house. Almost immediately he heard the sound of voices. He made his way to the kitchen. He found Abigail and Candy Annie huddled together like they were old friends getting together to catch up on all the gossip. The revelation that they were sisters had been completely ignored for the moment. They were like two very old friends.

Aunt Esther was still making her bread while the girls kibitzed. Her face was wreathed with smiles as she prepared another load of bread to go into the oven. She moved forward to McCall and took his hand. She gestured to the two girls.

"This is truly a miracle," she said. "The Lord has seen fit to bestow his blessings upon us. Did you know that Abigail that Anne were sisters?"

"I had suspected it," McCall said. "But I had no real proof."

"Look at their faces!" Aunt Esther exclaimed. "I don't think you need any more proof than your own eyes! Isn't it wonderful?"

"It is," McCall said. "And there is no doubt in your mind they are *really sisters*?"

"None whatsoever." Then her voice took on a more somber tone. She lowered her voice conspiratorially. "But once this reunion is over, what happens then? I want Anne to stay here with me, but I fear you are going to take her away."

"I'm not sure what the best course of action to take," McCall admitted. "Anne could stay here with you. She is appropriately dressed as a Mormon. It would mean giving up everything she has believed in. I not convinced that would be the best thing for her."

"She can stay here at the house for as long as she wants," Esther said. "Get to know her new sister better."

"I am concerned what action Sheriff Conway is going to take," McCall said. "When he finds out that Anne is his niece he might just drag her out of here. Don't let the homespun wisdom and cracker barrel philosophy fool you. He is a dangerous psychopath."

"But what can he really do to her?" Esther said, distressed. "She is family now."

"I am going to leave that up to Anne," McCall said. "If she wants to stay here with you, that's fine. If she wants to return to New York City with me, that's fine too. But she is going to make her mind up quickly. She is in a euphoria state of mind right now. But that won't last. The Sheriff may decide on a course of action that would be detrimental to her wellbeing. I won't allow that to happen."

"But how can you stop it?" Esther asked, nervously. "He is the Sheriff. He could arrest you and you'll be cooling your heels in a jail cell."

McCall put a steadying hand on Esther's shoulder. "I will take care of Sheriff Conway. *Candy Annie*, or just Anne as you call her, has a decision to make. Does she stay here, or do I take her with me?"

Esther looked at the two girls who were oblivious to their whispered conversation. "The Lord will provide us with the answer."

"You may be right," he said, gently. "But that's a decision you have to make right now."

XXI

GATHERING THE TROOPS

McCall moved over to where the two girls were standing. Before he could say a word, Candy Annie grabbed his arm. In her giddy excitement she was addressing him as if she and Abigail had only just met. "This is my sister, Abigail! Can you believe it? I didn't even know she even existed until now. This has been a wonderful blessing for me!"

"I want to thank you for bringing us together, Mr. McCall," Abigail said. "I guess I have been looking for a sign from the Lord that I had a purpose in this world. Now I have found it!'

She was overcome with emotion and tears flooded her eyes. Candy Annie grabbed Abigail's hand and held it tightly. She looked almost accusingly at McCall. "Did you know this was going to happen?"

"I thought that once the two of you had bonded the emotional floodgates would open," McCall said. "I didn't know how fast that acceptance would happen."

Aunt Esther moved up to them. Her hands trembled, but she was keeping herself composed. "It is a wonderful reunion for two souls who have joined together in this way. But I fear Mr. McCall has other plans for you."

McCall held both girls at arm's length, but he was mainly addressing Candy Annie. "You have a home here in Meadow Springs now, Candy Annie. If you decide to stay here at the compound, I won't stop you." Unconsciously he had been using Candy Annie's name. She was very silent now as he continued: "But if you want to leave with me it has to be in the next few minutes. You're not safe here." He looked at Abigail. "Neither of you."

"Because Sheriff Conway would never allow us to stay together," Abigail said, turning to Aunt Esther and then to McCall. "That's the truth, isn't it?"

"I am afraid the Sheriff would consider it his sworn duty to see that your lives were severely disrupted," McCall said. "It is a very tough decision that both of you have to make. You have found each other, but that won't last long. Do you stay in Meadow Springs, or do you leave here with me?"

"We don't have to make that decision right this minute!" Candy Annie objected.

Abigail said: "But we do!" She took her sister's hands in hers. "That is what Mr. McCall is trying to tell us. It is our decision to make. I know what I want to do!"

Candy Annie nodded, her eyes also brimming with tears. "So do I." she echoed. "We're soul mates."

The two sisters embraced. McCall turned back to Esther. "You have a say in this decision as well."

"When it comes to Abigail's happiness I only want the best for her," she said. "I will do what is right."

The two girls let go of each other.

"We're determined to be together," Candy Annie said.

"We're a team now," Abigail added.

"Fair enough." McCall said. "But there's no going back."

"We are very happy with our decision," Abigail gushed.

Candy Annie also nodded, smiling through her tears. "Very happy."

"I know you have a lot of friends you need to say goodbye to," McCall said to Abigail.

She looked embarrassed for a moment. She glanced down at the floor. "You're talking about my friends that I had mentioned to you? Ashtyn and Eden and Hannah and Kaidence and Naimi." She shook her head. "I just made those names up. I have no real friends here in the community. Just my friend Oakley and she is visiting with her father who lives in San Francisco. She is going to stay with her father until the autumn and then I don't think she will return to Meadow Springs. I'll write to her. I will take my Bible and my studies with me. That is all I will need."

"Maybe that is all any of us need," McCall said, philosophically.

Abigail looked over at Candy Annie. "You should change your clothes. You don't need to wear Amish clothes now. I'll go with you. My room is in the second building along from here."

Candy Annie turned to McCall, as if seeking his permission. "Go ahead," he said. "But get back here as soon as you can."

The two teenage girls raced from the kitchen and flew out the door of the house. Aunt Esther sighed. "I will miss both of them so much."

"Can't be helped," McCall said, shortly.

He felt like he was running out of time.

"You have turned our lives completely around," Esther said. "Which I know is a good thing. Maybe Sheriff Conway will leave us alone now."

"Don't count on it," McCall said. "The Sheriff will take his revenge out on you."

"You can't stop him doing that!" Esther objected.

"I can try. I am not finished with the Sheriff yet."

"I regret to say that my uncle is a very vindictive man," she said. "Mean-spirited and cunning, like a fox. I have been listening to his platitudes most of my life."

"I will deal with the Sheriff," McCall said. "Leave him to me. Is there a meeting place where you could go to where Abigail and Anne would feel safe? At least for the time being."

Esther sighed. "I don't know the answer to that. Most of the time I am alone in this house. But I do venture out when other members of the Church come calling. I join them for high tea with scones and raspberry jam. That way I can hear all the latest gossip which make me feel audacious and fearless."

That made McCall smile. He said: "As soon as Abigail and Anne are ready I want you to join your Mormon friends."

"All right."

"You can leave the house anytime you want to, isn't that right?"

"I am not a prisoner here," Esther said, offended. "I come and go as I please."

"That's good to hear," McCall said.

Aunt Esther picked up a shawl from a table and wrapped it around her shoulders. "The evenings are getting a little cooler. How long should I plan to be gone?"

"Maybe half an hour at the most," McCall said.

"But you are going to say goodbye?"

"I wouldn't leave without doing that," he promised.

Esther and McCall moved into the parlor of the house. Esther stepped out into the night. Two of her Mormon friends immediately sought her out. "Where have you have been hiding?" Clara demanded, taking Esther's arm.

"We have been asking about you," her friend Ivy said and took her other arm.

"I had some bread I had just put into the oven," Esther said, carelessly. "I just needed to get a breath of fresh air."

"I heard that your niece is visiting," Clara said. "How long is she staying here?"

"Only a few days," Esther said.

"The sewing circle has missed you," Ivy said.

"It's nice to be missed," Esther said with no irony in her voice. "I feel in the mood to take a walk."

Her friends accompanied her, chatting animatedly. McCall knew Esther's heart wasn't into the small talk. That was all for show. He moved to one of the windows overlooking the wide porch.

An ominous silence had permeated the stillness.

McCall hoped it was not an omen of what was still to come.

*   *   *   *

Mickey Kostmayer got up off the couch he had been dozing on. He ached all over, but the effects of the beating he had suffered were diminishing. He felt stronger. He unlocked the front door of the apartment and tossed the key onto a coffee table. Stairs led him down to the street. He was still groggy, but he was feeling better by the minute. He knew exactly where he was. Two blocks from the tavern. He walked swiftly until he came to *Katz's Delicatessen* and the *Dry Cleaners*. The *Hallmark Store* had a special on *Halloween Cards* and the *Cooperstown Bakery* was jammed with people queuing up for bagels and croissants. It felt good to Kostmayer to be alive. He opened the tavern door and moved inside.

The place was a madhouse. People were jammed into it. All of the barstools were taken. Kostmayer moved through the melee. Dixie spotted him and made a beeline for him. She clutched his arm as if she was going to break it.

"What are you doing here?" she demanded. "I left you sleeping on a couch at my place dead to the world! You were supposed to stay there until I came back!"

"I got lonely," Kostmayer said in a deadpan way. He looked around. "Those guys I followed out of here. Did they come back?"

"You mean the shit-for-brains lowlifes who beat the living crap out of you?" Dixie said, wryly. "Sure, they came back. They're sitting right over there. But you don't want to mess with those losers. They are bad news."

Kostmayer noted Jeremiah Reynolds and Jeff Fletcher sitting at one the back tables drinking Coors Light. "I'll stay out if their way," he promised. "I'll get a beer at the bar."

"For you that is dangerous," Dixie said, wryly. "These guys would just love an excuse to cause you some severe bodily harm."

Kostmayer smiled at her concern. "Only if they see me. Keep an eye on them."

"I hope you know what you're doing," Dixie muttered.

"That makes two of us," Kostmayer said.

He found a place at the bar where he could see Jeremiah and Fletcher in the mirror. He ordered a Stella Artois beer and took a swallow. Jeremiah and Fletcher suddenly stood up. They left by a back table near the entrance. Kostmayer finished up his beer and moved quickly to the front door after them. Dixie just shook her head and sighed.

"A possum has got more sense that you have," she said.

Outside the tavern Kostmayer was in time to see Jeremiah and Fletcher move down the street. He realized he still didn't know their names. Not that it mattered. A white Kia Sorento LX sport utility vehicle was parked outside. It wasn't new, probably seven or more years old, but in reasonable condition. Jeremiah unlocked the doors and he and Fletcher climbed in. They pulled out and headed west.

Kostmayer reached his Ford Explorer. He unlocked it, slid into the driver's side, fired it up and pulled out of the parking space. He followed Jeremiah and Fletcher at a safe distance.

* * * *

McCall watched from the window of the house as Sheriff Conway pulled up and got out of his police cruiser. McCall needed to give Abigail and Candy Annie time to get themselves together before he could spirit them away. At the compound the Mormons were playing volleyball and they had just added a Lacrosse game to their repertoire. Their high spirits were infectious. Deputy Jack Foster climbed out of his police cruiser. One of the Mormons, a man named Jacob, jogged over to where the Sheriff was standing.

"Evening, Sheriff."

"Evening, Jacob," Sheriff Conway said, affably. "Everything here good with you?"

"Couldn't be better," he said. "I don't suppose you'd like to join us for a game of volleyball?"

"If I wasn't on duty there's nothing I'd like better," he said. "But I'll have to take a rain check on that kind offer."

"Hannah has baked some of her gingerbread cookies," Jacob said. "And some homemade jam. Sure I can't tempt you?"

"That does sound tempting," the Sheriff said. "But I never stop the plough just to catch a mouse." He glanced around him. "There was a fellah wandering around the compound a while back. I had my eye on him. He was about my height and weight. Didn't want him bothering folks. Do you what happened to him?"

"There was a stranger here, but I didn't speak to him," Jacob said. "The last time I looked he was heading for that Jaguar parked in the trees. I think he was leaving, but then I got caught up in one of the volleyball games."

"I reckon he moved on," the Sheriff said. "I'll take a look around to see if I can see him at one of the other houses. Don't give it another thought, Jacob. Police business."

That seemed to placate Jacob who headed back to his volleyball game on the grounds. Deputy Jack Foster had joined the Sheriff. "I told you that stranger would be no trouble," he said. "He was just passing though."

"Do some mingling with the folks," Sheriff Conway said. "Make sure of that. I have some business of my own to take care of."

"Sure thing, Sheriff."

Deputy Foster strode over to where one of the volleyball games was in process. He was welcomed by the Mormons there which now included Aunt Esther. But Sheriff Conway wasn't going to escape that easily. A continent of Mormons had descended on him, all of them needing attention.

"Simmer down folks," the Sheriff said. "One of you at a time is plenty for this country boy to handle. What can I do for you?"

McCall ran back through the house, into the kitchen and let himself out onto the small porch. He almost collided with Abigail who was carrying a small leather canvas duffel bag filled to the brim.

"I am ready," she said. "I didn't have much to pack. We Amish girls travel light."

McCall looked around. "Where's Candy Annie?"

"I guess you're referring to Anne?" Abigail asked him.

"It's kind of a nickname for her."

"*Candy Annie*? I like that!" Abigail looked around, suddenly concerned. "She was getting some things together to take with her. I lost sight of her. She has been gone for quite a while. I thought she would be waiting for me out here. Maybe she had forgotten something."

"Go back into the house," McCall said. "Stay there until I get back."

"Where are you going?" she said, concerned.

"To run an errand. I won't be gone long. Go into the house and I am sure Anne will join you."

"There is a problem, isn't there?" Abigail asked him.

"No problem," McCall assured her. "Just do like I say."

Abigail took two steps, then turned back again. "I realize I had forgotten something myself. My diary was under my pillow. Not a great hiding place for it, but I can't leave without it. It has my whole life in there!"

"Go and get it and then come back here to the house," McCall said.

"I'll just be a second to find it!"

Abigail ran toward one of the houses in the quadrant.

McCall moved away. He was careful not to run into Sheriff Conway and disappeared into the towering elm trees.

*　*　*　*

Hayden Vallance was in place long before the raid in the warehouse. He had climbed up the outside stairs and left himself in onto the third floor. The various catwalks stretched out below him. The space was divided into two portions. Six foremen were supervising the cardboard boxes as they travelled on a conveyor belt. Two Chevrolet Silverado trucks stood at the loading doors where they were being loaded into the trucks. The cardboard boxes all were labelled, but there was a difference. They were painted black with orange decals and bigger than the rest of the contraband. These boxes had artillery shells in them, not heroin or cocaine. Next on the conveyor belt were cardboard boxes stenciled C-4. Another foreman was supervising the boxes. He opened one of the boxes at random. It contained Sarin containers stacked three feet high. Vallance had used the colorless, odorless nerve agent when he had been fighting guerillas in the South American jungles.

U.S. Marshals accompanied the coterie of agents that surrounded the warehouse. They were backed up by the Federal Task Force consisting of Andy Esterhaus, Matthew Cohen, Ben Reynolds, Gregory Fuller and Morgan Lynch. They still wore suits and ties but had donned camouflage Assault Military Camo coats.

Vallance checked his watch.

He counted down the seconds.

*　*　*　*

The white Kia Sorento pulled up to the white-washed building in the center of the compound. Jeremiah Reynolds and Jeff Fletcher climbed out. There was no sign now of Sheriff Conway, but his police cruiser was parked to one side on the grassy lawn. The Mormon faithful were still playing volleyball and throwing horseshoes around. Another badminton net had been set up. The big frame house looked somehow abandoned.

"I presume that little bitch Candy Annie is on the compound somewhere," Jeremiah said. "Maybe we should pay her a visit."

"Rattle her cage?" Fletcher said.

"Something like that. Remind her that we went to a lot of trouble on her behalf."

"The main house looks abandoned," Fletcher said. "But we could check it out."

The two thugs strode to the house. Jeremiah took out a Taurus 9mm Luger pistol as he entered with Fletcher.

XXII

PAYBACK

THE TASK FORCE HAD gathered outside the warehouse on Vallance's instructions. He kept in touch with them by speaking softly into a handheld portable two-way radio. He was up on the catwalk looking down at the activity below. Andy Esterhaus, Matthew Cohen, Ben Reynolds, Gregory Fuller and Morgan Lynch were all in position. But Vallance had a flag up. He said into the two-way radio: "Hold your positions."

He had just seen *Laredo Snake Man* enter the warehouse. He was dressed the same in a three-piece suit in his fancy waistcoat and high-heel cowboy boots. He moved over to where the foreman was loading up the boxes and had a brief word with him. Vallance didn't know if he would have to abort the mission, but he held out for a little longer. The foreman had heated words with Luther Oppenheimer which seemed to placate him. The conveyor belt moved once more. *Laredo Snake Man*, as Vallance called him, took over the chore of loading the boxes into the back of the Silverado truck. The work resumed around him. Vallance allowed him another moment to make sure he was staying in the warehouse. Then he bought the handheld portable two-way radio to his lips.

"Go!" he said.

The task force erupted into the warehouse in full force.

The terrorists were caught completely by surprise. They were rounded up basically before they had a chance to react. Four of the men who had been loading the boxes fired at the hanging globes, smashing them, plunging the warehouse into semi-darkness, but it was to no avail. The U.S. Marshals were taking no chances of letting these anarchists get away. It was all over in a matter of seconds. Only a handful of the gunmen had escaped. Hayden Vallance looked at the last place where he had seen Luther Oppenheimer and realized he had assessed a rear entrance on the catwalk. Vallance ran to the exterior door that led out onto the steel steps and clattered down them. But his quarry had disappeared. He re-entered the warehouse where the Federal Marshals were handcuffing the terrorists. He caught sight of Andy Easterhaus and Ben Reynolds. Both of them gave him high-five signs. The other Federal Marshals, including Matthew Cohen, Gregory Fuller and Morgan Lynch had their hands full taking the terrorists into custody.

Laredo Snake Man had vanished at the first sign of trouble, but Vallance knew where he could find him.

*   *   *   *

Sheriff Conway came out into the trees which now surrounded him. The steel grain storage silos were off to one side. The Sheriff made his way across to them in the sporadic moonlight. He moved over to the first silos which towered over him. He was relieved to see that the padlock was still in place. He inserted a key into it and the padlock split open. It didn't look as if it had been disturbed. Sheriff Conway left the open padlock on the ground and moved to the silos. He unlocked the door there.

The interior of the silo was in darkness. The Sheriff reached for the light switch. Nothing happened. The skylight at the top of the silo provided some wan light. The Sheriff moved slowly through the pale darkness. The hanging chain that had held the restraints was still in place. He thought he saw Candy Annie's figure dangling where he had left it. But the closer he got to it he realized there was *not* a figure hanging there at all. The arms were stretched out as if the figure was still there, but that was an optical illusion. The chain swung around a couple of times to give the appearance that a human being had been suspended there. But the figure's wrists were not secured.

McCall held his Glock 19 pistol at his side.

His voice echoed through the darkness. "Time for us to have a reckoning, Sheriff," he said.

Sheriff Conway pulled his heavy Colt .45 Revolver out of his holster. He moved farther into the shadows. All pretense of him being a "good-old-boy" had disappeared. His voice was chilling with understated menace.

"One of us is not going to leave this grain silo alive," he said. "We got a saying back home. *Pigs get fat, but hogs get slaughtered.*"

"Since we're trading down some homespun wisdom," McCall said, his voice also echoing in the darkness. "How did you get rid of Abigail's cousin? I don't believe she fell and hit her head on a rock. That's the myth you came up with."

Sheriff Conway moved deeper into the shadows. "I didn't kill her if that's what you're asking me," he said. "But I did let her bleed to death right there on the ground."

McCall's voice echoed again, but the Sheriff couldn't tell where it was coming from. "So you covered it up?"

"I had no choice," the Sheriff said.

"There is always a choice," McCall said.

"Anyway, that's ancient history," Sheriff Conway said. "Come out into the light so I can see you."

"I don't believe I'll do that," McCall said. "Might be detrimental to my health. Your cousin Esther and Abigail know the truth about what happened in that field."

"Good luck proving that."

A panel high in the skylight flared for a moment on McCall. The Sheriff changed direction, moving closer. "The truth hurts all of us," he said. "All I can see right now is that little dude from Oz standing behind the curtain. When I look again, he'll be gone."

A shadow moved. The Sheriff fired his Colt .45. Revolver in the darkness. The flash of the gun showed him that there was no one standing there. Sheriff Conway moved farther into the grain silo.

McCall had been waiting for his opportunity. He had circled around the grain storage silos and stepped through a narrow space that led him back to where Candy Annie had been hanging. Which meant that he was behind Sheriff Conway's figure. The Sheriff stood motionless, listening for a sound to let him know where his adversary was. Then he was moving forward again toward the back of the grain silos.

"Let's finish this here hoedown, son," he rasped, his voice shrill in the silence. "I'm an awfully good shot with a handgun. Time for you to turn mother's picture to the wall and get what's coming to you."

McCall could hear the subtle rustle of the Sheriff's gun belt in the darkness. He saw a vague shape materialize just for a moment, backlit in the radiance spilling from the skylight.

McCall would only have one shot at him.

"Sheriff!"

Sheriff Conway swung around, his .45 Revolver coming up into his hand.

Too late.

McCall fired his Glock at his quarry. The bullet knocked the Sheriff off his feet. He slid to the floor of the grain silo and didn't move. McCall approached him, realizing that he was a cunning old fox who might have been playing possum. He approached the lawman warily, then he lowered his Glock Revolver.

Sheriff Conway was dead.

McCall knelt beside him. He said softly: "We have a saying also, Sheriff. *'Enemies of the soul create monsters.'*"

The Sheriff stared up at him with sightless eyes.

McCall straightened up. He didn't have a lot of time before the Sheriff's Deputy, Jack Foster, returned to find out what happened to his boss. McCall retraced his steps to the big iron silo door and stepped through it. He picked up the padlock and snapped it shut. He made his way back through the orchard and out to where the five buildings stood. Deputy Foster had joined in the festivities around on the grassy lawn where the Mormons were playing volleyball. The Peace Officer was having a grand time while Sheriff Conway lay dead in the grain silo.

McCall ran toward the five buildings that made up the quadrant of the estate.

Inside the main house all of the lights had been turned out. Jeff Fletcher had found a fuse box on the kitchen wall and had extinguished all of them. The kitchen was left in darkness. Jeremiah Reynolds had moved up the staircase to the first floor. He was rummaging through drawers in a bedroom to see what he could find. These Mormons were fastidious people. But there was no jewelry to be found. He moved his search to the smaller bedroom on the first floor.

The back door was thrown open and Abigail let herself back into the house. She had her precious diary with her. She was surprised to find that the kitchen was in darkness. She ran through to the living room, still gripping her canvas duffel bag. The lights had been extinguished there also. Abigail thought that was very odd. She set the duffel bag down and flipped on a couple of table lamps. The lights were out all through the house. She heard some small sounds coming from the first bedroom. She started to run there, but a pair of powerful arms grabbed her from behind and held her in a vice-like grip. Jeff Fletcher leaned close to Abigail, his voice sibilant and menacing.

"Well, what do we have here?" he murmured. "One of the Amish girls trying to escape her destiny?" He raised his voice. "Hey, Jeremiah! I got something to show you. Downstairs in the living room. You'll get a kick of out this."

There was movement from upstairs. "I'll be right down!" Jeremiah shouted.

Abigail tried to escape from Fletcher's grasp, but he held her tightly. "What's your hurry, darlin'? We need to get to know each other better." He leaned in a little closer to her face. "Maybe I can take a peek under that prim and proper dress you're wearing? Bet I would find something that would make my day."

A sound turned him around. Kostmayer was coming through the overlapping shadows. He was carrying a Smith & Wesson 9mm gun in his hand. Fletcher jammed his gun up against Abigail's throat. "Just keep coming," he said, his voice hoarse. "Nice and easy."

Kostmayer froze where he stood. When he recognized him, Fletcher broke into a wide grin. "You just don't know when to quit! I'll give you high marks for tenacity. Toss the gun down onto the floor."

Kostmayer threw the gun to the floor. It skittered away from Fletcher.

He raised his voice. "You got to see this, Jeremiah! You won't believe it!"

Jeremiah came clattering down the stairs. He stopped dead when he saw Kostmayer and shook his head. "Where the hell did he come from?"

"Who cares?" Fletcher said. "He's not going anywhere."

"This is a problem," Jeremiah said. "I don't think we have the time to have to deal with it."

"The more the merrier," Fletcher said. "We'll kill two birds with one stone." He looked at Kostmayer. "It will give me a chance to finish the job we started with this deadbeat."

He had relaxed his grip on Abigail's throat. With a sudden move she twisted out of his grasp and stumbled down to the floor.

Fletcher whirled around.

At the same moment Kostmayer threw himself to the floor right where his gun had skittered away. He grabbed it before Fletcher could aim it at him and fired. Fletcher sprawled to the floor. Jeremiah pulled a Colt Python 357 Magnum Revolver from his belt. He aimed it directly at Kostmayer.

McCall shot him from fifty feet away.

Jeremiah collapsed beside his colleague.

Both of them were dead.

McCall picked Kostmayer up and helped him to his feet. He was still holding the fallen Smith & Wesson 9mm pistol in his hands.

"That was a pretty good shot," McCall said, conversationally. "And you were on your back. You haven't lost your touch."

"A lucky shot," Kostmayer said, faintly.

Abigail stood shaking, but she had composed herself admirably. McCall turned to her. "You're all right?"

"I'm fine," she said. "I can't believe I let that creep put his hands on me."

"I would say he has no further interest in you," McCall said. He looked back at Mickey Kostmayer. "Where did you come from?"

"I was just in the neighborhood," he said. "You know how it is. I had a score to settle with these guys."

"I'd say you did that," McCall said, wryly. "Let me put on some lights."

"The fuse box is in the kitchen," Abigail said.

McCall moved through the shadows. Kostmayer put his arms around Abigail and moved her away from the bodies of the dead men.

"I don't believe we have been formally introduced," he said. "I am Mickey Kostmayer. Friend of McCall's."

"That works for me," Abigail murmured.

At that moment the lights in the house came back on. McCall returned and this time he had Candy Annie with him who had entered the kitchen. Abigail flew into her sister's arms and held her fiercely.

Kostmayer looked at McCall. "What happened to Sheriff Conway?"

"I left him on the floor of the grain silo," McCall said. "He drew down on me."

"Some things never change," Kostmayer murmured.

Abigail broke from Candy Annie's arms. She looked at McCall for a moment as if she couldn't believe her ears. "Who killed him?"

"I did," McCall said. "Had no choice." He was still looking at Kostmayer. "Take the two girls out of here."

"What are you going to do?"

"Take out the garbage."

Kostmayer nodded and he turned to Candy Annie. "These circumstances are pretty strange, but it is nice to see you again, Candy Annie."

"It is just 'Anne' now," she said, demurely.

"When did that change?"

She looked fondly at her sister. "When I met my soul mate."

"That works for me," Kostmayer said. "You're all packed?"

"I am."

"Then let's get out of here."

He shepherded the two girls to the front door of the house.

McCall looked down at Jeremiah and Fletcher but made no comment.

There was nothing he could add to their demise.

*   *   *   *

Hayden Vallance took the ferry in Maine to Omega Island, adjacent to Hope Island, which was a gateway to the Polynesian Islands. It was a 25-minute trip. Vallance walked down the pier which was swarming with people. Several cottages were nestled together on the boardwalk with their red rooftops gleaming in the sun. A white-washed chapel had been built beside the cottages. But the centerpiece of the Island was an 11,795 square-foot mansion. It consisted of eight bedrooms, six bathrooms and various workers' quarters. Vallance noted a rustic tavern where tables were set out adjacent to the pier. Beside it was a replica of the HMS Bounty. That story had resonated with Vallance ever since he had been a boy. The ship's Captain, William Bligh, had set out to purchase breadfruit plants to be taken to the West Indies. His sailing vessel had been seized by acting lieutenant Fletcher Christian who had set him and his 18 Mutineers adrift in the ship's open launch. The Mutineers reached Pitcairn Island in the South Pacific and found a safe haven there. Vallance had always wondered what had happened to them.

Right now he had more pressing matters to deal with than the fate of the HMS Bounty's crew.

Vallance trekked toward the elegant mansion. The meandering path was obscured by flowering red maples, black cherry trees and immense white oak trees. He came a clearing in the forest and started looking for armed guards. He was not disappointed. The Security personnel on the island wore green uniforms with a decal on the pockets of a grey wolf. They wore GPS tracking systems. They carried Ak-47 Kalashnikov Tactical rifles. In their holsters they carried Sig Sauser pistols. Two of guards were patrolling the area so Vallance avoided them at all costs. He didn't want to get into a shooting war with armed Security Officers. He figured these guys were professionals who adhered to a strict code of discipline. They would not be looking for trouble.

Vallance skirted around the armed guards and proceeded to the mansion. He took a moment to take in the stunning view from the place offered. Floodlights were lit on the porch and spilled out into the extensive grounds. A low fence ran around the lawn. There was no movement from outside the building. Vallance jogged toward the entrance. It didn't look as if anyone was home, but Vallance knew that could be deceptive. There could be a reception committee waiting for him which he wanted to avoid. He jogged toward to the entrance of the mansion. Then he thought better of that and made it back to the rear of the house. Stables were erected there, but they were in darkness. French windows and marble columns towered to the second floor of the mansion. Lights blazed in the widows. Vallance moved to one of the sliding glass doors, thinking it would be locked.

It wasn't.

He stepped inside the mansion.

An ornate hallway greeted him. Pastel shades of pink, mauve and yellow assailed him from floodlights in the ceiling. A corridor led the way to the front of the mansion that was decorated with gorgeous oil paintings. Vallance was in no way a connoisseur, but he knew what he liked. There were *Picasso lithographs* of *Guernica, Don Quixote, Mother and Child, Blue Nude, Weeping Woman and Au Lapin Agile.* Doors led into a study. He assessed a breakfast nook and an open-plan kitchen. Vallance spied more exquisite lithographs in the open door of a library. He paused to listen intently. He heard no sounds from the rooms that he could see, but there was a faint rustle from downstairs. It sounded like a cry for help. He might have imagined that, but it didn't hurt to check it out. He moved down the thick carpet to the floor on the lower floor. Polished wood greeted him and there were more paintings on the walls. This time he noted *Rembrandt's: A Boy with Pipe, Portrait of a Seated Woman with a Pendant* and a *Self-Portrait.*

Vallance had to wait for his senses to adjust.

He heard it again. A soft, whimpering sound from one of the rooms off another shadowy corridor. He moved to the door of what had to be a wine cellar. It was locked. Vallance took out several small lock-pick tools from his pocket until he found the right one. He inserted it into the lock and worked it back and forth. The padlock was not new but if Hayden Vallance knew anything about locks, this one should split open. It took him another five minutes of working the key back and forth before the padlock snapped apart. He dropped the padlock to the carpet and hesitated with his hand on the doorknob. Now there was no sound coming from the room at all.

As McCall would say, *in for a penny, in for a pound.*

XXIII
DAMSEL'S-IN-DISTRESS

VALLANCE STEPPED MORE FULLY into the cellar. There was virtually no furniture in it. A rumpled narrow bed took up most of the space inside. A threadbare couch stood beside it under a low overhang. There was a cushion on the floor and a blanket on the bed. There were no windows in the room.

Vallance stopped dead at the sight that greeted him.

Three young women in their twenties were crowded into the little room which was basically designed as a closet. One of them lay on the bed. The second one of them lay down on the couch with no covers over her. The last of the prisoners lay down on the blanket. She had been the one who had cried out before silence and hopelessness had overtaken them. Vallance noted that the young women were shackled together like they were cattle.

They were naked.

Vallance let the horror of this scene resonate with him.

Laura Whittaker was a statuesque brunette with high cheekbones and soulful eyes. She was over six feet tall, but that was deceptive. Her features were emaciated with fatigue. Her large breasts were a mockery of her attractive looks. She looked up from where she was sitting in an old armchair from which stuffing spewed out. Sitting across from her was Melanie Shepherd, a model with lackluster eyes in a pretty face. Her complexion was waxen as if she was a mannequin doll. Her breasts were huge and gave her a kind of sunken, sullen look. Lying on the bed was Kate Davenport, a diminutive, pixie-like sprite with large circles under her beautiful eyes. Her breasts were enormous like the other three young women. Vallance realized that they had been carefully chosen for their outstanding figures.

An irrational rage had taken hold of him at this scene of depravity.

Laura was the only who made eye-contact with him. Her defiance was palpable on her face. "Get the hell away from me!" she snarled at him.

And she spit in his face.

Vallance let that go. He grabbed Laura's left wrist in a vice-like grip. "I'm not here to harm you," he said. "I am going to get rid of these manacles."

He knelt beside the armchair and took out the small lock-picking tools from his coat pocket. He selected one of them and went to work on Laura's wrists. Beside her, Melanie Shepherd had sat up a little higher on the floor. She just looked at Vallance like this was a trick that was going to bring her more grief. Kate Davenport lay on the bed as if she could not move a muscle. It took Vallance under three minutes to break the handcuffs from Laura's wrists. The skin around them was bruised but she massaged them, grateful for the respite.

"Who are you?" Melanie asked him from where she was sitting on the floor. Her anger was scathing. "Is this some kind of cruel joke that Luther Oppenheimer is playing at our expense?"

"He doesn't know I'm here," Vallance said, evenly. "Deep breathing. Let your nerves calm down."

He went to work on the handcuffs on Melanie's wrists and broke them apart. She massaged her wrists which were raw and discolored. Vallance moved over to the bed and gently lifted Kate Davenport up. Laura jumped up and caught her friend's arm and held her tightly. Vallance was the most worried about her condition than any of the others. There was no life in her eyes which just gazed out into space.

"How long has she been like this?" Vallance asked as he went to work on Kate's wrists.

"She has been suffering for a long time," Laura said. "Maybe months. Before I got imprisoned here.'

"How long have you been subjected to this ordeal?" Valance asked.

"We've lost track of time," Melanie said. "Maybe for six months. Maybe longer. The days and nights all feel the same. We're just dolls for Luther Oppenheimer to play with. He strips us naked and does whatever he wants to us."

"Not anymore," Valance said, and his voice had a harsh edge to it.

It took him another sixty seconds to break the wrist restraints from Kate's wrists. She finally looked over at him and the other girls as if she had not seen them in a long time. Laura and Melanie lifted Kate to her feet, throwing off the covers from her body. Kate was still pretty much out of it, but she was slowly responding to gentle commands.

"What happens to us now?" Laura asked. "We're naked because that was the way Luther wanted us to be. Fragile and vulnerable. That's part of the games that he played with us."

"That is going to change," Vallance said. He picked up the blanket that Laura had been sitting on in the armchair. "Put this around your body."

Laura shrugged the blanket around her shoulders. Vallance ripped the blanket from the narrow bed and held it out for Melanie to wrap herself in. He moved to the closet door in the small room and opened it. There were no clothes hanging there but there was another blanket folded on the top shelf. Vallance wrapped it around Kate's body. She held it tightly in her hands as if it were a lifeline. Her hands were shaking.

"What happens to us now?" Laura asked, still not believing that Vallance was not playing a sadistic trick on them.

"We get you out of here," Vallance said. "Stay close to me."

He moved to the door of the closet and opened it. There was no one outside in the dimly lit corridor. The young women, still draped in their sheets and a blanket, followed him. They climbed up the stairs to the ornate hallway. Vallance tried one of the doors that led into one of the bedrooms on the floor. It opened at his touch. He moved to a bureau and rifled through a chest of drawers. He came up with some clothes that he moved to a couch. He opened a closet door and found several pairs of sandals which he also brought to the couch.

"Nothing fancy," Vallance said. "Jeans and sweaters and leather slide sandals. That is all you need."

Kate had finally reacted to the others. She reached out a hand to grip Vallance's arm. When she spoke it was in a hushed, throaty whisper.

"Who are you?"

"The cavalry," he said with no hint of irony.

He moved away from the girls. Laura was momentarily panic-stricken. "Where are you going to be?" she asked.

"Taking care of business,' Vallance said, grimly. "When you're dressed, just stay here in this room. Don't open the door for any-one. *Not for anyone.* I will be back."

The young women threw off the sheets and the blanket on the floor and started to get dressed.

Vallance moved out of the room and into the main part of the house. He heard some movement above him. He climbed up a massive staircase to the second floor of the mansion. The doors were all closed but not locked. Vallance opened a door to an ornate library where leather-bound books filled the shelves. It was desert-ed. The next door he opened led to a breakfast room. That, too, was deserted. The room beyond that was a formal dining room with eight place settings. He closed that door and came to another door on the second floor. The small rustlings were coming from within that room.

Vallance took out his Glock 19 mm H&K pistol from his belt and opened the door.

He found himself in an office with several filing cabinets beside a floor-to-ceiling bookshelf. There was a massive L-Shape Execu-tive desk below a picture window. The grounds looked out across the spacious lawns. Luther Oppenheimer was packing up a leather briefcase and stuffing files into it. He looked up and was surprised at Vallance's intrusion.

He froze.

Vallance kept the door to the office open. He took another step into the room.

It was clear that Luther Oppenheimer did not know who he was. "What the hell do you want?" he demanded.

Vallance took another step into the inner sanctum without answering him.

He thought he saw a flicker of fear come into Luther's eyes.

"Who are you?" Luther demanded.

"No one you would want to know," Vallance said, calmly.

"There is cash in that desk," Luther said. "Take out whatever you need."

"I'm not here for your money," Vallance said. "I know you have plenty of that."

"Then what do you want?"

"Your son needed your guidance in the hospital," Vallance said. "But you turned your back on him. He was suffering. I guess that didn't register with you."

Luther didn't know what game Vallance was playing, but he was going to go along with it. "My son is a very sick young man. There is nothing I can do for him. How do you even know him?"

"I don't know him," Vallance said, evenly "I talked to him at Mercy Hospital. And you're right. He is very sick young man. You have done nothing to ease his suffering. He wanted to visit with his father. But you didn't have time for him. It was a duty call. You left him to die."

"I do have issues with my son, but that is not your concern," Luther said, his temper flaring. "I have done my best for him."

"It wasn't enough," Vallance said.

Luther glanced down at the middle drawer of his desk. Vallance thought he was assessing his chances to reach the gun hidden there. Obviously he thought they were pretty good. If Vallance noticed the hesitation he gave no sign of it.

"Maybe I have been a little cavalier with Clifford," Luther said and moved a step closer to the desk. "That is my son's name. It has been a traumatic time for both of us. I am heading out right this minute to go to the Mercy Hospital to see him. Does my son know you?"

Vallance shook his head. "No, he doesn't."

"Allow me the privilege to know your name so I can tell my son you have been asking about him."

"He won't care," Vallance said. "How about the young women you have kept prisoner here?"

Again that trickle of fear washed over Luther's features. "I don't know you are talking about."

"I'm talking about white slavery. Laura and Melanie have been incarcerated in this mansion for at least six months. I guess Kate was a new edition to your menagerie. How long have they been your sex slaves?"

"You're talking in riddles," Luther said. "I don't know anyone with those names."

Suddenly he reached down to the desk drawer and threw it open. He came out with a Russian Makarov semi-auto 9mm pistol. It was fitted with a silencer.

Vallance blew it out Luther's hands.

The gun skittered across the floor to just beyond the desk. Luther clutched his wrist where the bullet had grazed him.

"Pick it up," Vallance said. When the financier didn't move, Vallance shouted at him:

"*Pick it up!*"

Luther shook his head, desperate and frightened. He stumbled to the picture window which overlooked the extensive grounds. There was no question in Vallance's mind that he was going to shoot Luther Oppenheimer dead.

But he never got the chance.

From behind him in the ajar office door Laura Whittaker, dressed in designer jeans and a man's plaid shirt, picked up the fallen gun and fired it. It didn't have to be a marksman's shot. She was aiming dead center at Luther's face. The bullet exploded into him. He collapsed to the floor. Vallance whirled. He saw Laura lower the gun and drop it to the carpet. She was shaking again, but she had accomplished what she needed to do. Vallance holstered the H&K 9mm pistol and took Laura's arm to steady her.

She looked into his eyes. "He deserved to die," she said, softly.

"I understand," Vallance said. He had been going to do the same thing, but there was a difference. He was a mercenary. The fragile young woman in his arms had just committed murder.

"I had to take the bastard down," she said.

Vallance nodded. There was nothing more to say. "I need to get you, Melanie and Kate out of here."

He took Laura's arm and propelled her out of the study. He closed the door on Luther Oppenheimer. He and Laura moved down the sweeping staircase to the ground floor of the mansion. Melanie and Kate were waiting for them. They both had changed to jeans and button-down shirts in blue and gray.

"What happened to Luther?" Melanie asked in a whisper.

"He's dead," Vallance said.

"For real?" Kate asked, as if she didn't quite believe it.

"Yes. You need to come with me now."

Vallance propelled the three young women to the front door and opened it. The Security Guards were not patrolling at this moment. Vallance skirted the ornate fountains in the center of the property and climbed over the white picket fence that encircled it. The girls climbed up with him. Vallance led them into the deep foliage that surrounded the mansion. He headed for the path that came out just before the pier. The ferry was just finishing loading up with passengers. Vallance had a round-trip pass which he had already paid for. He escorted the three gorgeous women onboard. He looked out to see if any of the guards had returned, but they hadn't. He figured it would be a good half-hour before they came to investigate the mansion on their rounds.

The ferry departed. Vallance leaned on the deck. Laura and Melanie joined him. Kate hung back, still traumatized. Even though the young women were ecstatic to be free, the ordeal they had suffered weighed heavily on them. They looked to Vallance for some measure of comfort. He was expecting them to do to do that. He hugged all three of them in turn.

"You took out a vicious killer who had been tormenting you for months," Vallance said, quietly. "If you want to analyze these circumstances and put them under a microscope, that's up to you. Personally I'd say you avoided a minefield."

Kate, who until that moment had avoided contact with Hayden Vallance, kissed him in the cheek. "We owe you our lives," she whispered.

Laura and Melanie both kissed and hugged him.

"Sometimes you pick a winner," Vallance said, and he smiled.

The ferry docked forty minutes later. Vallance escorted his new-found friends off on the pier. They were a little disoriented in the crowd of people surging down to pick up the ferry for the trip back. Laura looked around, as if lost.

"We don't know where we are," she said.

"Safe," Vallance said, dryly.

"Thanks to you," Laura said.

"Where had the three of you come from?" Vallance asked them.

"We were on vacation here in Maine," Melanie said. "A friend of mine was putting us up in a New England Inn. Luther literally picked us up on our way to a party. He kidnapped us. We found ourselves on that island where you found us."

"Don't dwell on that," Vallance advised. "Turn the page. Where do you need to go right now?"

"We were staying with friends here in New England," Kate said. She had recovered somewhat from her ordeal. Her voice was getting stronger. "It's a house in the woods on a wonderful lake."

"Do your friends know where you are?" Vallance asked.

Laura shook her head. "I am sure they have tried to reach us, but once we had set out to explore the countryside they didn't know what happened to us."

"They knew we had a lot of friends to visit," Melanie said. "But we never got that far."

"We were in that creepy mansion for at least six months," Laura said.

Vallance took out his cell phone and handed it to the girls. "Let your friends know that you're safe. You can go to into all the details later. Who wants to do the honors?"

"I guess I am the spokesman for us," Laura said and took the cell phone from Vallance.

Vallance let them have some privacy as they called their friends. He leaned against the railing on the dock. The ferry was filling up quickly with passengers. Vallance gathered his thoughts together. There was a pit stop he had to make at the Mercy Hospital in Maine.

Laura touched Vallance's arm tentatively. He turned to see the three young women facing him. Their spirits had soared. "We just spoke to our friends in the country," Laura said. "They were relieved to hear that we were all right."

"Of course they don't know the whole story," Melanie said. "They're going to pick us up here on the pier. It will take them a couple of hours."

"Maybe we can find a place to eat," Kate suggested. Her natural exuberance had finally returned. "I'm famished."

Vallance smiled at them. "I will buy you dinner," he said. "There is a little seafood place at the end of the pier. The *Fisherman's Paradise* I think it's called. As long as you stop thanking me for rescuing you."

"But you *did* rescue us," Laura said.

"It's what I do," Vallance said and smiled at them.

"Then it's a date," Melanie said.

Vallance moved down the pier with the girls. He realized that when he left them he would never see them again. Which was fine with him. He was basically a loner. After their dinner Vallance took the girls back to Maine. He left them at the Hyatt Regency Hotel and Suites

"You aren't coming inside?" Laura asked him.

"Our friends want to meet you," Melanie said.

"They won't believe what happened to us!" Kate added.

"Even if I tell them, I am sure they won't believe it," Vallance said.

"But we'll see you again?" Laura asked him.

"To quote my favorite line from James Bond, *Never Say Never*," Vallance said.

"This is really goodbye?" Melanie said.

"You'll see me again," Vallance said. "Maybe when you are more settled and at peace with yourselves."

"Will that ever happen?" Kate asked and she sounded distraught.

"It will," Vallance promised them. "It's better this way. Take care of yourselves."

There were no more goodbyes. Vallance drove to the Mercy Hospital. He took the elevator to the fourth floor and headed to Clifford Morgan's room. Even as he got there he noted the ambiance had subtly changed. He realized what that meant, but he wanted to be sure. He went into the hospital corridor and found a nurse.

"I had been visiting a patient of yours," he said. "Clifford Morgan."

The nurse just nodded and sighed. Confrontations like this were always hard for her. "Mr. Morgan passed away last night," she said. "I am so sorry."

Vallance just nodded. "I had been expecting it."

"We're trying to get touch with his father. Do you have a number for him?"

"Disconnected," Vallance said, curtly. "Thanks for telling me."

Hayden Vallance took the elevator to the ground floor of the hospital and walked out into the night.

He had one more person he needed to see before he found Robert McCall.

XXIX

KACEY ROSE

McCALL STOOD OUTSIDE the back porch of the house with Abigail and Candy Annie beside him. The Deputy had joined the festivities on the makeshift volleyball court, although he did not join in the festivities themselves. McCall closed the door out to the porch behind him.

"Easy does it," McCall said, softly. "We need to get to where the cars are parked."

He tossed the keys to the Ford Explorer to Kostmayer. He had the keys to the Jaguar in his pocket. They made a dash away from the white-washed buildings toward where the cars were parked.

They didn't get far.

Deputy Foster turned around and spotted them. "Stop right there!" The Peace Officer immediately pulled his firearm from his holster which was a Colt .45 Revolver with an ivory handle. The volleyball game was suspended while the Mormons turned to see what had happened. McCall gauged the distance still to be covered to the parked cars and realized his passengers weren't going to make it in time. He drew his own Glock 19 to give them cover fire.

"Stay with me!"

Bullets riddled the ground around them. McCall sent his passengers down to the ground. He fired at Deputy Foster, but he was not out to hit him. He forced the Deputy to take cover. Some of the Mormons had gone into panic mode reacting to bullets being fired at them. McCall shouted at Kostmayer.

"Open the car door!"

Kostmayer got to his feet, couched low and ran for the Ford Explorer. The Deputy Sheriff did not have a clear shot. He ran to his Police Cruiser and grabbed the radio there to call for back-up.

"With me!" McCall said. "I'll see you back in Meadows Springs!"

Candy Annie and Abigail scrambled to their feet and finished their rush to the Ford Explorer. Kostmayer reached the car and opened it. Candy Annie and Abigail piled into the front seat. McCall jumped into his Jaguar. Kostmayer slammed the doors to the Ford Explorer and started it. In the Jaguar, McCall saw that Deputy Foster was running toward them. He fired at the vehicle, but the bullets exploded in the dirt. The Ford Explorer took off like a bat from Hell, followed by the Jag.

Deputy Foster reached the driveway. For some reason Sheriff Conway had been fixated on Robert McCall. The Deputy had given up trying to get a handle on the Sheriff's quirks. McCall had taken off, but they would catch up with him. The Sheriff was a wily old fox. Who knew what motivated a man like him? But Deputy Foster was alarmed that Sheriff Conway had not made an appearance. That was out of character for him. Eventually Deputy Foster would follow the Sheriff to the grain silos. He would discover the dead man and all Hell would break out. By that time it would be too late for the Deputy Sheriff to do anything about it unless his radio call was heeded.

McCall called Kostmayer from his Jaguar and put him on the speaker phone.

"Do you know the back roads into Meadow Springs?" Kostmayer asked.

"I do, but that won't help us unless we can get into town," McCall said. "Keep your eyes peeled for roadblocks."

"Why is the Sheriff hunting us down?" Abigail asked anxiously from the back seat.

"He's not," McCall said. "I left him dead in that grain silo."

"But that's terrible!" Candy Annie exclaimed.

"Sheriff Conway was gunning for me," McCall said. "I got to him first. Deputy Foster will discover the Sheriff's body in due course. I am hoping we will be long gone from here by then. Deputy Foster doesn't have that intel yet. By the time he realized that the Sheriff is missing hopefully it would be too late for him to do anything about it."

They rolled into Meadow Springs half an hour later. McCall parked the Jaguar and left the Ford Explorer outside the tavern.

Hayden Vallance waiting for to fly them back in the Visa Jet.

*　　*　　*　　*

The cemetery was in a graveyard a mile away from the center of Meadow Springs. It was secluded and sheltered by huge oaks. A kind of heavy ambiance permeated the gravestones. The rows of monuments were haphazardly placed in the trees and the tall grass was six feet tall. Hayden Vallance was looking for a tomb of black marble, and found it.

The person he was waiting for stepped out of the trees and moved over to the graveside. She had porcelain skin that seemed to glow in the moonlight. She knelt beside the memorial plaque where she had just put fresh lilies. Vallance didn't want to disturb her, but he needed information. She straightened from her quiet prayer and turned around. She seemed a little startled to see him. Vallance respected her stillness. Then she nodded as if she had been expecting him.

"How did you find me?" she asked him.

"It wasn't too hard," Vallance said. "I know you come to this cemetery when you're in Meadow Springs. You don't spend much time hanging out at that fairground in New York City. When McCall described you to me I knew immediately who he was talking about."

Kacey Rose regarded the mercenary frankly. She was wearing the same stone-washed jeans and no shoes. Her jet-black hair flowed down her back. The tattoos gleamed on her skin. She had ditched the fishnet stockings and her gold necklace. She still had the tattoos of gorgeous butterflies on her breasts, although the name *Kacey Rose* was no longer written in letters of blood. She had her shirt unbuttoned all the way to her navel which revealed the pubic hair that was displayed on her sheer panties. Vallance thought that she didn't leave much to the imagination.

"You had an encounter with Robert McCall," he said.

It was not a question.

"I did."

"Was he the hero you remembered?"

She nodded. "He was."

"Did you manage to get any information from him?" Vallance asked.

"I don't know if he was just stringing me along," Kacey said. "Maybe he was being obtuse. It was kind of shadowy in that fairground. McCall had to fight off some lowlifes who had attacked him from out of the darkness. He was concerned for my wellbeing and safety."

"That sounds like McCall," Vallance nodded. "But he doesn't know who you really are?"

"No and I don't want him to know," Kacey said. "At least, not yet. He is the quintessential Knight Errant. But whether he is inclined to rescue a damsel-in-distress remains to be seen. He is moody and mercurial, but beneath all of that there beats the heart of a very good person. Just ask Mickey Kostmayer or Jackson T. Foozelman."

"Be careful what you wish for," Vallance advised her. "Even a Knight Errant can find himself in dire peril from which there is no escape."

"I know that's true," Kacey said. "I'll just have to take my chances that Robert McCall is the man you say he is."

Vallance glanced down at the gravestone. It had obviously been placed there only hours ago. "Where did find the headstone?" he asked.

"I ordered it a month ago," Kacey said. "I travelled here from Meadow Springs. I live here."

"You didn't really get to know your brother, did you?" Vallance asked.

"No, I didn't," she said, sadly. "It is one of my greatest regrets."

Vallance knew she was talking about her brother whom he had met briefly in the Mercy Hospital. "You know he passed away this afternoon?" he said.

"I didn't know that until I came here to the cemetery," Kacey said. "I got a phone call tonight. A phone call I have been dreading."

"That must have been tough for you," Vallance said. "I know you and your brother were close."

"I know he didn't deserve to die alone and afraid," Kacey said, emotionally. "He deserved to find some happiness in this life, but that never happened."

"Maybe you will find it together," Vallance said. "You and McCall."

"Maybe," she said, softly.

Vallance straightened. "I am leaving here tonight."

"I knew you weren't going to stay long," Kacey said. "What happened to Luther Oppenheimer?"

Vallance chose his next words carefully. "He got shot dead in a mansion in Maine."

"Who shot him?"

"Three beautiful young women whom Luther Oppenheimer had been holding prisoner for months," Vallance said. "It's a long story, but it does have a happy ending." He regarded Kacey with troubled eyes. "Will you seek out McCall now that you found him again?"

"I don't have a choice," she said. Vallance noted a sadness to her that he had seen before. "He is my last chance to find happiness."

"Take care of yourself, Kacey," he said. "I won't always be around to look out for you."

"I can take care of myself," she retorted.

"That's good to hear," Vallance said. "I wouldn't want anything bad to happen to you. Robert McCall has shown that he can beat the odds, but that won't last forever."

Vallance moved away from the ghostly cemetery diffused with moonlight and was swallowed up in the darkness.

Kacey Rose looked after him.

A sense of dread had settled over her.

She needed to find Robert McCall before anything happened to him.

*　　*　　*　　*

When McCall returned to Meadow Falls the first thing he did was ditch the Ford Explorer. He didn't need it anymore. The Jaguar was fine for his purposes. He found a coffee house called the *Coffee*

Bean Emporium next door to the *Cooperstown Bakery*. Kostmayer, Candy Annie and Abigail would wait for him in there. He moved over to the tavern and entered it. Hayden Vallance was waiting for him in the crowded bar at a back table. He was nursing a Caffe Latte laced with Daiquiri Rum. McCall sat next to him.

"I was giving you another twenty minutes and then I was going to look for you," Vallance said. "Bring me up to speed. What happened to Mickey Kostmayer? I heard from our erstwhile waitress Dixie that he took off after those two hoodlums who were here in the tavern."

"He caught up with them," McCall said. "At the Mormon compound a few miles out of Meadow Springs. I gave him a hand, but he really didn't need it. Both of those guys are dead."

"And Sheriff Conway?" Vallance asked. "I hear he was gunning for you."

"Dead also," McCall said.

"You have been busy." Vallance took another swallow of his spiced Daiquiri Rum. "Did you bring back Candy Annie with you?"

"I did, except she doesn't want to be called 'Candy Annie' any longer." McCall smiled. "Just 'Anne' works fine for her. She is okay, a little traumatized from her ordeal, but I think she is ready to come home. I picked up another passenger on the way. An Amish girl in her twenties named Abigail. She and Anne are now best friends."

"Is this Amish girl going to leave with us?" Vallance asked him.

"That's the general idea," McCall said. "Nobody gets left behind." Vallance nodded. "Works for me."

"What happened to the drug bust you were orchestrating?" McCall asked.

"Went like clockwork," Vallance said. "The Feds swooped in and rounded up the bad guys. One of them, a mean son-of-a-bitch named Luther Oppenheimer got away, but I tracked him down."

"Meaning you were forced to kill him?"

"Actually I didn't have to," Vallance said. "I had help from three beautiful and soulful young women who had a score to settle with Luther."

"Where are they now?" McCall asked. "I have never known you to need any help from anyone."

"Special circumstances," Vallance said and shrugged.

"Are these young women still in New England?"

"As far as I know," he said. "Hopefully they're enjoying the hospitality of a quaint Inn somewhere in Connecticut and having the time of their lives. Laura, Melanie and Kate. Special people."

"You sound as if you had established a very special relationship with them," McCall said.

"I did," Vallance said. "I am sure I won't ever see them again, but that's okay." He finished off his cocktail. "Are we done here?"

"Unless you like spending time in Meadow Springs?" McCall said.

"That's not high on my list of things to do," Vallance murmured.

"There are still forces working against us," McCall said. "The sooner we can get out of here the better I'll like it."

Vallance stood up. "I had an uncle who used to say: 'If you're waiting for me, you're backing up.'"

McCall smiled. Dixie caught up with them as they moved to the tavern door. "For some reason I don't think you'll are coming back. Which is a shame because I was getting used to you guys being around. Is Mr. Kostmayer going to be okay?"

"He is going to be fine," Vallance assured her. "You have been a treasure, Dixie. We'll come back and look you up one these days."

"Better make it quick," Dixie said. "The way you fellas burn the candle at both ends, a polecat couldn't scratch at it without drawing blood."

Vallance kissed the server on the cheek. "Take care of yourself, Dixie."

"I will surely do that."

McCall and Vallance pushed open the tavern door.

Dixie sighed as if she would really miss them.

Kostmayer, Candy Annie and Abigail were just exiting the *Coffee Bean Emporium*. They jogged to where the Jaguar was parked.

"We'll have to ditch the Jag," McCall said. "I hate to do that, but that can't be helped. The Ford Explorer will have more room. It's time for us to get out of Dodge."

McCall opened the Explorer and they all climbed inside. It was a tight fit with the two girls and Candy Annie in the back seat. Kostmayer, Vallance and McCall climbed into the driver's side. McCall started the car. He pulled away from Meadow Springs. It took him thirty minutes to reach the airport. McCall ditched the Ford Explorer and left it on the tarmac. Vallance fired the Global Vista jet and headed for New York City.

* * * *

A week later McCall walked into Bentley's Bar and Grill at 77th Street and Broadway. It had been completely refurbished and had been given a major facelift. The waitresses wore aprons with white shirts with jazzy bowties. They had familiar faces that McCall knew well. Gina was an actress with soulful eyes who was always going to auditions for some musical or another. McCall knew she had appeared in a production of *Wicked* for a year. She was back now waiting on tables which Gina assured him was fine with her. She was up for a role in *Carousel* and she was hopeful that would work out for her. Another Bentley's server, Amanda, had a desultory way of looking at the world that belied her sweet nature. McCall remembered that Brahms had once described her as a vampire out looking for blood. The servers hugged McCall like he was an old friend, but they were crazy busy because the place had just reopened for business. It prompted McCall to think about Brahms. He wondered how he was doing without his beloved Hilda. He had reached out to Brahms when he had returned to New York, but the old spy was still on a pilgrimage to Jerusalem and the Holy Land. He had told McCall he would be back to pick up his life again, but McCall didn't think that was going to happen any time soon. Brahms had needed to find closure with Hilda gone and McCall had given him the space to do that.

McCall spied Candy Annie sitting at one of the tables in Bentley's with Abigail talking up a storm. They really had bonded in a special way that warmed McCall's heart. They were soul mates now. Both of them were living a dream that they had shared. Candy Annie had been living until recently under the streets of Manhattan.

Abigail had spent most of her years in the Amish community around Meadow Springs trying to escape her fate. The two of them had found each other and McCall thought that was a very good thing. The two of them were engrossed in their tales of strife and redemption. McCall thought it was better for him not to intrude until they called him over, which they were bound to do. He looked around for Mickey Kostmayer, but he had not arrived yet.

But Hayden Vallance was waiting for McCall at one of the tables.

XXIV
THE EQUALIZER

McCALL SAT DOWN and immediately Vallance signaled to one of the beleaguered servers to come over. It was Gina, who smiled when she saw it was McCall.

"Nice to see you again, Mr. McCall," she said. "We've been closed for renovations for six months, but we're back now and the place is hopping!"

"How is the work situation going?" McCall asked her.

"Oh, the usual," Gina said. "Auditions and workshop readings. I think I am going to step into the touring company of '*Hamilton*'. I am super-excited. Fingers crossed. What can I get you to drink? I know your friend is drinking a Vodka Gimlet."

McCall ordered a Brandy Alexander with Crème de Cacao and cream.

"Coming right up," Gina said and disappeared into the madhouse.

Vallance looked over to where Candy Annie and Abigail were sitting. "Our girls seem pretty happy," he said.

McCall followed Vallance's gaze. "They do," he said. "But I have the feeling that you aren't telling me the whole story. Is it a story I need to hear?"

"Your instincts are way off base this time," Vallance said.

"Are they? Sheriff Conway confided in me while he was stalking me in that grain silo," McCall said. "He wanted me to know that he was responsible for killing Abigail's cousin. She didn't fall off her horse and hit her head in a tragic accident. It was premeditated murder."

"You knew that going in?" Vallance said.

"I suspected it," McCall said. "But I didn't have any proof."

"Isn't the Sheriff's confession good enough for you?" Vallance asked him, mildly.

"I guess it will have to be. Any more surprises you have to lay on me?"

"That should be all for the time being," Vallance promised.

McCall looked over to where Candy Annie and Abigail Connor were engrossed in earnest conversation. "The only person who might benefit from this revelation about what happened thirty years ago was Sheriff Conway."

"Who is no longer with us," Vallance pointed out.

"That's true," McCall said. "I suspect Esther knew the truth, but she never told anyone how her cousin was murdered."

"Some things are better left alone," Vallance agreed.

At that moment Jackson T. Foozelman entered the restaurant. He was dressed to the nines in an Armani wool-and-mohair suit that McCall figured had to set him back $3000 dollars. He wore a cravat with a diamond stickpin holding it in place and polished Cole Haan slip-on loafers. Candy Annie was the first one to see him. She rushed over to his side and gave him a bear hug. When they parted Abigail had reached them.

Candy Annie introduced her to Fooz. "This is my friend Jackson T. Foozelman! He has been my companion since I was living under the streets of Manhattan!"

Fooz took Abigail's hand and kissed it. "Any friend of Candy Annie's is a friend of mine," he declared.

"It is just plain old Anne!" Candy Annie gushed. "The 'Candy Annie' moniker is ancient history now! You're looking so spiffy, Mr. Foozelman! All dressed up!"

"It's a special occasion," Fooz said with some reverence. "It isn't every day I get to see my favorite girl in a setting like this. I have something to give you."

He reached into the pocket of his coat and came up with a small ring box. From it he produced the charm bracelet he had been saving for Candy Annie. It sparkled as the light caught it in just the right way. Candy Anne was speechless. Fooz put it around her small wrist. It had two charms already on it: A *Murano Glass Sea Turtle Charm* and a *Harry Potter & Hogwarts Express Train Charm*.

"I know you have an affinity for trains," Fooz said. "This scenic route in Colorado travels across the Cumbres & Toltec Gorge past magnificent Evergreen and Aspen forest trees. The *Glass Sea Turtle* will remind you of me, slow and plodding and I know you are a big Harry Potter fan. The *Hogwarts Express Train Charm* just seemed to fit."

The charm bracelet dangled from Candy Annie's wrist. She threw her arms around the old man and hugged him. "I will cherish these gifts," Candy Annie whispered to him.

Fooz wiped a tear from his eyes.

At his table McCall witnessed this reunion with a smile. Gina returned to the table with a Brandy Alexander with Crème de Cacao for McCall and Vallance took another Vodka Gimlet.

"I'll be back to take your dinner order," Gina promised and disappeared.

McCall and Vallance each took a swallow of their drinks. McCall said: "I had a call from the Sheriff's Department outside Chicago. Deputies found two men in a patrol car in the bushes. They had been shot to death. The odd thing about it was that these cops weren't really cops at all. They wore uniforms and carried holsters and guns, but they were completely bogus. They were robbing motorists at gunpoint and leaving their victims dead by the side of the road. You wouldn't know anything about that?"

"Not a thing," Vallance said, deadpan. "It just shows you have to be very careful out there." He finished off his Vodka Gimlet. "Is there any more I can do for you?"

"I can't think of a thing," McCall said.

Vallance stood up. "It's time for me to leave."

"Where are you heading?"

"West Africa."

"What's there?"

"There's been an outbreak of the Ebola virus which has severe consequences for the people in the Cote d'Ivoire," Vallance said. "The disease had originally spread from an infected bat. I need to travel to a town where the Jihadists have been especially active. There has been unrest in Ethiopia and Somalia as well where food has been out of reach for many people. These conflicts need to be resolved."

"Sounds as if you have your work cut out for you," McCall said.

Vallance shrugged. "It's what I do."

"You help people," McCall said. "That is all I need to know."

Vallance smiled and shook McCall's hand. "Take care of yourself, McCall."

"I will."

Vallance moved through Bentley's Bar & Grill and exited the restaurant.

Candy Annie, Abigail and Fooz moved directly to McCall's table. He stood and embraced Candy Annie and gave Abigail a kiss on the cheek. Gina returned to serve them.

"What can I get for you guys?"

Candy Annie and Abigail ordered Mai Tai's and Fooz ordered a Moscow Mule Champagne Cocktail. A moment later Mickey Kostmayer joined the raucous group. He had fully recovered from the beating he had suffered at the hands of Jeremiah and Fletcher.

"Did the party start without me?" he asked, sitting at the table.

"No way!" Abigail said.

"It's not a party without you," Candy Annie said.

Kostmayer looked at their server. "I'll take a Tequila Sunrise."

Gina took their orders and was soon lost in the melee. Before McCall could finish the "roll call" they were joined by three very beautiful young women.

"We just got into the Big Apple," Laura Whittaker said. She glanced around Bentley's. "What a fabulous place!"

"I hope we're not late to join you," Melanie Shepherd said.

"We came here just as soon as we could," Kate Davenport added in her lilting voice.

McCall got to his feet to introduce them. "Let me do the honors. This is Laura, Melanie and Kate. They are special friends of Hayden Vallance. When did you guys get into New York?"

"We got here this evening." Laura said. "We just dumped our luggage at the hotel and took a cab to Bentley's!"

"I was afraid we had missed you!" Melanie said. "Our plane was twenty minutes late getting here from La Guardia!"

Kate looked around. "Is Hayden Vallance not here?"

"He had some pressing business that couldn't wait," McCall said and left it at that. "He will be sorry to have missed you."

Gina found them another table and put the tables together. The young women sat down. They were somewhat breathless from their trip across town in the Manhattan traffic.

"What can I get your guys to drink?" Gina asked.

Laura ordered champagne, Melanie vodka with a twist and Kate ordered absinthe. Gina gave McCall's arm a squeeze.

"It's nice to have you back with us at Bentley's, Mr. McCall," she said, as if she was being conspiratorial.

"Nice to be back," he said.

Then Gina was on her way back through the melee. The new gorgeous young women were all talking at once. McCall smiled while he finished his Brandy Alexander. He was heartened by the laugher and camaraderie that he heard from his guests.

McCall's cell phone rang. He barely heard it over the clamor in the bar. He debated whether to answer it or not, with all of this goodwill flowing, but it was his private number which few people possessed. McCall took the cell phone out of his sports coat pocket.

"This is Robert McCall."

"Sam Kinney!" the old spymaster said.

McCall had not heard from Sam since he went into hospital. His voice was scratchy and hoarse. "I need to see you right away," he said. "It's a matter of life and death."

McCall just nodded. Everything with Sam Kinney was life and death. "I'll be with you in twenty minutes," he said and hung up the cell phone. He got to his feet and made his apologies to the people at the table. "I'll be back," he promised them and left Bentley's via a back table.

Twenty minutes later McCall entered the Mercy Hospital and traveled up to the fourth floor. Sam Kinney's room was located just past the nurse's station. McCall had no trouble finding it. Flowers filled the room. Bouquets of elegant *Royal Bouquets, Moonlit Meadow Bouquets* and *Pink Daisy Floral Bouquets* were on display. McCall knew that Sam Kinney had a lot of friends, but he had no idea that he had this many! The old Spymaster was sitting up in bed, propped up with pillows, watching a rerun of *Gilligan's Island* with the sound turned low. He turned to McCall when he entered the room and lowered the sound some more.

"It's my favorite show," Sam said. "Bob Denver and Alan Hale Jr. were a hoot. Jim Backus knew how to deliver a droll line and Tina Louise could always get my blood flowing."

"How are you doing, Sam?" McCall asked, suppressing a smile. "It looks as if Inter Flora had a massive yard sale in here."

"I'm a popular guy," Sam said, modestly. "It is my winning smile and my years behind the reception desk at the Liberty Belle Hotel. Did the receptionist contact you?"

"Chloe didn't have to," McCall said. "We have an unofficial pact. If anything happens to you, and I am made aware of it, she gets in touch with me right away. The circumstances were not quite the same, but Chloe did get in touch with me as a backup. She is very fond of you, Sam."

"That's good to hear," he said. "Gives me a warm feeling inside. That and the chocolates that Chloe sent me. It's *Godiva* with white and dark chocolate and various kinds of fruit."

"I am having a sugar rush just thinking about it," McCall said, mildly.

"Damn it's good to see you, McCall," the old spy said. "I am on the mend. In a few days I will be back to my old self."

"I glad to hear it," McCall said. "But you didn't leave a sick bed to lure me here. You could have done that anytime. What's on your mind?"

Sam looked away, as if he was suddenly stricken with remorse. McCall gave him the space he needed. The episode of *Gilligan's Island* was now a low murmur. "I haven't been totally honest with you," he said.

"About what?"

"I guess about a lot of things. You are my dearest friend in the world, but sometimes there are secrets that have to be brought out into the open."

"Like what?"

"About your *sister*."

A cold chill coursed through McCall's veins. He moved deeper into the room and looked down at Sam Kinney.

"I don't *have* a sister," he said.

Sam nodded. "Yes, you do. It's a secret I have kept for twenty years. Your sister didn't want to deceive you, but it was a pact we agreed upon and that pact has been in place for a long time."

McCall sat down on the edge of the bed, as if trying to get to terms with this startling revelation. "You're saying that I have a *sister* that I never knew about all this time?" he asked, incredulously.

"That's right," Sam said. "I don't know much about who your father was, but I guess he died when you were a young man. Your mother still lives in Scottsdale, Arizona in Old Town behind the Scottsdale Museum of Contemporary Art. She has a gallery of western-themed paintings and sculptures in there including a piece by *Elie Hazak* of *Wyatt Earp in bronze* which is to die for. It's been a long time since I have seen your sister. We used to correspond on a regular basic, but you know how that goes. You lose track of the people in your life. The last time I heard from your sister she was getting married, but I don't believe that ever happened. I lost track of her for a long time. Then I got I note from her, not an email, you understand, but an actual note saying that she was in trouble."

Sam paused, as if trying to repair the damage he had just done to his best friend.

"Go on," McCall said, his tone more subdued.

"I would have reached out to you, but something was always holding me back," the old spymaster said. "I guess the years have weighed heavily on both of us. Then I got waylaid in that fairground and had the snot beat out of me. A hood was pulled over my head. I lost consciousness. Then you found me in the *Hall of Mirrors*. I don't how I got there. The spectacle of those gilt mirrors flattening you, shrinking you and elongating you has always been a recurring nightmare of mine. But you knew that because you were there at the fairground."

"I tracked you down," McCall said. "A beautiful and soulful young women named Kacey Rose helped me."

"Is that her real name?" Sam asked, as if he was intrigued.

"Probably not," McCall said. "But that doesn't matter now. I carried you out of the *Hall of Mirrors* and laid you down on the ground. Jimmy Murphy was with me. I brought you here to the hospital."

"I guess it was touch and go if I was going make it," Sam said. "But I did. So now you know the whole story."

"Except the part where you mention my *sister*," McCall said. "You couldn't have been mistaken about that?"

"I could be, but I am not. Your sister and I were friends all through her high school years," the old Spymaster confessed. "I know I should have told you about this a long time ago. My bad."

"What is her name?" McCall asked. "This sister I am supposed to have?"

"Allison Carmichael."

"The name doesn't ring any bells," McCall said.

"I would be astounded if it did," Sam said. "You don't know her, but she certainly knows you. At least by reputation."

"If this is all true, why hasn't she reached out to me?" McCall demanded. "Twenty years is a long time to keep a secret like that."

"I guess it was never the right moment," Sam said. "And she was frightened."

"Of what?"

"There is a dark past to this gal, but I don't know what it is," Sam confided. "I'm just a friend of the family. I don't know much about Allison's past. It was a long time ago. I get it all mixed up in my memory."

McCall stood up from the bed. "Do you know where Allison lives? Here in New York City?"

"No such luck," Sam said, ruefully. "She is living right now in Knoxville in Tennessee. I don't have an address for her, but I have the next best thing. Allison has a best friend, Evangeline, whom I never met, but she and Allison went to high school together. I got that address right here for you."

The old spymaster delved in the morning papers that were strewn on his bed along with discarded magazines and jigsaw puzzles which Sam was laboriously attempting to put together. Finally he came up with an address and handed it to McCall.

"This is the last known address for Allison," Sam said. "Her best friend is a gal named Evangeline. Nice people. Who would want to live in Tennessee?" he suddenly muttered. "They have got swamps and rattlers and I guess Davy Crockett lived there once upon a time. Always been a hero of mine. Died in the Alamo fighting for freedom. Now Jim Bowie, he was a two-fisted brawler, the real deal, a man you could put your trust in."

Sam was slowly running out of steam. His retention level was fading fast. McCall knew the signs. He got to his feet. "Time for me to leave."

"You will have to travel to Knoxville," Sam said. "I know Allison still lives there. This gal Evangeline also lives in Knoxville, but I don't know where to find either of them."

"I'll find them," McCall said, still assimilating the intel that Sam Kinney had just laid on him.

"Did you take care of that crooked Sheriff who was out gunning for you," Sam asked, completely changing the subject.

"I did," McCall said.

"I hope he wound up dead."

"He did. We'll leave it that."

"What will you do when you leave here?" Sam asked.

McCall shrugged. "I guess I will travel to Tennessee."

"I figured that was in the cards," Sam said. "I am sorry to lay such a guilt trip on you. But it was time for you to know the truth. You *do* have a sister and she is in trouble."

"How do you know she is in trouble?" McCall asked.

"I wouldn't have told you the whole sad story if she wasn't in danger."

McCall nodded. "I appreciate that, Sam."

"Let me know what happens."

"I will do. Get some rest now."

There was no response. McCall looked over at him, concerned, but the old man had fallen fast asleep. McCall turned the sound level down on the television as low it could go. The laugh track of the *Gilligan's Island* echoed perversely in the background. McCall made sure that a nurse would come by to look in on the old spy. Then he took the elevator to the lobby and walked out into the night. He needed to clear his head. He found a café around the corner from the hospital called the *12 Corners* on Mott Street near the East Village. McCall ordered a warm chocolate chip cookie and a croissant with cinnamon sugar and hazelnut caramel. Decadent but delicious. He realized that there was no reason for him to remain in New York City. He needed to find a sister whom he had never even heard about. He could not believe that Sam Kinney had kept this secret from him for so many years. McCall had to discover if this intel was real or simply the rambling of an old man. He resolved that he would take a plane to Tennessee the next day.

McCall exited the coffee shop. The night had turned chilly. He turned up the collar of his leather coat. He found a cab right away and told the driver to take him to the Liberty Belle Hotel.

A figure was waiting for him. He also took a cab to the Liberty Belle Hotel and watched McCall enter the lobby. He did not follow McCall... yet.

XXX
EVANGELINE

McCALL FLEW TO McGhee Tyson Airport in Tennessee. He hired a car, a Jaguar F. Type sports car and found himself in the trendy downtown area of Knoxville in Market Square. Allison's townhouse was at the end of Gay Street where elm and maple trees flourished. It was two stories with shutters painted in mauve. Two stairs led up to the front door. McCall found newspapers scattered on the porch. He rang the doorbell. The chimes sounded but it was clear that there was no one at home. He looked under the Welcome Home mat, but there was no handy key stashed there. He glanced down at the parked cars in the street, but there was no movement anywhere. It was a quiet, residential area. McCall reached into the pocket of his leather jacket and produced the small lock-picking tool he had used before. He took a skeleton key and went to work on the lock. It took him five minutes while he worked it back and forth, but finally the lock snapped apart. He straightened and checked the street again. No activity. He opened the door to Allison Carmichael's house and stepped inside.

There were more old newspapers scattered on the hall floor. He closed the door behind him. And listened. When he had been in Mickey Kostmayer's apartment he had grappled with an intruder. That error in judgment had almost cost McCall his life. But there was no threat that he could perceive now. He walked through the hallway which opened up to a spacious living room area with a study and three bedrooms beyond. The décor was tastefully furnished with old antiques, bookshelves, a leather couch and two armchairs. There was an 83-inch television that had pride of place in the apartment. McCall moved on to what was obviously the children's rooms. There was a *Monopoly Jurassic Park Edition Board Game* and a *Goosebumps Game* on the carpet. *A Jumanji Board Game*, a *Scrabble Board* and a *Haunted House Board Game* were off to one side. McCall moved into a modern tiled kitchen and opened the refrigerator. It was empty except for frozen entries. In the pull-out drawer were mustard and horseradish bottles, ketchup, maple syrup, corn on the cob, a package of butter and a dozen eggs.

McCall closed the refrigerator and looked in the cabinets. Silverware, knives, flour, cornflakes, various kinds of soups and packages of luncheon meats were in evidence. Also baked beans, hot dogs, potatoes, onions, fruit juice and rice and pasta. As well as tea and coffee, peanut butter, honey and several candles and matches. He moved back into the small hallway and sorted through the junk mail and the regular mail on a hall table. They were all addressed to Allison Carmichael at 730 North Cherry Street in Knoxville. There were a dozen flyers that extolled the delights of *spelunking*. The idea of finding himself trapped in a series of caves had never appealed to McCall. It had something to do with his fear of claustrophobia when he had been a child. He wondered if Allison and her children had succumbed to the joys of *spelunking*. Somehow he hoped not. He collected all of the flyers and folded them into his leather jacket pocket.

At the bottom of the discarded mail he came across a return address for David Carmichael. McCall knew Allison had been divorced. This had to be her ex-husband. The return address was also in Knoxville. McCall pocketed the letter without reading it. He felt he had done all he could in Allison's modest house.

So that left him with an address for Allison's best friend.

McCall found her on a street that housed the *East Tennessee Historical Society Museum*. Cherry trees were in full bloom. There was a festive air in the neighborhood with kids playing stickball in the street. Three steps led up to exterior French Doors with Victorian wrought-iron glass on either side. McCall pushed the doorbell. Footsteps clattered in the hallway and the door was thrown open.

McCall thought of all the times in his life that he had been surprised by events that had happened to him. He had been blindsided when he had encountered an assassin named Jovan Durovic near the Chateau Krazinski whom he had killed in a fight to the death. He had dealt with Alexei Berezovsky in the subway tunnels below the streets of Manhattan. That time he had managed to escape with his life. Another time he had barely escaped capture while he was trying to rescue Captain Josh Coleman in the town of Aleppo in Syria. The Army Officer had climbed aboard a helicopter piloted by Hayden Vallance. McCall was right beside him. The helicopter took off while Russian troops fired on them.

Josh Coleman had died in McCall's arms.

But he had not seen this present encounter coming.

Kacey Rose stood in front of him. She had ditched her fairground persona and had cleaned up her act. She was not wearing her usual provocative clothing. The tattoos adorning her body were gone except for two skulls and a skeleton with guttering candles on her breasts. She wore high-waist jeans and a Haband women's long-sleeve embroidered shirt in power blue. Her hair fell down to her shoulders in long, wavy curves. She was wearing stylish Sketchers taupe sandals on her feet.

She was astonished to see McCall standing on the threshold in front of her.

Finally she said: "You had better come in."

McCall stepped through the doorway and Kacey Rose closed the door behind him. She lived in a modest apartment that was bright and decorated with a flourish. Glass doors led out to a patio. A Steinway piano stood in one corner. Fresh flowers adorned a small end table. There was a Frigidaire in the kitchen flanked by porcelain marble counters. Walnut shelves were prominent on the bookshelves. McCall noted that there were several thriller paperbacks on the shelves written by *Harlan Cobin* and *Lee Dresser*. Also *Stephen King* and *David Baldacci*. He searched further until he found two of his favorite novels by *John Le Carre*: *Smiley's People* and *Tinker, Tailor, Soldier, Spy*. A glass-topped coffee table was located beside a leather couch and a loveseat. A Charleton 6-piece dining set was in evidence in the room along with two armchairs and an easy chair. Several lithographs graced the walls: *Starry Night, The Angel that Stopped Time, The Lighthouse Beam of Hope, The Sunshine Tree of Life* in dazzling colors and a Lithograph of *The Disillusioned Man* with an Angel standing at his shoulder. Finally there was a beautiful oil painting of a *Naked Girl Seen Through a Window* beside the piano.

"You have some beautiful lithographs," McCall remarked. "I always loved the *Disillusioned Man* with the *Angel* perched on his shoulder."

"One of my favorite paintings," she admitted.

"This is where you live?" he asked her.

"Good old Knoxville, Tennessee," she said. "I would say you were stalking me, but you didn't know my home address. Pretty good detective work."

"How long have you lived here?" McCall asked.

"Six years. I take the train into New York City at least twice a week. I lose myself in the Manhattan canyons. Most of the time I hang out at the fairground where we first met. Seeing you standing on my doorstep here in Knoxville is a trip. I never thought I would see you again."

"Why don't we start this conversation by you telling me your real name?" McCall asked. "It's not Kacey Rose."

"No, it's not. That's a stage name I picked out for the movies. Not that I have been in any movies as yet, but we all have our dreams, don't we? I thought Kacey Rose had a certain panache to it." She picked up a package of Camels from the coffee table and shook one out. "Do you mind if I smoke? I am up to two packages a day, but I am trying to cut back on my nicotine habit."

"I'm glad to hear it," McCall said.

She lit the cigarette and blew out a cloud of smoke.

"Your real name?" McCall prompted her.

"It's Evangeline," she said. "Evangeline Palmer."

"How long have you been hanging around the fairground?"

"Since the time I was fourteen," she admitted. "It is like a narcotic. The more I craved it the more I had to have. After that I moved on to designer drugs like fentanyl, Vicodin and oxycontin. Not a smart move on my part, I know, but I have cut back on those also. I am trying to clean up my act."

"It was a very convincing performance," McCall said with some irony. "I must say you are wearing less clothing than the last time I saw you."

Evangeline shrugged. "The tattoos came off. They were never a permanent fixture. I miss the prowling *Black Panther* and the *Bible quotes* and the N*aked Girl with the Folded Wings* W*earing Fishnet Stockings*. I still have the tattoos of the skulls and the skeleton with the four guttering candles on it on my breasts. They're pretty discreet. The morons at the fairground never even noticed them. I had my shirt unbuttoned all the way down to my navel. My pubic hair was prominently displayed beneath my lace panties, but that was for the benefit of the fairground denizens. I am really too modest to show major skin unless I am in the mood to be outrageous."

"You fooled me," McCall said, mildly.

"You weren't in the fairground long enough for me to size you up," she said. "But I know you are a good person."

"How do you know that?"

"I know it in my heart," she said. "That's the only place where it matters."

McCall noted the ornate necklace that Evangeline was wearing. It was made of ivory, silver and gold balls that hung down across her breasts. She noted his interest.

"Do you like my necklace?"

"It's beautiful," he said. "I've never seen anything like it before."

She reached behind her and unhooked the necklace from her throat. It had a heavy silver chain on it. When she untied it the necklace reached right down to below her breasts.

"It's a Bola," she said. "A primitive hunting weapon used by South American Gauchos to capture animals by entangling their legs. It's got weights on the ends of interconnected cords. I picked it up when I made a trip to Argentina last summer. Of course I don't use it for that purpose. I just thought it was a stylish piece of jewelry. Native Indians can bring down a camelid, that's a camel, that weighs 400 pounds by throwing a boleadora at its legs. Pretty cool."

"Very cool," McCall said.

"It came in handy when I was slapping around some of those lowlifes in the fairground. Hook me up again, can you?" McCall retied the necklace around Evangeline's neck and made sure the clasps were secure. "Thanks. It was a gift from Hayden Vallance.

He rescued me from some hoodlums who were harassing me in the fairground. He has been a good friend ever since."

"Hayden Vallance has no friends," McCall said with an edge to his voice. "He's a mercenary who fights other people's wars."

"That doesn't matter to me," Evangeline said. "I take people the way I find them. Even the ones who are a pain in the ass," she added, giving McCall an accusatory glance. Then she grinned. "But you are growing on me."

"Glad to hear it," he said. "Where did you meet Hayden Vallance?"

"In a cemetery."

McCall nodded, a little wryly. "That makes perfect sense."

"I guess it is a little creepy that I was out wandering around a graveyard in the middle of the night," she said. "But I love the silence that comes with the headstones. They have their own history. I am at peace there. There is a black marble sculpture that I always visit with a single name etched on it: '*Sherilyn!*' I have no idea who she was, but I created a whole persona for her. These are the gravestones that resonate for me."

"If Hayden Vallance sought you out in that graveyard there was a reason," McCall said.

"Maybe he's just fond of me," she said. She shook out another Camel cigarette and lit it. "I am trying to quit, I really am. I am up to two packages a day which not a good thing, but I am trying to clean up my act. I am sure you do not have any vices."

"Not ones I can talk about," McCall said and smiled. "Tell me more about your relationship with Hayden Vallance."

"You don't approve, do you?" Evangeline asked. "Why? Because he is a mercenary? He helps people who cannot defend themselves. That is what you do, isn't it? They call you '*The Equalizer*', don't they? Or a name like that. Very cool."

"Thanks, but I am not here to talk about me," McCall said. "Tell me more about your relationship with Hayden Valance."

She shrugged. "He has been there for me when I needed a shoulder to cry on. He doesn't judge me. I need heroes to look out for me. Benjamin Franklin was my favorite Revolutionary character. He said: '*Tell me and I forget, teach me and I may remember, involve me and I would learn.'* He took his life in his hands by flying a kite in a rainstorm. Both George Washington and Thomas Jefferson had slaves which was not cool. But I guess in those days it was acceptable. Benjamin Franklin was a person who recognized human fragility."

"Who are your other heroes?" McCall asked her.

"Babe Ruth and Mickey Mantle are on my list of serious icons," Evangeline said. "A couple of movie stars as well. Benedict Cumberbatch is a great actor. Humphrey Bogart and Kate Winslet are all close seconds. But assassins are the really modern gangsters. They can tear a hole in your soul if you let them. Do you know what I mean?"

"I am trying to keep up with your thought process," McCall admitted.

"Tough to do if you're me, I know that." Then she was off onto a new tangent. "I thought it was a terrible crime when John Wilkes Booth assassinated Abraham Lincoln. Booth was a member of a secret society called the *Knights of the Golden Circle*. Did you know that? He betrayed his country and all of its citizens. The play '*Our American Cousin*' was playing at the Ford Theater at the time. Lincoln was sitting in a booth with his wife Mary Todd Lincoln. Booth used a .41 derringer that he put at the back of Lincoln's head shouting: '*Sic Semper Tyrannis*' which was Latin for '*Thus Always to Tyrants*'. I never forgave him for that. Lincoln was a great man who should have lived a long life. But my favorite is still Benjamin Franklin."

"Do you know where Benjamin Franklin is buried?" McCall asked her.

"Of course I do," Evangeline said, as if offended. "His body is in the Christ Church Burial Ground in Philadelphia. I always longed to make a trip there to see it."

"Why would you do that?"

She crushed out another cigarette and lit a fresh one. "Because looking at the headstones in a graveyard has always resonated with me. A cemetery has history and poignancy. The souls buried there reach out to me from the grave. It does not matter what year they were abandoned by the living. They are reminders of the fragility of life. Hayden Vallance talked to me about that on one of our walks through the Old Dutch Church in Sleepy Hollow. He told me that a little girl haunts the graveyard there at dusk. That there is a stairway somewhere that leads directly down to Hell."

"But you don't believe those superstitions?" McCall said.

"Sometimes when I am alone in that graveyard I hear things that I can't explain," Evangeline said. "Eerie, supernatural voices wailing through the headstones just before dawn."

"What were you doing wandering around cemeteries in the middle of the night?"

"That's the time when the dead rise up," she said. "I have heard them before."

"You do have a vivid imagination," McCall remarked. "It will play on your nerves when you've vulnerable."

"I'm not frightened by ghosts," she said and lit up another Camel. "Only the phantoms that prowl the night."

"Those are nightmares that you have created in your mind," McCall said. "They are not real."

"They are very real to me," Evangeline said. "But I can't burden you with them."

"Living in the past has a way of catching up with you," he said.

"Because I lived part of the time in a fairground?" Evangeline said, bristling. "At least there I could lose myself on the rides and visit the *Hall of Mirrors* and become someone else."

"But you're not someone else," McCall pointed out, gently. "You have your own identity and your own lifestyle."

"That hasn't got me very far," she said, sadly. "You may be the only friend in my life. And Hayden Vallance, of course. He never mentioned me to you?"

"Need to know," McCall said. "Hayden Vallance played his cards pretty close to the vest when he had to. He has a soft spot for beautiful, willful women who come too close to the flame."

"I like the way you put things," Evangeline said, and she laughed. "Are you referring to your own life, Mr. McCall?"

"My life is complicated," he admitted.

"Maybe it's time for you to do something about it," she said.

That gave McCall pause. He thought about the people who had affected his life. Mickey Kostmayer was one, but he was headstrong and recalcitrant to deal with. Emma Marshall was Control's assistant, feisty and free-spirited, and he loved her dearly, but she always had an agenda. McCall had once rescued his old boss Control from a country house in the woods where some very bad guys had been keeping him a prisoner. It had taken the urbane Spymaster a long time to recover from that ordeal. Sam Kinney was still languishing in a hospital bed. Hoodlums had attacked him in that same fairground. Hayden Vallance was engaged on a crusade in an African country fighting for his own sense of justice. That left Robert McCall alone and vulnerable. He knew that loneliness was dangerous to the soul. But the peace it brought him made it possible for him to continue his quest to right wrongs for people who had nowhere else to turn.

"If you're asking me about my emotions," McCall said, quietly, "I am dealing with them the best that I can. You need to do the same thing."

"That's a nice sentiment, but you're not here to see me," Evangeline said. "Hayden Vallance said you have a sister you never knew about."

McCall nodded. "That intel came from Sam Kinney. It may just be just smoke and mirrors as far as I am concerned. You know who he is?"

"Of course I do," Evangeline said, offended again. McCall realized that her quick temper was a symptom of a much deeper emotion. "He is a pal of yours. We rescued him in that fairground together. I would not have forgotten that."

McCall opened the sliding glass door that led out onto the patio. He needed space to gather his thoughts together. The terrace overlooked neighborhood shops that included a laundromat, a florist and a place called *"Delmonico's Deli."* A Mom-and-Pop Spaghetti restaurant was on the opposite corner.

McCall tried another approach. "How well do you know Allison Carmichael?" he asked her.

"She is my best friend," Evangeline said and shrugged.

"I have a special reason for asking that."

"Because you have a sister that you did not know about?"
He nodded. "That's right."

"That must have been quite a shock."

"It takes some getting used to," McCall admitted. "Who else knows about my sister besides you?"

"Hayden Vallance," Evangeline said. "All roads seem to lead back to him." She finished her cigarette and lit another. "Allison has two kids. Kyle is ten and Emily is eight. They are fearless and go *spelunking* every chance they get. Do know what *spelunking* is?"

"I do," he said. "Cave exploring. Nothing I am in a hurry to do. The thought of spending time buried in the ground does not appeal to me."

"It didn't appeal to me either," she said. "Then I started visiting the underground caverns and found that there was a whole new world in there. It gave me a real rush. Now I go *spelunking* wherever I can. Usually I go with some friends who think it is a blast, but recently their own lives have been more important to them."

McCall moved back into the apartment and closed the sliding door behind him. "So now you spend your time in eerie graveyards," he said.

"It sounds a little creepy, I know," Evangeline admitted. "But there is a certain peace I find there."

"These caves you were talking about. Where are they located exactly?"

"In the *Craighead Caverns* right here in Tennessee," she said. "They are also known as the *Lost Sea Caves*. It is a massive underground series of spectacular caverns complete with stalactites and stalagmites and the whole nine yards. I went there once with Allison to check them out."

"What happened?"

"It scared the hell out of me," she admitted. "After that I told Allison I could not go *spelunking* with her again. She has got two kids and there was always something going on at her house. Allison is a free spirit. I am worried about her. I am confident that I can deal with any demons that Hell can send my way, but Allison has this vulnerable side to her. I am convinced that is because she spends so much time caving and getting into weird passages and tunnels. Allison is vulnerable. She can lose herself in her own world and that is not a good place for her to be."

"Why not?" McCall asked.

"Because she loses all sense of time. The shadows creep up on her when she is not looking and engulf her."

McCall smiled. "Aren't you being a little melodramatic?"

"You don't know what is in my head," Evangeline said, flaring again. "Little furry creatures are constantly gnawing at me."

McCall tried to get the girl back on track. "You were telling me about Allison Carmichael?"

"Yes, I was," she said. "Sorry. My emotions get all jumbled up in my head."

"Take your time," McCall said. "It's important for me to try to know you better."

"Why? Going to try and psychoanalyze me?"

"Just trying to get inside your head."

"A dangerous place to be," Evangeline said, darkly. 'Don't say I didn't give you fair warning."

"Duly noted," McCall said.

She sighed. "It is not easy being me. Which you are finding out. What else do you want to know about my life?"

"Tell me about it," McCall said.

"You may be disappointed."

"Somehow I don't think so."

"Why not?"

"Something about you," he said. "It is like tracking down a very perplexing mystery. I have all the clues but putting them together is a challenge.

"Think you can work it out?" Evangeline asked, as if she were still challenging him.

"I'll give it a shot," McCall promised. "Tell me about your friend Allison Carmichael. She is at the heart of this story you are telling."

"I told you, she is my best friend."

"Tell me more about her."

"Why?"

"Because I believe she has been abducted," he said, quietly. "Maybe I can find her."

XXXI

GRAVEYARD

It took a moment for Evangeline to compose her thoughts. "Allison is headstrong," she said. "I have tried to talk to her into coming to the surface and staying there, but she's so stubborn."

"A little like you," McCall said.

She nodded and smiled. "Just like me. You just figured that out?"

"I'm a slow learner sometimes," McCall said, ironically. "What happened with Allison?"

"I lost track of her," she confessed. "She and her kids went down into the caverns a week ago and I did not see them again. There is a support group that I meet with every week who know everything about caving. They are difficult to reach so I have left them alone for now. I have a map to follow. But it has been some time since I have ventured down into the caverns. I guess I have been getting my courage up to actually go back down there."

"When you're not getting into trouble with the lowlifes who frequent the fairground," McCall said.

"That's a low blow, but you're right," Evangeline said. "I think my fairground adventures are over for the time being."

"What is the name of the labyrinth of tunnels beneath the ground?"

"*Plymouth Caverns.*"

'Where are they located?" McCall asked.

"Right here in Knoxville. There is a whole underground series of caverns that stretches for miles. I have not been there myself yet, but according to Allison it is pretty speculator. There is a hidden entrance located somewhere here. Sometimes there is a police car parked outside to guide the tourists. Personally, I cannot see the fascination of being trapped underground in hot, stifling tunnels which could collapse at any moment."

"It wouldn't work for me," McCall admitted.

"But it's that danger that lure folks to go *spelunking*," Evangeline said. "It is like the ultimate rush. I am I afraid I would not find my way out of those caverns. It would be too *'Journey to the Center of the Earth'* for me. Unless I had to go down into the caverns because it was a matter of life and death."

"I don't think that is going to happen anytime soon," he said.

"The very thought of it gives me the creeps."

"And you haven't seen Allison at her home?"

"No, I haven't," Evangeline said. "I am really worried about her wellbeing. I am terrified that something awful has happened to her and her kids."

McCall picked up the letter that Evangeline had received and turned it around to show her. "Who is this from?"

She took the envelope from him. "His name is David Carmichael. He is an ex-marine who lives right here in Knoxville." She shook her head. "A nasty piece of work if you ask me. Loud and obnoxious, but he and Allison had something going for them once upon a time. David is Allison's ex-husband. I shudder to think of the family reunions they had when they were together."

"Did David approve of Allison's infatuation with *spelunking?*" McCall asked.

"He thought it was a terrible idea," Evangeline admitted. "In the end that was what broke them up. David filed for divorce. After that he visited Allison on a regular basis to see his kids. But they were afraid of him. He has a violent streak that was frightening at times. He slapped Allison around a couple of times even after their divorce."

"Did you call the police?" McCall asked.

"I don't want to bring the cops into it," she said. "I have enough trouble sorting the thoughts and emotions that are trapped in my head."

"You haven't tried to get in touch with Carmichael?"

"I leave him alone and he leaves me alone." Evangeline said.

McCall nodded. "I'll pay Allison's husband a visit."

It didn't sound like a threat, but there is no mistaking his intent. Evangeline crushed out her cigarette and took his hand. "I would be happy if you wasted him. He is a dangerous predator. I fear for Allison's safety."

"I'll use kid gloves with him," McCall promised. "I need you to stay here in your apartment until I can take care of this problem."

"Then we'll go back underground into the *Plymouth Caverns?*" she asked, hopefully.

"That would be the general idea. I know where David Carmichael lives now."

"I have a map here of the underground caverns," Evangeline said and dashed away. She returned with a well-worn map which she handed to McCall. "They've all got provocative names like '*Raccoon Mountain*', '*Slaughter Canyon Falls*' and '*Bell Witch Cave*'. This map should be your guide. Those caverns are difficult to find."

"I'll keep that in mind," McCall said. "David Carmichael may not be the predator you think he is. Just because he was once married to your friend Allison that does not mean he is dangerous."

"I am trying to tell you that he is very dangerous," Evangeline said. "Trust me."

"Then it would be better if I dealt with him."

"Good luck with that." Evangeline let go of McCall's hand. "I won't hold my breath."

McCall pocketed Allison's letter and moved into the small hallway. "I'll be back," he promised.

He closed the door of the apartment behind him.

"Just come back to me in one piece," Evangeline said, softly.

*   *   *   *

It took McCall twenty minutes to find the sepulchral graveyard. Huge oak trees obscured it which were not visible from the road. Wrought-iron gates protected the cemetery from casual visitors who might have wandered in. The burial ground was a maze of broken headstones and carved obelisks. Marble statues stood throughout the mausoleum. A pall of grief seemed to hang over the churchyard like a shroud. Thunderclouds had massed over the graves that threatened to erupt in violent fury. Fingers of lightning flickered as the electrical storm lashed the leaden sky over the mausoleum. The rain had not fallen yet, but the powerful elements continued to threaten the sky.

McCall had left his Jaguar F-type sports car on the edge of the massive oaks. He entered the sacred ground with a sense of impending disaster. It was not because he was frightened by the intense imagery he would encounter there. He had lived through violent electrical storms before. But the atmosphere in the graveyard was oppressive. A fine drizzle had started to fall to add to the ambiance of foreboding. It was the thought of the lost souls that played on McCall's mind. There was something about a necropolis that had always frightened him. It had started when he had been a boy. He thought it was the stillness that attracted him. The headstones of the burial ground had a sepulchral dread for him that permeated his soul. He knew from somewhere in his memory that the graveyard meant a *Sleeping Chamber*. He had not intended to visit the huge crypts in the cemetery, but something had drawn him to this eerie place. The headstones were haphazardly placed in the tombs. Some of them were wildly overgrown so that the dates on the tombstones were barely readable. Other grave markers were made of black marble, pristine and immaculate with their inscriptions and dates clearly defined.

McCall wandered through the various granite monuments until he found the gravesite he was looking for: *Major Nelson McCall*. A single rose adorned the placard with the dates: *1915-1985*. Beneath that was a memorial plaque that had etched on it: *Operation Iraq Freedom* and the words: *Deployed from Iraq to Heaven* beneath an American flag. The words: *Department of the Army – United States of America* had been carved at the bottom of tombstone.

McCall had never got to know his father well. He had been a tough disciplinarian who had been in the military all his life. Major Nelson McCall had never had the time to be a loving father to his son, but McCall cherished his memory nevertheless in his heart. He wondered whether his father had ever referred him as "*The Equalizer*". He thought probably not. His father had been fighting dementia at the time of his death. McCall had not visited his father's gravestone in a long time, which he now regretted. Major

Nelson McCall had instilled in his son the values of caring and respect which was something he would always carry with him.

A brisk wind stirred the leaves of the oak trees in the graveyard. McCall got a glimpse of of a figure moving away from him in the overlapping shadows. The shadowy wraith filled McCall with a sense of dread. It was as if one of the specters from out of his nightmares had suddenly come to life. He ran after the apparition who disappeared into the trees overhanging the churchyard. He came to one of wrought-iron gates that separated the cemetery. McCall opened the gate and ran through it. The undergrowth outside of the cemetery had wrapped itself around the hedge that ran from the graveyard through the willow trees. McCall followed the ghostly figure that disappeared out of sight. The foliage tangled under his feet. A corkscrew willow tree barred his path which twisted horizontally and then forked vertically.

There was no sign of the intruder.

McCall thought that the prevailing imagery of the graveyard had affected him. Then a figure moved again in the shrubbery. McCall plunged after him. He broke free into a clearing where he found himself surrounded by white oak and red maple trees. The apparition was only visible for a moment, but McCall had fixed his position. He stumbled through the clinging vines until he came to a hidden cave entrance. It was off the beaten track that led down into the heart of the mountain. He might have missed it if he had not been searching for it. The mountain itself towered above him for 1000 feet.

McCall plunged into the caverns that stretched out before him. Stalactites and stalagmites hung down in the mausoleum like mutated fingers that had broken off. The massive underground chamber had a cathedral-sized ceiling of layered bedrock with psychedelic patterns etched in them. Wooden ladders had been cut into the underground crypt, but they didn't very reach far into the chamber. The grotto directly in front of McCall led down to more fantastic, distorted images. The catacombs descended down in the necropolis in a sloping tunnel. He came to a halt, not wanting to press his luck by burrowing farther down into the abyss.

The figure that McCall had glimpsed had completely vanished.

He was not at all certain if he had seen him at all. Just more nightmare images conjured up in his imagination. McCall retraced his path back to the entrance in the jumble of rocks that surrounded the cave. He took another route that led him back to where he had first encountered the intruder. Something caught his attention. He knelt down and picked up a distinctive chrome satin pocket lighter that had the insignia *US Army* on it with a star. The intruder had obviously dropped it in the long grass. McCall realized that it could have lain there for a long time. He dropped it into his leather jacket just in case it was some kind a clue.

But to what?

McCall smiled to himself. He was getting jumpy. He returned to the sepulchral graveyard for a last look at his father's gravestone, then headed back to where he had parked his Jaguar.

*   *   *   *

The car came out of a side street and bore down on McCall like a bat out of hell. There was no warning. McCall had just crossed in front of the *Beloved Woman of Justice* sculpture that graced the thoroughfare outside the stately Courthouse in Knoxville. A pedestrian had stepped off the curb at the same time as McCall. She was in her twenties with an attractive figure who had not been looking where she was going. McCall grabbed her and flung her out of the path of the speeding vehicle. He fell beside her as the driver swerved just in time. He recognized the man behind the wheel immediately. Khalid Rehman Mohammed had tried to kill McCall for a second time. He sped down the street. McCall picked up the young woman and steadied her. The sports car, a Citroen Gran Turismo, turned the corner onto Bijou Street in the theater district and was gone.

"Where did he come from?" the girl said, clearly flustered at her brush with death. "I didn't even see him!"

"He was aiming for me," McCall said.

The girl looked at him, astounded. "You're not serious?"

"Deadly serious."

"Why would someone try to run you down?"

"Someone with a grudge against me," he said. "Are you all right?"

The young woman nodded, pulling herself together. "Yeah, I am okay, thanks to you. You have lightning-fast reflexes! One moment I was crossing the street and the next moment I was on my ass checking out the sky."

"As long as you're okay, that's all that matters," McCall said.

She gave him an appraising look and liked what she saw. "In the circumstances the least you can do is buy me a drink! It is not every day I get hauled up out of the street by a handsome stranger!"

McCall smiled. "Maybe some other time."

"Rain check?"

"Sure."

She held out her hand. "I'm Beth Daniels."

McCall shook her hand "Robert McCall."

"Would it be very forward of me if I asked you for your phone number?"

"Not at all."

She scribbled her number on the back of a bus ticket and handed it to McCall.

"I'm visiting my folks who live here in Knoxville," she said. "Then I'm returning to New York City. You can catch me at the Sherry-Netherlands Hotel on 5th Avenue. I just live in an apartment a stone's throw from there. Promise to look me up?"

"I'll give it serious consideration."

"I can't ask more than that," Beth said. "I'm sure I'll never see you again but take this bus ticket as a memento of our very brief encounter."

"No harm done," he said.

"Just to my nerves," she said and laughed. "Be seeing you. Remember about that rain check."

"I will."

McCall pocketed the ticket. Beth continued down the street. She did not glance back.

McCall looked after her and smiled, totally charmed.

In other circumstances he might have taken Beth Daniels' offer seriously.

But not today.

He waited to see if Khalid Rehman Mohammed would make a U-Turn and come back, but he didn't do that. McCall turned onto Market Street which was filled with boutiques and up market stores.

That made two times that Samantha Gregson had tied to kill him using Khalid Rehman Mohammad as a shield.

McCall vowed to himself there would not be a third time.

Khalid Rehman Mohammad pulled over to the curb on Seeley Street and Samantha Gregson slid into the car. She had seen the whole incident unfold. Mohammad expected her to be angry, but she was icy calm.

"That makes two times you've been missed your target," she said. "We will need to approach this differently. McCall's reflexes are too good. He can sense danger coming at him and reacts accordingly. I have underestimated him. I have no clue why he is here in Knoxville. He will take care of his current 'Equalizer' business, whatever that may be, and then he will return to New York City."

"What happens then?"

"We will be waiting for him."

"You are still determined to kill him?" Khalid Rehman Mohammad asked.

"That isn't going to change until I see him dead," Samantha vowed.

"It is dangerous to plan your revenge too far ahead," the terrorist warned. "Leave him to me. I will take care of him."

She looked at him and slowly nodded. "I won't give you another chance."

"One is all I will need."

Samantha squeezed his hand. "I am counting on you."

"I won't let you down," he promised.

Khalid Rehman Mohammed pulled out into the traffic.

Samantha thought there was murder in his eyes.

XXXII
RESCUE WORKERS

McCALL FOUND DAVID CARMICHAEL at the *Back Door Tavern* in downtown Knoxville. The place was crowded. Carmichael was holding court at a back table with two other men who were truck drivers on long hauls. He was buying the next round of drinks. McCall thought he was pretty hammered at this point. He was a good-looking man with dark brown eyes and a stubble of beard. He was wearing a plaid shirt, canvas trousers and loafers with no socks. McCall stepped up to him.

"David Carmichael?"

Carmichael glanced at McCall, but he did not recognize him. "Who's asking?"

"My name is Robert McCall. I need to talk to you about your ex-wife."

"I have nothing to say about her," Carmichael said, dismissing him. The bartender moved over to them. "Another round, Jack."

The bartender just nodded and moved away. McCall tried to be friendly, but his patience was wearing thin. "This will only take a few minutes of your time. Can we move to another table?"

Carmichael turned to look at McCall. "What part of 'Get Lost' didn't you understand? The 'Get' or the 'Lost'?"

McCall grabbed the man's wrist and held it in a vice-like grip. "I am trying to locate your ex-wife. She may be in some danger. I can break your wrist if that is what it takes to reach you. Your call."

Carmichael was immediately intimidated by the encounter. He had not been expecting it. He realized that McCall was not going to go away. He held his gaze for a moment, then he nodded. "We can talk here. There's a table in the corner."

The bartender brought Carmichael two beers. McCall released his wrist. The man turned back to the truckers. "I need to take care of this. Give me five minutes."

Carmichael moved over to the corner table and sat down. One of the truckers approached the bar and rescued the remaining two beers. He glanced at Carmichael with some disdain. McCall got the feeling that Carmichael was not popular even among his acquaintances. The truck driver returned to his pals. McCall sat down next to Carmichael. The raucous ambiance in the tavern was boisterous in the prevailing tension.

"Are you here to harass me about my alimony payments?" Carmichael demanded. "If you have you are out of luck. I send Allison a check for the rent every month. I have not missed a payment yet."

"I'm sure she appreciates that," McCall said. "But I am not here to discuss your financial arrangements. When was the last time she saw your ex-wife?"

"Last week if that is any business of yours," Carmichael said. "She was fine. Those brats of hers were tearing around the house screaming at the tops of their lungs. They are completely undisciplined. I have tried to reason with Allison, but she only hears what she wants to hear."

"When was the last time your ex-wife and your kids went *spelunking*?" McCall asked him.

"Is that what this is about?" Carmichael said, astonished. "I don't keep track how many times Allison has burrowed in the ground with the kids like a couple of rampant moles. It is unnatural to explore these underground caverns. I have told her a hundred times it's dangerous down there, but she doesn't listen." Suddenly he leant forward. "Don't tell me she has been trapped down in the *Plymouth Caverns*?"

"I don't know what has happened to your ex-wife and children," McCall confessed. "She was supposed to return to the surface a week ago."

A new note of concern had crept into Carmichael's voice. "You're saying that she might be missing?"

"She might be."

"With the kids?"

"If you haven't seen them in a week, I can only presume she is keeping them somewhere below ground," McCall said. "You have any idea where they could be in the labyrinth?"

"None whatsoever." Carmichael shook his head. "I knew this would happen. Allison takes her life in her hands every time she goes into those underground caverns. Have you alerted the authorities about this? They will need to send out search parties to look for her and the kids."

"That's the next thing I am going to do," McCall promised. "I was just covering all of my bases. It has been more than a week since your ex-wife and your children have disappeared."

"Why would you care what happens to my ex-wife and her kids?" Carmichael demanded. "I've never seen you before tonight."

"I promised a friend of your ex-wife's that I would look for them," McCall said.

Carmichael nodded. "You must be talking about Evangeline Palmer."

"That's right."

"She's like a *Black Mamba Spider* who crawls out of the darkness to strike at their victims," he said. "She is seriously deranged. I have told Allison to stay away from her."

"When did you do that?" McCall asked.

"The last time I saw her."

"And she got that message?"

"I made sure that she did," Carmichael said. "The next time I warned her there would be consequences."

"What kind of consequences?" McCall said.

"I had to call the cops at least two times in the past six months. I was forced to take out a restraining order to keep Allison away from my wife and her obnoxious friend Evangeline Palmer."

"Did you threaten either of them?"

"I didn't have to," Carmichael said. "Forget about Evangeline Palmer. She is bad news. My ex-wife Allison is highly-strung and impressionable. She takes everything to heart. I have to walk on eggshells every time I pay her a visit. There's no reasoning with her when she is in one of her moods. We share two children named Kyle and Emily. I need to see them and that has not been easy."

"But you have been doing that?" McCall asked.

"I have. Every chance I get. The children and I call it their Prairie Time. '*Little House on the Prairie*' is their favorite TV show. I would not jeopardize that for all the tea in China." Carmichael looked away. The raucous ambiance in the bar was still rowdy and boisterous. It cut through his chaotic thoughts like a knife blade. "Allison does everything she can to keep me away from them. It's a personal vendetta. But I'm not going to let her get away with it this time."

"Why is this time special?" McCall asked.

"I have plans for the family," Carmichael said, darkly. "I am not about to share those plans with a stranger. I'm not keeping Allison on a leash. She's probably out visiting her friends like Evangeline Palmer. But the truth is that Allison has no *real* friends. She lives for her children which could be argued was a laudable thing, except I know her better than that. She is conniving and manipulative and our children are the ones who are suffering. She plays on their affection. That has driven a wedge between us."

"Maybe there's a way for you and your wife to reconcile your differences?" McCall suggested.

"We tried therapy and that got us nowhere," Carmichael said. "I suspect Allison suffers from a bipolar disorder which is the real reason she has been uncommunicative and withdrawn during our marriage. Or else it is a rage that causes her to lash out at me. I don't know which and I don't care. This is none of your business, Mr. McCall. Is that message clear enough for you?"

"It would be if Allison and your children had been found."

"What the hell are you talking about?"

"She hasn't been home in the last twenty-four hours," McCall said. "I am trying to put together what may have happened to her."

"I could care less," Carmichael said cavalierly, but McCall knew that was not the truth. He turned away from McCall, taking another swallow of his beer. "Maybe Allison has gone on a trip around the world with her best bud Evangeline. Good riddance."

"But you don't really believe that is true," McCall said, evenly. "And you haven't answered my question. Do you know any reason why Allison and your children should be missing?"

"Who says they're missing?"

"I have reason to believe they're still below ground in the *Plymouth Caverns*."

That got Carmichael's attention. "Have you been to Allison's house?"

"I have," McCall said. "No one has been at her apartment for at least a week."

Carmichael got to his feet. "I had no idea anything had happened to them."

McCall also stood up. "I don't know what has happened to your family, but if I were you, I would make sure I found out."

"No, you're right," Carmichael said. "I'm going to call SAR and the search and rescue teams and bring them into the picture." His attitude had undergone a radical change. He reached out and took McCall's hand. "Thanks for bringing this to my attention. Sorry I was being a jerk before. What did you say your name was again?"

"Robert McCall."

"Thank you, Mr. McCall. Of course I am concerned about my ex-wife and my children. This is very disturbing news. I'll make some calls and see where the rescue teams can be contacted. I am in your debt, Mr. McCall."

"No problem," McCall said.

Carmichael moved through the noisy tavern, taking out his cell phone.

McCall didn't think for a moment that the man's concern for his ex-wife and children was genuine. But he was at a loss to figure out his next move. He exited the bar, but there was no sign of Carmichael on the street. Finally McCall drove back to Allison Carmichael's apartment. He rang the doorbell, but there was no response. He felt under the *Welcome Home Mat* and this time he found a yale key. He straightened up and unlocked the door. When he entered the apartment he found that everything was just as he had left it. There was no sign of Allison Carmichael or, for that matter, Evangeline Palmer. McCall moved out into the small hallway and discovered that Allison had left a note that was sitting out on the hall table. He picked it up with a sudden feeling of dread. It wasn't addressed to Allison, but to her friend Evangeline. It was written in Evangeline's quirky handwriting. It said: "*Going back into the underground tunnels to try and find my friend Allison and her children.*" That was all it said. McCall was used to Evangeline's capricious whims, but this time the note hit him with the force of an express train. He knew something was very wrong with this situation. For Allison Carmichael and for her friend Evangeline Palmer. He pocketed the note and let himself out of the apartment.

There was one place he had not tried yet.

McCall made some phone calls on his cell phone. He retraced his way to where he knew the underground caverns were located at the side of the mountain. A sense of foreboding accompanied his fear. He had always been a victim of claustrophobia ever since he had been a child. The thought of being confined to a small space had an ominous, sinister connotation for McCall. But it was a fear he had long ago come to deal with.

Rough-hewn rocks had been cut into the sheer rock that led down in a twisting spiral. Many of them were chipped and some of them had gaps which McCall had to leap over. He estimated the underground chamber descended for at least two or three miles below the surface. Finally he emerged out into a vast underground chamber. Blue silver spider webs crisscrossed the caverns in front of him. Spectral growths twisted making eerie, unnatural patterns on the rust-red rocks. Several wood bridges spanned a turgid lake that he could see in the shadowy caverns beyond him.

McCall noted that several of the rescue workers and structural engineers were working in the shrouded darkness. They had been alerted to expect his arrival. He introduced himself to them, shaking hands. He found that all of them were quirky and eccentric. Lucas Slater was their leader, a bull of a man who didn't need a bullhorn to put his views across. J.D. Shandon was a soft-spoken introvert who barely acknowledged his team. Carlos Berkeley was basically a loner who spoke only occasionally. Mark Washington was a firebrand kind of a guy who held the rescue team together.

The labyrinth opened out into a massive series of caverns three football fields long. Stalactites and stalagmites hung down above a lake that seemed to reach into infinity. The huge grotto had several spiked formations that resembled wild orchids. McCall turned away from the long staircase and looked out to where the caverns towered above him.

J.D. Shannon regarded McCall frankly. "We don't have many visitors down here in the caverns," he said. "There are guided tours that take the tourists into another part of the mountain."

"Having said that you'd be surprised how many lost souls we encounter every night," Carlos Berkeley said.

"We're in the business of finding people," Mark Washington said, his tone somewhat confrontational. "People who have ventured down into these caverns because they got lost or separated from their guides. I'm not counting the kooks and thrill-seekers that we see every day of our lives who think that these underground caverns need to be explored."

"Cut him a little slack," Lucas Slater advised. "This is a rescue facility, Mr. McCall. That's why we're here."

J.D. Shannon handed McCall a steel helmet, insulated freezer gloves with grip palm protection and orange goggles.

"You'll need to wear these down here in the tunnels," he said. "Air intakes are equipped with anti-intrusion grilles that protect entry of debris. The plasma orange Safety Helmets have to be worn at all times below ground."

McCall took the hard steel helmet and put it on. Shannon adjusted the straps on the helmet to fit snugly. "Okay, you're all set," he said. "Some of the rescue workers also wear lamp clips and a vision attachment."

"Where are we exactly?" McCall asked.

"In the *Plymouth Caverns*," Lucas Slater said. "But the description of them is misleading. These underground tunnels travel back several miles and circle back again in a circuitous route."

"How far back do these caverns radiate?"

J.D.'s quiet voice was subdued, as if he were awed by the enormity of their rescue task. "Maybe a hundred miles and more. The tentacles wrap around themselves. The tunnels twist and turn with offshoots going far back into the passageways."

"Then they just come to an abrupt end," Mark Washington said. His voice was still belligerent, echoing down the passageway. "That's why we don't encourage the public to venture down here. They do so at that their own risk."

"There is another member of my party who may be trapped underground in the caverns," McCall said. "Her name is Evangeline Palmer. She is a close friend of Allison Carmichael's. Do you know who she is?

"I afraid I don't," J.D, Shannon said.

"Allison and Evangeline are friends who may have ventured down here to these caverns. One of them, Evangeline Palmer, is headstrong and impulsive. I don't know Allison Carmichael, but she may be trapped down here as well."

"What are you basing this intel on?" Lucas Slater asked.

"Observation," McCall said. "Evangeline was headed down here to try to find her friend Allison."

"When was that?" J.D. Shannon asked, alarmed. "No one else should be down in these tunnels."

"I saw the note from Evangeline this evening," McCall said. "Whether she actually ventured into the caverns I can't say, but I'd say it's highly likely that she did."

"And her friend Allison Carmichael could be trapped in the labyrinth as well?"

"That's my guess," he said.

"Just what I needed to hear," Carlos Berkeley muttered. "Two more lost souls trapped in the tunnels." He turned to Mark Washington. "You had better add them to the list of missing persons."

"That list is getting too long for my liking," Washington said, darkly. "We're talking about at least eight people who have vanished in these caverns in the last few years."

"For all I know Evangeline may be home by now," McCall said. "She's headstrong and impulsive, but I am hoping common sense prevailed with her."

"But you have no intel about Allison Carmichael?" Lucan Slater asked him.

"No, I don't."

They had come to an eerie lake which lapped at their feet.

"I didn't expect to find a lake down here," McCall said.

"There are several of them," Washington said. "The series of caverns are honeycombed with shallow ponds or channels."

"How many bridges are located down here?" McCall asked.

"Probably a hundred," Carlos Berkeley said. "Maybe more."

"The lake here is deceptive because it's much deeper than it appears," J.D. Shannon said. "The grottos hem them in. We have to access it from these wooden bridges. The Great Salt Lake in Utah is still the biggest saline lake in North America."

"We're not here to give a history lesson," Lucas Slater said, his voice echoing back against the limestone walls. "This is a rescue mission."

The quartet skirted around the edge of the lake. Rainbowed hues towered above them in the fissures that dwarfed the rescue workers. Fantastic spirals and murals were displayed in the configuration of the rocks. McCall thought again that being trapped underground in these caverns was claustrophobic and unsettling.

Lucas said: "Just past this last wooden bridge the grotto opens up."

"Try not to look down onto the lake," Carlos Berkeley advised. "It will mesmerize you. All of the colors merge together. Keep to the bridges if you have to venture farther into the caverns. There are several of them."

"How much further do these tunnels travel?" McCall asked.

"It's impossible to tell," J.D. Shannon estimated. "I have searched these caverns many times and just when you are certain you have found a way back to the surface another tunnel opens up. It is not as simple as retracing your steps back to where you came out."

"The only landmarks available to us are the stone steps that lead up to the surface," Lucas Slater said. "And the various wooden bridges here that keep us orientated."

"So it is a maze," McCall concluded.

"From which there is no escape once you're in it," Slater added. "That's when the search-and-rescue dynamic falls apart. You can get hopelessly lost in these caverns if you take one wrong turn."

The quartet moved to where they had initially initiated their search. Lucas Slater unfolded a large map which he laid out onto a slab of graphite. Mark Washington took up the narrative: "Distance is deceptive here below ground. These dual-bore tunnels have arteries that can travel for miles in both directions. This is the best map I can supply you with. It has been extensively revised with more tunnels and arteries. It will lead you about twelve or fifteen miles deeper into the caverns before it branches out into veins of limestone. Even then there is no guarantee that you will not get lost. Landmarks have been listed here on the map, but they can twist and turn for hours for no apparent reason."

"Here's a case in point," Carlos Berkeley said. "This is an entrance to *Wolf Creek Pass* that has access down into the tunnels. But there are tubular veins that branch out in two different directions beneath the ground. If you travel down this route in particular it will take you on a circuitous journey that will eventually deposit you ten miles further beneath the ground."

"How long has Allison Carmichael been trapped down here in these tunnels?" McCall asked, faintly appalled.

"Six days," Lucas Slater said. "And now we have to add another lost camper to our list if your intel about Evangeline Palmer is correct. There are four teams of *Search and Rescue Personnel* scouring these tunnels with us. We haven't heard anything from Allison Carmichael or her two children."

"Their names are Kyle and Emily," J.D. Shannon added. "Those kids must be seriously traumatized by now."

"You've had no word from them at all?" McCall asked.

"Nothing," Carlos Berkeley said with finality.

"Maybe they have left some signs for you?"

"Like breadcrumbs scattered through the tunnels?" Mark Washington said, caustically. "Hey! Why didn't I think of that?"

"Save the sarcasm," J.D. Shannon said, annoyed. "We have a job to do here. That isn't helping us."

"Not to put a fine point on it," Lucas Slater said, "but it's as if Allison and her children have been swallowed up in the earth."

"Don't forget to add another lost soul to that list," Mark Washington reminded him. "Evangeline Parmer may be trapped down here in the caverns also. That makes eight people who have vanished into thin air. So now you're up to speed, Mr. McCall."

"It's a frightening scenario," McCall said.

"And it's only going to get worse," Washington said. "There is nothing you can do to help us. If you go accessing these tunnels we'll just have another MIA to track."

"Leave the searching to us," Carlos Berkeley advised. "Finding missing persons is what we do for a living."

"Stay out of it. Mr. McCall," J.D. Shannon said.

But McCall shook his head. "I can't do that. I'll take my chances in the tunnels."

"Then sign this waiver while you're down here," Mark Washington said. "Everyone who visits the *Plymouth Caverns* needs to do that."

McCall signed the waiver and handed it back to Washington. "I'm hoping I can locate these missing campers and bring them home."

"Good luck," J.D. Shannon said. "You're going to need it."

"Follow the wooden bridge at the lake," Carlos Berkeley said. "After that, you're on your own."

Lucas Slater folded the map they had been following and handed it to McCall. "We've given you fair warning," he said. "What you do now is up to you."

"I appreciate that," McCall said.

He put the folded map into his leather jacket and moved farther into the echoing caverns. The rescue workers watched his progress until he was past the lake and then his figure disappeared.

"One wrong turning and he'll become lost and disoriented," Mark Washington prophesied. "I am not going to go looking for him."

"No one asked you to," J.D. Shannon said, shortly. "He'll make it back to the lake. I'm pretty sure of that."

"But he'll be alone," Carlos Berkeley said. "Those missing children are lost. Maybe Evangeline Parmer as well."

"I think Mr. McCall is up to the challenge," J.D. Shannon said. "He seems to be very resourceful."

"He will need to be," Mark Washington said. "I wouldn't bet the farm on his chances."

"We'd better get back to ground zero," Lucas Slater suggested. "We'll have to leave Mr. McCall to the fates."

Carlos Berkeley shook his head. "It's our job to find them," he said with an edge to his voice. "That's why we're here."

"McCall will have to take his chances," Mark Washington said.

The quartet moved back to the echoing chamber of the labyrinth and their voices faded in the profound silence.

XXXIII

LOST

Allison Carmichael had completely lost her way. She had been wandering aimlessly through the forbidding caverns for what seemed to be an eternity. At every wrong turn she felt a profound sense of dread. Her children Kyle and Emily were missing. Kyle was ten years old and a thoughtful, reserved child. Allison thought of him as an old soul. He looked out for his sister Emily who was eight years old and a real terror. Allison loved them more than life itself. They had been right behind her when they had tried to traverse the diagonal opening that led to yet another series of caverns. Emily had stumbled to her knees on the uneven ground. Kyle had immediately moved to her side and caught her before she fell. He had steadied her, making sure she didn't trip again. She had nodded her head, irritated that she had fallen and that her big brother had to come to her rescue. Allison had carried on down the echoing passageway and did not see this happening. She came to a fork in the tunnel and squeezed through it between the towering boulders. She emerged into a bewildering series of new tunnels that towered fifty feet above her. She turned back to retrace her path through the narrow opening. When she had negotiated this passage and looked around for her children she could not see them anywhere. Panicked-stricken, she moved back to where she had last caught sight of them.

Her voice echoed. "Kyle! Emily!"

There was no response. She ran farther down the narrow path where dagger-like formations surrounded her. A ninety-foot column faced her that leaned precariously like the *Tower of Pisa*. She called her children's names again, but the words were torn from her throat and echoed eerily back through the caverns.

There was no response.

Allison stumbled onward. The cathedral-size ceilings were fifteen stories high at this point, dwarfing her small figure. Metal plaques were strategically placed throughout the caverns. Several of the passageways had picturesque names: *Devil's Springs Dome, Temple of the Twin Tower and the Bottomless Pit.* She moved past the *Frozen Waterfall* and *The Boneyard* which had fossilized outcroppings like giant Tyrannosaurus Rex teeth. Allison was getting more frantic with each passing minute. She didn't know if she was running away from Kyle and Emily or getting closer to them. Her sense of direction was seriously impaired in the never-ending maze. Finally she turned in all four directions and shouted in desperation: "Kyle! Emily! Where are you?"

She waited for a response from her children, but she knew in her heart that it was not coming. She had strayed too long in the labyrinth. She waited in vain for one of the rescue teams to find her, but that hadn't happened either.

Allison resolved to come back for her children if she could find a way out of this labyrinth. At the moment that seemed like a forlorn hope.

She stumbled forward and inadvertently stepped down into a quicksand quagmire.

Allison felt herself being sucked down into the bowels of the earth. She turned around as she sank deeper in the swamp. In desperation she grabbed a trailing vine to try and pull herself free. Inch-by-inch she ascended, wrapping her hands around the vine. The muddy ooze clawed at her body. It stank and the bog bubbled up around her like a living creature that emerged from the Gates of Hell. Finally, Allison clambered out of the treacherous morass and collapsed to the ground. The stinking ooze clung to her face and arms. She climbed to her feet, being careful not get herself mired again in the treacherous swamp. She moved deeper in the limestone caves. She did not think her legs would carry her much further. She just wanted to sit down in the midst of the towering geysers and accept her fate.

Finally she sank down to her knees. The sighing of the wind rose and fell as it whistled around her. It had an eerie, funereal feel, but yet it was strangely comforting. Like an old friend whispering to her. The shelves of sheer rock around her were like stepping-stones. They ascended upward in spirals splashed with fantastic colors in the maze. She could see *old faces* in the boulders that resembled *Indian Chiefs*. In her fevered imagination they surrounded her with a stony silence. The pointed stalactites and stalagmites seemed to be aimed down at her. She looked farther up and saw more geyser-like formations had formed around her in the echoing mausoleum.

Allison crawled up to her feet. There were precarious wooden bridges that spanned part of the chasm at this point in the lagoon. Gathering up her courage she ran across one of them. She did not know how long she had climbed up the treacherous steps, but it must have been at least two miles. She remembered that the underground chamber below her was one of the biggest in the caverns. Rough-hewn stone steps were cut into the rocks right above her that travelled up at least fifty feet in a twisting spiral.

Allison ascended the stairs with a renewed determination.

At last she came to some broken stones that continued to lead upward. She climbed a narrow staircase and faint moonlight drifted across the ground. She reached the top of the fragmented stairs and stumbled out of them into the night.

Above Allison the sky was studded with stars. She stumbled to her knees. It was a cliché to kiss the ground, and she knew that, but she couldn't help it. She was so grateful to be out of the underground complex and to be breathing fresh air again. She straightened and looked around her. The cavern entrance was half hidden by the mountain from which she had just emerged.

But her euphoria was short lived.

She still had no idea where her children were. They were buried somewhere in the catacombs. She realized she would have to return to the caverns. The idea of going back down into the crypts filled her with fear and apprehension. But she could not leave Kyle and Emily to their fate. She had to steel herself to venture down back into the underground maze once again.

What other choice did she have?

In the forlorn hope that her children had returned home, Allison took a cab to her house on Gay Street near the Lawson McGhee Library. She climbed the two steps to her front door. She reached down, found the Yale key that was hidden under the *Welcome Mat* and opened her front door. She ran straight into Kyle and Emily's room, but it was deserted. *Monopoly* and the other *Board Games* were strewn across the floor. Allison had a random thought that she needed to get her kids to pick up for themselves. She accessed her phone and tried reach their neighbors Monica and Stuart Abrams who lived across the street. Monica worked as a legal secretary and Stuart was an attorney. But they were never home. In desperation Allison called her cousin Carole Sheppard, who lived on Long Island, but she was just running out the door for a meeting at the Stuyvesant High School and she promised she would call back later. Allison hung up, frustrated and exhausted.

At that moment her front door chimed. With a soaring in her heart she ran to the door and threw it open. But it was not her children. A Police Officer stood on the threshold. He was attached to the *Criminal Investigations Division* and wore a badge pinned to his Commander's uniform that said: *Tactical Response Unit.* The Officer's name was Detective Jeff Martinez. Behind him two casually dressed Homicide Detectives were wearing their badges around their necks: Detective Jim Friedkin and Detective Lance Holloway. Allison knew Detective Jeff Martinez because he had organized volunteers in the neighborhood for a bake sale. The Peace Officer had a great relationship with the people in the Community. But at this moment he was all business.

"Mrs. Carmichael, I am going to have to ask you to come with me."

"Is this about my children?" Allison asked immediately. "We were trapped in the labyrinth beneath the *Plymouth Caverns* for several days. I finally managed to escape just now, but I don't know where my children are."

"Just come with us," Detective Jim Friedkin said, not unkindly. "We need to ask you some questions."

"I can't answer your questions until I know that my children are safe!"

Detective Holloway took Allison's arm. As opposed to his other colleagues, his manner was brusque. "We'll answer your questions back at the Knoxville Police Station."

"You don't understand!" she protested. "I need to stay home in case my children return!"

"Just come with us, Mrs. Carmichael," Detective Martinez said, more forcefully. "Don't make us put the cuffs on you in front of your neighbors."

Allison allowed herself to be led to two unmarked police cars with their lights flashing. She slid into the back seat and Detective Holloway climbed in beside her. Detective Friedkin slid into the front seat. Detective Martinez did the driving and they pulled away from Allison's house.

*   *   *   *

After searching the underground caverns in vain for any sign of Allison Carmichael, her children or Evangeline Palmer, McCall had called it a day. One of the rescue workers had told him to look out for a landmark after he had passed several wooden bridges. It was shaped like a *Bashful Elephant hiding its trunk*, but McCall never found it. He had retraced his steps back to where the underground lake was shrouded in shadows. He had been very careful to leave markers on the cavern walls so he wouldn't become hopefully lost. He crossed the last wooden bridge over the turgid lake and found himself back with the rescue teams. Lucas Slater and J.D. Shannon were heavily involved in a conversation with two other teams in the labyrinth. Carlos Berkeley was studying a map showing red flags to mark the places the rescue teams had been searching. Mark Washington looked up and acknowledged McCall. His voice as usual was brusque and dismissive.

"So you're back. Did you find your missing party?"

"Not a sign of them," McCall admitted. "I took various routes and I left markers to guide my way."

"What about your friend Evangeline Palmer?"

"She's among the missing."

"Sorry to hear that," Washington said. "The maze can be a daunting experience. I'm surprised you made it back to the lake and the wooden bridges. I thought I'd have to send a rescue party to try and find you."

"Thanks for your concern," McCall said, with an edge to his voice.

J.D. Shannon looked up from the map he was sharing with Carlos Berkeley and the other rescue teams. "You know your way back to the surface from here, Mr. McCall?"

"I do."

"Don't feel bad that you couldn't find our missing campers," J.D. said. "You could spend days down here and not see any sign of them at all."

"I am just glad to see that you made it back to the lake over the wooden bridges," Carlos Berkeley said. "The tunnels can be disconcerting. They never seem to be in the same place at the same time which defies logic. It's like the passageways have rerouted themselves into new patterns beneath the ground."

Lucas Slater arrived at this point. "What J.D. is trying to say is that you're pushing your luck, Mr. McCall. You know how many times we have lost people down here in the caverns? Probably a dozen who were never heard from again."

"Do yourself a favor," Washington said. "Don't come back."

"Sounds like good advice," McCall said, although he knew he would not be heeding it.

"There are several entrances to the caverns," J.D. said. "You happened to find one of them. You had better come with me."

"Thanks," McCall said.

J.D. led him to where there was a series of stairs that ascended up into the mountain. "These stone stairs will lead you back to the surface."

"I really appreciate your taking time to point me in the right direction," McCall said.

"No problem," he said. "It can be very tricky finding your way out of these caverns unless you know what you're doing. Good luck, Mr. McCall."

The rescue team went back to their maps. McCall made his back to the stone steps that led up to the surface. This time it took him longer than he had anticipated. He found that the caverns had a strange hypnotic effect on him. It stemmed from his terror of being trapped in claustrophobic places when he had been a child.

When he finally reached the entrance to the caverns he experienced a sense of profound relief.

McCall made his way to his parked Ford Explorer and climbed inside. He took a few deep breaths to try and center himself. The whole experience underground had been unnerving for him. He would have to venture back into the caverns again, but to do what? He was no further along in his quest to find Allison Carmichael. He had not seen her children. Evangeline Palmer was still on the missing list. In the end he decided to go back to Allison's house in the hope she had returned home.

McCall drove to Gay Street and parked under the flowering cherry trees. He climbed up the two stairs to the front door. He reached automatically under the *Welcome Mat* and found there was a Yale key hidden there that had not been there before. McCall glanced around him. A moving van had parked in the street. Two workers were unloading it. The neighborhood kids were playing basketball in a playground next to the two-story houses. A couple of older people now sat on the steps in front of one of the buildings. The husband waved at McCall. He waved back just to be friendly and opened the front door.

Everything in the apartment seemed to be the same as when he left it. There was no one in the children's rooms or in the kitchen. The pile of discarded newspapers and mail still lay on the hall table. McCall saw that a note had been hastily added to it. He picked it up. It was from Allison. It simply said: *"Back later."* The note had not been there when he had accessed the house the first time. Allison had obviously been home, albeit briefly, which meant she had escaped from the labyrinth. But he was still no closer to finding Allison, her children or Evangeline Palmer. The body count was adding up. And now Allison was missing. Playing a hunch, McCall took out his cell phone, found the number for the *Tactical Response Unit* of the *Knoxville Police Force* and dialed it. A Police Officer answered the call, but McCall immediately hung up. He needed to question the cops on a more personal basis. He left the apartment and moved down the stairs to the street. He slid inside his Ford Explorer and pulled away from the curb.

Twenty minutes later McCall was standing with Detective Jeff Martinez of the Knoxville Police Department. McCall's instincts had been correct. He had located Allison Carmichael. She was sitting in an interrogation room in the precinct. Two-way glass shielded him and Detective Martinez in the small office. Detectives Jim Friedkin and Detective Lance Holloway could be seen grilling Allison in an interrogation room. It was not going well. Jeff Friedkin was a forceful, no-nonsense Police Officer who possessed a laconic sense of humor. Lance Holloway was the opposite, dour and uncommunicative. McCall decided to leave out the part where he was also looking for Evangeline Palmer. That was more information than the Knoxville Police Department needed to assimilate.

"We've been questioning Allison Carmichael for three hours," Martinez said. "We keep going over the same ground and it's getting us nowhere. She insists the last time she saw her children was beneath the labyrinth at the *Plymouth Caverns*. They had wandered away from her and when she tried to find them again they had completely disappeared. Allison made her way back to one of the tunnels which eventually led her to the outside world. She returned to her house on Gay Street thinking her children might be there, but they weren't."

"Do you believe her story?" McCall asked.

"That she and her children had been trapped beneath those underground passageways?" Martinez asked. "I believe her when she tells me that is what *she* believes. Her story has not changed for three hours. If she is lying, then she is an accomplished actress who should be receiving an Academy Award for her performance."

"Which is it?" McCall pressed.

"Hard to say," the detective said. "My colleagues Detectives Friedkin and Detective Holloway are trying to give Allison the benefit of the doubt. She talked about being lost in the labyrinth which she said was terrifying. Then she said that her children had been with her the whole time. Then that story changed to them wandering away from her and she had searched for them in vain. Then her story switched back and she swore she had been trapped in the caverns with no hope of finding her way back to the surface. She had been totally lost in the passageways that she called *The Boneyard* and the *Devil's Springs Dome*. She described several cathedral-size caves around her that towered several stories high. She said there was a *Frozen Waterfall* where *Daggers of Stalactites and Stalagmites* had formed. She swore there was a place called *Red Rust Caverns* on a lake, but as far as I know in talking to the rescue teams there is no such lake. Allison described faces in the rock formations around her that resembled *Indian Chiefs* like *Geronimo* and *Sitting Bull*, but I think that was all in her imagination."

"She's frightened and disoriented," McCall said.

"Or she is playing us." Martinez looked at McCall. "What is your take on this? I've never seen you before today, but I made some phone calls to a Detective Steve Lansing in New York City. He said you were a good guy and a royal pain in the ass. He had a name for you I did not catch. It sounded like '*The Equalizer*,' or something like that. That ring any bells?"

"It does, but we're here to talk about Allison Carmichael," McCall said. "She's a client and I need to talk to her."

"So you have *clients*?" Detective Martinez said, ironically. "Does that make you some kind of a private eye?"

"Something like that."

"Why should I believe anything you say?"

"Because it's the truth," McCall said.

"That won't cut the mustard with me," he said.

"I have a special reason for keeping secrets," he said. "It's personal and it has nothing to do with Allison Carmichael or anyone else."

"You had better spell that out for me," Detective Martinez said, tersely. "Because from where I am sitting you are a prime suspect in a missing person's case. You want to elaborate on that scenario?"

McCall could not fend off the truth any longer.

"Allison Carmichael is *my sister*," he said, simply.

That gave Detective Martinez pause. "The defendant is your *sister*?"

"That's right. Let's not call her a defendant until I can prove her innocence."

"You could have mentioned that to me before this interview started."

"I didn't know she even existed until this evening," McCall admitted. "I was visiting with an old friend of mine who had been in the hospital in New York City recovering from pneumonia."

"What's his name?"

"Sam Kinney."

"And he'll vouch for you?"

"I am sure he will. We have been friends for a long time. Right now I need to talk to Allison. I might be able to sort out what is the truth and what is pure fiction."

Detective Martinez paused again, then he nodded. "Okay, come with me."

He led the way out of the interrogation room to where offices were located. Detectives Friedkin and Holloway were waiting for him. Detective Martinez turned to McCall.

"You can have five minutes with our witness," he said.

He opened the office door. McCall stepped into the interrogation room and Martinez closed the door behind him.

Detective Friedkin said: "You're going to be listening through the one-way glass?"

"You'd better believe it," Detective Martinez said, grimly.

XXXIV

ALLISON

McCALL ENTERED THE ROOM and closed the door behind him. Allison Carmichael did not get up. She looked at McCall as if she had reached the end of her endurance. The myriad freckles that were sprinkled across her face had been diminished until they barely registered. Her eyes were bloodshot. Her hands were tightly clenched into in her lap.

"How many of you does it take to question a suspect?" she asked, wearily. "Your colleagues took in turns to browbeat me. The same old questions over and over again. No, I don't know where my children are. Their names are Kyle and Emily, by the way. They were behind me in the underground caverns and then they just simply disappeared. I couldn't find them anywhere. Eventually I found a stone staircase in one of the grottos that must have been several miles long. I didn't know how far up it went, but I was out of options. I had to climb those stairs."

Allison paused, as if the strain of being interrogated had finally got to her.

"Go on," McCall said.

"That eventually led me to another cavern," she said. "It was like a great cathedral with antediluvian medieval arches. The spiral steps there had a yellow glow to them like some antique old clock that looked like it came out of an illustration for *Alice in Wonderland*. Most of the stairs were broken in places and decayed in others. That led me to another cavern in the mausoleum. I climbed up the stone staircase there which had to have been two or three miles high. I sensed I was getting close to an exit. Eventually I came out of the crypts into the open air. I think that just about covers it." She finally made eye contact with McCall. "Anything else you need to know you'll have to get out the rubber hoses and beat it out of me."

"I don't think they use rubber hoses anymore," he said, gently. He sat down beside her. "I am not here to force a confession out of you."

"Then why are you here?"

"Because you need my help," McCall said. "The probing questions from the cops will continue unless I can you get out of here. So let's start again. My name is Robert McCall."

"Is that name supposed to mean anything to me?"

McCall had been working out a way to break his news to her, but in the end he just opted for the truth. "You are my *younger sister*," he said, quietly.

It took Allison a moment to compose herself. "Don't be ridiculous. I have never seen you before in my life!"

"Believe me this came as a shock to me too," McCall admitted.

"Who told you this?" she demanded.

"A friend of mine named Sam Kinney. He works at the reception desk at the Liberty Belle Hotel in New York City. Some fairground louts took it in their heads to beat the old man up. I dealt with them, but it was touch-and-go if Sam was going to pull through."

"Did your friend make it?" Allison asked.

McCall liked her even more in that moment. He nodded. "He did. He's cankerous and unpredictable, but his heart is in the right place. He was the one who shared with me your true identity. It took him a long time to tell me the secret. I guess he didn't know how I would react, but I've got used to the idea now."

Allison finally found her voice. She shook her head. "I am sorry to disappoint you," she murmured. "But I don't have a sister."

McCall smiled. "I said the same thing."

"You're basing this information on the word of someone named Sam Kinney," Allison said, "who works at a hotel in New York City?"

"That's right."

"How reliable is he?"

"He wouldn't have told me this secret unless he knew it was the truth," McCall said, quietly. "I trust his word one hundred percent."

"And you really believe I am *your sister?*" Allison said, incredulously.

"It looks that way."

Allison shook her head. "You are obviously mistaking me for someone else."

"I don't think so," he said. "You're in your twenties and I am in my early fifties. I haven't seen you grow up, that's true. I didn't know you even existed before today. But I trust Sam Kinney's word on this."

"I don't know anything about you!" she protested.

"As me a question," McCall said.

"All right! Here's one you should be able to answer. My mother passed away several years ago. I am assuming you have a mother, right? Where is she at this moment?"

"Sadly, I never got to know her," McCall said. "She died when I was a young man, but that's a story that can keep for another day."

"You could be making all this stuff up!"

"I could, but I'm not. My father's name was Major Nelson McCall. He was a tough marine. Old school. I never got to know him until it was too late for me to reach out to him. He had been suffering with dementia before his death."

Allison shook her head. "I can hardly believe this is happening. There has to be a mistake."

"There's been no mistake," McCall said.

"You don't understand," she said. "I have never had anyone in my life who meant anything to me except my children."

"That is no longer true."

Allison shook her head, as if trying to clear it. "This will take some getting used to."

McCall nodded. "For the both of us," he said and smiled.

She suddenly faced him, but her hands had stopped trembling. "Do you know anything about my life? Who I am? My fears or my hopes and dreams?"

"I know very little about you," McCall confessed. "I know where you live here in Knoxville. I have been to your home."

"Describe it," Allison said, challenging him.

"A friendly environment, lots of clothes in the closets, two children's rooms that look as if a tornado had hit them," McCall said. "Kyle is ten and Emily is eight. I am sure you love them very much, but right now they are missing. You have no idea where they are. Your friend Evangeline Palmer is also missing, but she may return home again. I need to check that out. The cops aren't buying your story about what happened in the *Plymouth Caverns*. They believe that you have made the whole story up. That your children are probably dead because that is what their training has taught them."

"But you don't believe that?"

"I don't," McCall said. "I believe your children are trapped down in those subterranean caverns, lost and frightened, and we need to rescue them."

"But why should you do any of that?" Allison demanded, but there was suddenly a sense of hope in her voice. "Why should you help me?"

McCall shrugged. "It's what I do," he said, simply.

"I've never had anyone who really cared about me."

"You do now. If you really are my sister I need to look out for you. Which means we have to get out of these interrogating rooms."

"The Knoxville Police Department doesn't believe my story about being trapped in the *Plymouth Caverns*," Allison said. "I didn't know that Evangeline has been missing. Maybe she returned to her senses and went home. But as far as the cops are concerned, I left my children down in those subterranean caverns to die."

"But you didn't," McCall said. "I need to prove that."

"How?"

"I can be very persuasive," he said with a hint of irony. "Just leave this with me. Can you do that?"

"I can try," she said.

"Good enough. Wait here."

McCall exited the interrogation room and was met by Detective Martinez who had been waiting for him. McCall knew that he had reviewed his conversation with Allison. He was accompanied by Detectives Friedkin and Holloway.

"What's the verdict?" Martinez asked.

"I believe her story," McCall said.

"Why?"

"She has no reason to lie to me."

"Because you are *her uncle*?" Detective Holloway said. "We have no real proof of that. I reckon she's been playing you like a fiddle."

"Her story doesn't add up," Friedkin added. "Too many loose ends. Too many contradictions."

"It works for me," McCall said, evenly. "I don't want Allison going back into the *Plymouth Caverns* and start looking for her children. She'll be trapped underground and I'm not going to let that happen."

"You'll take responsibility for her?" Detective Martinez asked.

"I will."

"But you've said that she's a complete stranger to you."

"Not any longer."

The detective nodded, glancing at his colleagues. "Okay, cut her loose."

McCall moved back down the corridor to the interrogation room and entered it.

"I don't like it," Detective Friedkin said.

"She's not going anywhere," Detective Holloway said. "We know where to find Allison Carmichael if we need to question her further."

"Just make sure you know where she is when she leaves here," Martinez advised.

McCall walked out of the Knoxville Police Department with Allison. She had pulled herself together with an effort. She looked at the cops. "I wish you would believe me. I am telling you the truth."

"You're very convincing," Detective Martinez said. "Is it your intention to go back into those subterranean passageways again?"

"Yes," she said, firmly. "I have no choice."

"Good luck with that," Detective Holloway said.

"I hope you find your children," Detective Friedkin said.

"So do I," she murmured.

McCall opened the door and they moved to his car which was parked outside. In the precinct room behind them, Detective Friedkin turned to Martinez and shook his head. "I don't believe her for a second."

"She's a pathological liar," Holloway said. "Her kids are dead. I'd bet my badge on it."

"But we don't know any of that for sure," Detective Martinez said. "For all we know Allison Carmichael and her friend Evangeline Palmer hopped on a plane bound for Rio together."

"Don't count on it," Detective Friedkin said darkly.

"I'm not," Martinez said. "Put on a Bolo on Allison Carmichael. If she does go back into the *Plymouth Caverns*, I want to know about it."

*   *   *   *

Outside, McCall opened the Ford Explorer and Allison slid into the passenger's seat. He sat beside her, fired up the car and moved into light traffic in downtown Knoxville.

"I must know what has happened to my children," Allison said.

"You will," McCall said. "But I am not going take you to the *Plymouth Caverns* just yet. I got a revised map of the caverns from the rescue workers. We need to figure out where your children might be and devise a plan of action."

"I feel so helpless," she confessed.

"You're not helpless," he said. "Far from it."

She looked over at him. "I do feel safe with you. You're like my Knight Errant riding to my rescue. Right now you're all I have got. I am putting all my trust in you."

"You're feeling vulnerable and defenseless," McCall said. "That fear will subside."

"But you won't be here forever. I don't have a claim on your feelings or emotions. You won't always be there for me."

"I am here right now," McCall said, gently. "That's all you need to worry about."

Allison nodded, blinking back unwanted tears. "I have never had anyone who really cared about me."

McCall shrugged. "You're my younger sister. We need to stay together and figure out a plan of action."

"But why should you care what has happened to me?"

"One step at a time," McCall advised. "We'll return to your apartment on Gay Street. Think you can get your act together long enough to put on some coffee?"

Allison looked at him and now it was her turn to smile. "I think I could manage to do that."

"Good enough."

McCall parked on one side of Gay Street. He and Allison climbed the two steps to the front door. Allison reached automatically for her Yale key hidden under the *Welcome Mat*. She unlocked the door and she and McCall entered the familiar apartment. Whether it was from fatigue or desperation, Allison moved immediately to her children's rooms which were in shadows. The children were not there. She moved into the kitchen, took a Coffee Percolator and set the timer for five cups of coffee. In the living room, McCall took a 1000-piece San Francisco Trolley jigsaw puzzle that Allison and her children had half-finished and moved it to a sideboard. Allison came in from the kitchen.

"Coffee is brewing," she said.

"The Rescue Workers had a revised map that they gave to me," McCall said. He spread it across the dining table. "It outlines the new passageways and tunnels they had found down in the *Plymouth Caverns*."

Allison leaned over the map. "How detailed is it?"

"It's pretty extensive," McCall said. "The red areas are outlined. I'll need some time to go through them."

"What are you hoping to find?"

"Anything that brings us closer to finding your children."

She looked at him, as if reaching a decision. "You could have just walked away from this situation. I wouldn't have blamed you for a second."

"But I would," McCall said, quietly. "How's that coffee coming along?"

"Ready," she said and rushed back to the kitchen. She poured out the dark roast blend into Cambria Stoneware mugs. McCall had sat down at the dining table. He had taken a small magnifying glass from a drawer in the table. Allison returned with the coffee. McCall took a sip of his while studying the map. She sat down beside him.

"Are you making any progress?"

"I'm getting some details, but they don't make sense to me yet," McCall said. "The map has some provocative names on it. Do they mean anything to you?"

She looked at the map and nodded emphatically. "Yes, they do! Kyle was really taken with the names in the caverns. He liked '*The Boneyard*' and the '*Temple of the Sun*'. The '*Tarantula Lagoon*' was his favorite. He wanted to visit there before we left the geysers behind."

"How far did he get?" McCall asked.

"He is a born adventurer. I know he wanted to explore more of the underground passages to see where they led to, but Emily kept nagging him to abandon that quest. She just wanted to return to the surface and breathe the fresh air again."

"This name jumped out at me on the map," McCall said. "*Chisholm Trail Park*. It's a recent addition."

"Kyle wanted to go there," Allison said with growing excitement. "It reminded him of the westerns he grew up on. Emily is a tomboy who was always climbing apple trees at home, but Kyle was into his western myths. Wyatt Earp and Bat Masterson were his heroes. Gary Cooper and Shane would be high on that list. *High Noon* was his favorite movie. He would have wanted to visit a place that had the name '*Chisholm Trail*' in it. I'll bet you always loved westerns. It fits your persona."

McCall smiled. "I must admit I had some heroes growing up."

"Who were they?"

"I loved Burt Lancaster when he appeared in '*Elmer Gantry*'. Steve McQueen in '*The Great Escape*' and '*The Sand Pebbles*.'"

"You must have had some favorite television stars too?"

"Maybe '*The Man from U.N.C.L.E*' and Clint Walker as '*Cheyenne*.'"

"Where did the name '*The Equalizer*' come from?" she asked.

"Just a nickname I seemed to have acquired over the years."

"It suits you," she said. "Are you going to equalize the odds against me?"

"I am going to try. Does that name '*Chisholm Trail*' mean anything to you?"

Allison shook her head. "Not a thing."

"There are more provocative names on the map. Maybe they will mean something."

"What are they?"

"How about '*Restless Hollows*' or '*Rattlesnake Canyon*?'"

She shrugged. "Just names on the map. I don't know what any of them mean."

"Take another look," McCall urged.

Allison took the map in both hands. He handed her the magnifying glass. She studied the names. "For a treasure map, these names are pretty obscure. I guess I was hoping to find '*Long John Silver*' or some mention of '*Treasure Island.*'"

"Just take your time."

Allison shook her head. "I'm sorry. None of these names register with me."

McCall took back the map and refolded it. "Nothing to be sorry about," he said. "I would be surprised if they meant anything to you. It was worth a shot.'

"But the map could lead us to my children," Allison said, sounding distraught.

"It will. We have to find the right series of caverns that will lead us back down into in the labyrinth."

"When can we do that?"

"Right now is as good a time as any," McCall said, softly.

XXXV
LABYRINTH

McCALL FINISHED his coffee. Allison joined him, shrugging on a mountain classic water-resistant jacket. The nights were getting chillier. McCall drove back to the *Plymouth Caverns*. He parked and Allison waited while he had a word with the Police Officer who was on duty at the caverns. McCall had all the paperwork that the Rescue Teams had provided him with including the revised map which he also showed to the cop on duty. The Officer advised him that the caverns had been temporality closed to the public at this time. McCall explained the circumstances. He showed him the map and the various blueprints and his authorization to be there. The cop handed them back.

"You couldn't pay me enough to go into those underground tunnels," he said. "But if you're willing risk it, go ahead. The entrance is behind those traffic barricades."

"One of the Rescue Team members accompanied me," McCall said when Allison moved over to him. "She is also going underground."

"On your head be it," the Officer said.

He returned to the line of traffic that was waiting for him. McCall and Allison moved past the plastic cones to the entrance to the labyrinth. McCall knew there was no use in his insisting that Allison should not accompany him. He accessed the map and indicated the tunnel entrance.

"These rough-hewn stones lead to the stairs that descend down into the abyss," he said. "One of the rescue workers explained the necessity of adhering to strict safety guidelines in the tunnels. The air intakes are equipped with the anti-intrusion grilles that protect entry of debris. The plasma orange Safety Helmets must be worn at all times below ground. Some of the rescue workers also wear lamp clips and a vision attachment."

"Fine with me," Allison said.

Both McCall and Allison donned their protective helmets. McCall took out the handheld two-way Motorola VHF Analog Radio.

"We can keep in touch with these portable radios," he said. "You may find some difficulty with the reception down here in these underground caverns, but I think the signal will carry even if it is sporadic." He handed one of the radios to Allison and put the other one in the pocket of his leather jacket. "Ready to do this?"

"As ready as I will ever be," she said, but her determination had not wavered.

"Stay with me." McCall said.

Slowly they descended the huge stones into the caverns. After forty feet they came to an elevator set in the stone wall. Allison was astounded. "What's an elevator doing down here?"

"I came upon one of them when I first accessed the tunnels," McCall said. "It won't travel very far, but we need all the help we can get."

He opened the elevator cage and they moved into it. McCall pushed a button and the elevator descended at a rapid rate. Then they came to a halt. The elevator door opened. McCall and Allison found themselves in another underground tunnel. McCall pushed the *Up* button and the elevator rose to the rocky caverns.

"That was pretty cool!" Allison said.

"Stick with me," McCall said.

Blue-tinged spider's webs wove around them. That led down to more of the underground crypts. McCall held Allison's hand to stop her falling into the abyss. The passageways twisted like a serpent in the echoing necropolis. McCall estimated they had traveled the steep chasms for at least five miles. Finally they came to the end of the tunnel where large stones were chipped, broken and splitting. McCall and Allison stepped out into a tunnel that stretched out before them. As McCall had prophesied the two-way reception in the caverns was erratic. 70,000 Lumen LED

500-Watt area lights were set at intervals along the main tunnel. Allison shivered and pulled her coat tighter around her.

"Cold in here," she murmured.

"It'll get even colder now that we're underground," McCall said.

"I feel like a character out of Jules Verne's '*Journey to the Center of the Earth*'," she said.

"Remember to stay with me," McCall urged. "No wandering off."

"I'm not going to leave your side," she promised. "Where would I go? We're in this adventure together, aren't we?"

"Yes, we are," he said.

A natural formation greeted them as they moved down the echoing tunnel which was shaped like a *Bashful Elephant* carved out of the limestone rocks.

"We're in the right place," McCall said. "There can't be another *Bashful Elephant Sculpture* down here that looks as if it is hiding its face."

"It does look remarkably like that," Allison agreed.

They emerged fully into the massive caverns that stretched out before them. Huge stalactites and stalagmites hung down like obscene fingers of serrated rock. Several grottos could be seen that had swirls of fantastic colors. The ceiling at this point was honeycombed with other caverns that led off at tangents. McCall lit flares that he placed on the cavern floor.

"So we don't lose our way out of this maze," he explained.

"Good thinking," Allison murmured. She had been down in the caverns many times before, but she was awed by the enormity of the shelves of rocks that surrounded them. "I am seriously creeped out," she admitted.

"Nothing to be afraid of down here," McCall assured her. "Just stay close to me."

"As if I would leave your side," she said.

But after an hour of fruitless searching McCall could see that Allison had become dejected and disheartened. He knew they could inspect these caverns for several more hours and come up with nothing at all. It was a chance that McCall had known was in the cards. He had searched these caverns himself before and come up with nothing. The rescue workers had prophesied that this would happen to them. J.D. Shannon and Mark Washington in particular had warned McCall of the dangers of getting hopelessly lost in the caves. He was at the point of calling the search off. They could return tomorrow, but the longer Allison's children were gone the more likely it was that they were longer alive.

It was Allison who first saw the small figures clinging to a shelf of limestone twenty feet above them. She clutched McCall's arm hard enough to break it. "Up there!" she exclaimed in a voice hoarse with emotion.

McCall followed her gaze. The figures of Kyle and Emily were dwarfed on the spur of rock above them. They had not seen their mother yet. They were trying to navigate a narrow passageway that might lead them back down into the caverns.

"It looks as if they're trying to reach one of the cave entrances," McCall said, urgently. "These stone stairs lead right up to the place where they are trapped. Don't move from this spot."

He ran down one of the tunnels.

Allison shouted to her children: "Kyle! Emily!"

Finally Kyle looked down at the small figure of his mother and clutched his sister's arm.

"There's Mom!" He took another precarious step to her and shouted: "We're here, Mom! Trapped on this rock!"

From Allison's perspective her children were swallowed up in the shadows. Kyle held onto Emily. Both of them were clinging to life.

"Just hold tight to your sister!" Allison shouted back. "A friend of mine is coming to get you."

McCall climbed up the rough-hewn stone stairs which twisted around him. The stone steps were slippery and treacherous. Twice McCall stumbled and almost pitched down into the abyss below. The tunnels branched out in tangents the higher McCall ascended. He noted that there were more caverns at regular intervals. The grottos disappeared into the darkness around him. He had accessed his Motorola Zebra radio to guide him part of the way. The signal was sketchy as it threaded in and out, but it guided McCall until he came to more stone steps.

McCall caught his breath while he got his bearings. He didn't know whether to climb higher or to access one of the cavern entrances. He had to judge where he was in the maze which was confusing. He had marked various pieces of rock to guide him, but the tunnels were tricky to navigate. Finally he came to an immense cavern that was sheathed in darkness. McCall stepped carefully off the stone staircase. He plunged down into a passageway which came to a sudden end. He emerged out onto the rocks that clung precariously to the side of the mountain. It was a thirty-foot drop at this point back down to the cavern floor.

Kyle and Emily hung precariously onto some boulders that resembled stiletto daggers. They were cut off from the cave entrance by some thirty feet. McCall clambered over the rocks and came to the same place where the children were trapped. There was no going back. A fissure had opened up that at this point cutting off McCall's escape plan.

There was a danger that he would be marooned with them.

"We're too afraid to move!" Kyle shouted up at McCall. "The shelves of rock are splitting up. They won't support of our weight much longer."

His voice echoed across the abyss that separated him and his sister from the main cave entrance. McCall could see immediately the dilemma the children were facing. The rocks had crumbled around them until they were just splinters of granite. McCall noted the entrances to some of the caverns plunged right down to the valley floor. It was thirty feet from where Kyle and Emily were huddled. McCall needed to jump down to the sheer rock face to reach them.

"Brace yourselves!" he shouted. "Can you do that for me?"

"We'll try!" Kyle shouted back.

"I'll climb down to you!"

"Okay!"

Kyle gripped Emily's hand and held it tight.

McCall climbed down to where the needle-pointed rocks were situated. He gathered his courage around him and leaped down the side of the mountain. He landed precariously on the diamond-shaped rock. Kyle reached out to catch him. McCall hugged both him and Emily to his side.

"Nice jump!" Kyle said.

"Far out!" Emily said.

McCall felt his heart pounding in his chest. He looked down at the panorama of rocks that tumbled below them to the valley floor. The outcrop of rocks had not been far for him to leap, but the fall could have been treacherous. He knew that he and the children were not out of danger yet. It was another fifteen feet to where the lower cave entrance was situated.

Which was a long way down.

McCall released the children and held them at arm's length. "We can't go back up," he said. "There is a ledge of rock just below us which we could reach, but it will mean jumping down to it. Are you up for that?"

Kyle looked down at the stiletto of the rocks. He swallowed hard and nodded. "I'm up for it. There's an apple tree I used to climb when we lived in Maine. I could go up and down that apple tree in ten seconds flat!"

"Sounds good to me." McCall looked to Emily. "Are you good for this?"

Emily looked frightened as she glanced down at the abyss.

"I can't move!" she said, but her voice was still strong.

"I'll hand you down to us," McCall promised her. "Your brother goes first. Okay?"

"Okay," she said.

McCall took hold of Kyle's hand and moved right to the edge of the boulder. "Like you were climbing that apple tree in Maine," he said.

"Piece of cake," Kyle said with false bravado.

"On my count of three," McCall said. He held Kyle's hand and counted down. "Three, two, one…"

He and Kyle leapt down from the boulder and landed on the shelf of rock. McCall grabbed the boy, but he didn't need his help. He looked up at McCall with a look of exhilaration.

"Told you I could do it!" he said.

"You did great!" McCall indicated the cave entrance which was twenty feet from them. "Climb down to that cave entrance. You see it there?"

"I got it!"

"Be careful. These rocks are pretty treacherous."

"I won't fall!"

"Wait for us there."

Kyle carefully made his way to the cavern entrance. McCall was still precariously perched on the flat rock. He looked up at Emily and reached up for her.

"Your turn!"

But Emily just shook her head. "I can't do it!"

"Yes, you can," McCall said. "I'll catch you the same way I caught your brother. You heard Kyle. A piece of cake. You don't want to be braver than him, do you?"

"No way!" she said.

"Just jump down to me," McCall said.

Emily looked down at the shelf below her. She took a step closer to it.

"You won't let me fall?" she pleaded with him.

"I won't."

The young girl had gathered her courage. Finally, she jumped down to where McCall was waiting. He didn't even need to catch her because she scooted right away into his waiting arms. She also looked exhilarated.

"That was a blast!" she said, breathlessly.

"Glad you liked it!" McCall murmured.

"Stay with me," he said. "The cave entrance is right over there!"

Emily took his hand and held it tightly. McCall moved from the jumble of rocks with her to where Kyle was waiting. He clutched his sister's hand, but she pulled away from him.

"I was fine by myself!" Emily insisted. "I don't need to hold onto to my brother's hand!"

"Suit yourself!" Kyle retorted. "See how far you get in those tunnels without my help!"

"Save the bickering until we're on firmer ground," McCall suggested. "Both of you hold my hands!"

The children, somewhat chastened, took McCall's hands. Together they entered one of the caverns. A long, winding staircase faced them. It descended down into the bowels of the earth. McCall climbed down the descending staircase with the children. The cold limestone walls seemed to close in on them. The temperature had dropped at least twenty-five degrees. More rock walls encased them with psychedelic patterns that were embedded in the bedrock. McCall and the children descended together down the various levels until finally they emerged out from the cavern. More distorted images greeted them in the almost lunar landscape. Allison greeted her children with hugs and kisses, which was fine with Emily, but Kyle was ready to go back into the caverns and do some more exploring.

"Where did you find them?" Allison asked, joyfully.

"They were sitting on a shelf of rock that was isolated away from the caves," McCall said. "I don't know how they even got there."

"We found the cave entrance after we had been climbing in circles," Kyle said. "We wanted to see how far up the mountain we were. We thought there was a route that we could take to reach another cave entrance."

"But it was an optical illusion," Emily said. "That's the right word, isn't it?"

"Yeah, that's it," Kyle said. "The rocks were shaped like pointed daggers. We thought we could get below them, but there was no way that was going to happen."

"That was when we realized that we were trapped," Emily said.

"What were you doing on those rocks anyway?" Allison demanded. "You were supposed to stay where I could see you!"

"We got turned around," Kyle said, defensively. "Emily stumbled and almost fell, but I grabbed hold of her."

"I could have got up by myself!" she said, glaring at her brother. "I didn't need my big brother to come to my rescue!"

"And when we looked around," Kyle said, ignoring his sister's outburst, "we found that we were alone."

Now it was Allison's turn to be defensive. "I thought you kids were right behind me! I've always told you to stay with me in those caverns."

"We were… what is the right word, Em?"

"Disoriented."

"That's it," Kyle said. "You were supposed to be right there with us, Mom, but Emily tripped and fell on her face."

"Sure, blame it on me! "Emily said, flaring. "You were the one who was lagging behind."

"Maybe now isn't the time to argue among yourselves," McCall suggested, mildly.

"You're right!" Allison acknowledged, a little abashed. "We need to find our way to that flight of stairs that leads up to the surface."

"Those stairs look secure, but they're not," McCall said. "There are gaps in the stone. So we need to stay together."

"We'll follow your lead," Allison promised.

McCall led them to the entrance to the cave.

* * * *

Up on the shelf of rock a man could be seen standing, looking down at McCall and Allison. He was an ominous, sepulchral figure who stood motionless near one of the cave entrances. Allison's children could be heard talking non-stop as they clamored for attention. McCall herded them and Allison to one of the entrances to the caverns. For just a moment he looked up at where he had rescued them from the flat piece of rock. He thought he saw a figure silhouetted in the shadows, but when he looked back again the figure had vanished. He dismissed the momentary illusion. He moved over to where Allison and her family were standing at the cave entrance. He joined them, indicating the stone steps that led back into the darkness.

"This flight of stairs should lead us back up to the elevator that we took before," McCall said. "But there may be other caverns that will bar our path. In that case we'll have to retrace our steps and find another way to the surface."

"We'll follow your lead," Allison said, taking charge of her children.

"Stay close to me," McCall said.

"We're not going to leave your side, believe me," Allison promised. "You got us this far."

McCall stopped, sensing again a presence in the caverns. He turned around in a hundred-degree angle. Allison clutched his arm, pulling Kyle and Emily closer to her.

"What is it?" she asked, anxiously.

"I thought I saw a figure standing on one of the ledges above us."

Allison followed his gaze. "I don't see anyone."

"He was only visible for a moment," McCall said. "But he was there."

"Maybe one of the rescue teams you told me about," she said.

"Those teams are working down in one of the caverns," he said. "They wouldn't come this far up the mountain."

"Then who was it?" Allison asked, anxiously.

"I don't know," McCall said. "But I feel as if someone had just walked over my grave."

"That's creepy," Emily said.

"Everything to you is creepy," Kyle said.

"Children, behave yourselves," Allison said.

"I may have been imagining it," McCall said to calm her fears. But he realized in that moment that they weren't alone on the mountain. "Just a trick of the light. Nothing for you to worry about." He turned back to Kyle and Emily. "You kids stay close to me."

"Yes, sir," Kyle said, and he nudged his sister. "Just keep holding my hand!"

"It's sweaty and clammy!" Emily protested.

"That's enough!" Allison said, admonishing her children. "We're lucky that we have Mr. McCall to guide us."

"Let's get out of here as quickly as we can," McCall said.

He entered the entrance to the caverns with Alison and her children. They were soon swallowed up in the darkness as they ascended up toward the surface.

The sinister figure who had been waiting for them on the side of the mountain stepped back out of the shadows.

He could afford to wait a little longer.

Allison and her family would be dead soon enough.

XXXVI
AFTERMATH

McCall and Allison returned to her apartment where she insisted that Kyle and Emily get ready for bed immediately. They protested loudly, but Allison had been adamant. They'd had enough excitement for one day to last them a lifetime. She escorted McCall to her front door.

"What are you going to do now?" she asked him.

There was apprehension in her voice. McCall took her hands and held them tightly.

"Evangeline Palmer is still missing," he said. "She left me a note saying she was returning to the underground caverns. I need to find her."

"I keep expecting her to walk through that front door," Allison said. She regarded McCall frankly. "But I have a suspicion that you know what has happened to her."

"I might have an idea," he admitted, "but right now it's just a theory. I need to check it out."

"Evangeline has been my best friend forever," Allison said. "I am fearful that something terrible has happened to her."

"Leave it with me," McCall said. "Take care of your children. They need you right now. They've been through a lot."

"You'll get in touch with me?" she asked him.

"As soon as I have some news for you."

She released his hands. "God bless you, Mr. McCall," she said softly.

And she kissed him gently on the cheek.

"I'll be in touch with you," he said and moved through the door that led out to the street.

McCall returned immediately to where the uniformed Police Officer was stopping traffic. Two more uniformed cops had pulled in to assist him. A line of vehicles was being turned away. McCall parked some distance away. He realized that he wasn't going to be allowed access to the caverns. He would need to find another way into the underground labyrinth. He still had the Motorola VHF analog radio with him. He left the police activity behind and plunged into the dense foliage around him.

McCall made his way through the rubble-strewn boulders and the vegetation that clung to the side of the mountain. He was retracing his route to where he had found the cave hidden in the woods. It took him longer than he had anticipated. The dense foliage crowded in around him. Then he came to a familiar landmark, the *Bashful Stone Elephant* buried in the woods. He reached the willow tree that was nestled in the white oak and red maple trees. A few yards further he came to the corkscrew willow tree which twisted horizontally and then forked vertically. He knew he was in the right place. The foliage wrapped around his legs as he plunged deeper into the dense foliage. He still had the rough map with its circuitous route through the boulders.

He broke free from the dense undergrowth. The mountain towered above him. It did take him long to find the cave entrance. It was hidden in a series of rocks that ended at the mouth of the cave itself. McCall entered and descended down a long tunnel that led down into the heart of the mausoleum. He stepped out into another tunnel buried in the echoing necropolis.

McCall found himself in yet another underground passageway that led directly into the mountain. The labyrinth that branched out before him was dank and dripping with moisture. He noted again the LED 500-watt area lights were strategically placed at various points in the tunnel ceiling. He descended down another steep incline. Frozen icicles were honeycombed throughout the passageway. He ran down the echoing tunnel and emerged out into the massive caverns.

They towered a hundred feet above him. The blue *Spider's Webs* caught the refracted light. He found another *Stone Bashful Elephant* in the rocks, its trunk wrapped around one of the dagger-shaped boulders. More eerie obelisks greeted him like malignant growths that had taken root in the caverns ahead. There was something sinister in the way the various cocoons snaked through the boulders. There were dozens of them like ancient mummies buried in virtual layers with their bandages intact. McCall felt like a grave robber who had stumbled onto the ancient resting place of *Pharaoh Amenhotep*. He recognized at least a dozen wooden bridges that spanned a turgid lake. He realized that he had come at least a mile underground to have reached the lake.

The silence had gathered around him. It was intense and almost intangible. It gave McCall an uneasy, queasy feeling. He had expected to hear faintly the murmurs of voices from the rescue team. But there was nothing. He took out his Glock 19 pistol and ran through the cathedral-sized ceiling which towered high above him. Stalactites and stalagmites had formed a web of intricate patterns around his running figure. He reached the lake that lapped gently in the stillness. He ran across the first of the wooden bridges. He plunged through an immense tunnel of rock that momentarily barred his path. He emerged on to another small lake that was nestled in the catacombs. He crossed the arched trestle bridge he found there. That had led him back to the caverns where he had spoken to the rescue workers working in the underground caverns. The lighting in the cavernous space was sporadic. The overhead LED 500-Watt work area lights had been dimmed. They gave out a sorrowful, melancholy aura that permeated the murky gloom.

That was when McCall came upon the first body.

Carlos Berkeley had been struck in the head and had collapsed to the rocky floor. McCall turned him over. His lifeless eyes stared up as if he had been betrayed. There was another body fifty feet away. McCall moved to where Lucas Slater was lying prone on the ground. His face had been caved in from a savage blow to the head. There was nothing McCall could do for either of them. Then he heard a groan from behind him in the fractured shadows. He ran forward and saw that it was J.D. Shannon, who was still alive.

McCall knelt beside him. He helped the rescue worker to sit up. He was dazed and disoriented, but he did not appear to be badly hurt. There was a nasty bruise under his left eye where he had been struck. McCall held onto him to stop him from falling. The rescue worker looked up as if he didn't know where he was.

"I'd call the paramedics and have them meet us outside the caverns."

"What happened to me?"

"You were attacked. The assailant must have fled when I entered the underground complex."

J.D. was still disoriented. "Someone grabbed me and dragged me down to the ground. I never even saw his face. He tried to kill me."

"But he didn't succeed," McCall said. "I want you to take a couple of deep breaths."

J.D. nodded. He looked behind him. He noted Carlos Berkeley's body lying in a pool of blood. "Carlos Berkeley is dead," McCall said. "So is Lucas Slater. Killed by the same intruder you encountered."

"But why?" J.D. gasped. "Who could have done such a terrible thing?"

"I don't have an answer for you right now," McCall said. "I'm going to find out. Can you stand up?"

J.D. nodded and allowed McCall to help him back onto his feet. There was the sound of running footsteps. McCall whirled around to see Mark Washington run up to them. He took in the scene with none of his usual snide remarks. He looked over at Carlos Berkeley's body.

"My God," he said, softly.

"Do you know happened here?" McCall asked him.

"I heard a commotion when I re-entered the caverns," Washington said. "I had to go up to the surface to get another map that Carlos had requested. Is he dead?"

"He is," McCall said.

"And Lucas Slater too?"

"Both of them."

Washington looked at J.D. Shannon. "Are you okay?"

"I'm okay," J.D. said.

"You look as if you hit a brick wall."

"It felt that way," J.D. said.

His left eye was slowly closing. Washington reached over.

"I've got hold of you," Washington said. "Lean on me."

J.D. nodded, still stunned by what had happened.

"Who else was with you down here in the catacombs?" McCall asked him.

"There were six of us," J.D. said. He had regained some of his composure. "Two of the rescue teams had just returned to the surface. It's disorienting down here in the caverns. We usually try to rotate with the Delta Force Teams."

"We had just passed the baton to the next team of rescuers," Washington said.

"Both of you need to return to the surface," McCall said.

"I'll call the paramedics and have them meet us on the surface," Washington said.

He moved off into the darkness and accessed his cell phone.

McCall still had hold of J.D. "Can you stand up?"

"I can try," J.D. murmured.

McCall gently hauled him up to his feet. He was unsteady, but he nodded. "I'm all right."

He kept hold of J.D.'s arm. "You need medical attention."

"My colleagues are dead," J.D. Shannon said, and shook his head. "What kind of monster could have carried out such a barbaric atrocity?"

"I'll find out," McCall said.

Washington returned quickly. "I spoke to the paramedics. They'll be waiting for us when we get back to the surface."

"Good enough," McCall said.

"Where will you be?" Washington asked him.

"I believe the killer is still down in these caverns."

"Do you have any idea who he is?" J.D. asked.

"I have an idea who it could be," McCall said. "If I'm right, I need to find him. I believe he is keeping my friend Evangeline Palmer a prisoner down here in the crypts."

J.D. was still traumatized. McCall took hold of his arm. "Stay with me."

"I've got him," Washington assured him.

McCall let Mark Washington and J.D. Shannon move with him to the rough-hewn stairs that led up to the surface.

Evangeline's breathing had become a nightmare. A plastic bag had been placed over her head which only allowed her to take breaths every other second. As if she were blowing out a candle. The muscles in her neck and shoulders had been traumatized and ached fiercely. Pain throbbed in her head. Her entire world had become centered on her labored breathing. Nothing else mattered. The plastic bag over her head deflated and refilled again with air like a bellows. The continual expansion and contraction of her lungs threatened to send her into cardiac arrest. She had tried to wrench the plastic bag from her head without success. It was tied in such a way that allowed her to maintain the panicked breathing she needed to sustain her life. It was a monotonous exercise that kept repeating itself over and over again until she thought she would scream.

Then the plastic bag was suddenly removed from her head.

Evangeline gasped for air. She took several deep breaths, her lungs heaving. Finally she regulated her breathing to the point where it was not painful and looked around her.

The scenery was magnificent.

She was stranded in an immense cavern beneath the earth. Confetti-like splinters of rock towered above her that were several stories high. They resembled faces cut into the granite like macabre *Carnival Masks from Hell*. Dripping icicles like pointed daggers hung down from the high ceiling over her head. In Evangeline's fevered mind they resembled the faces of a *wolf* and a *Peregrine Falcon*. Totem pole structures reached down for her from the vaulted ceiling over her head like malevolent tentacles. She observed that the cocoon-like protuberances were scattered throughout the caverns. Spectral tentacles hung down in intricate *Spider's Webs* above her that gave out an eerie blue light. These Christmas-tree-like squibs were like serrated confetti that surrounded her, then disappeared into the murky gloom.

Evangeline didn't see the shadowy figure that had approached her.

He moved past the guard rail that closed off a wrought-iron gate made of galvanized steel. It towered above Evangeline for twenty feet. A heavy combination padlock closed off the gate. The path behind it fell away into the shadows. The intruder pointed a Smith & Wesson .38 revolver at her. Its barrel carried a five-shot capacity.

Evangeline had been unconscious when the intruder had carried her into the underground vault. He had dumped her on her ass like she was a sack of potatoes. She had stirred finally at that point and tried to crawl to her feet. He struck her with a haymaker punch that completely jarred her.

That was when he had put the plastic bag over her head. He had tied it in such a way that it would inflate and collapse every one-and-a-half seconds. Evangeline had stumbled down onto her knees. She had gasped for breath. The intruder had been careful not to let the plastic bag strangle her. The rhythmic pattern of her gasped breaths had been carefully measured. After more seconds of this torture he had taken pity on her and untied the plastic bag from around her head. She had collapsed to her knees again, gasping for each breath. She stayed like that for a long time. The intruder gave her some space. Finally, she managed to get to her feet. She took stock of her surroundings in the sinister underground cavern. The metal guardrail ended a few feet from her. Evangeline was unsteady on her feet, but she was determined to confront her tormentor. He moved closer to her in the malignant darkness. The .38 snub-nosed revolver in his hand did not waver an inch from her body. She noted her captor was a good-looking man in his early thirties with a strong face and startling blue eyes. Laughter-lines that were etched around his face crinkled when he smiled.

Evangeline had never seen him before in her life.

She faced her tormentor in the unnatural blue light that permeated the underground mausoleum. Her voice sounded hoarse and rasping to her in the sudden stillness.

"Who are you?" she demanded. "Why have you kept me a prisoner here?"

"You're not a prisoner," the young man said, affably. "You can leave here at any time once I have concluded my business."

"What business is that?"

"You'll find out."

"You tried to strangle me!" Evangeline almost shouted at him. Her voice was shrill and strident. "You tied a bag around my head! I was gasping for air!"

"I can always put the plastic bag back over head," he offered. "But I thought you might like to take a break. It must be lonely down here in these underground crypts. Kind of eerie and surreal with phantoms reaching out for you from out of the darkness."

Evangeline's voice was a little less shrill now. She had regained her composure, but her breathing still rasped in her throat. She looked past her tormentor to where the guardrail disappeared into the shadows.

"I guess you wondered where I came from," the young man said as if they were having a pleasant conversation. "The heavy wrought-iron metal gate behind me is at least twenty feet high. I have the only key to the steel combination padlock. I promise to set you free once my work is done here."

Evangeline needed to keep this psychopath talking. She edged a little closer to him, glancing down at the Smith & Wesson .38 revolver in his hand. It had not wavered even a millimeter.

"What work? What are you talking about?" she demanded.

"Payback," he said tersely. His mood had swung from elation to being morose and melancholy. Evangeline didn't think it would take much for the young man to suddenly become a raging maniac. She would have to watch herself carefully with him.

"What kind of a payback?"

"The emotional stress you have caused for both of us. Don't think for a minute that I don't know what are doing," he said in the same friendly tone. "Get him to talk to you. You'll have a better chance to turn the tables on him if he opens to you. Is this the game you're playing?"

"I am not playing any games with you," she said.

"That's a good thing. It won't work on me, Evangeline my sweet. I know everything that I am doing. But do try to get into my head. I'm enjoying the experience."

"We've broken the ice now," Evangeline said. "You know you can talk to me."

"I am not going to play your little game!" he suddenly shouted. "When are you going to learn that? Are you going to make a grab for my gun?"

"I wouldn't do that," she said, as if offended. "That would be suicide. I just want to talk to you."

Now he was back to being a sane, rational human being again. "You want to find out what makes me tick. Sure, I get it. All the repressed emotions that are swirling around in my head. But you don't get around me that easily. By the way, I loved your tattoos. Especially the prowling black panther and the naked girl with the folded wings wearing fishnet stockings."

"I usually have my shirt unbuttoned down to my navel," Evangeline admitted, pulling her shirt out to expose her large breasts. She was wearing black lace panties and nothing else. "I never wear a bra. What's the point of having great breasts if you don't show them off? Was this what you wanted to see?"

He laughed as if he was enjoying her attempt to seduce him. "Nice try. I must say you're very beautiful. Another time I would take you up on your offer. But not tonight. I still have unfinished business to care of."

"What kind of business?" she asked, suddenly frightened again.

"Personal," he said and suddenly he was raging at her again. "I don't care to share my thoughts and fears with you!"

"Okay," Evangeline said, quickly. "Fair enough. But at least tell me your name. You can do that, can't you?"

Suddenly he was introspective again. He nodded. "Sure, I can do that. It's a reasonable request."

When he didn't continue, she asked him: "So what is it?"

"My name is David," he said. "David Carmichael."

The name didn't mean anything at all to Evangeline.

"We haven't met before, have we?" she asked, just to keep him talking.

"No, we haven't met before. Maybe we'll get acquainted sometime in the future. But I doubt that will happen. Hostages usually come to a sticky end, don't they? That would be too bad. I kind of like you. You've got sass and style."

Sudden terror again clawed at Evangeline's throat. She tried to disguise it with a devil-may-care-attitude, but she knew that David saw right through her bravado.

"What are you going to do to me?"

"Interesting question," he said, as if he was weighing the pros and cons of her dilemma. "Haven't decided yet. You're going to stay right here until my business has been concluded."

Evangeline dreaded to ask him the question that was on her lips, but she needed to ask it anyway. "What business is that?"

"Leveling the play field," he said. "Too many loose ends. The rescue teams had their own agenda, but unfortunately they didn't play by the rules."

She was ahead of him now. "You killed them, didn't you?"

"Only two of them," he said, reasonably. "Carlos Berkeley threatened me. I had to take him out. Lucas Slater came to his rescue. Bad idea. I had to cut his throat. There were others on the rescue team. I had to get out of there fast so there was no time to finish the job. But they're not going anywhere. If they have returned to the surface they'll be back to mourn their fallen colleagues. It's dark and scary in those underground tunnels. I'll just bide my time. Another opportunity will present itself."

"But why kill them?" Evangeline demanded, her voice catching in her throat. "They did nothing to you. The rescue teams are there in the tunnels to help people."

"They got in my way," David said, nonchalantly. "Another bad idea."

"They were just doing their jobs," she said, helplessly.

"That's true. I'll give you that. But let's talk about your savior, Robert McCall."

More warning signs flashed through Evangeline's mind. "I hardly know him. He is a stranger to me."

"You're lying!" David suddenly shouted at her. "I think he means a great deal to you. He's your knight errant, isn't he? Riding in on his white charger to rescue his damsel-in-distress. But you know what? When I get through with Robert McCall he won't be anything special to anyone. Just a failed do-gooder who tried to do the right thing and failed miserably."

"Why are you doing all this?" Evangeline asked in desperation.

David moved right up to her, squeezing her face. The gun in his hand didn't waver an inch. "Because there is nothing to stop me. Once McCall is dead, I'll come back for you, Evangeline. You never know, I might take pity on you and set you free. It will depend how you treat me. I don't mean sexual favors or special privileges. Just two human beings looking out for each other."

He stepped away from her. Evangeline knew now that David Carmichael was seriously deranged. She would need to play along with him and gain his trust until she could escape from this nightmare.

"I'll do anything you say," she said.

He had contained his rage now. He just smiled and nodded. "I know that you will."

He moved away, fading back into the shadows. Evangeline had a moment of sheer panic. "Don't leave down here!"

"Feeling a little lonely?" he asked, his voice echoing in the stillness. "That's completely understandable. But you won't be alone for long. Then we'll have another chat. I look forward to it."

"Please!" Evangeline begged. "Stay with me. I want to understand where you're coming from!"

"From a dark place," he said and hissed the words at her. "Don't you get that by now?" He grinned at her from the darkness. "As Arnold Schwarzenegger would say: '*I'll be back!*'"

Evangeline was afraid to go after him. She heard the key turn in the lock. She ran forward but David Carmichael had moved through the wrought-iron gate and closed it behind him.

Evangeline pulled on the heavy-duty combination padlock to no avail. She glanced up at the wrought-iron fence that towered twenty feet above her. The path through the caverns disappeared into the spectral shadows. The wrought-iron gate ended abruptly a few feet from her.

She was trapped.

Evangeline sank down to the ground, hugging her arms around her body.

But she was already planning how to escape from this madman.

XXXVII
DEATH MATCH

WHEN MCCALL EMERGED from the mountain peak with J.D. Shannon and Mark Washington he found the paramedics waiting for them. An ambulance had backed into the space between tall oaks and the paramedics swarmed around the injured rescue workers. They treated J.D. Shannon for tachycardia to lower his heart rate and attached him to an IV drip medication. Two patrol cars pulled up and four uniformed Police Officers got out in a hurry. McCall took Mark Washington's arm and moved away from the paramedics and the police activity. The rescue worker looked back at J.D. Shannon and watched the paramedics go to work on him.

"J.D. and I go back a long way," he said. "We graduated from Med School together."

"He is going to be all right," McCall said. "Is there another way to access the underground tunnels?"

"Yeah, there's another entrance about half-a-mile further down the mountain," Washington said. "Tough to see it from here. I marked it down on that map I gave you."

"Show me the map again," McCall asked.

He glanced up as the Police Officers moved onto the scene to where the paramedics were working on J.D. Shannon. McCall and Washington were momentarily shielded from them. Washington took one of his maps and held it up for McCall.

"We're here," he said. "The entrance to the caverns is right here. You wouldn't see it if you weren't looking for it. It's located about a hundred yards up the mountain slope. There's a cave entrance that is partially hidden by the mountain."

"I was there not long ago," McCall said. "I think I can find it again. Can I have this map?"

"Sure, be my guest," Washington said.

He refolded the map and handed it over to McCall. The rescue worker looked over at the paramedics and the Police Officers. Washington shook his head. "I can't believe Carlos Berkeley and Lucas Slater are dead."

"The authorities will want to hear your story," McCall said. "Stall them if you can."

"I'll do my best. What will you do now?"

"Go back down into the underground tunnels. Keep the cops busy. I was never here above ground."

"I'll play it anyway you want," Washington said. "All I care about now is my partner J.D. pulling through."

"He'll be okay," McCall said.

"Are you really going back into the tunnels?" Washington asked him.

"I am."

"Good luck."

Washington moved back to where the paramedics were working. McCall ran over to where his Jaguar was parked. He was running out of time. Evangeline would be dead unless he pulled off a miracle. He slid into the vehicle and gunned it away before any of the Police Officers had time to see him.

McCall was pretty sure where the entrance was located on the mountainside. He had accessed it before when he had followed the mysterious figure through the trees. There was no doubt in his mind who that figure had been. The forest track was off the beaten track about three-quarters up the side of the mountain. This time McCall had no trouble finding the right place. Washington's map guided him through the familiar cluster of white oaks and red maple trees. He parked the Jaguar and climbed up the rugged peak until he came to the hidden cave entrance. If McCall hadn't been looking for the location he would have never seen it. He descended down into the underground cavern.

The prior time McCall had been down there he had not ventured far into the cave, but now it was a different story. He moved up the steep gradient and was immediately brought up short. He came to another elevator in the mountain. It was positioned just below the ground level entrance. McCall pressed the *Down* button. The elevator door opened immediately. He entered and the door closed them behind him. McCall pushed the *Down* button. The high-speed elevator descended at an alarming rate. It rocketed down for 762 feet and then came to an abrupt stop. The elevator door opened automatically. McCall stepped out. The door closed and the elevator ascended.

McCall took stock of where he was. Another passageway led down farther into the necropolis. More of the Lumen 500-Watt area lights were strung along the tunnel. McCall took his Glock 19 pistol out of his pocket and ran the length of the passageway. He emerged from the side of the mountain and found himself not far from where he had encountered the wooden bridges that spanned the turgid lake.

The view around him was staggering.

McCall passed under frozen waterfalls that seemed to be suspended in time. The cathedral-sized ceilings that towered over his head had to be at least fifteen stories high. He had to transverse several Christmas-tree-like caves that opened up in front of him. Limestone had been shaped through the centuries into distorted patterns like bunches of twigs tied together. Large deposits of quartz, chalk and coral glowed in the subdued light like so many jewels that had been carelessly strewn through the caverns. Limestone corals and fossils were splashed throughout the necropolis. Stalactites and stalagmites formed a web of intricate patterns around him. They towered over his head as he descended even deeper into the underground labyrinth. More of the cavern entrances were apparent the farther up he travelled.

Funnel-eared bats suddenly swarmed out of one of the many cave entrances. Their wings flapped around McCall's face. He had to fight his way through them. Fruit bats and even ghost-faced bats hung down from the high caverns which made McCall shudder. Then he was through the worst of the loathsome creatures.

He came upon another elevator that stood in a recess in the cavern in front of him. It was an antique *Victorian Art-Deco Birdcage Elevator* with iron cage gates. McCall thought it had not been in use for some time. It was decorated with ornate *Peacock-style artwork*. He opened the gates. Inside he found the bronze interior had the original *1960's Art-Deco design* with elevator call buttons. There were only two floors, a basement and a lower-level basement in the vast subterranean landscape. He entered the elevator and pressed the bronze button to take him down to the sub-basement. The antiquated elevator descended down into the lower level. When he reached it McCall pulled the iron gates apart and stepped out. As soon he closed the elevator door it ascended again.

McCall moved through the overlapping shadows. He reached an entrance and emerged out onto a terrain like something out of *Fahrenheit 451*. Huge Christmas-like protuberance were scattered against the gothic lunar landscape. More *Spider's Webs* like shredded confetti hung from the ceiling that towered above him for 1000 feet. Shrouded figures like bizarre mummies were wrapped up at various levels in the futuristic surreal landscape. Skull-like monsters and grotesque mutants inhabited the menacing shadows. The obelisks were rust-red in the caverns like huge totem poles growing haphazardly in the interior.

McCall moved down a narrow limestone path. More of the LED 500-Watt area lights were in evidence, but they were spaced infrequently now. Many of them had blown out. An iron guardrail gleamed dully in the darkness. McCall came to an ornamental wrought-iron gate made of galvanized steel. A heavy combination padlock secured it. There was no other sound in the somnolent caverns. The silence was eerie and ominous.

McCall took out his skeletal lock-pick tools and went to work on the combination padlock. He broke apart the lock in less than three minutes and dropped the lock onto the ground. He opened the iron gate and stepped through. The darkness was like a palpable force. He listened for some sign that Evangeline was a prisoner on this lower level, but there was nothing. Just the profound silence that cloaked the caverns. If David Carmichael was also in the eerie necropolis he was not making a sound.

McCall moved further along the narrow path, but the ominous hush was absolute. He did not think Evangeline had escaped from her captor. The lock on the ornamental gate had not been tampered with. That meant that she was still Carmichael's prisoner.

McCall turned around and retraced his steps back toward the iron gate. As he did so his foot disturbed something lying on the ground. He knelt down. The jewels on Evangeline's ornate necklace caught the pale light in the cavern. McCall picked it up and turned it around in his hands. He didn't think that she had lost it. It meant a great deal to her. Obviously, she had pulled the necklace from her throat and dropped it where she hoped McCall would find it. The Bolo was made of ivory, silver and gold balls. It gleamed in the darkness. It felt heavy in McCall's hands. He dropped it into the pocket of his leather jacket and straightened. He moved back to the ornate gate and slipped through it, replacing the heavy padlock. Once again he followed the narrow path to where the elevator was located. He opened the heavy gates and ascended back to the Mezzanine level. He opened the elevator door and stepped out into the glowing caverns that surrounded him. The elevator door closed behind him.

McCall climbed a steep gradient and had to hold onto the iron guardrail. Another magnificent view of the caverns rose steeply in front of him. Stalactites and stalactites hung down in icicle-shaped splendor at various places on the landscape. Rust-red deposits of chalk and marble were in evidence among the hidden grottos. The *Blue-Spider's Webs* were intermingled with what looked like organ pipes that hung down at various levels. Frozen wax obelisks decorated the walls. Protuberances like gigantic totem poles appeared throughout the cavern. McCall noted a huge skull that was wrapped in bandages and gauze with immense teeth and whiskers. It was an optical illusion, but it appeared like a vision straight from Hell.

David Carmichael was waiting for McCall.

His figure moved into and out of the shadows like a vengeful phantom.

He was not alone.

Evangeline was still his prisoner.

Carmichael had thrown her down to the ground and tied her ankles together. Then he had hauled her up by her bare feet. He had attached the rope to a pulley that raised her up six inches into the air. She dangled upside-down with her head just touching the ground.

She was naked.

McCall moved in and out of the overlapping shadows. He could hear Evangeline's rasping voice as she gasped for air. She swung back and forth in humiliating small arcs. The sight was mortifying to him in its savage disregard for life.

David Carmichael faced McCall with a smirk on his face. He held the .38 revolver at chest level. It did not waver for a millisecond.

"Put your gun down on the floor and kick it away," he said. "If you don't comply I will put a bullet at the back of Evangeline's head. Your call."

McCall did have a choice. He dropped his Glock 19 pistol on the ground and kicked it away from him. Carmichael gazed at him as if he had just scored a major victory.

"I had a chrome lighter in the pocket of my jacket," Carmichael said. "Did you pick it up by any chance?"

McCall reached into his pocket and produced the chrome lighter. "You dropped it in the tall grass near the cave entrance."

"Toss it over."

McCall tossed the lighter over to him. Carmichael shook out a cigarette and lit it. He dropped the lighter back into his pocket. "Thanks. It has some sentimental value to me." He glanced down to where Evangeline swung back and forth like an obscene marionette. There was a shit-eating grin on his face. "I like the way she rotates back and forth without my having to do anything to her." His voice echoed in the confines of the underground cavern. He looked back at McCall. "Time for you to get down onto your knees, mother-fucker."

"Let her go," McCall said. "This is just between us."

"You'd like that, wouldn't you?" Carmichael said. "But I'm not going to play your game. Unless you can leap tall buildings at a single bound, you have nothing to tell me. I am holding all the cards. We'll play this out my way."

Surreptitiously, McCall pulled the antique Gaucho Bola out of his leather jacket. He shielded his hand from Carmichael who was looking back down at Evangeline as if working out her ultimate fate. The pools of darkness were intermittent in the echoing chamber. McCall gathered the delicate ivory, silver and gold balls and held them hidden in his left hand. He remembered that his friend Gunner had once used a Bolo when disarming a would-be assassin. Whether McCall could throw the Bolo in the right place was problematic, but he knew he had only one shot to try and turn the tables on this madman.

Carmichael turned back to face McCall.

"Time for you do die," he said.

He aimed the gun at McCall.

McCall threw the Bola with unerring skill at him. The weighted balls wrapped around Carmichael's throat. He clawed at the interconnected Boleadoras. He gasped for breath and stumbled down to his knees. His body convulsed. He tried to pull the braided cords of the Bolo off his throat. In the same moment McCall dove down to the floor, grabbed the Glock 19 pistol, turned on his back and fired.

The force of the bullet exploded against Carmichael's forehead.

He was dead before he hit the ground.

McCall got to his feet and moved to where Evangeline was swinging by her wrists. He grabbed her, took out the slim throwing knife he carried and slit the ropes holding her just above the ground. Gently he brought her naked body to the floor. She turned over and reached for him. She was gasping and shivering with fright. McCall took her into his arms and held her tightly.

"I've got you now," he said. "Just hold onto me."

It took a couple of moments for Evangeline to break from him.

"Good thing you've seen my body in all its glory," she murmured. "No surprises there."

"Can you get up?" McCall asked.

"I can try."

He helped her to get to her feet. Evangeline swayed a little in his arms, but he held onto her tightly.

"I'm okay," she murmured.

She looked down at David Carmichael. She reached down and scooped up the ivory, silver and gold Bolo and straightened. She turned back to McCall and dropped the Bolo into his hands.

"What is that?" she asked.

"A Bolo," McCall said. "Used by Filipino Guerrillas to capture animas by entangling their legs."

"Or their throats," Evangeline said.

She shivered involuntarily. McCall took off his leather jacket and pulled it around her shoulders. "Let's get out of here."

She looked down at David Carmichael's lifeless body. "He was going to kill me."

"I wasn't going to let that happen," McCall said. "There is an elevator just outside the caverns that will take us right up to the surface."

"Stay with me," she asked him, softly.

"I won't leave your side," he promised.

She looked down at her one-time captor. "He told me he had killed a couple of rescue workers in the underground tunnels."

"He did," McCall said. "Two of them escaped. I took them back to the surface."

"He said his name was David Carmichael," Evangeline said. "I had never even seen him before today. He had been waiting for me. I guess he had been stalking me. He told me all the terrible things he was going to do to me."

"Put that out of your mind for now," McCall said.

"I need to know why," Evangeline said. "For my own peace of mind. Why did he try to make me his prisoner? Why did he try to torture me?"

"I don't know," McCall said. "We'll never know the answer to that."

"I think I met him once when I was in the fairground," she said. "Just one of the lowlifes who wanted my body. I guess he was just biding his time. To find the perfect time to make me his slave. It's a wonder I escaped from the fairground at all."

"None of that matters now," McCall said. "You were smart and played the game in a way Carmichael wasn't expecting. You turned the tables on your tormentor. End of story."

"You did that," she said. "You were there for me."

"I will always be there for you," McCall said, gently.

She nodded and pulled McCall's leather jacket tighter around her. "Let's get out of here."

McCall put his arms around her. Together they descended to the level of the first elevator.

XXXVIII

NEMESIS

McCall delivered Evangeline back to her home in Knoxville, Tennessee. She was still shaken from her ordeal with David Carmichael, but she was coping with the trauma he had caused her in her own way. McCall stood in the doorway of her apartment but was reluctant to cross the threshold. She sensed his tension and just nodded.

"This is where we say goodbye to each other," she said.

"There is some unfinished business I need to take care of," McCall said.

"Equalizer business?" she asked him with no trace of irony.

"You could call it that."

"Will you return to New York City now?"

"I will."

"I go there at least once a week," Evangeline said. "Where I can get into all sort of trouble. But I'll avoid getting involved in the fairground again. That has serious consequences I can't deal with now."

"That's probably for the best," McCall said.

She moved close to him and put her hands on his shoulders. "But you don't get out of my life that easily," she added. "I'll turn up like the bad penny to torment you."

"I will look forward to that," he said.

"This unfinished business of yours that you have to take care of," Evangeline asked. "Does that include bad people trying to kill you?"

"Possibly."

"Then care of yourself," she murmured. "You are very precious to me."

"I'll take that into consideration," McCall said.

Evangeline leaned over and kissed McCall on the lips as if her life depended on it. When she came up for air she stepped back from him. "Now, that wasn't so bad, was it?"

"Not bad at all," McCall said, and he smiled. "Take care of yourself. We'll meet up again back in New York City."

"Count on it," she said, and she laughed. "You don't get rid of me that easily."

"Goodbye, Evangeline."

McCall left her in the doorway of her apartment and moved back toward where he had parked the Jaguar. He didn't look back, but he didn't have to.

He knew she was crying.

McCall returned the Jaguar to the dealer and then boarded a train to New York City. He reached Penn Station and took a cab to the Liberty Belle Hotel. He entered his suite that Sam Kinney had arranged for him, dropped off his suitcases and left almost immediately. He knew where to find Khalid Rehman Mohammed. The terrorist parked his car in the basement at 555 Tenth Avenue. McCall watched the building for three days until Khalid Rehman Mohammed returned to his apartment. He had parked his rental vehicle which happened to be a 2022 Porche 718 Cayman sports car. McCall took the stairs to the basement of the building in time to see him heading to his car. McCall came up behind him and used a back fist to the forehead to stun his pineal gland and paralyze his arm through the median nerve. A sword-hand to his throat finished him off. He slumped down to the garage floor. McCall made sure he was still breathing; his pulse rate low, but adequate. He carried him in a fireman's lift to the stairs. He couldn't access the elevator for fear of being discovered so he carried the terrorist all the way up the fifty-six floors. There was a brick and balustrade balcony that had a metal staircase welded to the side of the building. McCall found a door that he could access and took the metal stairs up to the roof. The roof itself was covered with mechanical equipment and cables. By this time Khalid Rehman Mohammed had stirred. McCall climbed to the edge of the precipice. He dangled the terrorist upside-down over the railing. Khalid Rehman Mohammed was terrified. He gazed down at the sheer drop to the street in absolute mortal fear of his life. McCall still held the man's legs in a vice-like grip.

His voice was soothing and matter of fact.

"Here is what is going to happen," he murmured. "You are going to abandon your Porsche and take a cab to the airport. You'll get the next flight out of the city and never come back. If you do return for any reason I will kill you. Are you with me so far?"

The terrorist, in a hoarse voice, said: "I am with you."

"There wouldn't be no second chances," McCall said. "You're going to be wearing the same clothes you're wearing now. I'll make sure you have the fare for the cab. You'll take a flight out of Manhattan to a new location somewhere out of the country. Where that location will be is up to you. If you return to New York City for any reason you'll suffer the consequences. Just nod your head if you understand?"

Khalid Rehman Mohammed nodded, which took every ounce of willpower he possessed.

For just a moment McCall was tempted to toss the terrorist off into space. Then he hauled him back over the guardrail and dumped him onto the roof. He put a black hood over his head and dragged him to his feet. He marched him back to the stairs leading from the roof and all the way down to the lobby. McCall removed the black hood. He manhandled Khalid Rehman Mohammed outside. A yellow cab pulled up. McCall thrust the terrorist into it.

"JFK," McCall told the driver. "My friend is in a hurry to catch a plane."

McCall slammed the cab door. The cabbie took off. That was the last McCall ever saw of Khalid Rehman Mohammed. There was still a chance that the terrorist would return and try to kill his target, but McCall thought that in the circumstances that possibility was very unlikely.

When McCall returned to the Liberty Belle Hotel he had an urgent message from Hayden Vallance. He knew Vallance had got himself involved in a conflict in Northern Nigeria. From his terse account the battle had not been going well against the *Boko Haram Terrorist Organization*. Ten thousand people had been killed and three mission people had been displaced from their homes. It was the deadliest terror spot in the world according to the *Global Terrorist Index*. McCall had the coordinates to reach him, but he didn't know if Vallance had been killed in the conflict. His message said simply: *"Need your help. I am beleaguered on all sides. Get here if you can."*

There was no question in McCall's mind that he had to respond to Vallance's desperate plea for help. Twenty-four hours later he was in the jungle fighting a rearguard action with Government forces against the terrorists. Vallance had been injured in the heavy fighting with the rebel forces. The leader of the insurrection was a man named Jaak Olesk. McCall had come up against him before. Vallance said the terrorist had organized the attacks on the Government forces. He wanted McCall to find him and take him out.

"I'm not a hired assassin," McCall said. "If Jaak Olesk coordinated the attacks on the Government forces this is a war I don't want to be a part of."

"He's a very bad guy," Vallance said. "He massacred women and children here in Nigeria a week ago. There was nothing I could do to stop him. He's forceful and vengeful. That was when I rallied the Government forces here. The rebel attack was beaten back, but Jaak Olesk disappeared in the midst of the fighting."

"Do you know where he is now?" McCall asked.

"My intel said that he was in the city of Abuja, but I can't verify that," Vallance said. "He's a phantom who strikes with deadly accuracy, then disappears from the battlefield like a wisp of smoke."

"If I can find him, what do you want me to do?" McCall asked.

"Terminate his existence."

"I'll settle for trying to find him," he said. "After that, all bets are off."

"Fair enough," Vallance retorted.

McCall knew where to find Jaak Olesk. He travelled to Nigeria and then took the Ibadan train service in Lagos. That let him out in Abuja at the Nigerian railway station. He took another train in the *Ebute Meta Junction* until he found 12, Anvoluwapo Street, not far from the De Blueezzz Hotel and the Nigeria Cathedral of Christ.

A hostage situation was taking place. Jaak Olesk had laid siege to the *Kalakuta Republic Museum*. The two-story Colonial Mansion was set back from the street. It housed some of Fela Amikulapo Kuti's paintings and belongings. That included his paintings, historical documents, photographs, murals, album covers and musical instruments. McCall had been a fan of Fela's for a long time. He was a freedom-fighter and political activist who McCall had admired. His mission had been to promote the music and resources of the African people in their struggle against neo-Colonial tyranny.

The museum was also a showcase for Fela's shoes and fur coats. There was a rooftop café at the top of the white-washed building that had been abandoned. The ornate building had iron railings and two prominent balconies. Government troops had surrounded it. McCall's liaison with the Government Forces had been with a *Colonel Ojukna Amed*. He had the grace of a leader who reminded McCall of the late Sidney Poitier. There was a lot of activity around the grounds of the estate. McCall showed Colonel Ameda a card he carried with him.

"What is the status here?"

"Hostage situation," Colonel Ujukna Amed said. "We've surrounded the building with Government troops. There has been no dialogue between us and the armed terrorist. We don't even know his name. You have to leave us now, Mr. McCall. We will deal with this situation."

McCall nodded and stepped away from the building. He had once been invited to attend a State dinner on Lagos Island. He knew the layout of the grounds outside the museum. Behind the building was a grove of Monterey Cypress trees. McCall plunged into them. He knew there was an entrance below ground that he had stumbled upon when he had been wandering through the woods. He remembered there was a trapdoor in the trees that led to a wine cellar below ground. It took him a little time to find it. It was overgrown with tangled vines and leaves. The hidden entrance was padlocked. McCall didn't think anyone had disturbed it for years. The padlock had a 4-digit combination in black which was rusted and overgrown with shrubs. McCall took out the skeleton key he had used on the padlock before and went to work on it. It took him almost five minutes to break the lock apart. He dropped the lock down onto the ground and lifted the trapdoor beneath. It revealed stairs that descended in pitch black into the earth.

McCall brought out a pencil flashlight and descended the staircase. At the bottom there were recessed lights in the ceiling that revealed a narrow corridor in the earth. McCall followed it and came to a place where another flight of iron stairs led up. He climbed them. He pulled on the rusting doors until they finally opened. He made his way out of the underground cellar. He dropped the cellar door so that it was flush with the ground.

McCall's flashlight probed the darkness. He took out the Glock 19 pistol from his jacket and moved through the mangrove and palm trees. He opened the door and stepped through the entranceway into Government House. The silence in the building was oppressive. Through one of the front windows McCall saw Jaak Olesk standing in an ornate study looking out at the grounds. The terrorist stood well back from the window. The Government troops had positioned themselves around the building. Colonel Ujukna Amed had a bullhorn to his lips while his troops rallied around him.

"This is Colonel Yjukna Amen," he said. "I am speaking to the terrorist who calls himself Jaak Olesk. You have barricaded yourself in the Embassy and present a threat of violence to the guests in the mansion. These are acts of aggression that will not be tolerated."

Jaak Olesk gave no sign that he had even heard the warning. He was still standing in his place by the window with the door to the room wide open. There was an eerie stillness about him that gave McCall pause. But the terrorist was not looking behind him. McCall moved quickly to the back of the house. The door there was bolted but not locked. McCall turned the key in the lock and entered the Embassy room.

There were a dozen people inside. All of them were wearing evening wearing attire. Some of them had name tags on their lapels: *Christian Noyer*, the *Governor of the Banque de France, Kersti Kaljulaid,* the *President of Estonia, Christine Lagarde,* France's

Finance Minister, Masaaki Shilakawfi, the *Governor of the Bank of Japan,* the *U.S. Special Envoy to Afghanistan,* the *Prime Minister of Turkey, Binali Yildirim,* the *French Minister in Italy, Jean-Marc de la Sabliere, Israeli Minister Saiman Peres* and the U.S. *Ambassador Richard Jones.* McCall gathered the distinguished guests together and held up his hand for silence. He used hand signals only. He ushered the guests out of the banquet room and led them as a group through the house.

Jaak Olesk had closed the door of the study which McCall was thankful for. He opened a door that led down to the cellar. He provided two flashlights for the illustrious guests to guide their way.

"Follow the path in the cellar," he whispered. "It will take you to another door that will lead you upstairs back to the ground level. Just stay on your path."

One of the guests, *Christian Noyer,* suddenly gripped McCall's hand. "*Kersti Kaljulaid* isn't with us!"

"Who is that?" McCall asked, urgently.

"She is the President of Estonia," *Christine Lagarde,* another of the guests, whispered. "She had to go to the bathroom."

"I'll catch up with her," McCall said. "All of you move quickly to the cellar steps."

The influential guests found the cellar entrance and climbed down into it.

McCall turned back into the house. Jaak Olesk had left the door to the ballroom open again. But this time the room was deserted. McCall ran down the narrow corridor to the back of the house. He threw open the ballroom door. Jack Olesk was holding Kersti Kaljulaid a prisoner. She was formally dressed for the occasion in a smart business suit. McCall recalled that she had been award-ed the *Rainbow Hero Award* for her support of the gay LGBTQ community in Estoria.

Jaak Olesk had a Damascus hunting knife pressed at her throat.

McCall took another step closer. "Let Ambassador Kaljulaid go," he said. "This doesn't have to end badly for you."

Olesk's voice, which echoed in the room, was tinged with hyste-ria. "I will kill her!" he shouted.

"Your hostages are all gone," McCall said. "Throw down the knife."

Kersti Kaljulaid was wearing an ornate Victorian cameo rhinestone broach on the lapel of her suit. Discreetly she unpinned it, looking at McCall for guidance. He nodded imperceptibly. She stabbed the pin into Jaak Olesk's hand. The terrorist howled as the sharp brooch pieced his skin. He took his hand away. Kersti Kaljulaid moved out of his grasp.

McCall brought up the Glock 19 pistol and fired.

Jaak Olesk was dead before he hit the polished ballroom floor.

McCall moved to Kersti Kaljulaid and took her hand. She appeared undaunted by her close call with death. He picked up the fallen broach and pinned it gently back on her lapel.

"Are you all right, Ms. Ambassador?" he asked.

"Never better," she murmured. "Is he dead?"

"He is," McCall said. "Come with me."

He took her arm, but she was doing just fine without his help. He moved her from the ballroom down the corridor with him. This time he opened the front door of the building and delivered Kersti Kaljulaid into the arms of the waiting Government Forces. They were immediately surrounded by more troops. Colonel Yiukna Amen had taken charge. By this time the rest of the hostages had emerged from the storm cellar. They clustered around Kersti Kaljulaid to make certain she was safe. McCall moved back through the house and out through a side entrance. He glanced back behind him. All of the hostages had been accounted for. McCall disappeared onto the grounds of the embassy before any of the hostages could find him to offer him their heartfelt thanks.

That left him the last of the unfinished business he needed to take care of.

McCall booked into the Hotel Luxembourg Parc in Paris. He looked around the small suite. There were gorgeous trees and shrubbery in front of the building. He opened the French windows to a terrace which overlooked the front of the hotel. There were other balconies on the other floors. He noted a speculator half-moon sculpture of wrought-iron below on the terrace. It depicted a somewhat unflattering mural of a woman's face. McCall closed the French doors. The junior suite had a plasma TV and a state-of-the art sound system. There was a DVD Player on a table. A Nespresso coffee maker was beside the television.

McCall checked out the marble bathroom. It was exquisite. He closed the bathroom door, moved to the French doors and looked out. Paris lay before him. He had always loved this city. But tonight it had a sinister purpose that he was very aware of. He moved to a bureau and found it was stocked with Hennessy XO cognac, Courvoisier and several bottles of French wine. He took a brandy bottle from the refrigerator which he had ordered in advance, pulled out the cork and poured himself a large glass of Hennessy brandy. He placed it on a small end table. He fitted a silencer onto his pistol and screwed it in. Then he made himself comfortable in an easy chair and turned out all of the lights.

McCall had no qualms about what he was going to do. Samantha Gregson had organized her *Memento Mori* thugs to be assassins. They had been close to killing innocent people in Greece and Rome. She had killed Daniel Blake at the Chateau in Pylos in Russia using a high-powered rifle. She had smuggled an explosive device onto the train in Montreal that McCall had discovered. He had managed to disarm the device with Gunner's help, but it had been a near thing. Samantha was waiting for the right opportunity to dispose of McCall for good.

McCall settled down to wait for her.

He had finished the brandy and was starting on another bottle when he heard Samantha Gregson's key in the door. McCall gently put down the brandy glass onto the end table.

He waited.

Samantha entered the suite and threw her overcoat on a Louis V chair. She moved into the bathroom and turned on the marble shower. The thrumming of the shower did wonders for her shattered nerves. She had always loved the Hotel Luxembourg Parc in Paris. It was like coming home for her. Paris was Paris, after all. She had never tired of the grandeur of the city. But tonight she was tired. Robert McCall was like a malignant tumor she had to get rid of. It shouldn't be long until he was dead. She had faith in

Khalid Rehman Mohammed, but she didn't entirely trust him. In the end she had decided to kill McCall herself at the first opportunity that presented itself.

Samantha moved back into the suite. She had intended to open the French doors to look down at the terrace below. But a sense of danger assailed her. She picked up her purse and took out a Compact 9mm pistol from inside it. At first she didn't recognize McCall in the shadows of the room. Then she focused on his shrouded figure which was unmoving in the easy chair. She aimed her gun at him.

McCall shot Samantha Gregson dead.

He slowly rose out of the easy chair. His would-be assassin lay crumpled on the plush carpet at his feet. He picked up the Compact pistol she had dropped from her nerveless hand. He emptied the nine rounds onto the floor. He moved into the marble bathroom and turned off the shower. Then he returned to the suite and placed the empty pistol beside Samantha's prone hand. He had not fired his Glock 19 so there no was way the French police could trace the weapon back to Samantha. McCall paused to look down at Samantha's body. He felt no remorse for the act he had committed. She had left him no choice.

He had accomplished what he needed to do.

McCall put the Glock 19 pistol back into his leather jacket, let himself out of the suite and closed the door quietly behind him.

XXXI
RESOLUTION

McCALL RETURNED TO his apartment in New York City. Everything was as he had left it. For a moment he felt a sense of loss, although there was no justification for it. He needed somewhere to unwind and let his emotions take over. He grabbed a cab to 77th Street and entered Bentley's Bar and Grill. The place was hopping tonight. He spied his two favorite servers Gina and Amanda. They were serving the customers with their usual style and verve, but they didn't have time to stop and chat with McCall. He sat up at the bar. The bartender moved over to him.

"We haven't seen you in a while," Terry said. "What can I get for you, Mr. McCall?"

"A whiskey sour."

"Sure, coming right up."

He moved away. A moment later Mickey Kostmayer sat down at the bar beside him. McCall ordered a Coors light beer for him.

"I have been worried about you," Kostmayer said. "You suddenly vanished from the face of the earth. I left several messages for you, but none of them were answered. I know not to question you when you want to be left alone, but I had a strange feeling that you were in trouble. Would I be right about that?"

"You might be," McCall said. The bartender returned with a Brandy Alexander. "Enjoy," he said.

McCall took a swallow of his cocktail.

"Want to share any of the details with me?" Kostmayer asked.

"Not particularly."

He smiled. "I didn't think so. While you were away, Candy Annie and Abigail moved into an apartment on Clinton Street next to the Bakery on the Lower East Side. They have been having a grand time."

"I'm glad to hear it," McCall said.

Mickey glanced across where a young woman had moved over to the empty stool at the bar. "You have got a visitor," he said.

McCall looked to see Allison Carmichael had just arrived. He stood up and offered her a bar stool. She seemed hesitant but she sat down. Kostmayer looked back at McCall. "Are you going to introduce me?"

"This is Allison Carmichael," McCall said.

Kostmayer shook hands. "Pleased to meet you. You're a friend of McCall's?"

"I'm her uncle," McCall told him.

That hit Kostmayer like a lightning bolt, but he recovered quickly. "You never cease to surprise me, McCall. I'll leave you folks to enjoy your evening. I'll catch you later."

He moved away and Allison took his vacated stool at the bar.

"What are you doing here?" McCall asked.

"I wanted to see you. That's okay, isn't it?"

"It's all right with me."

"I don't mean to spring my company on you," Allison said.

"Don't think another thing about it," McCall said. "Can I get you a drink?"

"I just want to talk to you," she said.

He nodded. "It's kind of noisy in here. Let's go for a walk."

"I would like that very much," she said.

They exited Bentley's Bar and Grill and walked down 77th Street before entering Central Park. They strolled to Strawberry Fields and from there to the beautiful Bow Bridge. Allison was animated and engaging, but McCall knew there was a lot on her mind.

"Where are your kids?" he asked her.

"I dumped them off at Evangeline's place," she said. "It seems you were responsible for saving her life. I didn't know that meant you actually had saved her from mortal danger, but I thought you probably had. You want to tell me about it?"

"Nothing to tell," McCall murmured. "Evangeline had demons she needed to deal with. I helped her do that."

"I know there is more to that story that you're telling me."

"You're better off not knowing all the details," McCall said.

"Because the truth is gnarly?" she asked him.

McCall smiled. "Something like that."

"So you are still protecting me," Allison said. "From the demons and monsters that might do me harm ."

"I'm trying to," he said. "You came all the way from Knoxville to see me."

"Maybe I just missed you," Allison said and took his arm. "We went through a lot together."

"We did," McCall said. "But that's not the reason."

They looked over the Bow Bridge where a couple in a rowboat had just emerged from under it. Allison leaned on the bridge. Her mood was mercurial.

"After all that we've shared together," she told him, "I still don't know who you really are. You're a mystery to me. I want to get to know you better."

"No, you wouldn't," McCall said, softly.

"Evangeline said you were troubled with dark memories," Allison said. "I know that is true, but there must be a way to reach you. You're a great person. I am not saying that because you are my uncle. You mean a lot to me."

With that Allison leaned over and kissed McCall on the lips. It wasn't exactly a chaste kiss and there was definitely passion in it. When Allison finally came up for air she looked back out at a rowboat which had just passed under the bridge.

"What was that for?" McCall asked, somewhat taken aback.

Allison shrugged. "Just think of us as kissing cousins."

"But you're not my cousin," McCall protested.

"I know, you're my uncle and there's a huge age difference between us," Allison said. "But somehow I don't think of you as a distant relative. You're my knight in shining armor coming to rescue me in a cruel world."

McCall smiled at her. "You do put things in a romantic perspective."

She turned back to him. "You're not mad, are you?"

"Let's just say that dealing with you has some unique advantages," McCall said, wryly. "You're certainly headstrong and cavalier."

"But you like me, right?" Allison asked.

"I like you a lot," McCall admitted. "I'm glad you're in my life."

"Me too," Allison said and took his arm. "That restaurant where I met you had some great vibes. Bentley's, right?"

"That's right."

"Do you think we could go back there?" she asked. "I'd like to check it out."

"We can do that," McCall said. "But no kissing or making a pass at me."

"I'll be on my best behavior," she promised. "First could we take a carriage ride through Central Park? I've always wanted to do that!"

"Not a problem," McCall said.

He escorted Allison back over Bay Bridge, past Strawberry Fields and out to where the horses and carriages were tethered on 7th Avenue and 59th Street.

After their carriage ride through Central Park, McCall and Allison returned to the bar at Bentley's Bar and Grill. There wasn't a table to be had. The place was really jammed to the rafters. McCall looked around. Mickey Kostmayer was holding court at two tables. With him was the ubiquitous figure of Jackson T. Foozelman who immediately got up. He was elegantly dressed for the occasion in his mohair suit and a cravat complete with a watch chain and gold cufflinks that looked like he had borrowed them from James Bond. Sam Kinney stood up beside him, not quite so dressed up, but with Sam it was hard to tell. He always wore the same outfit to work which was a tuxedo with a Rochester silk red bowtie. He looked a little pale after his hospital ordeal. Dixie, who had nursed Kostmayer back to health, was thrilled to be included in the group. She had arrived in New York City and McCall thought it was a little overwhelming for her. But she was having a grand time.

Three gorgeous women stood up from the table. McCall knew that Hayden Vallance had rescued them from a mansion on Omega Island where they had been imprisoned. Laura Whitaker was a statuesque brunette with soulful eyes. Melanie Shepherd was a model with a gorgeous figure. Her eyes were hazel. Kate Davenport had a pixie-like quality to her which was infectious. McCall had somehow inherited them from Hayden Vallance, but he wasn't complaining. All of the young women were stunning. Candy Annie had leaped to her feet to be a part of the celebrations along with Abigail Connor. McCall had grown fond of them since he had rescued them from the treacherous Sheriff Collins in Meadows Springs.

All of them were talking at once when Allison Carmichael joined them. Fooz had made himself the unofficial spokesman for the group, introducing them to Candy Annie. Laura Whitaker and Melanie Shepherd were pals by this time. Kate Davenport was introverted, but she was enjoying her new friends. Dixie was droll and exuberant. Sam Kinney virtually ignored Fooz and shook hands with Allison. There was not a lot of love lost between Sam Kinney and Jackson T, Foozelman.

With the introductions out of the way, two tables had been brought together for the boisterous crowd. Allison sat down between Fooz and Sam Kinney. McCall suspected that was a good thing before both of them had a chance to come to blows. Allison was treated as the guest of honor at the table. Both of the cocktail waitresses had converged on them to take their orders. All of the participants were talking at once. Explosive laughter punctuated the good-natured camaraderie.

McCall had stepped back to the bar. His felt his presence was not needed for these festivities. Which was fine with him. He exited Bentley's Bar and Grill and walked back to the Liberty Belle Hotel. He ran into Chloe at the front desk and who always looked pleased to see him.

"I didn't realize you had come back to us," she said. "Is everything all right at your suite?"

"It's fine," McCall said. "Good to see you again, Chloe."

"When we don't you see in the hotel for a few weeks I worry about you."

"Nothing to worry about," he assured her.

"Take care of yourself, Mr. McCall."

"I'll promise to do that," McCall said.

Chloe watched him move to the bank of elevators. There were times when she didn't believe she would see him again.

McCall entered his suite on the 17th floor. Everything was as he had left it. There was a bottle of Dom Perignon vintage 1961 champagne chilling in an ice bucket which Sam Kinney had provided. McCall opened the bottle of champagne, poured himself a glass and accessed his messages. He had over twenty of them. McCall went through them quickly, then he came back twice to a phone message that seemed out of place to him. It was from Fort Bragg in North Caroline which was the home to the *US Army Special Operations Command.* Lieutenant Colonel Kathy Rigby had written a terse message to Robert McCall. It consisted of five words: *"Please find my kid sister."* The message had intrigued him. He called Allison Carmichael at Bentley's Bar and Grill. When she answered the phone, he asked her if she was going to be staying long in New York City. "I didn't know what I was going to do when I saw you," she admitted.

"I have a suite at the Liberty Belle Hotel here in New York," he said. "You can stay there for as long as you need to. A great girl named Chloe works in reception at the hotel. She will see that you get settled in okay."

"Okay, but where will you be?" she asked, concerned.

"I have to go out of town for a few days," he said.

"That means that you're going to do something dangerous," Allison said.

"Just checking on some things," McCall said. "Nothing for you to worry about."

"You're my uncle," she insisted. "I have to look out for you."

"I always come back," he told her, gently. "Enjoy your stay in New York City."

"Just take care of yourself," Allison pleaded. "You mean the world to me."

"That's good to hear," McCall said. "To quote my friend Mickey Kostmayer, who should be sitting with you right now at the bar in the restaurant: *'I'll be back.'*"

"I'll hold you to that promise," she said.

McCall hung up. He took the elevator to the ground floor and exited the hotel. He walked to the Sherry-Netherland Hotel at 5th Avenue and 59th Street. The New York Bar there was elegant and stylish. Stools were lined up with white tablecloths on the tables. The place was jammed to the rafters. McCall found a seat at the bar. Beth Daniels had been sitting nursing a cocktail. She looked at McCall in surprise. Her face was immediately wreathed in smiles.

"I really didn't think I would ever see you again!" she said. "Wow, this is great!"

"I told you I would take a rain check," McCall said. The bartender came over. "Nice to see you back in New York, Mr. McCall," he said. "What can I get you to drink?"

"Rob Roy with scotch, light on the vermouth with a cherry."

"Coming right up!"

The bartender moved away. Beth smiled at McCall. "You had business to attend to in Lexington, Kentucky. Did that work out okay?"

McCall shrugged. "As good as it could be in the circumstances."

"What circumstances are those?"

"It's a long story," he said and smiled.

"I've got all the time in the world!" she said. "I want to hear your whole story."

"No, you wouldn't," he said, quietly

"You're very mysterious," Beth said. "But I can live with that."

Their drinks came at that moment. She and McCall clinked glasses and he took a swallow of his Rob Roy cocktail. Beth did most of the talking, which McCall found charming and endearing. An hour later he and Beth Daniels left the Sherry-Netherlands and strolled down 5th Avenue. Beth asked if he would be offended if she came to his hotel suite for a goodnight cocktail. McCall thought that would be fine. The sparks were flying between them. McCall escorted Beth to the bank of elevators and they travelled up to the 17th floor. Beth looked around, impressed.

"Nice apartment," she said. "What a cool place to live!"

"It suits my needs," he said. "What can I fix you to drink?"

"A scotch and soda with a twist," she said.

McCall fixed up her drink and mixed a Manhattan cocktail for himself. They clinked glasses. Beth only took a sip of her drink, then she put the glass down on the coffee table. She moved into

McCall's arms and kissed him. It was a great kiss. She moved from him, took a moment as if reaching a decision, then she unbuttoned her shirt and took it off. It dropped to the floor. She removed her bra, then her skirt and panties. She moved naked into McCall's arms and kissed him again. When they parted McCall held her at arm's length.

"This has nowhere to go," he told her, gently. "I'm leaving in the morning."

"Then we should make tonight something special," she murmured. "Does that work for you?"

He smiled. "I'll give it my best shot."

They collapsed onto the sofa in each other's arms.

In the morning McCall had awakened to find Beth gone. She had left him a note. It said: "*Don't be a stranger.*" McCall smiled. The tryst had been fun and rewarding, but he knew it had nowhere to go.

He dressed and lightly packed. He took the elevator to the ground floor. He waved to Chloe at the reception desk and took a cab to JFK. He was concerned about the note that Colonel Kathy Rigby had left for him. It had said: "*Please find my kid sister.*" The plea from her had been unmistakable.

Which was why Robert McCall was on the next plane to Fort Bragg, North Carolina.

Like it or not, McCall thought, he was back in the "Equalizer" business.